名人演說一百篇

100 FAMOUS SPEECHES

一百叢書②

英漢對照 English-Chinese

石幼珊譯・張隆溪校

名人演說一百篇
100 FAMOUS SPEECHES

臺灣商務印書館發行

《一百叢書》總序

　　本館出版英漢(或漢英)對照《一百叢書》的目的,是希望憑藉着英、漢兩種語言的對譯,把中國和世界各類著名作品的精華部分介紹給中外讀者。

　　本叢書的涉及面很廣。題材包括了寓言、詩歌、散文、短篇小說、書信、演說、語錄、神話故事、聖經故事、成語故事、名著選段等等。

　　顧名思義,《一百叢書》中的每一種都由一百個單元組成。以一百為單位,主要是讓編譯者在浩瀚的名著的海洋中作挑選時有一個取捨的最低和最高限額。至於取捨的標準,則是見仁見智,各有心得。

　　由於各種書中被選用的篇章節段,都是以原文或已被認定的範本作藍本,而譯文又經專家學者們精雕細琢,千錘百煉,故本叢書除可作為各種題材的精選讀本外,也是研習英漢兩種語言對譯的理想參考書,部分更可用作朗誦教材。外國學者如要研習漢語,本叢書亦不失為理想工具。

商務印書館香港分館
編輯部

前　言

　　演說詞是一種重要的文件，具有自己的特
點。在現有的記錄中，西方的演說最早見於古
希臘羅馬共和國議會的辯論，是古希臘羅馬貴
族民主政治的一種產物。從一開始，演說就有
着重要的社會作用。隨着歷史的發展，演說又
成了民主政治的一種形式。一般的演說詞，都
是經過深思熟慮寫成的講稿，以嚴密的思維邏
輯吸引人；但也有隨機而作的即興發言，以強
烈的感情、機智的幽默和生動的語言打動聽
衆。

　　本書選譯了一百篇外國著名演說詞。發表
的時間從公元前四百多年到現代，前後二千多
年，包括古希臘、羅馬、中世紀德意志帝國、
意大利以及近現代法國、蘇聯等國家的演說
家。由於這是中英對照的文集，因此佔篇幅最
多的當然還是英國人和美國人的演說，約佔百
分之七十。其他演說詞則是由英譯文轉譯。

　　這些演說家有奴隸主，也有奴隸；有國家
總統、將軍、首相，也有革命領袖；有哲學
家，也有科學家；還有作家、律師和學者……。
演說的內容，有政治的論爭，也有科學的探討；
有對先烈的緬懷，也有對後輩的激勵；有雄辯

的說理，也有深沉的抒情；有熱烈的頌揚，也有嚴厲的貶斥……。

這一百篇演說詞的作者，多是各個時代、各個階層的代表人物。我們可以讀到闡述深刻的哲理和閃光的思想。這些哲理、思想曾豐富了人類精神文明的寶庫，是全人類的共同財寶。有的演說詞反映了某些國家在重要歷史關頭或重大歷史事件上的立場、戰略和政策。這些，都是極有價值的文獻。當然，有的演說詞不可避免地反映演說家個人的觀點。有的演說詞語言優美，娓娓動聽，然而和演說家的行動兩相對照，就可以發現說的和做的完全是兩回事。從這意義上說，本書選譯了少量這樣的演說詞，也可以起歷史見證的作用。

除了因集中同一講者的演說詞而稍有調動外，本書大體按各篇演說詞發表日期的先後作順序編排。

由於篇幅關係，書內部分較長的演說詞不得不作適當的刪略。刪略時，以保持文意完整連貫爲原則，刪去的部分以連續號（……）代替。現書內兩段之間的連續號表示原文的一段或連續數段略去了，句末的連續號則表示刪略了該段的一句或多句句子。

本書翻譯過程中，得趙紹熊、王岷源、張祥保諸位教授以及龔文庠先生、李德煜博士的

2

寶貴幫助，尤其是張祥保敎授，從選材、翻譯到註釋都提了不少寶貴意見，使本書得以完成，謹在此對他們致衷心的感謝。

石幼珊

CONTENTS

2

6

1 The Funeral Oration of Pericles

Thucydides

. . .

Our constitution does not copy the laws of neighboring states; we are rather a pattern to others than imitators ourselves. Its administration favors the many instead of the few; this is why it is called a democracy. If we look to the laws, they afford equal justice to all in their private differences; if to social standing, advancement in public life falls to reputation for capacity, class considerations not being allowed to interfere with merit; nor again does poverty bar the way; if a man is able to serve the state, he is not hindered by the obscurity of his condition. The freedom which we enjoy in our government extends also to our ordinary life. There, far from exercising a jealous surveillance over each other, we do not feel called upon to be angry with our neighbor for doing what he likes, or even to indulge in those injurious looks which cannot fail to be offensive, although they inflict no positive penalty. But all this ease in our private relations does not make us lawless as citizens. Against this fear is our chief safeguard, teaching us to obey the magistrates and the laws, particularly such as regards the protection of the injured, whether they are actually on the statute book, or belong to that code which, although unwritten,

一 在培里克利葬禮上的演說詞

修昔底德

......

　　我們的憲法不抄襲鄰國。我們不模仿別人，
相反，却是別人的典範。我們的政府爲大多數
人設想而非爲少撮人，這就是我們政府被稱爲
民主政體的原因。法律方面，所有個別情況不
同的人都得到同等公平看待。社會地位方面，
在公衆生活中獲得擢升的人均具眞才實學而非
徒負虛名。一個有才幹的人不該受其所屬階級
影響；貧窮也不可阻擋其前進道路。有才能爲國
家服務的人不會因出身低微而受困阻。我們不
僅在政府工作中享受自由，在日常生活裏也可
享受得到。我們絕不會因嫉妒而互相監視，不
會因鄰人做自己喜歡的事而生氣，甚至不喜歡
常常臉露不豫之色。這種臉色並無實際的懲罰
作用，却着實令人反感。我們隨和地與人交往，
可是，不會因此成爲毫無法紀的公民。正因害
怕變成毫無法紀，反成爲捍衞我們法律的主要
力量，敎導我們遵從行政機構和法律。我們特
別遵守那些保護受害人的法律，不論其是否明

　　修昔底德（公元前471～400），古希臘著名歷史
學家。

　　培里克利（公元前495～429），雅典重要政治家，
雅典與斯巴達爆發戰爭的第一批犧牲者之一。

yet cannot be broken without acknowledged disgrace.

Further, we provide plenty of means for the mind to refresh itself from business. We celebrate games and sacrifices all the year round, and the elegance of our private establishments forms a daily source of pleasure and helps to banish the spleen; while the magnitude of our city draws the produce of the world into our harbor, so that to the Athenian the fruits of other countries are as familiar a luxury as those of his own.

If we turn to our military policy, there also we differ from our antagonists. We throw open our city to the world, and never by alien acts exclude foreigners from any opportunity of learning or observing, although the eyes of any enemy may occasionally profit by our liberality; trusting less in system and policy than to the native spirit of our citizens; while in education, where our rivals from their very cradles by a painful discipline seek after manliness, at Athens we live exactly as we please, and yet are just as ready to encounter every legitimate danger. In proof of this it may be noticed that the Lacedaemonians do not invade our country alone, but bring with them all their confederates; while we Athenians advance unsupported into the territory of a neighbor, and fighting upon a foreign soil usually vanquish with ease men who are defending their homes. Our united force was never yet encountered by any enemy, because we have at once to attend to our marine and to dispatch our citizens by land upon

載於法典。即使這類法律屬於不成文，要是我們違反了，便會蒙受恥辱。

此外，我們提供多種方法，使人從紛繁的事務回復身心清新。我們終年舉行娛樂活動和祭神典禮。優雅的住宅成爲我們日常歡愉生活的泉源，驅散我們的憂悶。我們這規模宏大的城市吸引得世界各國把產品運來我們的港口，讓我們雅典人可以經常享用其他各國及本國的產品。

我們的軍事政策也跟我們的敵人不同。我們的城市向世界敞開大門。雖然敵人或會因我們的自由開放而窺探得益，我們從不訂出無理的法令，阻止外國人到來學習和觀察。相較來說，我們不大依靠政策制度，反而較爲信賴我們公民天生的愛國精神。教育方面，我們的對手[1]以嚴酷的紀律自小訓練公民英勇精神。我們在雅典完全隨自己喜歡而生活，却同樣能隨時面對任何眞正危險。爲了證明這一點，大家可以注意到拉塞第莫尼人要侵略我們的國家時，是與所有同盟者一起成行而非單獨前來。我們雅典人進入鄰國國土時，不需別人支援。我們在國外打仗，往往不費氣力便征服了那些保衛自己家園的人。敵人從未遭遇過我們的整支部隊，因爲我們既要守護海上，又要從陸地

（1）指居住於希臘南部，以勇武著稱的拉塞第莫尼人。

a hundred different services; so that, wherever they engage with some such fraction of our strength, a success against a detachment is magnified into a victory over the nation, and a defeat into a reverse suffered at the hands of the entire people. And yet if with habits not of labor but of ease, and courage not of art but of nature, we are still willing to encounter danger, we have the double advantage of escaping the experience of hardships in anticipation and of facing them in the hour of need as fearlessly as those who are never free from them.

. . .

派遣公民執行上百種不同任務。這樣，無論在那裏碰到我們這些武裝力量分隊，戰勝我們的分隊可擴大視爲戰勝我們的國家，相反，落敗便等於敗在我們全體人民手上。然而，儘管我們習慣於安閒而不慣勞苦，我們的勇氣來自天生而非訓練，我們還是願意面向危險。我們具有雙重有利條件：一是善於預見並避免艱難的處境，二是在需要時，我們能夠同經常警戒的人一樣，無畏地迎接艱險。

......

2 Apology

Socrates (from Dialogues of Plato)

Let us reflect in another way, and we shall see that there is great reason to hope that death is a good; for one of two things — either death is a state of nothingness and utter unconsciousness, or, as men say, there is a change and migration of the soul from this world to another. Now if you suppose that there is no consciousness, but a sleep like the sleep of him who is undisturbed even by dreams, death will be an unspeakable gain. For if a person were to select the night in which his sleep was undisturbed even by dreams, and were to compare with this the other days and nights of his life, and then were to tell us how many days and nights he had passed in the course of his life better and more pleasantly than this one, I think that any man, I will not say a private man, but even the great king will not find many such days or nights, when compared with the others. Now if death be of such a nature, I say that to die is gain; for eternity is then only a single night. But if death is the journey to another place, and there, as men say, all the dead abide, what good, O my friends and judges, can be greater than this? If indeed when the pilgrim arrives in the world below, he is delivered from the professors of justice in this world, and finds the true judges who are said to give judgment there, Mino and Rhadamanthus and Aeacus and Triptolemus, and other sons of God who were righteous in their own life, that pilgrimage will be worth making.

這是柏拉圖記錄蘇格拉底臨終的辯訴詞。蘇格拉底（公元前470～399），希臘的哲學家和演說家。公元前399年以＂瀆神違教＂之罪被控入獄，不久被判服毒。

二　申　辯

蘇格拉底（引自柏拉圖對話錄）

我們如果從另一角度來思考死亡，就會發覺有絕大理由相信死亡是件好事。死亡可能是以下兩種情形其中之一：或者完全沒有知覺的虛無狀態；或是大家常說的一套，靈魂經歷變化，由這個世界移居到另一世界。倘若你認爲死後並無知覺，死亡尤如無夢相擾的安眠，那麼死亡眞是無可形容的得益了。如果某人要把安恬無夢的一夜跟一生中的其他日子相比，看有多少日子比這一夜更美妙愉快，我想他說不出有多少天。不要說是平民，就是顯赫的帝王也如此。如果這就是死亡的本質，那麼死亡眞是一種得益，因爲這樣看來，永恒不過是一夜。倘若死亡一如大家常說那樣，只是遷移到另一世界，那裏聚居了所有死去的人，那麼，我的諸位朋友、法官，還有什麼事情比這樣來得更美妙呢？假若這遊歷者到達地下世界時，擺脫了塵世的判官，却在這裏碰見眞純正直的法官邁諾、拉達門塞斯、阿克斯[1]、特立普托里瑪斯[2]，以及一生公正的諸神兒子，那麼這歷程

柏拉圖是蘇格拉底的弟子，亞里斯多德的老師，著有《理想國》、《法律篇》等。

（1）希臘神話中的冥府三大判官。

（2）古希臘英雄，半人半神的人物。

What would not a man give if he might converse with Orpheus and Musaeus and Hesiod and Homer? Nay, if this be true, let me die again and again. I myself, too, shall have a wonderful interest in there meeting and conversing with Palamedes, and Ajax the son Telamon, and any other ancient hero who has suffered death through an unjust judgment; and there will be no small pleasure, as I think, in comparing my own suffering with theirs. Above all, I shall then be able to continue my search into the true and false knowledge; as in this world, so also in the next; and I shall find out who is wise, and who pretends to be wise, and is not. What would not a man give, O judges, to be able to examine the leader of the great Trojan expedition; or Odysseus or Sisyphus, or numberless others, men and women too! What infinite delight would there be in conversing with them and asking them questions! In another world they do not put a man to death for asking questions: assuredly not. For besides being happier than we are, they will be immortal, if what is said is true.

Wherefore, O judges, be good cheer about death, and know of a certainty, that no evil can happen to a good man, either in life or after death. He and his are not neglected by the gods; nor has my own approaching end happened by mere chance. But I see clearly that

---

（1）希臘神話中善奏豎琴的歌手。

（2）希臘神話中的歌手兼預言家。

（3）古代希臘詩人，著名作品有《工作與日子》(Works and Days) 和《神譜》(Theogony)。

（4）古希臘偉大詩人，作品有史詩《伊利亞特》(The Iliad) 和《奧德修記》(Odyssey)。

（5）古羅馬神話中的海神，負責保護海港。

（6）荷馬史詩中特洛伊戰爭的著名英雄。

就確實有意義了。如果可以跟俄耳甫斯[1]、繆薩尤斯[2]、赫西阿德[3]、荷馬[4]相互交談，誰不願意捨棄一切？要是死亡眞是這樣，我願意不斷受死。我很希望碰見帕拉默底斯[5]、蒂拉蒙的兒子埃杰克斯[6]以及受不公平審判而死的古代英雄，和他們一起交談。我相信互相比較我們所受的苦難會是件痛快的事情。更重要的是，我可以像在這世界一樣，在那新世界裏繼續探求事物的眞偽。我可以認清誰是眞正的才智之士，誰只是假裝聰明。法官們啊，誰不願捨棄一切，以換取機會研究遠征特洛伊[7]的領袖、奧德修斯[8]、西昔法斯[9]和無數其他的男男女女！跟他們交談，向他們請教，將是無窮快樂的事情！在那世界裏，絕不會有人因發問而獲死罪！如果傳說屬實，住在那裏的人除了比我們快樂之外，還會永生不死。

法官們啊，不必爲死亡而感喪氣。要知道善良的人無論生前死後都不會遭逢惡果，他和家人不會爲諸神拋棄。快要降臨在我身上的結

---

(7) 特洛伊遠征起因於特洛伊王的兒子拐走了斯巴達王的妻子，結果希臘兵藏於大木馬內攻入特洛伊城，將全城焚燬。

(8) 荷馬史詩中希臘小島伊薩卡(Ithaca)的國王，特洛伊遠征的領袖之一。

(9) 希臘神話中奧德修斯的父親，被罰不斷從山下推動同一塊大石上山頂。

the time had arrived when it was better for me to die and be released from trouble; wherefore the oracle gave no sign. For which reason, also, I am not angry with my condemners, or with my accusers; they have done me no harm, although they did not mean to do me any good; and for this I may gently blame them.

Still I have a favour to ask of them. When my sons are grown up, I would ask you, O my friends, to punish them; and I would have you trouble them, as I have troubled you, if they seem to care about riches, or anything, more than about virtue; or if they pretend to be something when they are really nothing, — then reprove them, as I have reproved you, for not caring about that for which they ought to care, and thinking that they are something when they are really nothing. And if you do this, both I and my sons will have received justice at your hands.

The hour of departure has arrived, and we go our ways — I to die, and you to live. Which is better God only knows.

局絕非偶然。我清楚知道現在對我來說，死亡比在世爲佳。我可以擺脫一切煩惱，因此未有神諭顯現。爲了同樣的理由，我不怨恨起訴者或是將我判罪的人。他們雖對我不懷善意，却未令我受害。不過，我可要稍稍責怪他們的不懷善意。

可是我仍然要請你們爲我做一件事情。諸位朋友，我的幾個兒子成年後，請爲我教導他們。如果他們把財富或其他事物看得比品德爲重，請像我煩勸你們那樣煩勸他們。如果他們自命不凡，那麼，請像我譴責你們那樣譴責他們，因爲他們忽視了該看重的事物，本屬貌小而自命不凡。你們倘能這樣做，我和我的兒子便會自你們手中得到公義。

離別的時刻到了，我們得各自上路──我走向死亡，你們繼續活下去。至於生與死孰優，只有神明方知。

3 The Public Spirit of the Athenians

The Athenians never were known to live contented
in a slavish though secure obedience to unjust and
arbitrary power. No. Our whole history is a series of
gallant contests for preeminence: the whole period of
our national existence hath been spent in braving
dangers, for the sake of glory and renown. And so
highly do you esteem such conduct, as characteristic
of the Athenian spirit, that those of your ancestors who
were most eminent for it are ever the most favorite
objects of your praise. And with reason: for, who can
reflect, without astonishment, on the magnanimity of
those men who resigned their lands, gave up their city,
and embarked in their ships, rather than live at the
bidding of a stranger? The Athenians of that day looked
out for no speaker, no general, to procure them a state
of easy slavery. They had the spirit to reject even life,
unless they were allowed to enjoy that life in freedom.
For it was a principle fixed deeply in every breast, that
man was not born to his parents only, but to his
country. And mark the distinction. He who regards
himself as born only to his parents waits in passive
submission for the hour of his natural dissolution. He
who considers that he is the child of his country, also,
volunteers to meet death rather than behold that
country reduced to vassalage; and thinks those insults
and disgraces which he must endure, in a state enslaved,
much more terrible than death.

. . .

三 雅典人為公衆服務的精神

德摩士梯尼斯

雅典人從不向專橫無義的政權卑恭屈膝，以求安逸。不，我們歷史記載的是一系列英勇傑出的事跡：立國以來，我們一直勇敢地克服艱險以保持國家榮譽。你們極其崇敬這類行為，認為這是雅典精神的特徵。在這方面有超卓表現的先輩，歷來是最受頌揚的人物。你們的想法自有道理。對於那些寧願離鄉背井，遠航他方而不願俯首聽命於異族的人，誰能不詫異於他們的崇高舉動呢？當日的雅典人並未渴求什麼議長或將軍為他們謀取不難忍受的奴隷地位。他們具有生而不得自由毋寧死去的精神。牢固於每人心底的原則是人生來不僅屬於父母，且屬於國家，請注意其間的差別。如果一個人認為自己生來僅為父母，他就只會被動地靜待自然死亡。可是，如果他認為自己也屬國家的兒女，便會自願赴死，也不願看到自己的國家淪為附庸。國家處於奴役的地位時，他會感到所蒙受的侮辱與羞恥比死亡更難忍受。

……

德摩士梯尼斯（公元前384？～322），古希臘哲學家、演說家。他深感馬其頓人對希臘的威脅，力圖保衞希臘自由。本篇選自他譴責馬其頓王腓力二世的一系列文章。

4 On the Crown

Demosthenes

. . .

I should conclude, AEschines, that you undertook this cause to exhibit your eloquence and strength of lungs, not to obtain satisfaction for any wrong. But it is not the language of an orator, AEschines, that has any value, yet the tone of his voice, but his adopting the same views with the people, and his hating and loving the same persons that his country does. He that is thus minded will say everything with loyal intention: he that courts persons from whom the commonwealth apprehends danger to herself, rides not on the same anchorage with the people, and therefore has not the same expectation of safety. But − do you see? − I have: for my objects are the same with those of my countrymen; I have no interest separate or distinct. Is that so with you? How can it be − when immediately after the battle you went as ambassador to Philip, who was at that period the author of your country's calamities, notwithstanding that you had before persisted in refusing that office, as all men know?

And who is it that deceives the state? Surely the man who speaks not what he thinks. On whom does the crier pronounce a curse? Surely on such a man.

雅典政治家泰西凡（Ctesiphen）鑒於德摩士梯尼斯為雅典所作的貢獻，建議贈以金冠。政敵埃斯吉尼斯認為這建議違法。本文是公元前 330 年德摩士梯尼

四　金冠辯

德摩士梯尼斯

……

埃斯吉尼斯，我可以下斷言，你是利用這件事來顯示你的口才和嗓門，而不是爲了懲惡揚善。但是，埃斯吉尼斯，一個演說家的語言和聲調的高低並沒有什麼價值。能夠以人民的觀點爲自己的觀點，以國家的愛憎爲自己的愛憎，這才有意義。只有心裏懷着這點的人才會以忠誠的心志說每一句話。要是對威脅共和國安全的人阿諛奉承，同人民離心離德，那自然無法指望與人民一道得到安全的保障了。但是，——你看到了嗎？——我却得到了這種安全保障，因爲我的目標與我的同胞一致，我關注的利益跟人民無異。你是否也是這樣呢？這又怎麼可能？儘管衆所周知，你原來一直拒絕接受出使腓力[1]的任務，戰後你却立刻就到腓力那裏作大使了，那時給我們國家帶來大難的罪魁禍首正是他。

是誰欺騙了國家？當然是那個內心所想與口頭所說不一的人。宣讀公告的人該對誰公開

斯的辯護詞，辯論結果決定贈與德摩士梯尼斯金冠。

（1）腓力二世（公元前382～336），馬其頓王，雅典的敵人。

What greater crime can an orator be charged with than that his opinions and his language are not the same? Such is found to be your character. And yet you open your mouth, and dare to look these men in the faces! Do you think they don't know you? — or are sunk all in such slumber and oblivion as not to remember the speeches which you delivered in the assembly, cursing and swearing that you had nothing to do with Philip, and that I brought that charge against you out of personal enmity without foundation? No sooner came the news of the battle, than you forgot all that; you acknowledged and avowed that between Philip and yourself there subsisted a relation of hospitality and friendship — new names these for your contract of hire. For upon what plea of equality or justice could AEschines, son of Glaucothea the timbrel-player, be the friend or acquaintance of Philip? I cannot see. No! You were hired to ruin the interests of your countrymen: and yet though you have been caught yourself in open treason, and informed against yourself after the fact, you revile and reproach me for things which you will find any man is chargeable with sooner than I.

Many great and glorious enterprises has the commonwealth, AEschines, undertaken and succeeded in through me; and she did not forget them. Here is the proof — On the election of a person to speak the funeral oration immediately after the event, you were proposed, but the people would not have you, notwithstanding your fine voice, nor Demades, though he had just made the peace, nor Hegemon, nor any other of your party — but me. And when you and Pythocles came forward in a brutal and shameful manner (O merciful heaven!) and urged the same accusations against me which you now do, and abused me, they elected me all the more.

詛咒？當然是上述那類人。對於一個演說家，還有比心思與說話不一更大的罪名嗎？你的品格却正是這樣。你還膽敢張口說話，敢正視這些人！你以爲他們沒有認清你嗎？你以爲他們昏昏沉睡或如此健忘,已忘記你在會上的講話？你在會上一面詛咒別人，一面發誓與腓力絕無關係，說我告發你是出於私怨，並無事實根據嗎？等到戰爭的消息一傳來，你就把這一切都忘記了。你發誓表示和腓力很友好，你們之間存在友誼──其實這是你賣身的新代名詞。埃斯吉尼斯，你只是鼓手格勞柯蒂亞的兒子，又能夠在什麼平等和公正的懇詞下成爲腓力的朋友或知交呢？我看是不可能的。不,絕不可能！你是受僱來破壞國人利益的。雖然你在公開叛變中被當場捉獲，事後也受到了告發，你却還以一些別的人都可能犯而我却不會犯的事來辱罵我、譴責我。

埃斯吉尼斯，我們共和政體的許多偉大光榮事業是由我完成的,國家沒有忘記我的業績。以下事例就是明證：選舉由誰來發表葬禮後的演說時，有人提議你，可是，儘管你的聲音動聽，人民不選你；也不選狄美德斯，儘管他剛剛達成和平；也不選海吉門或你們一伙的任何人，却選了我。你和彼梭克列斯以粗暴而又可恥的態度（慈悲的上天啊！）列出你現在所舉的這些罪狀來譴責、辱罵我時，人民却更要選

The reason — you are not ignorant of it — yet I will tell you. The Athenians knew as well the loyalty and zeal with which I conducted their affairs as the dishonesty of you and your party; for what you denied upon oath in our prosperity you confessed in the misfortunes of the republic. They considered, therefore, that men who got security for their politics by the public disasters had been their enemies long before, and were then avowedly such. They thought it right also that the person who was to speak in honor of the fallen and celebrate their valor should not have sat under the same roof or at the same table with their antagonists; that he should not revel there and sing a paean over the calamities of Greece in company with their murderers, and then come here and receive distinction; that he should not with his voice act the mourner of their fate, but that he should lament over them with his heart. This they perceived in themselves and in me, but not in any of you: therefore they elected me, and not you. Nor, while the people felt thus, did the fathers and brothers of the deceased, who were chosen by the people to perform their obsequies, feel differently. For having to order the funeral banquet (according to custom) at the house of the nearest relative to the deceased, they ordered it at mine. And with reason: because, though each to his own was nearer of kin than I was, none was so near to them all collectively. He that has the deepest interest in their safety and success had upon their mournful disaster the largest share of sorrow for them all.

舉我。原因你不是不知道，但我還是要告訴你。雅典人知道我處理他們的事務時的忠誠與熱忱，正如他們知道你和你們一伙的不忠。共和國昌盛時你對某些事物發誓拒認，國家蒙受不幸時，你却承認了。因此，對於那些以共和國災難來取得政治安全的人，我們的人民認爲遠在他們如此做時已是人民的敵人，現在則更是公認的敵人。對於那向死者演說致敬、表揚烈士英勇精神的人，人民認爲他不應和烈士爲敵的人共處一室，同桌而食；他不該與殺人兇手一起開懷飲宴，並爲希臘的大難唱歡樂之歌後，再來這裏接受殊榮；他不該用聲音來哀悼烈士的厄運而應以誠心吊唁他們。人民在我和他們自己身上體會得這一點，却無法在你們任何人中尋得。因此他們選了我，不選你們。人民的想法如此，人民選出來主持葬禮的死者父兄的想法也一樣。按照風俗，喪筵應設在死者至親家屬中，但人民却命令將筵席設在我家。他們這樣做有道理：因爲單獨來說，各人與死者的親屬關係要比我密切，可是，對全體死者而言，却沒有人比我更親了。最深切關心他們安危成就的人，對他們死難的哀痛也最深。

5 To His Soldiers

Hannibal

. . .

Here, soldiers, where you have first met the enemy, you must conquer or die; and the same fortune which has imposed the necessity of fighting holds out to you, if victorious, rewards than which men are not wont to desire greater, even from the immortal gods. If we were only about to recover by our valor Sicily and Sardinia, wrested from our fathers, the recompense would be sufficiently ample; but whatever, acquired and amassed by so many triumphs, the Romans posses, all, with its masters themselves, will become yours. To gain this rich reward, hasten, then, and seize your arms, with the favor of the gods.

Long enough, in pursuing cattle among the desert mountains of Lusitania and Celtiberia, you have seen no emolument from so many toils and dangers; it is time to make rich and profitable campaigns, and to gain the great reward of your labors, after having accomplished such a length of journey over so many mountains and rivers, and so many nations in arms. Here fortune has granted you the termination of your labors; here she will bestow a reward worthy of the service you have undergone. Nor, in proportion as the war is great in name, ought you to consider that the victory will be difficult. A despised enemy has often maintained a sanguinary contest, and renowned states and kings have been conquered by a very slight effort.

漢尼拔（公元前247～183），北非迦太基大將。
他在公元前 218 年率兵橫越阿爾卑斯山進攻意大利時
對兵士發表本篇演說。此次遠征以失敗告終。

五　致衆士兵

漢尼拔

……

　　士兵們，這裏是你們與敵人初遇的地方，在這裏，你們若不能取勝，便只能就義成仁。命運之神使你們不得不戰，但現在你們倘若得勝，她對你們的犒勞要比人們希望從永生之神那裏得到的還要多。哪怕我們憑着勇氣，只收復在祖先手裏失去的西西里省和薩丁省[1]，這報酬也夠豐厚的了；但是，羅馬人在多次勝利中向我們索取積聚的一切，連同他們自己，都將歸你們所有。爲了得到這份豐厚的報酬，快快拿起武器吧！神將賜福給你們。

　　你們在盧西塔尼亞[2]和切爾蒂伯利亞[3]荒涼的羣山中放牧牛羣已經很久了，你們備嘗辛苦，歷盡艱險，但毫無收益。現在是發財致富，打勝仗、取俘獲的時候了，因爲你們跋山涉水、長途勞頓，攻城圍國。命運之神決定在這裏結束你們的勞頓，論功行賞。這場戰爭雖是赫赫有名，但你們不應爲取勝感到困難。被人藐視的軍隊往往具有強大的戰鬥力，聲威遠震的國家與帝王却常毀敗於一旦。

（1）今意大利境內。

（2）今葡萄牙境內。

（3）今意大利境內。

. . .

I do not regard it, soldiers, as of small account that there is not a man among you before whose eyes I have not often achieved some military exploit; and to whom in like manner, I, the spectator and witness of his valor, could not recount his own gallant deeds, particularized by time and place. With soldiers who have a thousand times received my praises and gifts, I, who was the pupil of you all before I became your commander, will march out in battle array against those who are unknown to and ignorant of each other.

On whatever side I turn my eyes I see nothing but what is full of courage and energy: a veteran infantry; cavalry, both those with and those without the bridle, composed of the most gallant nations, — you, our most faithful and valiant allies, you Carthaginians, who are about to fight as well for the sake of your country as from the justest resentment. We are the assailants in the war, and descend into Italy with hostile standards, about to engage so much more boldly and bravely than the foe, as the confidence and courage of the assailants are greater than those of him who is defensive. Besides, suffering, injury and indignity inflame and excite our minds: they first demanded me, your leader, for punishment, and then all of you who had laid siege to Saguntum; and had we been given up they would have visited us with the severest tortures.

That most cruel and haughty nation considers everything its own, and at its own disposal; it thinks it right that it should regulate with whom we are to have war, with whom peace; it circumscribes and shuts us up by the boundaries of mountains and rivers which

……

士兵們，你們沒有一人不親眼看到我的一些戰績；同樣，我也目睹過你們每人勇敢殺敵的英雄氣概，我能一一細述你們在何時何地的戰功。我不認為這是一件小事。我曾千百次讚揚和獎賞你們。我現在是你們的統帥，但以前曾是你們的學生。有這樣的兵士和我在一起，那支官兵互不相識了解的軍隊是不堪一擊的。

我舉目四顧，看到的都是勇氣百倍、精力充沛的人：身經百戰的步兵和各英雄民族組成的馬上馬下的騎兵。你們，我們最忠誠果敢的同盟伙伴，還有你們，迦太基人啊，你們將要懷着義憤為自己國家而戰。我們在戰爭中是進攻者，將高舉軍旗向意大利衝殺過去。我們比敵人更大膽無畏，因為進攻者總是比防禦者更有信心和勇氣。此外，我們所受的苦難、損害和侮辱激起我們胸中的怒火，促使我，你們的主帥，痛懲敵人，也要求曾包圍猛攻薩貢塔姆[1]的你們一起這樣做。如果我們不這樣做，我們的內心痛楚早就會把我們折磨得苦不堪言。

那最殘忍和傲慢的民族把一切視作己有，認為一切都聽任他們主宰。他們認為我們同誰作戰、同誰和好都理應由他們來作安排。他們以山脈與河流為邊界將我們圍禁封鎖起來，但

_____

（1）古羅馬地名。

we must not pass, and then does not adhere to those boundaries which it appointed. Pass not the Iberius; have nothing to do with the Sagauntines. Saguntum is on the Iberius; you must not move a step in any direction. Is it a small thing that you take away my most ancient provinces — Sicily and Sardinia? Will you take Spain also? And should I withdraw thence, will you cross over into Africa?

Will cross, did I say? They have sent the two consuls of this year, one to Africa, the other to Spain: there is nothing left to us in any quarter, except what we can assert to ourselves by arms. Those may be cowards and dastards who have something to look back upon; whom flying through safe and unmolested roads, their own lands and their own country will receive: there is a necessity for you to be brave, and, since all between victory and death is broken off from you by inevitable despair, either to conquer, or, if fortune should waver, to meet death rather in battle than in flight. If this be well fixed and determined in the minds of you all, I will repeat, you have already conquered; no stronger incentive to victory has been given to man by the immortal gods.

他們却可以隨意越出劃定的邊界。他們說不許越過伊比利亞；不許碰一碰薩貢廷。薩貢塔姆位於伊比利亞境內，無論是東南西北那個方向，你們都不能越雷池一步！難道奪去我們歷史悠久的省份西西里和撒丁是一件小事嗎？你們還要把西班牙取去吧？假如我從那裏撤退，你們是否要橫渡重洋，入侵非洲呢？

我剛才說他們要橫渡重洋，是嗎？他們今年已向非洲和西班牙各派了一位執政官。除却靠軍隊維護得屬於我們自己的地方，再無其他土地留給我們了。還有後路的人可能成爲懦夫或膽小鬼，他們可以從未被圍困的安全途徑脫逃，回到接納他們的家鄉與國土。可是，你們必須勇敢作戰，因爲勝利與死亡之間的一切中間道路已經不可避免地完全堵死，要末奪取勝利，要末不幸戰死沙場，也不能在逃跑中被殲殺。假如你們下定決心做到上述所說，我重複一遍，你們已取得勝利了。永生之神從未如此有力地激勵人爭取勝利。

6 In Defense of the Rhodians

I know that most men in the hour of success and
prosperity become exalted in spirit and feel excessive
pride and haughtiness. Since, then, we have fared so
well in our late war, I am anxious that we should commit no blunder in our deliberations to dim the luster
of our triumph, and that we should not manifest our
joy with too great exuberance. Adversity brings men to
their senses, and shows them what must be done; but
prosperity is apt to turn men, in the excess of their
joy, aside from the path of cool deliberation and sound
judgment. It is for this reason that I urge and persuade
you to postpone the determination of this matter until
we recover from our excessive joy and regain our usual
self-control.

I admit that the Rhodians did not wish to see us
conquer the king of Persia. But the Rhodians are not
alone; many other peoples and many other nations
have expressed that same wish. And I am inclined to
believe that their attitude in this war was due not to
any desire to affront us, but to the very natural fear
that of there was no one in the world whom we feared,
and we should have our way, they, like many other
nations, would soon become the slaves of our imperial
rule. They were prompted only by a desire to preserve
their liberty. And yet they never openly aided the
Persian king.

六 為洛迪安人申辯

馬柯斯‧朴斯厄斯‧凱圖

我知道多數人在取得勝利和成就的時刻都會得意洋洋、驕傲自大、目中無人。鑒於我們上次戰爭作戰極其順利，我深切希望我們不要因考慮欠周而犯錯誤，使我們輝煌的勝利黯然失色；我希望我們不要得意忘形。逆境使人頭腦清醒，明白必須做什麼事情；順境却容易令人得意忘形，偏離冷靜的思考和可靠的判斷。正因上述理由，我敦促勸告你們，待過份的興奮消退，回復我們往常的自制能力時，再就這問題作出決定。

我承認洛迪安人不願看到我們戰勝波斯王。可是，不單洛迪安人如此，許多其他民族和國家均表達相同的願望。我頗相信洛迪安人以上述的態度看待這場戰爭，並非有意冒犯我們。相反，那是一種很自然的恐懼，害怕我們一旦在這世上無所忌憚，便會為所欲為。他們害怕很快就會像其他許多民族一樣，成為我們帝國統治下的奴隸。保持自由的願望驅使他們如此，可是，即使這樣，他們並未公開支援波斯王。

凱圖（公元前234～149）羅馬政治家、將軍。洛迪安人拒絕在波斯戰爭中幫助羅馬人，凱圖在本文為洛迪安人申辯。

Pause now for a moment, and consider how much more solicitous we are about our private interests than the Rhodians have been about their welfare. If any one of us foresees a possible injury to his private interests, he struggles might and main to avert it. Yet the Rhodians have patiently submitted to such a possible injury to their welfare.

Shall we now give up all at once the great advantages of our friendship with the Rhodians, and deprive them, too, of equal advantages? Were we not the first to do in fact the very thing which we now say the Rhodians wished to do?

. . .

It certainly is not proper that a man should be held in esteem merely because he says he has had a disposition to do good when in fact he has not done so. Shall the Rhodians, then, be in a worse position, not because they have actually done wrong, but because they are said to have the desire to do so?

"But these Rhodians," they say, "are proud" — a reproach that touches me and my children. Suppose they are proud. What is that to us? Are we to lose our temper because some one else is prouder than we?

請你們稍停片刻，想想我們多關切自身的利益，遠超洛迪安人考慮他們的利益。假如我們任何一人預見自己的利益可能受損，他會竭盡全力避免這不幸。然而洛迪安人明白他們的利益可能受損，却一直耐心忍受。

我們現在是否要一下子放棄跟洛迪安人友好而得的多樣好處，並剝奪爲他們帶來的同樣好處呢？那樣一來，我們說洛迪安人想要做的事，事實上我們自己不是先就做了嗎？

……

一個人說他打算做好事而事實上沒有做，對這樣的人報以尊敬當然是不恰當的。那麼，洛迪安人並沒有做錯事，而只是有人說他們想做，難道竟能因此而對他們報以敵意嗎？

"但是這些洛迪安人呀，可眞驕傲"，他們說。這個譴責倒說中了我和我的孩子們。就算他們驕傲吧，那又和我們有什麼相干呢？是不是因爲有人比我們更驕傲，我們就該發脾氣呢？

7 Denunciation of Verres

Marcus Tullius Cicero

An opinion has long prevailed, Fathers, that, in public prosecutions, men of wealth, however clearly convicted, are always safe. This opinion, so injurious to your order, so detrimental to the State, it is now in your power to refute. A man is on trial before you who is rich, and who hopes his riches will compass his acquittal; but whose life and actions are his sufficient condemnation in the eyes of all candid men. I speak of Caius Verres, who, if he now receives not the sentence his crimes deserve, it shall not be through the lack of a criminal, or of a prosecutor; but through the failure of the ministers of justice to do their duty. Passing over the shameful irregularities of his youth, what does the quaestorship of Verres exhibit but one continued scene of villainies? The public treasure squandered, a Consul stripped and betrayed, an army deserted and reduced to want, a province robbed, the civil and religious rights of a People trampled on! But his praetorship in Sicily has crowned his career of wickedness, and completed the lasting monument of his infamy. His decisions have violated all law, all precedent, all right. His extortions from the industrious poor have been beyond computation. Our most faithful allies have been treated as

七 對弗里斯的控告

馬柯斯・圖利厄斯・西塞羅

各位元老，長時期以來大家有這樣的見解：有錢人犯了罪，不管怎樣證據確鑿，在公開的審判中總還是安然無事。這種見解對你們的社會秩序十分有害，對國家十分不利。現在，駁斥這種見解的力量正掌握在你們手中。在你們面前受審的是個有錢人，他指望以財富來開脫罪名；可是在一切公正無私的人心中，他本身的生活和行為就足以給他定罪了。我說的這個人就是凱厄斯・弗里斯。假如今天他並未受到罪有應得的懲處，那不是因為缺乏罪證，也不是因為沒有檢察官，而是因為司法官失職。弗里斯青年時放蕩無行，後來任財務官時，除為惡之外又豈有其他？他虛耗國庫，欺騙並出賣一位執政官，棄職逃離軍隊使之得不到補給，劫掠某省，踐踏羅馬民族的公民權和宗教信仰權！弗里斯在西西里任總督時，罪惡滿盈，使他的劣跡遺臭萬年。他在這期間的種種決策違反了一切法律、一切判決先例和所有公理。他對勞苦人民的橫征暴斂無法計算。他把我們最

西塞羅（公元前106～43），羅馬著名政治家與哲學家。弗里斯於公元前73年任西西里總督。當時羅馬官員貪污的情形很普遍，弗里斯是其中著者。

enemies. Roman citizens have, like slaves, been put to death with tortures. Men the most worthy have been condemned and banished without a hearing, while the most atrocious criminals have, with money, purchased exemption from the punishment due to their guilt.

I ask now, Verres, what have you to advance against these charges? Art thou not the tyrant praetor, who, at no greater distance than Sicily, within sight of the Italian coast, dared to put to an infamous death, on the cross, that ill-fated and innocent citizen, Publius Gavius Cosanus? And what was his offence? He had declared his intention of appealing to the justice of his country against your brutal persecutions! For this when about to embark for home, he was seized, brought before you, charged with being a spy, scourged, and tortured. In vain did he exclaim: "I am a Roman citizen! I have served under Lucius Pretius, who is now at Panormus, and who will attest my innocence!" Deaf to all remonstrance, remorseless, thirsting for innocent blood, you ordered the savage punishment to be inflicted! While the sacred words, "I am a Roman citizen," were on his lips, — words which, in the remotest regions, are a passport to protection, — you ordered him to death, to a death upon the cross!

O liberty! O sound once delightful to every Roman ear! O sacred privilege of Roman citizenship! Once sacred, — now trampled on! Is it come to this? Shall an inferior magistrate, a governor, who holds his whole power of the Roman People, in a Roman province, within sight of Italy, bind, scourge, torture, and put to an infamous death, a Roman citizen? Shall neither the

忠誠的盟邦當作仇敵對待。他把羅馬公民像奴隸一樣施以酷刑處死。許多傑出的人物不經審訊就被宣佈有罪而遭流放，暴戾的罪犯却用錢行賄得以赦免。

弗里斯，我現在要問你對這些控罪還有什麼辯解的話說？不正是你這暴君，膽敢在意大利海岸目力所及的西西里島上，將無辜不幸的公民帕畢列阿斯‧加弗斯‧柯申納斯釘在十字架上，使他受辱而死嗎？他犯了什麼罪？他曾表示要向國家法官上訴，控告你殘酷迫害！他正要爲此乘船歸來時，就被捉拿到你面前控以密探之罪，受到嚴刑拷打。雖是徒然無效，他仍宣稱：「我是羅馬公民，曾在魯克斯普列蒂阿斯手下工作。他現刻在盤諾馬斯，他將證明我無罪！」你對這些抗辯充耳不聞，你殘忍已極、嗜血成性，竟下令施此酷刑！「我是一個羅馬公民！」這句神聖的話，即使在最僻遠之地也還是安全的護身憑證。但柯申納斯語音未絕，你就將他處死，釘在十字架上！

啊，自由，這曾是每個羅馬人的悅耳樂音！啊，神聖的羅馬公民權，一度是神聖不容侵犯的，而今却橫遭踐踏！難道事情眞已至此地步？難道一個低級的地方總督，他的全部權力來自羅馬人民，竟可以在意大利所見的一個羅馬省份裏，任意綑縛、鞭打、刑訊並處死一位羅馬公民嗎？難道無辜受害者的痛苦叫喊，旁

cries of innocence expiring in agony, the tears of pitying spectators, the majesty of the Roman Commonwealth, nor the fear of justice of his country restrain the merciless monster, who, in the confidence of his riches, strikes at the very root of liberty, and sets mankind at defiance? And shall this man escape? Fathers, it must not be! It must not be, unless you would undermine the very foundations of social safety, strangle justice, and call down anarchy, massacre, and ruin, on the Commonwealth!

觀者的同情熱淚，羅馬共和國的威嚴以至畏懼國家法制的心理都不能制止那殘忍的惡人嗎？那人恃仗自己的財富，打擊自由的根基，公然蔑視人類！難道這惡人可以逃脫懲罰嗎？諸位元老，這一定不可以啊！這樣做了，你們就會挖去社會安全的基石，扼殺正義，給共和國招來混亂、殺戮和毀滅！

8 The First Oration Against Catiline

Marcus Tullius Cicero

When, O Catiline, do you mean to cease abusing our patience? How long is that madness of yours still to mock us? When is there to be an end of that unbridled audacity of yours, swaggering about as it does now? Do not the mighty guards placed on the Palatine Hill — do not the watches posted throughout the city — does not the alarm of the people, and the union of all good men — does not the precaution taken of assembling the senate in this most defensible place — do not the looks and countenances of this venerable body here present, have any effect upon you? Do you not feel that your plans are detected? Do you not see that your conspiracy is already arrested and rendered powerless by the knowledge which every one here possesses of it? What is there that you did last night, what the night before — where is it that you were — who was there that you summoned to meet you — what design was there which was adopted by you, with which you think that any one of us is unacquainted?

You were, then, O Catiline, at Lecca's that night; you divided Italy into sections; you settled where every one was to go; you fixed whom you were to leave at Rome, whom you were to take with you; you portioned out the divisions of the city for conflagration; you undertook that you yourself would at once leave the city, and said that there was then only this to delay you, that I was still alive. . . .

八 對凱蒂林控告的第一次講話

馬柯斯・圖利厄斯・西塞羅

凱蒂林啊，你究竟還要我們忍耐到何時？你還要顛狂胡鬧地愚弄我們多久？你狂妄而肆無忌憚的行為到什麼時候才算了結？難道巴勒坦山上的強大警衛，滿佈全城的守望哨崗，人民的警戒，所有善良者的聯合，元老集會時所採的嚴密預防措施，在座諸公的威嚴儀態，對你都無足輕重嗎？你難道還不感到詭計已被查明了嗎？你沒看見在座眾人均已識破你的陰謀，使之不能得逞了嗎？你昨晚和前夜在什麼地方，幹了什麼，召見了什麼人，策劃了什麼，所有這一切，你以為有哪一樣我們不知道？

啊，凱蒂林，你那天晚上在列斯加的住處。你們把意大利分成一片片，商定把所有人打發去的地點；決定某人將留在羅馬，某人將跟從你們離開。你們把羅馬城劃分為一個個區，準備縱火。你準備立即離開本城，還說唯一能阻延你的，就是我還活着。……

本文發表於公元前63年。

凱蒂林（公元前108～62），羅馬政治家，曾為非洲總督。西塞羅偵得他用錢財及許以官爵等方式競選，對他提出控告。元老院於公元前62年將凱蒂林判以死刑。

As, then, this the case, O Catiline, continue as you have begun, leave the city at last: the gates are open; depart. That Manlian camp of yours has been waiting too long for you as its general. And lead forth with all your friends, or at least as many as you can: purge the city of your presence; you will deliver me from a great fear, when there is a wall between me and you. Among us you can dwell no long — I will not bear it, I will not permit it, I will not tolerate it.

. . .

凱蒂林呵，旣然如此，繼續你已經開始那樣，最後離開這城市吧：城門現在大開，你們走吧。你們的門蘭軍營等待你當他們的主帥已久。讓你的所有朋友都跟你走吧，或至少你能帶走多少就帶多少；讓這座城不留下一點你的痕迹；你我之間隔着一道城牆，你才算讓我擺脫心腹大患。你不能再留在我們這裏了，我受不了，我不允許，不能容忍。

　　……

9 Speech to Augustine and His Followers

Ethelbert

Your words are fair, and your promises — but because they are new and doubtful, I cannot give my assent to them, and leave the customs which I have so long observed, with the whole Anglo-Saxon race. But because you have come hither as strangers from a long distance, and as I seem to myself to have seen clearly, that what you yourselves believed to be true and good, you wish to impart to us, we do not wish to molest you; nay, rather we are anxious to receive you hospitably, and to give you all that is needed for your support, nor do we hinder you from joining all whom you can to the faith of your religion.

九　對奧古斯廷及其隨員的歡迎詞

埃塞爾伯特

你們的說話和諾言都合乎情理。可是，這些話，我們以前未有所聞，不免有些疑慮，所以我不能表示贊同，不能拋棄我和全體盎格魯薩克遜民族長久以來遵從的習俗。不過，你們是來自遠方的異鄉人，我也似乎清楚看得出你們希望向我們傳揚自己深信的眞與善，因此，我們不願干擾你們。相反，我們切望友好地接待你們，給你們所需的一切支持。你們可盡力使人皈依你們信奉的宗教，我們不會阻礙你們。

埃塞爾伯特（560？～616），英格蘭王。

奧古斯廷，意大利傳教士，597年到英格蘭傳敎。埃塞爾伯特接待並信奉了他們宣揚的敎義，成爲首位信奉基督敎的英格蘭國王。

10　The Rage of Battle

Duke William of Normandy

Normans! bravest of nations! I have no doubt of your courage, and none of your victory, which never by any chance or obstacle escaped your efforts. If indeed you had, once only, failed to conquer, there might be a need now to inflame your courage by exhortation; but your native spirit does not require to be roused. Bravest of men, what could the power of the Frankish king effect with all his people, from Lorraine to Spain, against Hasting my predecessor? What he wanted of France he took, and gave to the king only what he pleased. What he had, he held as long as it suited him, and relinquished it only for something better. Did not Rollo my ancestor, founder of our nation, with our fathers conquer at Paris the king of the Franks in the heart of his kingdom, nor had the king of the Franks any hope of safety until he humbly offered his daughter and possession of the country, which, after you, is called Normandy.

威廉大公（1027～1087），諾曼底人首領羅倫（Rollo 860～930）的後代。黑斯廷斯（Hastings）之戰發生於1066年10月14日，威廉大公率領的軍隊與英王哈羅率領的軍隊大戰於此，這是諾曼底征服英國的決定性戰役。本篇是威廉作戰前對士兵的演說。

十　黑斯廷斯之戰

諾曼底威廉大公

　　諾曼底人！一切民族中最勇敢的人！我從不懷疑你們的勇氣，深信你們將取得勝利。直至現在，還未有任何意外或障礙阻止你們努力贏得勝利。如果你們確曾有一次落敗了，或許現在就需要我來激勵你們，但是，你們本來就士氣高昂，不必靠人鼓動。最勇敢的人啊！法蘭克王[1]動員了他從勞倫[2]到西班牙的所有人力，可曾抵擋住我先王黑斯廷[3]的進攻？當年在法國，生殺予奪，一由於他，法王只能靠他的賞賜度日。凡他佔有的，只要適合他的需要，他就一直佔有。只有為了換取更好的東西時，他才願意放棄原有之物。我們國家的創立者，我的祖先羅倫王，不曾率領我們的先父在法國心臟巴黎戰勝了當時的法蘭克王嗎？法王不是卑順地獻出了女兒和國家，才保住性命嗎？這國家後來就以你們民族命名，稱為諾曼底公國。

（1）日耳曼人在西羅馬滅亡後建立了許多封建王國，
　　法蘭克王國是其中最大的一個。

（2）地名，在今日法國東北部。

（3）九世紀末北歐威金斯海盜（Vikings）的領袖，縱
　　橫於法國、西班牙與意大利海岸。

Did not your fathers capture the king of the Franks
at Rouen, and keep him there until he restored
Normandy to Duke Richard, then a boy; with this
condition, that, in every conference between the king
of France and the Duke of Normandy, the duke should
wear his sword, while the king should not be permitted
to carry a sword nor even a dagger. This concession your
fathers compelled the great king to submit to, as binding
for ever. Did not the same duke lead your fathers to
Mirmande, at the foot of the Alpes, and enforce submission from the lord of the town, his son-in-law, to
his own wife, the duke's daughter? Nor was it enough
for you to conquer men, he conquered the devil himself,
with whom he wrestled, cast down and bound him with
his hands behind his back, and left him a shameful
spectacle to angels. But why do I talk of former times?
Did not you, in our own time, engage the Franks at
Mortemer? Did not the Franks prefer flight to battle,
and use their spurs? While you — Ralph, the commander
of the Franks having been slain — reaped the honour
and the spoil as the natural result of your success. Ah!
let any one of the English whom, a hundred times,
our predecessors, both Danes and Normans, have
defeated in battle, come forth and show that the race
of Rollo ever suffered a defeat from his time until
now, and I will withdraw conquered. Is it not, therefore, shameful that a people accustomed to be conquered, a people ignorant of war, a people even without
arrows, should proceed in order of battle against you,
my brave men? Is it not a shame that king Harold,
perjured as he was in your presence, should dare to
show his face to you? It is amazing to me that you have
been allowed to see those who, by a horrible crime,
beheaded your relations and Alfred my kinsman, and
that their own heads are still on their shoulders. Raise
your standards, my brave men, and set neither measure

再後，你們的先父又在魯昂俘獲法蘭克王，把他囚禁，直至他將諾曼底公國歸還當時年幼的理查大公。雙方並定下以後法國國王和諾曼底公爵舉行會議時，公爵可以佩劍，法王却連一把匕首也不得攜帶。那高貴的法王不得不讓步，同意這具有永久約束力的盟約。這位公爵後來不是領軍到阿爾卑斯山下的莫門第，迫使統治該城的公爵子婿聽命於他的妻子，亦即公爵的女兒嗎？你們只是征服凡人，羅倫公爵却能戰勝魔鬼。他同魔鬼搏鬥，把魔鬼打翻在地；雙手反剪，讓魔鬼受辱於衆天使之前。可是，我何必追溯往事呢？在我們的時代，你們不曾在摩梯梅大敗法蘭克人嗎？他們不是倉惶潰逃，怯於交戰嗎？你們不是殺死了法蘭克人的主帥拉爾夫，然後如常地滿載榮譽和戰利品凱旋而歸嗎？啊，英國人曾上百次敗於我們的祖先丹麥人和諾曼底人。任何一位英國人能站出來證明羅倫的民族自立國以來曾嘗一敗，我就馬上認輸撤退。我的勇士們啊！一個屢戰屢敗、對軍事一無所知、連弓箭都沒有的民族竟能陳兵列陣擋住你們，這豈不是奇恥大辱嗎？背信棄義的哈羅王竟敢露面和你們作戰，豈不叫人羞恥？令我十分驚異的是，將你們的親屬和我的族人艾爾弗雷德斬首，犯下滔天大罪的兇犯仍未授首。勇士們，高舉戰旗，奮勇前進吧！

nor limit to your merited rage. May the lightning of your glory be seen and the thunders of your onset heard from East to West, and be ye the avengers of noble blood.

你們叱咤之聲將震動山河，東西迴蕩；你們刀劍之光將上沖牛斗！為我高貴的死傷戰士復仇吧！

11 A Second Crusade

St. Bernard

You cannot but know that we live in a period of chastisement and ruin; the enemy of mankind has caused the breath of corruption to fly over all regions; we behold nothing but unpunished wickedness. The laws of men or the laws of religion have no longer sufficient power to check depravity of manners and the triumph of the wicked. The demon of heresy has taken possession of the chair of truth, and God has sent forth His malediction upon His sanctuary.

Oh, ye who listen to me, hasten then to appease the anger of Heaven, but no longer implore His goodness by vain complaints; clothe not yourselves in sackcloth, but cover yourselves with your impenetrable bucklers: the din of arms, the dangers, the labors, the fatigues of war are the penances that God now imposes upon you. Hasten then to expiate your sins by victories over the infidels, and let the deliverance of holy places be the reward of your repentance.

If it were announced to you that the enemy had invaded your cities, your castles, your lands; had ravished your wives and your daughters, and profaned your temples — which among you would not fly to arms? Well, then, all these calamities, and calamities still greater, have fallen upon your brethren, upon the family of Jesus Christ, which is yours. Why do you

十一　第二次十字軍東征

聖伯納德

　　你們必然認識到我們生活在一個災難深重、面臨毀滅的時代。人類之敵使得世界所有地區散發着腐朽的氣息。我們面前，滿目都是未受懲戒的邪惡。人類的法律和宗教的規條已無力阻止道德淪落、邪惡得逞。異教的魔鬼佔據了真理的寶座，上帝已將咒詛降到他的聖殿。

　　聽我說話的人們啊，你們快快使上天息怒吧，但不要只靠幾句空洞的訴怨來求得他的慈悲。披上喪服於事無補，穿上你們那刺不透的盔甲吧。白刃相交、行軍勞頓、危難困苦就是上帝要求你們的贖罪苦行。快快戰勝異教徒，以洗清你們的罪孽。奪回聖地將是你們懺悔的獎賞。

　　如果有人向你們宣告敵人已經侵佔了你們的城池與土地，凌辱了你們的妻女，褻瀆了你們的神廟，有誰會不飛奔前去拿起武器？現在，所有這些災難，甚至更大的災難已經降臨你們兄弟身上，降臨到耶穌基督的家庭——也就是

聖伯納德（1091？～1153），法國教士，羅馬教皇的顧問。從十一世紀開始，羅馬天主教為了收復聖地耶路撒冷，前後進行十次十字軍東征。本文是第二次出征前聖伯納德向軍隊佈道。

hesitate to repair so many evils — to revenge so many outrages? Will you allow the infidels to contemplate in peace the ravages they have committed on Christian people: Remembering that their triumph will be a subject for grief to all ages and an eternal opprobrium upon the generation that has endured it. Yes, the living God has charged me to announce to you that He will punish them who shall not have defended Him against His enemies.

Fly then to arms: let a holy rage animate you in the fight, and let the Christian world resound with these words of the prophet, "Cursed be he who does not stain his sword with blood!" If the Lord calls you to the defense of His heritage think not that His hand has lost its power. Could He not send twelve legions of angels or breathe one word and all His enemies would crumble away into dust? But God has considered the sons of men, to open for them the road to His mercy. His goodness has caused to dawn for you a day of safety by calling on you to avenge His glory and His name.

Christian warriors, He who gave His life for you, today demands yours in return. These are combats worthy of you, combats in which it is glorious to conquer and advantageous to die. Illustrious knights, generous defenders of the Cross, remember the examples of your fathers who conquered Jerusalem, and whose names are inscribed in Heaven; abandon then the things that perish, to gather unfading palms, and conquer a Kingdom which has no end.

你們自己的家庭。你們為什麼還在猶豫，不去消除罪惡，懲處暴行？難道你們能容許異教徒踐踏了基督子民後依舊心安理得，逍遙法外嗎？請記住，他們的得勝將使我們的子孫長恨無窮。我們這一代若容許他們得勝，便將成為千古罪人。是的，耶穌基督命我向你們宣佈他要懲罰那些不抗敵保護他的人。

快快拿起武器吧。願神聖的怒火使你們在戰鬥中勇武有力，願基督徒的世界迴響起先知的預言：“刀劍不染血的人要受詛咒。”如果我主召喚你們起來保衛他的財產，你們切勿以為他已失去手中力量。他豈不能派遣無數天使或一聲令下就使敵人頃刻之間化為齏粉？可是上帝顧惜他的子民，給他們仁慈的出路。他召你們為恢復他的榮耀和聖名而戰，使你們有一天得到平安。

基督的勇士們，為你們獻出生命的基督今天要求你們以生命回報。你們值得進行這場戰鬥，因為戰勝則無比光榮，死亦受福無窮。顯赫的騎士，十字架的英勇捍衛者啊，緊記你們先輩征服耶路撒冷的榜樣，他們的名字已經銘刻在天堂。拋棄塵世終將消滅的一切吧，你們該奪取的是常青之樹，要征服的是永恒的王國。

12 Bondmen and Freemen

When Adam delved and Eve span,
Who was then the gentleman?

From the beginning all men by nature were created
alike, and our bondage or servitude came in by the
unjust oppression of naughty men. For if God would
have had any bondmen from the beginning, he would
have appointed who should be bond, and who free.
And therefore I exhort you to consider that now the
time is come, appointed to us by God, in which ye
may (if ye will) cast off the yoke of bondage, and
recover liberty. I counsel you therefore well to bethink
yourselves, and to take good hearts unto you, that
after the manner of a good husband that tilleth his
ground, and riddeth out thereof such evil weeds as
choke and destroy the good corn, you may destroy
first the great lords of the realm, and after, the judges
and lawyers, and questmongers, and all other who have
undertaken to be against the commons. For so shall you
procure peace and surety to yourselves in time to come;
and by despatching out of the way the great men,
there shall be an equality in liberty, and no difference
in degrees of nobility; but a like dignity and equal
authority in all things brought in among you.

十二　奴隸與自由民

約翰・波爾

亞當和夏娃男耕女織時，
有誰是什麼紳士？

上帝造人之初，一切人生來本屬平等，後
來惡人不正義的壓迫，我們才陷於奴役束縛的
境地。如果上帝一開始就要創造奴隸，他必然
會指定誰為奴隸，誰享自由。上帝任命的時刻現
已到來，因此我要勸你們考慮，只要你們願意，
就可以擺脫身上的枷鎖，恢復自由。我建議你
們深思熟慮、鼓足勇氣、振作精神。你們要學
習一個好莊稼人的榜樣，先耕耘田地，再拔除
損壞莊稼的莠草。你們也可以先鏟除國內的大
貴族，然後除去法官、律師，貪得無厭者，和一
切壓抑平民百姓的人。時候一到你們將可以得
到和平與安穩。除去那些大人物後，你們就能
得到自由平等，再沒有高低貴賤的不同等級。剩
下的只是你們對一切事物的同等尊嚴和權威。

波爾（ ？～1381 ），英國牧師與社會改革家。
1376年被逐出教會，後復被捕，受酷刑而死。波爾於
1381年在倫敦附近向農民發表本篇演說。

13 Before the Diet of Worms

Martin Luther

. . .

Yet, as I am a mere man, and not God, I will defend myself after the example of Jesus Christ who said: "If I have spoken evil, bear witness against me" How much more should I, who am but dust and ashes, and so prone to error, desire that every one should bring forward what he can against my doctrine.

Therefore, most serene emperor, and you illustrious princes, and all, whether high or low, who hear me, I implore you by the mercies of God to prove to me by the writings of the prophets and apostles that I am in error. As soon as I shall be convinced, I will instantly retract all my errors, and will myself be the first to seize my writings, and commit them to the flames.

What I have just said I think will clearly show that I have well considered and weighed the dangers to which I am exposing myself; but far from being dismayed by them, I rejoice exceedingly to see the Gospel this day, as of old, a cause of disturbance and disagreement. It is the character and destiny of God's word. "I came not to send peace unto the earth, but a sword," said Jesus Christ. God is wonderful and awful in His counsels. Let us have a care, lest in our endeavors to arrest discords, we be bound to fight against the holy word of God and bring down upon our heads a frightful deluge of inextricable dangers, present disaster, and

馬丁‧路德（1483～1546），德國新教派的創立人及領袖。他從青年時代就激烈反對羅馬天主教，1520年被教皇驅逐出教會。本篇是他於1521年在沃姆斯帝

十三 在沃姆斯國會上的講話

馬丁‧路德

……

我只不過是個凡夫俗子，我不是上帝，因此，我要像耶穌那樣爲自己辯護，他曾說："如果我說了什麼有罪的話，請拿出證據來指證我。"[1] 我是一個卑微、無足輕重、易犯錯誤的人，除了要求敵人提出所有可能反對我教義的證據來，我還能要求什麼呢？

至尊的皇帝陛下，各位顯赫的親王，聽我說話的一切高低貴賤人士，我請求你們看在慈悲上帝的份上，用先知和使徒的話來證明我錯了。只要你們能使我折服，我就會公開承認我所有的錯誤，首先親手將我寫的文章付之一炬。

我剛才的說話清楚地表明，對於我處境的危險，我曾仔細權衡輕重、深思熟慮；可是我不但沒有被這些危險嚇倒，相反，極欣慰地看到今天基督的福音仍如古代一樣，引起了動盪與紛爭。這是上帝福音的特質，注定如此。耶穌基督曾說："我到世上，不是送來和平而是送來刀劍。"天意神妙而可敬可畏。我們應當謹慎，以免因制止爭論而觸犯上帝的聖誡，引來不能解脫的危險、當前的災難以至永遠的毀

_____

國國會受審的講話。

（1）《聖經》，約翰福音，第十八章第二十三節。

everlasting desolations. ... Let us have a care lest the reign of the young and noble prince, the Emperor Charles, on whom, next to God, we build so many hopes, should not only commence, but continue and terminate its course under the most fatal auspices. I might cite examples drawn from the oracles of God. I might speak of Pharaohs, of kings of Babylon, or of Israel, who were never more contributing to their own ruin that when, by measures in appearances most prudent, they thought to establish their authority! "God removeth the mountains and they know not" (Job IX, 5).

In speaking thus, I do not suppose that such noble princes have need of my poor judgment; but I wish to acquit myself of a duty that Germany has a right to expect from her children. And so commending myself to your august majesty, and your most serene highnesses, I beseech you in all humility, not to permit the hatred of my enemies to rain upon me an indignation I have not deserved.

Since your most serene majesty and your high mightinesses require of me a simple, clear and direct answer, I will give one, and it is this: I cannot submit my faith either to the pope or to the council, because it is as clear as noonday that they have fallen into error and even into glaring inconsistency with themselves. If, then, I am not convinced by proof from Holy Scripture, or by cogent reasons, if I am not satisfied by the very text I have cited, and if my judgment is not in this way brought into subjection to God's word, I neither can nor will retract anything; for it cannot be right for a Christian to speak against his conscience. I stand here and can say no more. God help me. Amen.

滅。……我們應當謹慎，使上天保祐我們高貴的少主查理士皇帝不僅開始治國，且國祚綿長。我們對他的希望僅次於上帝。我願引用神喻中的例子。我要說古埃及的法老王、巴比倫諸王和以色列諸王。他們外貌明智，想建立自己的權勢，結果成為滅亡的主因："上帝在他們不知不覺中移山倒海。"（約伯福音，第九章第五節）

我這樣說，並不表示各位高貴的親王需要聽取我粗淺的判斷。我這樣做，是出自我對德國的責任感。國家有權期望自己的兒女盡公民的責任。因此我來到陛下和各位殿下尊前，謙卑地懇求你們禁止我的敵人因仇恨而將我不該受的憤怒之情傾瀉於我。

既然至尊的皇帝陛下、諸位親王殿下要求我簡單明白、直接了當地回答，我遵命作答如下：我不能向教皇或元老院屈從，放棄我的信仰，理由是他們錯誤百出、自相矛盾的情形有如昭昭天日般明顯。如果找不出聖經的道理或無可辯駁的理由使我折服，不能用我適才引述的聖經文句令我滿意信服，無法用福音或聖經改變我的判斷，那麼，我不能夠，也不願收回我說過的任何一句話，因為基督徒是不能說違心之言的。這就是我的立場，我沒有別的話可說了。願上帝祐我，阿們。

14 True and False Simplicity

François Fénelon

. . .

Simplicity is an uprightness of soul that has no reference to self; it is different from sincerity, and it is a still higher virtue. We see many people who are sincere, without being simple; they only wish to pass for what they are, and they are unwilling to appear what they are not; they are always thinking of themselves, measuring their words, and recalling their thoughts, and reviewing their actions, from the fear that they have done too much or too little. These persons are sincere, but they are not simple; they are not at ease with others, and others are not at ease with them; they are not free, ingenuous, natural; we prefer people who are less correct, less perfect, and who are less artificial. This is the decision of man, and it is the judgment of God, who would not have us so occupied with ourselves, and thus, as it were, always arranging our features in a mirror.

To be wholly occupied with others, never to look within, is the state of blindness of those who are entirely engrossed by what is present and addressed to their senses; this is the very reverse of simplicity. To be absorbed in self in whatever engages us, whether we are laboring for our fellow beings or for God — to be wise in our own eyes reserved, and full of ourselves, troubled at the least thing that disturbs our self-complacency,

十四　眞的與假的單純

弗朗索瓦·費奈隆

……

　　單純是靈魂中一種正直無私的素質；它與眞誠不同，比眞誠更高尙。許多人眞心誠懇，却不單純。他們只望別人按他們的本來面目認識他們，不願意遭人誤解。他們總在想着自己，總在斟酌辭句、反省思量、審視行爲。唯恐過頭，又怕不足。這些人眞心誠懇，却不單純。他們不能和人坦然相處，別人對他們也小心拘謹。他們不坦率、不眞誠、不自然。我們倒寧願同不那麼正直，不那麼完美，也不那麼矯揉造作的人相處。世人以此準則取人，上帝也以此作判斷。上帝不願我們用這樣多的心思於自己，好像我們要時時對鏡整理自己的容顏。

　　完全集中注意他人而不內省是某些人的一種盲目狀態。這些人全神貫注於眼前事物以及感官感受到的一切。這恰好是單純的反面。以下是兩種相反極端的例子：其一是不管爲同類還是上帝効力，均全然忘我地投入；另一是自以爲聰明含蓄，心中充滿自我，只要自滿的情緒

費奈隆（1651～1715），法國著名神學家與作家，曾任主教。1689年，獲路易十四委任爲其孫的教師，後被放逐。

is the opposite extreme. This is false wisdom, which, with all its glory, is but little less absurd than that folly, which pursues only pleasure. The one is intoxicated with all it sees around it; the other with all that it imagines it has within; but it is delirium in both. To be absorbed in the contemplation of our own minds is really worse than to be engrossed by outward things, because it appears like wisdom and yet is not, we do not think of curing it, we pride ourselves upon it, we approve of it, it gives us an unnatural strength, it is a sort of frenzy, we are not conscious of it, we are dying, and we think ourselves in health.

Simplicity consists in a just medium, in which we are neither too much excited, nor too composed. The soul is not carried away by outward things, so that it cannot make all necessary reflections; neither does it make those continual references to self, that a jealous sense of its own excellence multiplies to infinity. That freedom of the soul, which looks straight onward in its path, losing no time to reason upon its steps, to study them, or to contemplate those that it has already taken, is true simplicity.

. . .

受到絲毫干擾便心煩意亂。這是虛假的聰明；表面上堂而皇之，實際上跟純爲追求享樂的愚蠢行爲同樣荒唐。前者昏昏然陶醉於眼前看到的一切，後者陶醉於自認爲內心已佔有的一切。這兩者都是虛妄的。一心只注意內心的冥思默想確比全神貫注於外界事物更有害，因爲這樣看來聰明而實則不然；我們不以此爲非、不想改正，反引以爲榮；我們肯定這種行爲；它給我們一種不自然的力量；這是一種瘋狂狀態，我們却不自覺；我們病入膏肓却還自以爲身體強健。

單純存在於適度之中，我們在其中旣不過份興奮，也不過份平靜。我們的靈魂不因過多注意外界事物而無法作必要的內省；我們也並不時刻考慮自己，使維護自己美德的戒備心理無限膨脹。我們的靈魂要是能夠無羈無絆，直視眼前的道路，並不白白浪費時間於權衡研究腳下的步伐，或是回顧已經走過的道路，這才是眞正的單純。

......

15 Speech on Necker's Financial Plan

Comte de Mirabeau

The minister of finance has presented a most alarming picture of the state of our affairs. He has assured us that delay must aggravate the peril; and that a day, an hour, an instant, may render it fatal. We have no plan that can be substituted for that which he proposes. On this plan, therefore, we must fall back. But, have we time, gentlemen ask, to examine it, to probe it thoroughly, and verify its calculations? No, no! a thousand times no! Haphazard conjectures, insignificant inquiries, gropings that can but mislead — there are all that we can give to it now. Shall we therefore miss the decisive moment? Do gentlemen hope to escape sacrifices and taxation by a plunge into national bankruptcy? What, then, is bankruptcy, but the most cruel, the most iniquitous, most unequal and disastrous of imposts? Listen to me for one moment!

Two centuries of plunder and abuse have dug the abyss which threatens to engulf the nation. It must be filled up — this terrible chasm. But how? Here is a list of proprietors. Choose from the wealthiest, in

---

米拉波（1749～1791），全名爲奧諾雷・加布里埃爾・維克托・里凱蒂・米拉波（Honoré Gabriel Victor Riquetti Mirabeau），法國政治家，頗受羣衆愛戴。

十五　關於奈克的經濟計劃

米拉波伯爵

　　財政部長為我們的財政狀況描繪了一幅觸
目驚心的圖畫。他肯定地告訴我們，任何延宕
必然使危機惡化。只要再拖延一天，甚至一分
一秒，都會帶來致命的後果。我們沒有其他辦
法可以代替他提出的計劃。因此，我們只能靠
這計劃了。可是，有些先生問：我們可有時間
審查及徹底研究這計劃，並核實其計算方法嗎？
沒有了，一點點時間都沒有了！我們現在所能
做的，只是提出一些隨意的猜測和無關緊要的
質詢；這樣做只能誤導他人。我們是否應為此
而錯失關鍵重大的時機呢？諸位先生是否願意
全國經濟總破產，也不願意犧牲和交付稅款？
總破產還不就是最厲害、最不公平、最不合理、
帶來大災大難的徵稅嗎？請忍耐片刻聽我說幾
句話吧。

　　兩個世紀以來的橫徵暴斂挖下了一個要吞
沒我們國家的深淵。這可怕的深坑必須填平。
但是怎麼填？這裏有一份財產所有人的名單。
從中挑出最富有的人來吧，這樣可以使要犧牲

　　法國革命前，面臨嚴重經濟危機，財政部長奈克
提出徵收高額所得稅。本篇是米拉波於1771年9月在
國民會議上支持奈克的演說。

order that the smallest number of citizens may be sacrificed. But choose! Shall not a few perish, that the mass of the people may be saved? Come, then! Here are two thousand notables, whose property will supply the deficit. Restore order to your finances; peace and prosperity to the kingdom! Strike! Immolate, without mercy, these unfortunate victims! Hurl them into the abyss! — it closes!

You recoil with dismay from the contemplation. Inconsistent and pusillanimous! What! Do you not perceive that, in decreeing a public bankruptcy, or, what is worse, in rendering it inevitable without decreeing it, you disgrace yourselves by an act a thousand times more criminal, and — folly inconceivable! — gratuitously criminal? for, in the shocking alternative I have supposed, at least the deficit would be wiped off.

But do you imagine that, in refusing to pay, you shall cease to owe? Think you that the thousands, the millions of men, who will lose in an instant, by the terrible explosion of a bankruptcy, or its revulsion, all that formed the consolation of their lives, and perhaps their sole means of subsistence — think you that they will leave you to the peaceable fruition of your crime? Stoical spectators of the incalculable evils which this catastrophe would disgorge upon France; impenetrable egotists, who fancy that these convulsions of despair and of misery will pass, as other calamities have passed — and all the more rapidly because of their intense violence — are you, indeed, certain that so many men without bread will leave you tranquilly to the enjoyment of those savory viands, the number and delicacy of which you are so loath to diminish? No! you will

的公民人數減至最少。只要挑出來就行了！爲了使廣大人民得救，難道不應該犧牲少數人嗎？那末，來吧，這裏有兩千個顯要人物，他們的財產可以彌補財政赤字，恢復國家的經濟秩序、和平與繁榮！出手打吧，不要心軟！犧牲這些不幸的受害者，把他們投到深淵裏去，深淵也就填平了！

你們被這計劃嚇得畏縮。你們多麼矛盾、懦弱呵！怎麼，你們難道沒有想到，如果公佈全國經濟破產，或更壞的是未作公佈而無可避免地破產了，你們會極其丟臉，因爲你們犯了比罪犯差上一千倍的行爲，那實在愚不可及且毫無補益。我建議的辦法雖然令人震驚，但畢竟可以消除財政赤字！

你們以爲拒絕付款就不欠債了嗎？想想看，那突然爆發的可怕破產，或因破產而生的劇變，會令成千上萬的人頃刻之間失去帶給他們生活慰藉，甚至是唯一賴以生存的事物。難道你們以爲他們會讓你們安安穩穩地享用犯罪的果實嗎？這場降臨到法蘭西頭上的災難，將造成數不清的惡果。對此冷漠的旁觀者，麻木不仁的自私自利者，你們以爲這場使人傷心絕望的大變故會像其他災難那樣終將過去，甚至因其變動劇烈而更快過去；難道你們眞有把握這許多忍飢受餓的人會讓你們安穩地享受種種美味佳餚，份量一點不少，味道絲毫不差嗎？不，你

perish, and, in the universal conflagration, which you do not shrink from kindling, you will not, in losing your honor, save a single one of your detestable indulgences. This is the way we are going.

And I say to you, that the men who, above all others, are interested in the enforcement of these sacrifices which the government demands, are you yourselves! Vote, then, this subsidy extraordinary; and may it prove sufficient! Vote it, in as much as whatever doubts you may entertain as to the means — doubts vague and unenlightened — you can have none as to the necessity, or as to our inability to provide — immediately, at least — a substitute. Vote it, because the circumstances of the country admit of no evasion, and we shall be responsible for all delays. Beware of demanding more time! Misfortune accords it never. . . .

們會滅亡的！在這場你們自己伸手燃點的遍地焚燒大火中，你們不僅聲名掃地，你們那可厭的紙醉金迷的生涯也將燒得乾乾淨淨。這就是我們正在走的路。

我還要告訴你們，對於擬行政府要求的這些犧牲，最有利害關係的正是你們自己！那麼，投票通過這項額外補貼案吧，但願這能補足虧缺！儘管你們對這項措施有懷疑，模模糊糊、不明真象的懷疑，但在這緊迫情況下，你們別無選擇了。我們也未能立時找出其他可以替代這措施的辦法。那麼，你們就投票吧，因為國家的形勢不允許我們迴避這問題，我們要對一切延誤的後果負責。小心有人要求拖延時間！災難從不讓人有從容三思的餘地。……

16   The Liberty of the Press

Thomas Erskine

. . .

The proposition which I mean to maintain as the basis of the liberty of the press, and without which it is an empty sound, is this: that every man, not intending to mislead, but seeking to enlighten others with what his own reason and conscience, however erroneously, have dictated to him as truth, may address himself to the universal reason of a whole nation, either upon the subject of government in general, or upon that of our own particular country: that he may analyse the principles of its constitution, point out its errors and defects, examine and publish its corruptions, warn his fellow-citizens against their ruinous consequences, and exert his whole faculties in pointing out the most advantageous changes in establishments which he considers to be radically defective, or sliding from their object by abuse. All this every subject of this country has right to do, if he contemplates only what he thinks would be for its advantage, and but seeks to change the public mind by the conviction which flows from reasonings dictated by conscience.

If, indeed, he writes *what he does not think;* if, contemplating the misery of others, he wickedly con-

十六 論出版自由

托馬斯・厄斯金

……

我主張出版自由必須有以下基礎，否則只能成爲空話。這就是：每一個人，只要不是有意地把別人引入歧途，而是以心中認爲正確的理性和良知來啓發他人，不管他的想法原是多麼錯誤，他也可以向全國普遍具理性的國民發表自己的見解。他可以就一般的政府發表見解，也可以就我們這特定的國家政府發表見解。他可以分析本國憲法的原則，指出國家存在的錯誤和不足之處，審查國家的腐敗現象並公之於世，警惕國人注意其極嚴重的後果，盡力提出最有利的改革措施，以克服他認爲是最根本的缺陷或因政府工作人員濫用職權所生的偏差。上述一切，我國的每一個公民都有權去做，只要他認爲對國家有益並根據出自良知的理性去說服公衆，改變他們的看法。

然而，如果他寫出來的不是他眞心所想，如果他看見別人痛苦時，口是心非地譴責他理

厄斯金（1750～1823），英國律師，法官。本篇是他在1792年12月18日爲湯姆士・佩恩所寫《人權》一書辯護的演詞。湯姆士・佩恩，英裔美國人，支持法國革命。

demns what his own understanding approves; or, even admitting his real disgust against the government or its corruptions, if he *calumniates living magistrates,* or holds out to individuals that they have a right to run before the public mind in their conduct; that they may oppose by contumacy or force what private reason only disapproves; that they may disobey the law, because their judgment condemns it; or resist the public will, because they honestly wish to change it — he is then a criminal upon every principle of rational policy, as well as upon the immemorial precedents of English justice; because such a person seeks to disunite individuals from their duty to the whole, and excites to overt acts of *misconduct* in a part of the community, instead of endeavouring to change, by the impulse of reason, that universal assent which, in this and in every country, constitutes the law for all.

. . .

Let me not, therefore, be suspected to be contending that it is lawful to write a book pointing out defects in the English Government, and exciting individuals to destroy its sanctions and to refuse obedience. But, on the other hand, I do contend that it is lawful to address the English nation on these momentous subjects; for had it not been for this inalienable right (thanks be to God and our fathers for establishing it!), how should we have had this constitution which we so loudly boast of? If, in the march of the human mind, no man could have gone before the establishments of the time he lived in, how could our establishment, by reiterated changes, have become what it is?

智所贊同的事物；如果他對政府或其中的腐敗現象真心憎惡而誹謗現職官員；如果他支持某些人，認為他們有權不顧公衆的想法為所欲為，認為他們可以頑抗，甚至以武力反對自己私心不喜的一切；如果他們認為法律欠善，便可以不守法；只要他們真覺得民意需要改變，便可以隨便反抗民意。如果這樣，那末，無論從哪一種合理政策原則的角度來衡量，或是從英國法律有史以來的任何判決先例來看，他都是個罪犯。這樣的人有意使個人背棄對整體的責任，煽動社會某些人公然犯不端的行為。他們並非憑理性的推動，努力去改變衆人的一致看法。正是這一致的看法構成英國或其他任何國家的全民法律。

……

因此，我並非主張寫書指摘英國政府的缺點，也不是鼓動人們破壞和違背政府法令，請不要誤會我認為那是合法的行為。但是，另一方面，我確實堅決主張在這些重大問題上，對全英國人民提出自己的見解是合法的。因為，倘若沒有這種不可剝奪的權利（感謝上帝和我們的祖先確立了這種權利！），我們又怎麼可能有這部如此值得自豪的憲法？如果在人類智力前進的道路上，從未有人能走在他那個時代的各項制度前頭，我們的制度又怎麼可能通過反復更改，成為今天的面貌？假如從未有人能

If no man could have awakened the public mind to errors and abuses in our Government, how could it have passed on from stage to stage, through reformation and revolution, so as to have arrived from barbarism to such a pitch of happiness and perfection, that the Attorney-General considers it as profanation to touch it further, or to look for any further amendment?

. . .

使公衆認識到政府的失誤和弊病，這個政府又怎能經歷一個個階段的革新與改良，從野蠻時代到達目前這個高度幸福完美的狀況，使得我們的總檢察長認爲只要再碰一碰它，只要再尋求一點點改革，就是褻瀆神明，犯了瀰天大罪？

......

17 Objects to Taxation Without Representation

William Pitt

. . .

I will only speak to one point — a point which seems not to have been generally understood, I mean to the *right*. Some gentlemen seem to have considered it as a point of honor. If gentlemen consider it in that light, they leave all measures of right and wrong, to follow a delusion that may lead to destruction. It is my opinion that this kingdom has no right to lay a tax upon the colonies. At the same time, I assert the authority of this kingdom over the colonies to be sovereign and supreme, in every circumstance of government and legislation whatsoever. They are the subjects of this kingdom, equally entitled with yourselves to all the natural rights of mankind and the peculiar privileges of Englishmen; equally bound by its laws and equally participating in the Constitution of this free country. The Americans are the sons, not the bastards, of England! Taxation is no part of the governing or legislative power. The taxes are a voluntary *gift* and *grant* of the Commons alone. In legislation the three estates of the realm are alike concerned; but the concurrence of the peers and the Crown to a tax is only necessary to clothe it with the form of a law. The gift and grant

---

皮特（1703～1778），曾任英國陸軍大臣和內閣首相。本文是皮特於1766年1月4日在下議院的演說，反對英國向北美頒佈的印花稅法。該法規定所有法律證件、商業單據，都必須繳納印花稅。

十七 反對徵收印花稅

威廉・皮特

……

我只準備說一點，這一點看來沒有被人普遍理解，這就是關於權利的問題。有幾位先生似乎把這看成是有關榮譽的問題。假如他們那樣想，就等於拋棄了衡量一切是非的標準，沉迷於幻想之中，而臨毀滅而無所覺察。我認爲這王國無權向各殖民地徵稅。同時，我又完全肯定，不論政府和立法機構情況如何，這王國對各殖民地享有至高無上的權威。殖民地人民都是這王國的臣民，跟你們一樣享有一切天賦的人權和英國人特有的權利；他們受自己國家的法律約束，也同樣分享、分擔英國這自由國家憲法所規定的權利和義務。北美人民是英國的親生兒，不是私生子！徵稅權不是統治權與立法權的一部分。稅租是自願捐獻的贈款[1]，惟有下議院才能接受。英國的三個等級[2]同樣有立法權；可是，貴族議員和王室批准稅收的權力只是法律形式所需。贈禮和捐款只屬於下

（1）英國法律規定只有下議院有立法權，國家徵稅由立法機構決定，因此說只有下議院才能接受稅收。
（2）即上院主教議員、上院貴族議員和下院議員（或平民）。

is of the Commons alone.

In ancient days, the Crown, the barons, and the clergy possessed the lands. In those days, the barons and the clergy gave and granted to the Crown. They gave and granted what was their own! At present, since the discovery of America, and other circumstances permitting, the Commons are become the proprietors of the land. The Church (God bless it!) has but a pittance. The property of the Lords, compared with that of the Commons, is as a drop of water in the ocean; and this House represents those Commons, the proprietors of the lands; and those propeietors virtually represent the rest of the inhabitants. When, therefore, in this House we give and grant, we give and grant what is our own. But in an American tax, what do we do? "We, your Majesty's Commons for Great Britain, give and grant to your Majesty" — what? Our own property! No! "We give and grant to your Majesty" the property of your Majesty's Commons of America! It is an absurdity in terms.

The distinction between legislation and taxation is essentially necessary to liberty. The Crown and the peers are equally legislative powers with the Commons. If taxation be a part of simple legislation, the Crown and the peers have rights in taxation as well as yourselves; rights which they will claim, which they will exercise, whenever the principle can be supported by power.

There is an idea in some that the colonies are *virtually* represented in the House. I would fain know by whom an American is represented here. Is he represented by any knight of the shire, in any county in this kingdom? Would to God that respectable representation was augmented to a greater number! Or will you tell him that he is represented by any representative of a borough? — a borough which,

議院議員。

古時候的王室、貴族和教會擁有土地。那時，貴族與教會向王室納貢。他們繳納屬於自己的東西！自從發現美洲以後，加上其他情況，土地歸平民擁有了。上帝保祐，教會擁有的土地眞是少得可憐。貴族的地產與平民相比，也不過是滄海一粟。本院代表土地擁有者平民；土地擁有者實質上代表了其餘的所有居民。因此，我們在下院決定貢納的是我們自己的東西。但是，如果我們向北美徵稅，那是什麼意思呢？"我們，您大不列顛國王陛下的下院議員，向陛下進貢。"進貢的是什麼？我們自己的財產嗎？不是的！"我們向陛下您進貢北美平民的財產！"這說法是荒唐的。

清楚地區分立法權與徵稅權，對於維護自由極其重要。國王和貴族同平民一樣享有立法權。如果徵稅權只是立法權簡單的一部分，那麼國王和貴族就同你們一樣有權徵稅了。只要權力可以支持這原則，他們就要要求徵稅權利，享受徵稅權利。

有些人認爲下議院實際上已經代表了殖民地人民。我倒想知道到底是誰在這裏代表北美人？是這王國中某州某郡的哪一位代表北美人說話嗎？要是那樣，但願這些代表的人數大大增加！也許你們會告訴一位北美人說，某市鎮的代表已在這裏替他說話了。但是這代表可能

perhaps, its own representatives never saw! This is what is called the rotten part of the Constitution. It cannot continue a century. If it does not drop, it must be amputated. The idea of a virtual representation of America in this House is the most contemptible idea that ever entered into the head of a man. It does not deserve a serious refutation.

The Commons of America, represented in their several assemblies, have ever been in possession of the exercise of this their constitutional right of giving and granting their own money. They would have been slaves if they had not enjoyed it! At the same time, this kingdom, as the supreme governing and legislative power, has always bound the colonies by her laws, by her regulations, and restrictions in trade, in navigation, in manufactures, in everything, except that of taking their money out of their pockets without their consent.

. . .

Upon the whole, I will beg leave to tell the House what is my opinion. It is that the Stamp Act be repealed absolutely, totally, and immediately. That the reason for the repeal be assigned — viz., because it was founded on an erroneous principle. At the same time, let the sovereign authority of this country over the colonies be asserted in as strong terms as can be devised, and be made to extend to every point of legislation whatsoever; that we may bind their trade, confine their manufactures, and exercise every power whatsoever, except that of taking money from their pockets without consent.

從沒到過這市鎮來！這就是憲法上失策的地方，這情況不能長久延續下去。如果再不停止，就必須刪掉。認爲下院裏確實有北美的代表因而下院有權決定徵稅，這想法非常可鄙，不值一駁。

北美平民在北美各州州議會中有自己的代表，他們一直享有憲法所賦與的納稅權利。如果他們不享有此種權利，早就成爲奴隷了[1]！與此同時，作爲最高統治與立法力量的英國，一直以各種法律、規章及各方面的限制，包括貿易、海上交通、製造業等方面，來約束管理各殖民地。可是，未得北美平民的同意，英國沒有權力去掏北美平民的腰包。

……

總之，我請求議會容許我陳述意見，那就是：印花稅法必須絕對地、完全地、立即地廢除。廢除的理由已經明確指出，即，這法案是以錯誤的原則爲根據。與此同時，讓我們以最強烈的詞句再次肯定我國對殖民地的最高權威，並從一切立法的觀點加以確認這點。我們可以約束他們的貿易，限制他們的企業，行使我們的一切權力，但却無權未經他們的同意掏他們的腰包。

（1）在蓄奴國家中奴隷無納稅權。

18 America Unconquerable

William Pitt

This, my Lords, is a perilous and tremendous moment. It is no time for adulation. The smoothness of flattery cannot save us, in this rugged and awful crisis. It is now necessary to instruct the Throne, in the language of TRUTH. We must, if possible, dispel the delusion and darkness which envelop it; and display, in its full danger and genuine colors, the ruin which is brought to our doors. Can Ministers still presume to expect support in their infatuation? Can Parliament be so dead to its dignity and duty as to be thus deluded into the loss of the one, and the violation of the other; — as to give an unlimited support to measures which have heaped disgrace and misfortune upon us; measures which have reduced this late flourishing empire to ruin and contempt? *But yesterday, and* England *might have stood against the world: now, none so poor to do her reverence!* France, my Lords, has insulted you. She has encouraged and sustained America; and whether America be wrong or right, the dignity of this country ought to spurn at the officious insult of French interference. Can even *our* Ministers sustain a more humiliating disgrace? Do they dare to resent it? Do they presume even to hint a vindication of their honor, and the dignity of the State, by requiring the dismissal of the plenipotentiaries of America? The People, whom they

十八　北美是不可征服的

威廉·皮特

各位議員，這是個危機四伏的非常時期。現在不是歌功頌德的時候。在這道路坷坎、征途巇峻的時刻，甘言諛詞不能解救我們。現在必須向我王曉以真情。如有可能，我們就一定要設法使王室拋棄幻想，不受蒙蔽；我們要將大禍臨門的真相完全暴露出來。各位部長大人，你們難道還能昏昏然自以為可以得到國會的支持嗎？難道國會對自己的尊嚴與職責觀念如此牢固，竟會受騙以致喪失尊嚴、背棄職責嗎？對於帶給我們屈辱累累、厄難重重的措施，竟會無限度支持嗎？這些措施已經使我們這個一度繁榮昌盛的帝國陷入災禍，蒙受羞辱。昨日，英國猶巍然屹立，可與世界抗衡，今天，已無人低下地向她致敬了。各位大人，法國侮辱了你們，並慫恿支持北美；且不談北美的是非曲直，為着保持我國的尊嚴，你們也該斥責法國插手我國內政務的侮人行為。我們的各位部長大人是否還能容忍這樣的屈辱呢？他們是否連不滿的表示也不敢流露呢？為了表示有意挽回他們的聲譽與國家的尊嚴，他們敢要求法國黜逐

本文是皮特在上議院的一篇著名演說。對於北美獨立問題，他比較開明，主張同北美和談。

affected to call contemptible rebels, but whose growing power has at last obtained the name of enemies, — the People with whom they have engaged this country in war, and against whom they now command our implicit support in every measure of desperate hostility, — this People, despised as rebels, or acknowledged as enemies, are abetted against you, supplied with every military store, their interests consulted, and their Ambassadors entertained, by your inveterate enemy, — and our Ministers dare not interpose with dignity or effect!

My Lords, this ruinous and ignominious situation, where we cannot act with success nor suffer with honor, calls upon us to remonstrate in the strongest and loudest language of truth, to rescue the ear of Majesty from the delusions which surround it. You cannot, I venture to say it, you *cannot* conquer America. What is your present situation there? We do not know the worst; but we know that in three campaigns we have done nothing, and suffered much. You may swell every expense, and strain every effort, still more extravagantly; accumulate every assistance you can beg or borrow; traffic and barter with every little pitiful German Prince, that sells and sends his subjects to the shambles of a foreign country: your efforts are forever vain and impotent, — doubly so from this mercenary aid on which you rely; for it irritates to an incurable resentment the minds of your enemies, to overrun them with the sordid sons of rapine and of plunder, devoting them and their possessions to the rapacity of hireling cruelty! If I were an American, as I am an Englishman, while a foreign troop was landed in my country, I never would lay down my arms! — never! never! never!

北美的全權大使嗎？各部長慣於輕蔑地把北美人民稱為亂黨，但是他們已經強大起來，成為我們的敵人了。為了與北美人民對敵，各部長已把我們的國家拖入戰爭，還要我們盡全力支持他們無望的軍事行動。這個被斥為反叛、且作敵人的民族受法國慫恿起來反對你們。你們的死敵法國供給他們一切軍需，與他們商討利益，款待他們的大使，我們的衆位部長大人却不敢嚴正有力地出面干預！

諸位議員，這種使我們既不能動而取勝，又不能挫而不屈的處境，要求我們以最強烈的措辭和最響亮的聲音說出事實眞相，使陛下開目啟聽，去除幻想。我敢說你們無法征服北美。你們目前在北美的處境如何？最壞的情況我們還不知道，但已知在三次戰役中，我們一無所獲並損失慘重。你們可以更加不惜代價地增加一切可用的開支，用盡一切力量，乞求、借貸一切助力，同那些把炮灰送到外國的、地小力微的德國王子做買賣。但是，你們的努力是永不會奏效的，特別是你們倚賴這種傭兵的援助，其作用適得其反；因為你們用掠奪成性的卑賤兵士去滋擾他們，把他們及其財產置於傭兵的蹂躪之下，只會更加激起你們敵人無法平息的仇恨。倘若我是北美人，正如我現在為英國人一樣，當外國軍隊侵入我國國境，我絕對不會放下武器。永遠、永遠、永遠不會！

19　Give Me Liberty or Give Me Death

Patrick Henry

...Let us not,I beseech you,sir,deceive ourselves longer. Sir, we have done everything that could be done to avert the storm which is now coming on. We have petitioned; we have remonstrated; we have supplicated; we have prostrated ourselves before the throne, and have implored its interposition to arrest the tyrannical hands of the ministry and Parliament. Our petitions have been slighted; our remonstrances have produced additional violence and insult; our supplications have been disregarded; and we have been spurned, with contempt, from the foot of the throne! In vain, after these things, may we indulge the fond hope of peace and reconciliation. There is no longer any room for hope. If we wish to be free — if we mean to preserve inviolate those inestimable privileges for which we have been so long contending — if we mean not basely to abandon the noble struggle in which we have been so long engaged, and which we have pledged ourselves never to abandon until the glorious object of our contest shall be obtained — we must fight! I repeat it, sir, we must fight! An appeal to arms and to the God of Hosts is all that is left us!

They tell us, sir, that we are weak; unable to cope with so formidable an adversary. But when shall we be stronger? Will it be the next week, or the next year? Will it be when we are totally disarmed, and when a British guard shall be stationed in every house? Shall we gather strength by irresolution and inaction? Shall

---

帕特里克・亨利（ 1736～1799 ），北美律師及政治家。北美獨立前，不少人主張請願和談以減輕英國

十九 不自由，毋寧死

……各位先生，我懇求你們不要再欺騙自己了。為了阻止這現正來臨的風暴，一切我們能力做到的都已做了。我們曾請願，抗議，懇求；我們也曾在英王寶座前俯伏屈膝，哀求英王逮住內閣和國會的魔掌。但是，我們的請願白費唇舌，我們的抗議招來更多的鎮壓和羞辱，我們的懇求受到漠視，我們在寶座前被輕蔑地一腳踢開！儘管我們一廂情願得到和平與諒解，但這一切都已無望了。如果我們希望得到自由，如果我們真要維護長期以來為之奮鬥、使之不受侵犯的神聖權利，如果我們不致於卑鄙地想放棄我們進行已久、誓言不達目的決不休止的崇高鬥爭，我們就必須作戰！先生，我重覆一句，我們必須作戰！我們只有訴諸武力，求助於萬軍之主上帝了！

先生，他們說我們力量弱小，不是這強敵的對手。但是什麼時候我們才會強大起來？下星期還是明年？是不是要等到我們完全被解除武裝、家家戶戶都駐扎了英國士兵的時候？我們遲疑不決、無所作為就能積聚力量嗎？我們

的壓迫。亨利堅決主戰，反對妥協。本文是他1775年3月23日在弗吉尼亞州議會發表的演說。

we acquire the means of effectual resistance by lying supinely on our backs and hugging the delusive phantom of hope, until our enemies shall have bound us hand and foot? Sir, we are not weak if we make a proper use of those means which the God of nature hath placed in our power. Three millions of people, armed in the holy cause of liberty, and in such a country as that which we possess, are invincible by any force which our enemy can send against us. Besides, sir, we shall not fight our battles alone. There is a just God who presides over the destinies of nations, and who will raise up friends to fight our battles for us. The battle, sir, is not to the strong alone; it is to the vigilant, the active, the brave. Besides, sir, we have no election. If we were base enough to desire it, it is now too late to retire from the contest. There is no retreat but in submission and slavery! Our chains are forged! Their clanking may be heard on the plains of Boston! The war is inevitable — and let it come! I repeat it, sir, let it come.

It is in vain, sir, to extenuate the matter. Gentlemen may cry, Peace, Peace — but there is no peace. The war is actually begun! The next gale that sweeps from the north will bring to our ears the clash of resounding arms! Our brethren are already in the field! Why stand we here idle? What is it that gentlemen wish? What would they have? Is life so dear, or peace so sweet, as to be purchased at the price of chains and slavery? Forbid it, Almighty God! I know not what course others may take; but as for me, give me liberty or give me death!

高枕而臥、苟安僥倖，等到敵人使我們束手就擒時，我們就能找到有效的禦敵辦法？先生，如果能恰當地利用萬物之主賦予我們的力量，我們並不弱小。我們有三百萬為爭取神聖自由而武裝起來的戰士，我們擁有這樣的國家，那麼，不論敵人派來任何軍隊都不能戰勝我們。此外，我們並非孤軍作戰。公平的上帝主宰一切國家的命運，他會召喚我們的朋友起來和我們並肩戰鬥。先生，不一定強者才會取得勝利，高度警覺、生氣勃勃、勇敢無畏的人也會得勝。況且，我們已經別無選擇了。即使我們卑鄙怯懦，希望尋找別的道路，但現在要退出戰鬥也太遲了。後退就是投降！後退就將淪為奴隸！我們的枷鎖已經鑄成，琅璫的鐐銬聲在波士頓的平原上也可清晰聽聞！戰爭已經無可避免——讓它來吧！先生，我重覆一遍：讓它來吧！

先生，大事化小，小事化無的做法無濟於事。各位先生可以叫喊和平，和平！但是和平並不存在。事實上戰爭已經開始！不久北方颳起的風暴即將帶來震耳的隆隆炮聲。我們的弟兄已經開赴戰場，為什麼我們還在這裏投閒置散？諸君究竟希望什麼？他們會得到什麼？難道生命真的這樣珍貴，和平真的這樣美好，竟值得用枷鎖與奴役為代價？全能的上帝啊，制止他們這樣做吧！我不知道別人選擇走什麼樣的道路，但對我來說，不自由，毋寧死！

20 Better To Die Than Not Live Free

Camille Desmoulins

There is one difference between a monarchy and a republic, which alone should suffice to make people reject with horror all monarchical rule and prefer a republic regardless of the cost of its establishment. In a democracy, the people may be deceived, yet they at least love virtue. It is merit which they believe they put in power as substitutes for the rascals who are the very essence of monarchies. The vices, concealments, and crimes which are the diseases of republics are the very health and existence of monarchies. Cardinal Richelieu avowed openly in his political principles, that "kings should always avoid using the talents of thoroughly honest men." Long before him Sallust said: "Kings can not get along without rascals; on the contrary, they should fear to trust the honest and upright." It is, therefore, only under a democracy that the good citizen can reasonably hope to see a cessation of the triumphs of intrigue and crime; and to this end the people need only to be enlightened.

There is yet this difference between a monarchy and a republic: the reigns of Tiberius, Claudius, Nero,

---

德穆蘭（1760～1794），法國大革命中雅各賓派的一位領袖。因反對羅伯斯庇爾鎮壓反革命，被送上斷頭台處死。本文發表於1788年2月，發表後兩天，革命羣衆便攻佔了巴士底獄。

（1）黎塞留紅衣主敎（1585～1642），法王路易十三的總理大臣。

（2）沙拉斯(Caius Sallust Cripus，公元前86～34)，古羅馬歷史學家。

二十 生不自由，不如死去

卡米耶·德穆蘭

君主制與共和制之間有一點區別。僅僅這點區別就足以使人懷着恐懼擯棄君主統治，不惜犧牲一切以建立共和制了。民主政體的人民可能會受騙，但至少他們珍愛美德。他們相信把權力交給了有道德的人，而不是交給作為君主制基礎的流氓惡棍。邪惡、詭譎、犯罪等等對共和國來說是癰疽，對君主政治來說却是健全和賴以生存的要素。黎塞留紅衣主教[1]公開承認他的政治原則是"君主應永遠避免任用絕對誠實的人材。"遠在他說這話之前，沙拉斯[2]就說過："君主身邊不能缺少惡棍流氓。相反，他們倒不敢任用誠實與正直的人。"因此，只有在民主政體下，善良的公民才有可能看到陰謀與罪犯不能得逞。為了達到這目的，唯一要做的是啟發人民。

君主制與共和制之間還有一點區別：提伯利烏斯[3]、克勞狄斯[4]、尼祿[5]、卡里古拉[6]、

---

(3) 提伯利烏斯（公元前42～公元37），古羅馬的第二代皇帝。

(4) 克勞狄斯（公元前10～公元54），羅馬皇帝，提伯利烏斯之侄。

(5) 克勞狄斯之父。

(6) 卡里古拉（12～41），羅馬皇帝，提伯利烏斯之繼位人。

Caligula and Domitian all had happy beginnings. In fact, all reigns make a joyous entry, but this is only a delusion. Royalists therefore laugh at the present state of France as if because of its violent and terrible entry it could not always last.

Everything gives umbrage to a tyrant. If a citizen have popularity, he is becoming a rival to the prince. Consequently, he is stirring up civil strife, and is a suspect. If, on the contrary, he flee popularity and seclude himself in the corner of his own fireside, this retired life makes him remarked, and he is suspect. If he is a rich man, there is an imminent peril that he may corrupt the people with his largesses, and he becomes a suspect. Are you poor? How then! Invincible emperors, this man must be closely watched; for no one is so enterprising as he who has nothing. He is a suspect! Are you in character somber, melancholy, or neglectful? Then you are afflicted by the condition of public affairs, and are a suspect.

. . .

Tacitus tells us that there was anciently in Rome a law specifying the crimes of "lèse-majesté." That crime carried with it the punishment of death. Under the Roman republic treasons were reduced to four kinds, viz.: abandoning an army in the country of an enemy; exciting sedition; the maladministration of the public treasury; and the impairment by inefficiency of the majesty of the Roman people.

But the Roman emperors needed more clauses, in

多米尼克[1]的統治都以善始。事實上，一切統治開始之時都比較開明，但這只是一種假象而已。保皇黨人嘲笑法國目前的狀況，認爲它始於暴力、恐怖，便不能持久。

所有事情都使專制君主生氣。受人愛戴的公民會成爲君主的敵手，他會引起內亂，因此就是一個可疑分子。相反來說，假如他不求聞達，深居簡出，這種退隱生活使他引人注目，因此他是可疑分子。假如他很富有，那末他就極可能以慷慨餽贈來腐蝕人民，因此，他也是一個可疑分子。你窮嗎？那又怎麼樣！永遠勝利的諸位皇帝啊，這人可要嚴密監視，因爲沒有人比一無所有的人更雄心勃勃了，他是個可疑分子！你生性陰沉、憂鬱，或是不修邊幅嗎？那末你一定是因爲不滿國事而苦惱了，你是個可疑分子。

……

塔西佗[2]告訴我們，古羅馬有一條法律，專門治"不敬君主"之罪。犯上這罪要判處死刑。古羅馬共和國的叛逆罪有四種，那就是：在敵國領土上離開軍隊私逃；煽動叛亂；管理國庫不善；由於不稱職而損害了多數羅馬人的利益。

但是羅馬皇帝們需要更多法律條款，以便

（1）多米尼克（51～96），羅馬皇帝。

（2）塔西佗（55～117），古羅馬歷史學家。

order that they might place cities and citizens under proscription. Augustus was the first to extend the list of offenses that were "lèse-majesté" or revolutionary, and under his successors extensions were made until none was exempt. The slightest action was a state offense. A simple look, sadness, compassion, a sigh, or even silence became "lèse-majesté" and disloyalty. One must show joy at the execution of a parent or friend lest one should perish. Citizens, liberty must be a great benefit, since Cato disemboweled himself rather than have a king. And what king car we compare in greatness and heroism to the Caesar whose rule Cato would not endure? Rousseau truly says: "There is in liberty as in innocence and virtue a satisfaction one can only feel in their enjoyment and a pleasure which can cease only when they have been lost."

---

(1)奧古斯都（公元前63～公元14），凱撒養子。凱撒被刺後，成爲羅馬第一任皇帝。

(2)卡圖（公元前95～46），羅馬政治家，反對專制，給一些城市和公民多加罪名。奧古斯都⁽¹⁾最先擴大了"不敬君主"罪或"革命分子"的範圍。他的後任者繼續擴大這種罪的範圍，以至無人可倖免。最輕微的行動便構成反對國家之罪。看一眼、露出一點愁容、表示一點同情、歎一口氣甚至一聲不響都是犯了"不敬君主"和不忠之罪。處死你的父母或朋友，你也必須表示歡欣之情，否則你自己也就完了。公民們，自由必定有很大的好處，因為卡圖⁽²⁾寧願剖腹自殺，也不願受國王統治。有哪一個國王比得上偉大凱撒的英雄氣概呢？但卡圖仍不能忍受凱撒的統治。盧梭⁽³⁾說得很對，"自由和清白或美德一樣，只有在你享有它們時，才會得到滿足，一旦失去它們，你就會感到歡樂停止了。

主張共和。

（3）盧梭（1712～1778），法國啟蒙思想家、哲學家、教育學家、文學家。

21 To Dare Again, Ever To Dare

Georges Jacques Danton

It seems a satisfaction for the ministers of a free people to announce to them that their country will be saved. All are stirred, all are enthused, all burn to enter the combat.

You know that Verdun is not yet in the power of our enemies, and that its garrison swears to immolate the first who breathes a proposition of surrender.

One portion of our people will guard our frontiers, another will dig and arm the entrenchments, the third with pikes will defend the interior of our cities. Paris will second these great efforts. The commissioners of the Commune will solemnly proclaim to the citizens the invitation to arm and march to the defense of the country. At such a moment you can proclaim that the capital deserves the esteem of all France. At such a moment this national assembly becomes a veritable committee of war. We ask that you concur with us in directing this sublime movement of the people, by naming commissioners to second and assist all these great measures. We ask that any one refusing to give personal service or to furnish arms shall meet the punishment of death. We ask that proper instructions be given to the citizens to direct their movements. We ask that carriers be sent to all the departments to notify them of the decrees that you proclaim here. The tocsin we shall sound is not the alarm signal of danger, it orders the charge on the enemies of France. To conquer we have need to dare, to dare again, ever to dare! And the safety of France is insured.

丹敦（ 1759～1794 ），原爲律師，後爲法國大革命中雅各賓派領袖之一，曾鼓動羣衆攻佔巴士底獄。

二十一　勇敢些，再勇敢些！

喬治・雅克・丹敦

　　一個自由民族的政府官員能夠向人民宣告國家將得到拯救，似乎是最稱心的事了。於是所有人都被激勵起來，熱情奔放地投身於鬥爭中。

　　你們知道凡爾登城目前尚未陷入敵手，守衛部隊誓稱要處死第一個說出投降二字的人。

　　我們一部分人將守衛邊界，一部分人構築工事，設塹防禦，其餘持長矛者將擔任城內的警衛工作。巴黎將支持我們的巨大努力。各公社委員要向公民發出莊嚴號召，要求他們拿起武器奔赴保衛祖國的戰鬥。在這時刻，你們可以公開宣告，我們的首都值得全法蘭西敬重。在這時刻，國民會議成了名符其實的作戰委員會。我們要求你們一同領導這場崇高的人民運動，指定一定的委員支持和協助實現所有這些偉大的措施。任何人拒絕供職或提供武器，我們要求判處他們死刑。我們要求恰當地指示公民領導各種活動。我們要求派人到一切部門去傳達你們在這裏公佈的各項指令。我們不敲報險的警鐘而要吹響向法蘭西的敵人衝鋒的軍號。為了勝利，我們需要勇敢，更勇敢，永遠勇敢！這樣，法蘭西的安全就能得到保障。

1794年死於斷頭台。本文是他1792年在國民會議上的發言。

22 His Last Speech

Maximilien Robespierre

The enemies of the Republic call me tyrant! Were I such they would grovel at my feet. I should gorge them with gold, I should grant them impunity for their crimes, and they be grateful. Were I such, the kings we have vanquished, far from denouncing Robespierre, would lend me their guilty support. There would be a covenant between them and me. Tyranny must have tools. But the enemies of tyranny — whither does *their* path tend? To the tomb, and to immortality! What tyrant is my protector? To what faction do I belong? Yourselves! What faction, since the beginning of the Revolution, has crushed and annihilated so many detected traitors? You, the people — our principles — are that faction! A faction to which I am devoted, and against which all the scoundrelism of the day is banded!

The confirmation of the Republic has been my object; and I know that the Republic can be established only on the eternal basis of morality. Against me, and against those who hold kindred principles, the league is formed. My life? Oh, my life I abandon without a regret! I have seen the Past; and *I foresee the Future.*

羅伯斯庇爾（1758～1794），全名爲馬克西米連·
瑪麗·伊西多爾·德·羅伯斯庇爾（Maximilien François
Marie Isidore de Robespierre），法國大革命領袖，

二十二　最後的演說

馬克西米連・羅伯斯庇爾

共和國的敵人說我是暴君！倘若我眞是暴君，他們就會俯伏在我的脚下了。我會塞給他們大量的黃金，赦免他們的罪行，他們也就會感激不盡了。倘若我是個暴君，被我們打倒了的那些國王就絕不會譴責羅伯斯庇爾，反而會用他們那有罪的手支持我了。他們和我就會締結盟約。暴政必須得到工具。可是暴政的敵人，他們的道路又會引向何方呢？引向墳墓，引向永生！我的保護人是怎樣的暴君呢？我屬於哪個派別？我屬於你們！有哪一派從大革命開始以來查出這許多叛徒，並粉碎、消滅這些叛徒？這派別就是你們，是人民——我們的原則。我忠於這個派別，而現代的一切流氓惡棍都拉幫結黨反對它！

確保共和國的存在一直是我的目標；我知道共和國只能在永存的道德基礎上才能建立起來。爲了反對我，反對那些跟我有共同原則的人，他們結成了聯盟。至於說我的生命，我早已把生死置之度外了！我曾看見過去，也預見

處死了法王路易十六及丹敦等人。1794年7月24日被擁護丹敦的人逮捕，次日，被送上斷頭台。本篇是他臨刑前兩天發表的演說詞。

What friend of his country would wish to survive the moment when he could no longer serve it — when he could no longer defend innocence against oppression? Wherefore should I continue in an order of things, where intrigue eternally triumphs over truth: where justice is mocked; where passions the most abject, or fears the most absurd, override the sacred interests of humanity? In witnessing the multitude of vices which the torrent of the Revolution has rolled in turbid communion with its civic virtues, I confess that I have sometimes feared that I should be sullied, in the eyes of posterity, by the impure neighborhood of unprincipled men, who had thrust themselves into association with the sincere friends of humanity; and I rejoice that these conspirators against my country have now, by their reckless rage, traced deep the line of demarcation between themselves and all true men.

Question history, and learn how all the defenders of liberty in all times, have been overwhelmed by calumny. But their traducers died also. The good and the bad disappear alike from the earth; but in very different conditions. O Frenchmen! O my countrymen! Let not your enemies, with their desolating doctrines, degrade your souls, and enervate your virtues! No, Chaumette, no! Death is *not* "an eternal sleep!" Citizens! Efface from the tomb that motto, graven by sacrilegious hands, which spreads over all nature a funeral crape, takes from oppressed innocence its support, and affronts

將來。一個忠於自己國家的人，當他不能再爲自己的國家服務，再不能使無辜的人免受迫害時，他怎麼會希望再活下去？當陰謀詭計永遠壓倒眞理、正義受到嘲弄、熱情常遭鄙薄、有所忌憚被目爲荒誕無稽，而壓迫欺凌被當作人類不可侵犯的權勢時，我還能在這樣的制度下繼續做些什麼呢？目睹在革命的潮流中，沙泥俱下，魚龍混雜，周圍都是混跡在人類眞誠朋友之中的壞人，我必須承認，在這樣的環境下，有時我確實害怕我的子孫後代會認爲我已被他們的污穢沾染了。令我高興的是，這些反對我們國家的陰謀家，因爲不顧一切的瘋狂行動，現在已和所有忠誠正直的人劃下了一條深深的界限。

只要向歷史請教一下，你便可以看到，在各個時代，所有自由的衞士是怎樣受盡誹謗的。但那些誹謗者也終不免一死。善人與惡人同樣要從世上消失，只是死後情況大不相同。法蘭西人，我的同胞啊，不要讓你的敵人用那爲人唾棄的原則使你的靈魂墮落，令你的美德削減吧！不，邵美蒂[1]啊，死亡並不是"長眠"！公民們！請抹去這句用褻瀆的手刻在墓碑上的銘文，因爲它給整個自然界蒙上一層喪禮黑紗，使受壓迫的淸白者失去依賴與信心，使死亡失

（1）邵美蒂（1763～1794），巴黎公社領導成員之一。

the beneficent dispensation of death! Inscribe rather thereon these words "Death is the commencement of immortality!" I leave to the oppressors of the people a terrible testament, which I proclaim with the independence befitting one whose career is so nearly ended; it is the awful truth: "Thou shalt die!"

去有益的積極意義!請在墓碑刻上這樣的話吧：
"死亡是不朽的開端。"我爲壓迫人民者留下
駭人的遺囑；只有一個事業已近盡頭的人才能
毫無顧忌的這樣說，這也就是那嚴峻的眞理：
"你必定要死亡！"

23 Farewell Address

George Washington

. . .

I have already intimated to you the danger of parties in the state, with particular reference to the founding of them on geographical discriminations. Let me now take a more comprehensive view, and warn you in the most solemn manner against the baneful effects of the spirit of party, generally.

This spirit, unfortunately, is inseparable from our nature, having its root in the strongest passions of the human mind. It exists under different shapes in all governments, more or less stifled, controlled, or oppressed; but, in those of the popular form, it is seen in its greatest rankness, and is truly their worst enemy.

The alternate domination of one faction over another, sharpened by the spirit of revenge, natural to party dissension, which in different ages and countries has prepetrated the most horrid enormities, is itself a frightful despotism. But this leads at length to a more formal and permanent despotism. The disorders and miseries, which result, gradually incline the minds of men to seek security and repose in the absolute power of an individual; and sooner or later the chief of some prevailing faction, more able or more fortunate than his competitors, turns this disposition to the purposes of his own elevation, on the ruins of public liberty.

二十三 告別演說

喬治·華盛頓

......

我曾明白告訴你們，在國家內部存在各種派別的危險，尤其是那種基於地區偏見而形成的不同派別。現在讓我以考慮得更全面的觀點，以最鄭重的態度概括地提醒你們注意黨派精神的有害影響。

不幸的是，這種精神和我們的天性分不開，植根於人類最強烈的感情之中。它以不同形式存在於所有政府，只是或多或少地受到壓抑或控制而已。但是，在民主形式的政府裏，它滋生蔓長，確實成為危害這些政府的最大敵人。

派系紛爭自然產生報復情緒，這在不同國家不同時代曾造成可怖的暴行。由於這種報復情緒的支配，兩派你勝我敗的交替執政本身就是一種可怕的暴政。最終還會導致一種更為正式的永久性獨裁暴政，因為派別紛爭帶來了動盪和苦難，使人逐漸傾向於個人的絕對權力以尋求安全與保障。遲早有某個執政黨的首腦，因能力或運氣比他的競爭對手更好，利用上述普遍情緒破壞公眾自由，以達到個人升擢的目的。

喬治·華盛頓（1732～1799），美利堅共和國的創立人，美國第一任總統（1789～1797）。本文為華盛頓退休前於1796年9月17日發表的演說。

Without looking forward to an extremity of this kind, (which nevertheless ought not to be entirely out of sight,) the common and continual mischiefs of the spirit of party are sufficient to make it the interest and duty of a wise people to discourage and restrain it.

It serves always to distract the public councils, and enfeeble the public administration. It agitates the community with ill-founded jealousies and false alarms, kindles the animosity of one part against another, foments occasionally riot and insurrection. It opens the door to foreign influence and corruption, which find a facilitated access to the government itself through the channels of party passions. Thus the policy and the will of one country are subjected to the policy and will of another.

There is an opinion, that parties in free countries are useful checks upon the administration of the government, and serve to keep alive the spirit of liberty. This within certain limits is probably true; and in governments of a monarchical cast, patriotism may look with indulgence, if not favor, upon the spirit of party. But in those of the popular character, in governments purely elective, it is a spirit not to be encouraged. From their natural tendency, it is certain there will always be enough of that spirit for every salutary purpose, and there being constant danger of excess, the effort ought to be, by force of public opinion, to mitigate and assuage it. A fire not to be quenched it demands a uniform vigilance to prevent its bursting into a flame, lest, instead of warming, it should consume.

. . .

即使我們不預期事情發展至上述極端的地步（不過，我們不該完全忽視這種極端的可能），黨派風氣常不斷引起禍患，也足以使明智的民族出於責任感和自身利益去防範它、抑制它了。

黨派風氣往往使各種公共會議不能集中討論問題，削弱公共行政機構的功能。它使國民為毫無根據的嫉恨和虛驚所困擾；它煽動一派仇恨另一派，有時甚至挑起騷動與叛亂。它打開方便之門，使國家受外國影響與腐蝕。通過黨派情緒的渠道，外國事物輕易找到打進政府的入口。這樣，一個國家的政策和意志便會為另一國家的政策意志所左右。

某些人認為自由國家存有黨派，有助於監督檢查政府的行政事務，並可保持自由精神。這種意見在一定限度內可能是對的。在君主政體的政府中，愛國者對黨派精神如不是特別喜愛，至少也可以容忍。可是，對於民主性質或純粹由選舉產生的政府，這種黨派風氣却不宜提倡，因為這些政府自有足夠的黨派精神達成每一有益的目的。問題倒在於黨派風氣常有過份的危險，我們應該努力以公衆輿論壓力去緩和它，抑制它。一堆未熄滅的火須得大家始終小心戒備，防止它燃成熊熊烈焰，否則，它不僅不能使人取暖，反而會燒燬一切。

……

24 A Speech Delivered in Council with Governor Harrison

Tecumseh

It is true I am Shawnee. My forefathers were warriors. Their son is a warrior. From them I only take my existence; from my tribe I take nothing. I am the maker of my own fortune; and oh! that I could make that of my red people, and of my country, as great as the conceptions of my mind, when I think of the Spirit that rules the universe. I would not then come to Governor Harrison, to ask him to tear the treaty and to obliterate the landmark; but I would say to him: Sir, you have liberty to return to your own country. The being within, communing with past ages, tells me that once, nor until lately, there was no white man on this continent. That it then all belonged to red men, children of the same parents, placed on it by the Great Spirit that made them, to keep it, to traverse it, to enjoy its productions and to fill it with the same race. Once a happy race. Since made miserable by the white people, who are never contented, but always encroaching. The way, and the only way, to check and to stop this evil, is for all the red men to unite in claiming a common and equal right in the land, as it was at first,

特庫姆塞（ 1768？～ 1813 ），印第安人蕭尼族酋
長，主張印第安人擁有土地所有權，聯合各部爲此鬥
爭。1813年，與哈里遜州長作戰陣亡。本篇爲在此以

二十四 與哈里遜州長會談時的發言

特庫姆塞

確實，我是個蕭尼族⁽¹⁾人。我的祖先都是
戰士。他們的子孫也是戰士。他們只是生育了
我；我從我的部落什麼也沒有得到，我這份家
業是我自己掙來的。啊，當我想到主宰萬物的
神時，我多麼希望我能使我的紅種人民和我的
國家無限強大起來，達到我能想像的限度啊！
這樣我就不用來到哈里遜州長面前，請求他撕
毀條約，撤去佔地的界石了；相反，我會對他
說：先生，您儘可以回到您自己的國家去。聯
想到以往的世世代代，我的內心告訴我，這大
陸直到近年才有白種人的足跡。當時這大陸完
全屬於紅種人，他們都是同種祖先的後代。創
造他們的偉大的神把他們放在這塊土地上，讓
他們保有、開發這大陸，享用這片土地所生產
的果實，在這陸地生兒育女、滋繁族類。我們
曾在這裏安居樂業。但自從白種人來了以後，我
們就過着悲慘的生活。他們侵佔掠奪、永無饜
足之時。要制止他們這種罪行，唯一的辦法是
紅種人團結起來，要求對土地享有共同的平等
權利。這在一開始時就是如此，也應該永遠如

前一次談判的發言。

（1）蕭尼族是美國的印第安人中的一族。蕭尼是今美
    國的一個城市。

and should be yet; for it never was divided, but belongs to all for the use of each. That no part has a right to sell, even to each other, much less to strangers; those who want all, and will not do with less.

The white people have no right to take the land from the Indians, because they had it first; it is theirs. They may sell, but all must join. Any sale not made by all is not valid. The late sale is bad. It was made by a part only. Part do not know how to sell. It requires all to make a bargain for all. All red men have equal rights to the unoccupied land. The right of occupancy is as good in one place as in another. There cannot be two occupations in the same place. The first excludes all others. It is not so in hunting or traveling; for there the same ground will serve many, as they may follow each other all day; but the camp is stationary, and that is occupancy. It belongs to the first who sits down on his blanket or skins which he has thrown upon the ground; and till he leaves it no other has a right.

此。這塊土地從來未被分割,却完整地屬於大家,供每個人使用。無論哪一族的人都沒有出賣土地的權利,即使是內部買賣也不可以,更不用說賣給外來人了。外來人却要完全佔有土地,少一點也不行。

白人無權從印第安人手中奪去土地,因為土地原屬於印第安人;土地是他們的。印第安人可以出賣土地,但必須得全體人民同意,否則便屬無效。過去出賣的土地是不合法的,那是經部分人達成的交易。部分人不可能懂得如何賣地,那需要全體人民來為全族議價。所有紅種人對空置的土地都有同等的權利。這種權利在任何土地都是一樣。同一塊土地不能有雙重的佔有者。最先佔有土地的人可排斥一切後來者。打獵與旅行的情況不同;在這情形,同一塊土地可供許多人同時使用,他們可以終日彼此相隨。但營地是固定的,駐扎營地就表示佔有了那塊土地。第一個把氈毯或獸皮鋪在地上,再坐在上面的人就可佔有那塊土地。除非他離去,其他人無權佔有該地。

25 On Dissolution of the Continental System

George Canning

. . .

It is at the moment when such a trial has come to its issue, that it is fair to ask of those who have suffered under the pressure of protracted exertion (and of whom rather than of those who are assembled around me — for by whom have such privations been felt more sensibly?) — it is now, I say, the time to ask whether, at any former period of the contest, such a peace could have been made as would at once have guarded the national interests and corresponded with the national character? I address myself not to such persons only as think the character of a nation an essential part of its strength, and consequently of its safety. But if, among persons of that description, there be one who, with all his zeal for the glory of his country, has yet at times been willing to abandon the contest in mere weariness and despair, of such a man I would ask, whether he can indicate the period at which he now wishes that such an abandonment had been consented to by the Government and the Parliament of Great Britain?

Is it when the continent was at peace — when, looking upon the map of Europe, you saw one mighty and connected system, one great luminary, with his attendant satellites circulating around him; at that period could this country have made peace, and have

二十五　論歐洲大陸體系的瓦解

喬治·肯寧

……

　　現在，考驗已到了快結束的時候，應該問一問備嘗艱苦的人們——尤其要問問那些不在座的人，因為有誰比他們受到更大的困苦？——在這次戰爭的過去任何一個階段，有沒有一種旣能得到和平，同時又能維護國家利益、不辱國家尊嚴的兩全其美的辦法？我不去向那種主要只從國家的力量與安全來看她的尊嚴的人。但是，如果這種人當中有這樣的一個人，他雖然對於國家的榮譽抱有滿腔熱忱，却時時只由於極端疲憊和信心不足便甘願放棄鬥爭，那麼，我便要問問他，他能否指出希望在哪一個時候大不列顛政府和國會應該同意放棄鬥爭？

　　是不是歐洲大陸還處於和平的時期？那時你在歐洲的地圖上可以看到一個強大的互相連結的體系，一個巨大的天體[1]，周圍環繞着許多衞星。在那個時候，我國能得到和平，能維

　　肯寧（1770～1827），英國政治家，反對法國大革命及雅各賓派。本文提及英國對拿破崙一世的戰爭，肯寧當時任外交部長及海軍財政大臣。

（1）指法國。

remained at peace for a twelvemonth? What is the answer? Why, that the experiment was tried. The result was the renewal of the war.

Was it at a later period, when the Continental system had been established? When two-thirds of the ports of Europe were shut against you? When but a single link was wanting to bind the Continent in a circling chain of iron, which should exclude you from intercourse with other nations? At that moment peace was most earnestly recommended to you. At that moment, gentlemen, I first came among you. At that moment I ventured to recommend to you perseverance, patient perseverance; and to express a hope that, by the mere strain of an unnatural effort, the massive bonds imposed upon the nations of the Continent might, at no distant period, burst asunder. I was heard by you with indulgence — I know not whether with conviction. But is it now to be regretted that we did not at that moment yield to the pressure of our wants or of our fears? What has been the issue? The Continental system was completed, with the sole exception of Russia, in the year 1812. In that year the pressure upon this country was undoubtedly painful. Had we yielded, the system would have been immortal. We persevered, and, before the conclusion of another year, the system was at an end: at an end, as all schemes of violence naturally terminate, not by a mild and gradual decay,

持十二個月的和平嗎？答案是什麼？唉，我們已經試驗過了，結果是重新開戰。

那麼，是不是應該在後來，在大陸體系[1]已經建立起來的時候呢？是不是應該在三分之二的歐洲港口已經向你關閉起來的時候？是不是在只需一環[2]就能把整個大陸連成一條鐵鏈，使你不能同各國交往的那個時候？在那時候，人家倒是十分熱情地向你們提出和平。先生們，正是在那個時候，我初次來到你們之中。那時，我冒昧地勸告你們要有耐心，要堅持下去；我說我懷有一個希望，因為這個巨大的聯合體是勉強形成的，是強加給大陸國家的，可能不久就會四分五裂。當時你們是姑妄聽之，我不知道你們有幾分相信。但是，當時我們沒有屈服於窘迫與恐懼的壓力之下，難道今天應該感到遺憾？結果如何呢？大陸體系在1812年確實建立起來了，唯獨俄國例外。那一年，我國承受的壓力無疑是難忍的。倘使我們當時作了讓步，這個體系就會永遠存在下去。但是，我們堅持下來了，於是，第二年還未過去，這個體系就土崩瓦解了。它瓦解了，正如一切暴力體系必然終將解體那樣，它不像終於天年的生命，和

───────────────

（1）從1806至1812年法國的拿破崙與德國、波蘭等歐洲國家聯合起來，在經濟上抵制英國的政策。
（2）指俄國。當時沒有參加大陸體系。

such as waits upon a regular and well-spent life, but by sudden dissolution; at an end, like the breaking up of a winter's frost. But yesterday the whole Continent, like a mighty plain covered with one mass of ice, presented to the view a drear expanse of barren uniformity; today, the breath of heaven unbinds the earth, the streams begin to flow again, and the intercourse of human kind revives.

Can we regret that we did not, like the fainting traveller, lie down to rest — but, indeed, to perish — under the severity of that inclement season? Did we not more wisely to bear up, and to wait the change? . . .

緩地、逐漸地衰亡，而是突然地分崩離析；它瓦解了，好似冬日的寒霜，太陽出來便銷鎔蒸發。還是在昨日，整個歐洲大陸像廣闊的平原覆蓋在一塊巨大的堅冰之下，呈現出荒涼慘淡的景象；今天，天上吹來的和煦溫風，將這塊大地解凍，於是，河水又潺潺奔流，人類再次恢復交往。

我們在那嚴酷的季節下沒有屈服，沒有像疲憊已極的異鄉遊子那樣躺下歇息──那種歇息無異於死亡──難道今天我們反而感到後悔嗎？我們當時沒有氣餒，我們堅持下來，靜待變化，難道不是更明智嗎？⋯⋯

26 Farewell to His Old Guard

Napoleon Bonaparte

Soldiers of my Old Guard: I bid you farewell. For twenty years I have constantly accompanied you on the road to honor and glory. In these latter times, as in the days of our prosperity, you have invariably been models of courage and fidelity. With men such as you our cause could not be lost; but the war would have been interminable; it would have been civil war, and that would have entailed deeper misfortunes on France.

I have sacrificed all my interests to those of the country.

I go, but you, my friends, will continue to serve France. Her happiness was my only thought. It will still be the object of my wishes. Do not regret my fate; if I have consented to survive, it is to serve your glory. I intend to write the history of the great achievements we have performed together. Adieu, my friends, would I could press you all to my heart.

二十六　向舊日的侍衛隊告別

拿破崙・波拿巴

　　我的老衞隊士兵們：我向你們告別。二十年來，我一直陪伴你們走在光榮的道路上。在最近的這些年月裏，你們一如我們全盛時期那樣，始終是勇敢與忠誠的模範。有了像你們這樣的兵士，我們的事業是不會失敗的。但是這樣戰事就不會結束，却要成爲內戰，法國就會蒙受更深的苦難。

　　爲了國家的利益，我已經犧牲了我的一切利益。

　　我要離去了，但是你們，我的朋友，還要繼續爲法蘭西服務。過去我唯一想到的是法蘭西的幸福。今後，這仍將是我的願望。不要爲我的命運惋惜；我之所以同意活下去，那也是爲了你們的光榮。我準備將我們過去共同取得的偉大成就寫下來。別了，朋友們，但願我能把你們都緊緊地抱在心裏。

　　拿破崙（ 1769～1821 ），法國軍事家和政治家。1799年發動政變，1804年稱帝。1815年滑鐵盧戰役失敗後，被流放於聖赫勒拿島（ St. Helen）。本文爲他前往聖赫勒拿島前的講話。

27 The Monroe Doctrine

James Monroe

. . .

We owe it, therefore, to candor and to the amicable relations existing between the United States and those powers to declare that we should consider any attempt on their part to extend their system to any portion of this hemisphere as dangerous to our peace and safety. With the existing colonies or dependencies of any European power we have not interfered and shall not interfere. But with the Governments who have declared their independence and maintained it, and whose independence we have, on great consideration and on just principles, acknowledged, we could not view any interposition for the purpose of oppressing them, or controlling in any other manner their destiny, by any European power in any other light than as the manifestation of an unfriendly disposition toward the United States.

In the war between those new Governments and Spain we declared our neutrality at the time of their recognition, and to this we have adhered, and shall continue to adhere, provided no change shall occur which, in the judgment of the competent authorities of this Government, shall make a corresponding change on the part of the United States indispensable to their security.

The late events in Spain and Portugal show that Europe is still unsettled. Of this important fact no stronger proof can be adduced than that the allied powers should have thought it proper, on any principle satisfactory to themselves, to have interposed by force

二十七　門羅主義

詹姆士・門羅

……

出於我們坦率的天性，加上我國和歐洲各國間的友好關係，我們宣佈：如果歐洲列強企圖把其制度擴張到本半球的任何區域，我們便認為這危及我們的和平與安全。對於歐洲任何國家現有的殖民地與附屬國，我們不曾干涉過，今後也不會干涉。可是對於有些已經宣佈獨立並維持其獨立的政府[1]，我們憑正義的原則認真考慮後，已經予以承認。我們認為，任何歐洲國家旨在壓迫這些政府，或以任何其他方式控制其命運，皆是對美國不友好的表現。

我們承認這些新政府之時，就已宣告對它們同西班牙之間的戰爭持中立態度。我們現在仍然持這種態度。如果形勢不變，我們將繼續堅持這種態度。但如本政府主管當局判斷為維護國家安全而必需改變，美國將作相應的改變。

西班牙與葡萄牙近來發生的事件說明歐洲局勢仍不穩定。這重要事實最有力不過地證明了各同盟國只依據符合自己心意的原則，便武

門羅（1758～1831），美國第五屆總統。本文為1823年12月2日門羅致美國國會第七年度咨文。

（1）指中、南美洲各新獨立國家政府。

in the internal concerns of Spain. To what extent such interposition may be carried, on the same principle, is a question in which all independent powers whose governments differ from theirs are interested, even those most remote, and surely none more so than the United States.

Our policy in regard to Europe, which was adopted at an early stage of the wars which have so long agitated that quarter of the globe, nevertheless remains the same, which is, not to interfere in the internal concerns of any of its powers; to consider the government de facto as the legitimate government for us; to cultivate friendly relations with it, and to preserve those relations by a frank, firm, and manly policy, meeting in all instances the just claims of every power, submitting to injuries from none. But in regard to these continents circumstances are eminently and conspicuously different. It is impossible that the allied powers should extend their political system to any portion of either continent without endangering our peace and happiness; nor can anyone believe that our southern brethren, if left to themselves, would adopt it of their own accord. It is equally impossible, therefore, that we should behold such interposition in any form with indifference. If we look to the comparative strength and resources of Spain and those new Governments, and their distance from each other, it must be obvious that she can never subdue them. It is still the true policy of the United States to leave the parties to themselves, in the hope that other powers will pursue the same course. . . .

力干涉西班牙內政。因此，根據上述原則的干涉行動可以擴展到那種程度，便成為一切獨立國家所關心的問題。這些獨立國家的政府架構跟上述國家有別，甚至距離很遠，其中美國距離尤遠。

歐洲長期以來戰禍頻仍，我們對歐洲的政策是在歐洲戰亂早期確定的。現在我國國策仍然不變，那就是不干涉該地區任何國家的內政，承認實際存在的政府即是合法政府，與之發展友好關係，並以坦率、堅定與果斷的政策保持這種關係；在任何情況下滿足每一國家的正當要求，但對任何損害我們的行為則絕不屈服。然而，南北美洲的形勢明顯有所不同。如果各同盟國要將他們的政治制度擴展到這兩大洲的任何部分，就不可能不危及我們的和平與幸福。此外，沒有人會相信，如果聽任我們南方的兄弟自由選擇，他們會自願選擇那種政治制度。因此，無論是何種形式的干涉，要我們漠然置之，也同樣不可能。如果我們比較一下西班牙和這些新成立政府的力量、資源以及其間相隔的距離，可以看到，西班牙顯然無法令這些新政府屈服。美國的真誠政策仍然是對他們雙方都不加干涉；我們希望別的國家亦採取同一政策。……

28 Celebrates the American Heritage

Daniel Webster

. . .

Sink or swim, live or die, survive or perish, I give my hand and my heart to this vote. It is true, indeed, that in the beginning we aimed not at independence. But there's a divinity which shapes our ends. The injustice of England has driven us to arms; and, blinded to her own interest for our good, she has obstinately persisted, till independence is now within our grasp. We have but to reach forth to it, and it is ours. Why, then, should we defer the Declaration? Is any man so weak as now to hope for a reconciliation with England, which shall leave either safety to the country and its liberties, or safety to his own life and his own honor? . . . The war, then, must go on. We must fight it through. And, if the war must go on, why put off longer the Declaration of Independence? That measure will strengthen us. It will give us character abroad. The nations will then treat with us, which they never can do while we acknowledge ourselves subjects in arms against our sovereign. Nay, I maintain that England herself will sooner treat for peace with us on the footing of independence than consent, by repealing her acts, to acknowledge that her whole conduct toward us has been a course of injustice and oppression. Her pride will be less wounded by submitting to that course of things which now predestinates our independence than by yielding the points in controversy to her rebellious

---

韋伯斯特（ 1782～1852 ），曾任美國國務卿。本文發表於1826年8月2日的集會，為紀念7月4日美國獨立宣言簽訂50週年和同日美國第二、三任總統亞

二十八 美國的革命傳統

……

　　無論生死存亡、成功失敗，我將舉雙手贊成獨立宣言。不錯，開始時我們並沒有以獨立為目標。但是，上帝為我們安排了結局。英國的不義行為迫使我們拿起武器；他們堅持頑固立場，無視自己的利益所在，反而使我們得益，直到我們的獨立已經在望，只要伸出雙手，它就在我們掌握之中。既然如此，為什麼還要推延通過獨立宣言？難道現在還有人如此軟弱，竟希望同英國和解？這種和解既不能使國家得到安全與自由，又無法保障個人的生命與榮譽。……因此，戰爭必須進行下去。我們要作戰到底。如果這樣，為什麼還要推遲發表獨立宣言？宣言將增強我們的力量，為我們贏得國際地位。外國將與我們來往。如果我們把自己看作是武裝背叛宗主國的亂臣，我們就得不到這樣的國際地位。我認為英國不僅會同意，甚至更願意在獨立基礎上同我們媾和。英國將撤銷各項法案，承認對我們的行為全屬不義和高壓。英國接受我們由於她的不義與高壓而謀求的獨

當斯、傑弗遜同時逝世。講話中引用了亞當斯說過的話，但作為韋伯斯特自己的話講出。

subjects. The former she would regard as the result of fortune, the latter she would feel as her own deep disgrace. Why, then — why, then, sir, do we not, as soon as possible, change this from a civil to a national war? And since we must fight it through, why not put ourselves in a state to enjoy all the benefits of victory, if we gain the victory?

If we fail, it can be no worse for us. But we shall not fail. The cause will raise up armies; the cause will create navies. The people — the people, if we are true to them, will carry us, and will carry themselves, gloriously through this struggle. I care not how fickle other people have been found. I know the people of these colonies, and I know that resistance to British aggression is deep and settled in their hearts and cannot be eradicated. Every colony, indeed, has expressed its willingness to follow, if we but take the lead. Sir, the Declaration will inspire the people with increased courage. Instead of a long and bloody war for restoration of privilege, for redress of grievances, for chartered immunities, held under a British king, set before them the glorious object of entire independence, and it will breathe into them anew the breath of life. . . .

Sir, I know the uncertainty of human affairs, but I see, I see clearly, through this day's business. You and I, indeed, may rue it. We may not live to the time when this Declaration shall be made good. We may die; die, colonists; die, slaves, die, it may be, ignominiously

立，要比屈服於叛臣的作亂較有體面。前者，她可以看成是命運的結果，後者却是她的奇恥大辱。旣然如此，主席先生，我們爲什麼還不盡快把這場內戰轉變爲一場國際戰爭呢？旣然我們要作戰到底，爲什麼在勝利到來的時候，不享受勝利的一切利益呢？

如果我們失敗了，情況也不會比現在更壞。但是，我們是不會失敗的。這場戰事可以號召徵集兵士，建立海軍。如果我們忠於人民，人民將支持我們，並奮戰到底，直至光榮地取得勝利。我不管其他民族如何反覆無常，我只知道，反抗英國壓迫欺凌的情緒埋在我們各殖民地[1]的人民心底，不可消除。實際上，每個殖民地都已表示決心，只要我們一聲令下，他們就會揭竿而起。主席先生，獨立宣言將鼓舞人民，使他們勇氣倍增。他們不必再在英王的恩賜下，爲恢復某些權利，消除某些弊端和不公平，免納某些特種租稅而進行漫長的血腥戰爭了。在他們面前的光榮目標是完全獨立，這目標將使他們精神振奮，生氣勃勃。……

主席先生，人世間的事變化莫測，但是我今日已能看清大勢。你我可能因爲看不到宣言的實現而遺恨千古。我們可能先此而死去，作爲殖民地人民而死，作爲奴隸而死，甚至可能

───────────────

（1）當時英國在北美有十三個殖民地。

and on the scaffold. Be it so. Be it so. If it be the pleasure of heaven that my country shall require the poor offering of my life, the victim shall be ready at the appointed hour of sacrifice, come when that hour may. But while I do live, let me have a country, or at least the hope of a country, and that a free country.

But, whatever may be our fate, be assured, be assured, that this Declaration will stand. It may cost treasure; and it may cost blood; but it will stand, and it will richly compensate for both. Through the thick gloom of the present I see the brightness of the future as the sun in heaven. We shall make this a glorious, an immortal day. When we are in our graves, our children will honor it. They will celebrate it with thanksgiving, with festivity, with bonfires, and illuminations. On its annual return they will shed tears, copious, gushing tears, not of subjection and slavery, not of agony and distress, but of exultation, of gratitude, and of joy. Sir, before God, I believe the hour has come. My judgment approves this measure, and my whole heart is in it. All that I have, and all that I am, and all that I hope, in this life, I am now ready here to stake upon it; and I leave off as I began, that, live or die, survive or perish, I am for the Declaration. It is my living sentiment, and, by the blessing of God, it shall be my dying sentiment; independence now, and independence forever.

蒙受恥辱，死在斷頭台上。縱然如此，我亦無所悔憾！如果天意要我爲國捐軀，我將於指定的時刻從容就義。但是，在我有生之日，讓我有一個自己的國家吧，至少讓我有希望得到一個國家，一個自由的國家。

　　但是，無論我們個人的命運是禍是福，請堅信，堅信宣言必將巍然屹立。爲達成宣言，我們可能耗費錢財，可能犧牲流血；但是，宣言必將屹立，並加倍償還所耗的錢財和生命。透過目前陰沉的形勢，我看到了光明的遠景，有如昭昭天日。今天將作爲——光榮不朽的日子載入史冊。當我們長眠地下之時，我們的子孫將紀念這日子。他們將感激滿懷、載歌載舞、高燃篝火、張燈結綵慶此佳節。年年此日，他們將痛灑熱淚、濕袖沾襟。這眼淚，不再是奴役的屈辱之淚，不再是痛苦憂傷之淚，而是歡欣鼓舞，感恩戴德與喜慶歡樂的熱淚。主席先生，我對上帝發誓，我深信時刻已經到來。我斷定這宣言是好的，我全心全意擁護它。我將所有的一切，我的全部稟性、我一生的希望都傾注在這宣言上。我要重複我開始時說過的話：無論生死存亡、成功失敗，我堅決支持獨立宣言。這是我的生平夙願，願上帝賜福我，使它也成爲我臨終時的遺志吧；爭取立刻獨立！永遠保持獨立！

29 The American Union

Daniel Webster

I profess, Sir, in my career hitherto, to have kept steadily in view the prosperity and honor of the whole country, and the preservation of our Federal Union. It is to that Union we owe our safety at home, and our consideration and dignity abroad. It is to that Union we are chiefly indebted for whatever makes us most proud of our country. That Union we reached only by the discipline of our virtues, in the severe school of adversity. It had its origin in the necessities of disordered finance, prostrate commerce, and ruined credit. Under its benign influences, these great interests immediately awoke, as from the dead, and sprang forth with newness of life. Every year of its duration has teemed with fresh proofs of its utility and its blessings; and although our territory has stretched out wider and wider, and our population spread further and further, they have not outrun its protection, or its benefits. It has been to us all a copious fountain of national, social, personal happiness. I have not allowed myself, Sir, to look beyond the Union, to see what might lie hidden in the dark recess behind. I have not coolly weighed the chances of preserving liberty, when the bonds that unite us together shall be broken asunder. I have not accustomed myself to hang over the precipice of disunion, to see whether, with my short sight, I can fathom the depth of the abyss below: nor could I regard him as a safe counsellor in the affairs of this Government whose thought should be mainly bent on considering, not how the Union should be best preserved,

二十九　美利堅聯邦

丹尼爾・韋伯斯特

先生，我可以公開聲明，我在我的事業中歷來堅定地着眼於整個國家的繁華、尊嚴以及聯邦的長治久安。正是有了這聯邦，我們才在國內得保安全，在國外受到尊重。主要因爲有了這聯邦，我們才能夠以國家自豪。我們經受嚴峻的磨煉，堅持培養自己的美德，才得以形成這聯邦。基於當時財政紊亂、商業衰竭和信貸崩潰，產生了聯邦。在聯邦的庇護下，我們的財政、商業、信貸事業迅猛振興，死而復甦，欣欣向榮。自有聯邦以來，年年都有新的事實證明它的惠益和福祉；我們的疆土日益擴展，人口日益繁增，但我們仍在聯邦庇護之下，受惠於它。聯邦是我們國家、社會和個人幸福取之不竭的甘泉。先生，我無法想到聯邦不存在的可能，或是它不存在時的黯淡情景。我無法冷靜地衡量，把我們聯結在一起的紐帶一旦斷裂，還有多大可能保持我們的自由。我還不慣於設想聯盟一旦瓦解可能發生的危機，我短淺的目光實在測不出瓦解後脚下那無底深淵的深度。如果一位政府官員主要不是着眼於如何盡力維護聯邦的統一，却設想聯邦破裂後我們的

美國內戰後南北雙方成立美利堅聯邦。

but how tolerable might be the condition of the People when it shall be broken up and destroyed.

While the Union lasts, we have high, exciting, gratifying prospects spread out before us, for us and our children. Beyond that I seek not to penetrate the veil. God grant that, in my day, at least, that curtain may not rise! God grant that on my vision never may be opened what lies behind! When my eyes shall be turned to behold, for the last time, the sun in Heaven, may I not see him shining on the broken and dishonored fragments of a once glorious Union; on States severed, discordant, belligerent; on a land rent with civil feuds, or drenched, it may be, in fraternal blood! Let their last feeble and lingering glance, rather, behold the gorgeous Ensign of the Republic, now known and honored throughout the earth, still full high advanced, its arms and trophies streaming in their original lustre, not a stripe erased or polluted, not a single star obscured, — bearing, for its motto, no such miserable interrogatory as —*What is all this worth?* — nor those other words of delusion and folly — *Liberty first and Union afterwards,* — but everywhere, spread all over in characters of living light, blazing on all its ample folds, as they float over the sea and over the land, and in every wind under the whole Heavens, that other sentiment, dear to every true American heart — Liberty *and* Union, now and forever, one and inseparable!

民族將處於如何不堪的處境，那末，我不能認爲他是一個可靠的政府官員。

聯邦存在一天，我們和子孫後代的面前，就展現一片繁榮昌盛、激動人心的可喜遠景。我不願透過帷幕去看這遠景以外的東西。願上帝賜福於我，至少在我有生之年不要揭開這層帷幕！願上帝賜福，使我永遠看不到帷幕後的慘狀！在我將死時，當我彌留的目光仰視天上太陽之際，但願陽光照射的聯邦，並未從光榮燦爛變爲可恥的紛紛碎片；願陽光不是照射在分裂和互相爭吵殘殺的各州之上；不會照射在內部紛爭、同胞濺血的國土之上！讓我彌留之際的目光，看到的依然是這面美麗的、爲世界各國公認並尊崇的共和國大旗迎風高舉；星條旗上的紋章裝飾，依舊光彩鮮亮，沒有一條條紋污殘，沒有一顆明星失色；旗幟上標誌着的箴言旣不是"這一切有什麼價值？"的可悲疑問，也不是"先有自由後有聯邦"的虛妄愚言，而是標誌着另一種情操的大旗，在普天之下飛揚招展，在陸地，在海洋，光芒四射，生氣勃勃。這種情操是每個美國人心底都懷有的眞情：自由與聯邦，渾爲一體，世世代代，永不可分！

30 The American Scholar

Ralph Waldo Emerson

. . .

Thus far, our holiday has been simply a friendly sign of the survival of the love of letters amongst a people too busy to give to letters any more. As such it is precious as the sign of an indestructible instinct. Perhaps the time is already come when it ought to be, and will be, something else; when the sluggard intellect of this continent will look from under its iron lids and fill the postponed expectation of the world with something better than the exertions of mechanical skill. Our day of dependence, our long apprenticeship to the learning of other lands, draws to a close. The millions that around us are rushing into life, cannot always be fed on the mere remains of foreign harvests. Events, actions arise, that must be sung, that will sing themselves. Who can doubt that poetry will revive and lead in a new age, as the star in the constellation Harp, which now flames in our zenith, astronomers announce, shall one day be the polestar for a thousand years?

. . .

I read with some joy of the auspicious signs of the coming days, as they glimmer already through poetry and art, through philosophy and science, through

三十　論美國學者

拉爾夫・華爾多・愛默生

......

迄今為止，我們的節日一直只是一種友善的象徵，表示我們這忙碌得無暇顧及文學的民族，仍然對文學存着一點愛好。這點愛好極有寶貴的意義，顯示我們對文學有一種永不泯滅的本能。但是，也許早該發生變化，而且必會發生變化的時刻到了；這大陸上沉睡的知識分子早應覺醒，睜開沉重的鐵眼皮，供給世界一些機械技術以外更美好的事物，滿足各國期待已久的願望。我們在學術上依賴別人，長期學習別國的日子快結束了。我們周圍千千萬萬人正投身在火熱的生活中，不能總吃外國文化的殘羹剩飯。我們也有許多事變與活動，要我們去歌唱，它們也要歌唱自己。誰能懷疑詩歌在新時代裏將復興，像天文學家報告正在天頂熠熠閃耀的天琴星座那樣，終有一天成為光照千古的明星，指引我們前進呢？

......

我懷着喜悅看到未來的種種吉兆，它們已經透過詩歌和藝術、哲學和科學、教會和政府

愛默生（1803～1882），美國詩人，散文家。本文發表於1837年8月31日"美國大學優秀生全國聯誼會"（Phi Beta Kappa，簡稱 ϕBK）上。

church and state.

One of these signs is the fact that the same movement which effected the elevation of what was called the lowest class in the state, assumed in literature a very marked and as benign an aspect. Instead of the sublime and beautiful, the near, the low, the common, was explored and poetized. That which had been negligently trodden under foot by those who were harnessing and provisioning themselves for long journeys into far countries, is suddenly found to be richer than all foreign parts. The literature of the poor, the feelings of the child, the philosophy of the street, the meaning of household life, are the topics of the time. It is a great stride. It is a sign — is it not? — of new vigor when the extremities are made active, when currents of warm life run into the hands and the feet. I ask not for the great, the remote, the romantic; what is doing in Italy or Arabia; what is Greek art, or Provencal minstrelsy; I embrace the common, I explore and sit at the feet of the familiar, the low. Give me insight into to-day, and you may have the antique and future worlds. What would we really know the meaning of? The meal in the firkin; the milk in the pan; the ballad in the street; the news of the boat; the glance of the eye; the form and the gait of the body; — show me the ultimate reason of these matters; show me the sublime presence of the highest spiritual cause lurking, as always it does lurk, in these suburbs and extremities of nature; let me see every trifle bristling with the polarity that ranges it instantly on an eternal law; and the shop, the plough,

閃現出來。

這些徵兆之一就是所謂國家最低層的階級已通過運動提升了地位，這運動也同時令文學呈現顯著和有益發展的面貌。人們着意發掘並譜寫成詩章的，不是崇高優美的陽春白雪，而是發生在身旁、卑微而平凡的事物。那些束裝遠游、寄情異國的人踩在脚下不屑一顧的事物，忽然被人發現其實遠比一切外國事物更絢爛多彩。窮人的文學、童稚的感情、街頭的哲學、家庭生活的意義，都是當代的題材。這是一個躍進。生命的暖流已經流入手脚，身體四肢都已活躍起來，這難道不是一種新的活力迹象嗎？我不奢求偉大的、遙遠的、浪漫的事物，不追求意大利或阿拉伯的成就、希臘的藝術，或普羅旺斯[1]的吟游詩歌；我要擁抱平凡，我要探索人所共知的平凡事物。你們盡可佔有古代和未來的世界，讓我洞察今天的生活吧。我們要從哪裏去眞正了解意義呢？那就是桶中的飯菜、鍋裏的牛奶、街頭小調、馬路新聞、目光一閃、身體形體、走路姿態——把這些微末瑣事的最終道理寫出來，把隱藏其中最崇高的精神因素寫出來吧，因爲最崇高的東西往往隱藏在自然界最偏遠最微末的地方。讓我看到每件日常瑣事都直接聯繫着一條永恒的法則。一間店舖、

_____

（1）法國一地區。

and the ledger referred to the like cause by which light undulates and poets sing; — and the world lies no longer a dull miscellany and lumber room, but has form and order; there is no trifle, there is no puzzle, but one design unites and animates the farthest pinnacle and the lowest trench.

This idea has inspired the genius of Goldsmith, Burns, Cowper, and in a newer time, of Goethe, Wordsworth, and Carlyle. This idea they have differently followed and with various success. In contrast with their writing, the style of Pope, of Johnson, of Gibbon, looks cold and pedantic. This writing is blood-warm. Man is surprised to find that things near are not less beautiful and wondrous than things remote. The near explains the far. The drop is a small ocean. A man is related to all nature. This perception of the worth of the vulgar is fruitful in discoveries. . . .

（ 1 ）奧立佛・哥爾德斯密（ 1728～1774 ），英國18世紀後期重要作家。

（ 2 ）羅伯特・彭斯（ 1759～1796 ），英國18世紀後期著名詩人，對民間文學貢獻很大。

（ 3 ）威廉・庫柏（ 1731～1800 ），英國詩人。

（ 4 ）約翰・沃爾夫岡・歌德（ 1749～1832 ），德國詩人及思想家。

（ 5 ）威廉・華滋華斯（ 1770～1850 ），英國浪漫主義

一把犁耙和一本帳簿同樣會引起光波蕩漾，值
得詩人謳歌。這樣，世界就不再是一間堆滿零
亂雜物、死氣沉沉的陋室，却是井然有序。世
界無所謂瑣事細節，也無所謂疑案難題，最高
的與最低的天地萬物聯成一體，有相同的生命
設計。

　　哥爾德斯密[1]、彭斯[2]、庫柏[3]以及近代
的歌德[4]、華滋華斯[5]、卡萊爾[6]等這些天才，
就是由上述觀念激發出來的。他們從不同的角
度遵循上述觀念，各取得不同成就。同他們的
著作相比，蒲柏[7]、約翰遜[8]、吉本[9]的文體
顯得冷冰冰地帶着學究氣。他們的著作却都是熱
血沸騰的。人們驚異地發現，身邊的事物並不
見得不如遠處的美麗與新奇。近的東西解釋遙
遠的事物。一滴水就是一個小小的海洋。一個
人聯繫着整個自然界，從平凡事物中感受價值，
可以結出累累碩果。……

　　詩人，＂湖畔派＂詩人的代表。
（6）托馬斯·卡萊爾（1795～1881），英國作家、歷
　　　史學家和哲學家。
（7）亞歷山大·蒲柏（1688～1744），英國詩人，啟
　　　蒙運動時期古典主義的代表。
（8）撒姆耳·約翰遜（1719～1784），英國作家，批
　　　評家。
（9）愛德華·吉本（1737～1794），英國歷史學家。

31 To the Young Men of Italy

Giuseppe Mazzini

When I was commissioned by you, young men, to proffer in this temple a few words sacred to the memory of the brothers Bandiera and their fellow martyrs at Cosenza, I thought some of those who heard me might exclaim with noble indignation: "Wherefore lament over the dead? The martyrs of liberty are only worthily honored by winning the battle they have begun; Cosenza, the land where they fell, is enslaved; Venice, the city of their birth, is begirt by foreign foes. Let us emancipate them, and until that moment let no words pass our lips save words of war."

But another thought arose: "Why have we not conquered? Why is it that, while we are fighting for independence in the north of Italy, liberty is perishing in the south? Why is it that a war, which should have sprung to the Alps with the bound of a lion, has dragged itself along for four months, with the slow uncertain motion of the scorpion surrounded by a circle of fire? How has the rapid and powerful intuition of a people newly arisen to life been coverted into the weary, helpless effort of the sick man turning from side to side?" Ah! Had we all arisen in the sanctity of the idea

三十一　致意大利青年

朱瑟佩・瑪志尼

年青人，我受你們委托，在這神廟裏，為紀念班狄拉兄弟及在柯先薩與他們同時蒙難的烈士作簡單獻詞，我想，有些聽到我講話的人可能會激於義憤說：“傷悼逝者有什麼用處？對為自由而獻身的烈士，最有價值的悼念是為他們未竟的事業取得勝利；現在，先烈們殉難之地柯先薩還在受奴役；先烈們出生的城市威尼斯還在外敵圍困之中。讓我們解放這些地方吧！在這之前，除了戰爭二字，一句閒話也不要出口！”

但是，有人提出了另一個問題：“為什麼我們還沒有取得勝利？為什麼我們在意大利北方為獨立而戰時，南方却失去了自由？為什麼我們本應像雄獅那樣一舉將戰場推到阿爾卑斯山麓，現在却拖延了四個月，像被一圈火圍住的蝎子趑趄不前？我們這個剛剛復興的民族原來具有朝氣勃勃、敏感果斷的民族意識，為什麼會一落千丈，好似病入膏肓的人，輾轉反側、呻吟床蓆？”啊，如果我們所有人都已振奮精

瑪志尼（1805～1872）意大利愛國者及革命家。

1848年歐洲爆發革命，他在意大利成立羅馬共和國，不久失敗。本文是他1848年在米蘭為紀念反抗奧地利入侵而犧牲的愛國志士的講話。

for which our martyrs died; had the holy standard of
their faith preceded our youth to battle; had we reached
that unity of life which was in them so powerful and
made of our every action a thought, and of our every
thought an action; had we devoutly gathered up their
last words in our hearts, and learned from them that
liberty and independence are one; that God and the
people, the fatherland and humanity, are the two
inseparable terms of the device of every people striving
to become a nation; that Italy can have no true life
till she be one, holy in the equality and love of all her
children, great in the worship of eternal truth, and
consecrated to a lofty mission, a moral priesthood
among the peoples of Europe — we should now have
had, not war, but victory; Cosenza would not be compelled to venerate the memory of her martyrs in secret,
nor Venice be restrained from honoring them with a
monument; and we, gathered here together, might
gladly invoke their sacred names, without uncertainty
as to our future destiny, or a cloud of sadness on our
brows, and say to those precursor souls: "Rejoice! For
your spirit is incarnate in your brethren, and they are
worthy of you."

. . .

And love, young men, love and venerate the ideal.
The ideal is the word of God. High above every country,
high above humanity, is the country of the spirit, the
city of the soul, in which all are brethren who believe
in the inviolability of thought and in the dignity of our

神，樹立起烈士們曾爲之獻身的信念；如果烈
士曾高舉的聖旗已經引導我們的青年奔赴疆
場；如果我們已經達到使烈士如此堅強有力，
使我們每一行動都基於同一思想，每一思想都
形成一致行動的精誠團結；如果我們已把他們
的遺言銘刻心頭，向他們學習，認識到自由與
獨立永不可分，認識到對於每一個要自強建國
的民族，上帝和人民、祖國和人類兩者是不可
分的；如果我們認識到意大利若不成爲一個整
體，不崇尙平等、愛護子民、信奉永恒眞理、
忠於自己偉大事業，並成爲歐洲各民族中具有
高度道德信仰的民族，意大利就不可能得到眞
正的生命。如果我們認識到和做到上述的一切，
戰爭早就成爲過去，勝利早就在握了。那時，柯
先薩不用秘密地紀念自己的烈士，威尼斯敢於
公開爲他們樹起紀念碑。我們可以聚集在這裏
興高采烈地稱頌他們的英名，不用愁眉不展地
爲莫測的未來命運憂心忡忡了。我們會對先驅
們說："願你們的英靈歡欣鼓舞，因爲你們的
精神已經溶化到弟兄們身上，他們無愧爲你們
的後來者。"

······

青年人啊，熱愛理想、崇敬理想吧。理想
是上帝的語言。高於所有國家和人類的是精神
的王國，是靈魂的故鄉。在其中，所有人都是
兄弟，相信思想不容侵犯，相信我們不朽的靈

immortal soul; and the baptism of this fraternity is martyrdom. From that high sphere spring the principles which alone can redeem the peoples. Arise from the sake of these, and not from impatience of suffering or dread of evil, anger, pride, ambition, and the desire of material prosperity are arms common alike to the peoples and their oppressors, and even should you conquer with these today, you would fall again tomorrow, but principles belong to the peoples alone, and their oppressors can find no arms to oppose them. Adore enthusiasm, the dreams of the virgin soul, and the visions of early youth, for they are a perfume of paradise which the soul retains in issuing from the hands of its Creator. Respect above all things your conscience; have upon our lips the truth implanted by God in your hearts, and, while laboring in harmony, even with those who differ from you, in all that tends to the emancipation of our soil, yet ever bear your own banner erect and boldly promulgate your own faith.

Such words, young men, would the martyrs of Cosenza have spoken, had they been living amongst you; and here, where it may be that, invoked by our love, their holy spirits hover near us, I call upon you to gather them up in your hearts and to make of them a treasure amid the storms that yet threaten you; storms which, with the name of our martyrs on your lips and their faith in your hearts, you will overcome.

God be with you, and lest Italy!

魂是神聖尊嚴的。死節殉難是得到這種兄弟關係的洗禮。唯有出自那種崇高境界的原則能夠拯救各民族。你們要為實現這些原則而奮起，不要因為邪惡、憤怒、自大、野心以及物質慾望使你們受苦、使你們害怕、使你們難以忍受而奮起。因為這些都是人民與壓迫者可以共同使用的武器，即使你們今天用這些武器取得勝利，明天你們還是會失敗的。唯有原則單屬於人民，壓迫者找不到戰勝原則的武器。崇高奔放的熱情，追求貞潔靈魂的理想和青春的憧憬吧，因為這是靈魂從造物者手中得到的天堂的芳香。你們必須尊重良心，視良心高於一切其他事物。我們口中只能說上帝種於我們心田中的真理。在解放我們國土的一切努力中，要團結一致，甚至要團結和你們意見分歧的人，同時又要高舉你們自己的旗幟，大膽地傳播你們的信仰。

年青人啊，如果柯先薩的烈士仍然活着，他們也會對你們說這番話。現在，他們聖潔的靈魂被我們的愛所感動，可能正翱翔在我們的頭頂。我號召你們銘記這番話並牢牢珍藏於心。我們口呼烈士的英名，心懷烈士的信仰，就定能戰勝將臨的狂風暴雨。

願上帝與你們同在，與意大利同在！

145

32　To His Soldiers

Giuseppe Garibaldi

We must now consider the period which is just drawing to a close as almost the last stage of our national resurrection, and prepare ourselves to finish worthily the marvelous design of the elect of twenty generations, the completion of which Providence has reserved for this fortunate age.

Yes, young men, Italy owes to you an undertaking which has merited the applause of the universe. You have conquered and you will conquer still, because you are prepared for the tactics that decide the fate of battles. You are not unworthy men who entered the ranks of a Macedonian phalanx, and who contended not in vain with the proud conquerors of Asia. To this wonderful page in our country's history another more glorious still will be added, and the slave shall show at last to his free brothers a sharpened sword forged from the links of his fetters.

. . .

Providence has presented Italy with Victor Emmanuel. Every Italian should rally round him. By the side of Victor Emmanuel every quarrel should be forgotten, all rancor depart. Once more I repeat my battle cry: "To arms, all — all of you!" If March, 1861,

---

加里波第（1807～1882），意大利愛國者。1849
年2月，在加里波第建議下，意大利成立了羅馬共和
國。同年6月，法國干涉軍進攻羅馬，加里波第逃亡
至南美洲。本文爲紀念意大利愛國者擊敗了奧地利的
侵略而作。

三十二 致衆士兵

朱瑟佩・加里波第

這個歷史時期已經快要結束，我們必須把這時期看作是國家復興的最後階段，同時作好準備去完成無數優秀前輩設計的宏偉藍圖，無愧於他們的期望。上天有意把完成這宏偉藍圖的任務留給我們這幸運的一代。

是的，年青人，意大利由於有了你們，得以成就這項寰宇稱頌的偉業。你們已經克敵制勝，還要取得更大的勝利。因爲你們精嫻戰術，穩操勝券。你們比之古希臘的馬其頓[1]勇士毫不遜色，擊敗了來自亞洲的驕橫征服者。在我國歷史這輝煌的一頁之上，還要增添新的更輝煌的一頁，奴隸們終於要讓已經獲得自由的兄弟看到他們用身上的鐐銬鑄造成的一把利劍。

……

上天已經把維多・伊曼紐爾[2]賜給意大利，每個意大利人都應團結在他的周圍。在維多・伊曼紐爾身旁，一切爭執都應當忘却，一切宿恨都應該拋棄。我再次發出戰鬥的吶喊："所有人，全都拿起武器來！"倘若到了1861年3月，

（1）巴爾幹半島中部的國家，以勇敢善戰著稱。
（2）指維多・伊曼紐爾二世（1820～1878），意大利國王，最先統一意大利並與法、英、土聯盟抗奧，取得勝利。

does not find one million of Italians in arms, then alas for liberty, alas for the life of Italy. Ah, no, far be from me a thought which I loathe like poison. March of 1861, or if need be February, will find us all at our post — Italians of Calatafimi, Palermo, Ancona, the Volturno, Castelfidardo, and Isernia, and with us every man of this land who is not a coward or a slave. Let all of us rally round the glorious hero of Palestro and give the last blow to the crumbling edifice of tyranny. Receive, then, my gallant young volunteers, at the honored conclusion of ten battles, one word of farewell from me.

I utter this word with deepest affection and from the very bottom of my heart. Today I am obliged to retire, but for a few days only. The hour of battle will find me with you again, by the side of the champions of Italian liberty. Let those only return to their homes who are called by the imperative duties which they owe to their families, and those who by their glorious wounds have deserved the credit of their country. These, indeed, will serve Italy in their homes by their counsel, by the very aspect of the scars which adorn their youthful brows. Apart from these, let all others remain to guard our glorious banners. We shall meet again before long to march together to the redemption of our brothers who are still slaves of the stranger. We shall meet again before long to march to new triumphs.

我們還不能徵集到一百萬意大利軍隊，自由將會喪失，意大利將要滅亡。啊，不，讓我絕不要有這種邪毒的念頭。到了1861年3月，必要時是2月，我們所有人，卞拉塔菲米、巴勒莫、安科納、沃爾圖諾河、卞斯特爾菲達都、和伊塞尼亞等地的意大利人和我國的每一個人，除了儒夫與奴才之外，都會和我們一起站到各自的崗位上。讓我們團結在光榮的帕勒斯特羅的英雄[1]周圍，給搖搖欲墜的暴政大厦以最後的一擊。然後，我豪邁英勇的青年志願軍啊，請你們在十次戰鬥勝利的光榮時刻，再接受我最後的告別吧。

我從內心深處說出這些最真誠摯愛的話。今天我不得不暫時離開幾天。等到戰鬥打響，你們會看到我又來到你們中間，站在爲爭取意大利自由而作戰的戰士身旁。讓家裏有緊迫事情而必須回家的人回去吧，讓爲國光榮負傷的人回去吧，他們無愧於自己的祖國。他們必定會在後方繼續爲國家服務，他們那年青額上的傷痕就是忠於意大利的光榮標記。除了他們之外，讓其餘的人都留下來捍衛我們光榮的旗幟吧。不久我們就會重聚一起，共同進軍去解救那仍在異族奴役下的兄弟。不久我們就會重聚一起，向新的勝利進軍。

（1）指伊曼紐爾，帕勒斯特羅是意大利地名。

33 Welcome to Louis Kossuth

William Cullen Bryant

Let me ask you to imagine the contest, in which the United States asserted their independence of Great Britain, had been unsuccessful, that our armies, through treason or a league of tyrants against us, had been broken and scattered, that the great men who led them, and who swayed our councils, our Washington, our Franklin, and the venerable president of the American Congress, had been driven forth as exiles. If there had existed at that day, in any part of the civilized world, a powerful republic, with institutions resting on the same foundations of liberty, which our own country-men sought to establish, would there have been in that republic any hospitality too cordial, any sympathy too deep, any zeal for their glorious but unfortunate cause, too fervent or too active to be shown toward these illustrious fugitives? Gentlemen, the case I have sup-posed is before you. The Washingtons, the Franklins, the Hancocks of Hungary, driven out by a far worse tyranny than was ever endured here, are wanderers in foreign lands. Some of them have sought a refuge in our country — one sits with his company our guest to-night, and we must measure the duty we owe them by the same standard which we would have had history apply, if our ancestors had met with a fate like theirs.

. . .

勃列愛因（ 1794～1878 ），美國詩人、新聞記者。
本文為1851年紐約出版界歡迎匈牙利革命領袖柯蘇特
（ 1802～1894 ）流亡到美國的講話。

三十三 歡迎路易斯·柯蘇特

威廉·柯林·勃列愛因

請允許我要求你們設想一下，如果當年美國向大不列顛爭取獨立的鬥爭遭到了失敗，軍隊因內部叛變或專制集團的壓制而潰散，軍隊統帥、議會領袖，我們的華盛頓、富蘭克林和尊敬的國會主席等偉大人物被迫流亡國外，情況會是怎樣。如果當時在文明世界的某個地區，有個強大的共和國，它的制度也同樣建立在我國同胞努力追求的自由基礎之上。那麼，在那共和國裏，對那樣光榮傑出的逃亡者，對他們那光榮而不幸受挫的事業，有什麼款待會過份殷勤，什麼同情會過份深厚，什麼感情會過份熱烈、激烈呢？各位先生，我設想的這種情況，現正在你們眼前。匈牙利的華盛頓們、富蘭克林們和漢柯克[1]們被他們的專制政治逐出國土，流落異鄉。這種專制比我們過去所受的更爲殘暴。他們中有幾位正在我國避難，有一位今晚和他的同伴作爲我們的客人和我們一起坐在這裏。我們應衡量一下，如果我們祖先遇到同樣厄運時，會得到怎樣的接待規格，便應以同等的規格來接待這些匈牙利流亡者。

……

（1）約翰·漢柯克（1737～1793），美國政治家，獨立宣言的簽署人。

I recollect that while the armies of Russia were moving like a tempest from the north upon the Hungarian host, the progress of events was watched with the deepest solicitude by the People of Germany. I was at that time in Munich, the splendid capital of Bavaria. The Germans seemed for the time to have put off their usual character, and scrambled for the daily prints, wet from the press, with such eagerness that I almost thought myself in America. The news of the catastrophe at last arrived; Görgey had betrayed the cause of Hungary, and yielded to the demands of the Russians. Immediately a funeral gloom settled like a noonday darkness upon the city. I heard the muttered exclamations of the people, "It is all over — the last hope of European liberty is gone."

Russia did not misjudge. If she had allowed Hungary to become independent, or free, the reaction in favor of absolutism had been incomplete; there would have been one perilous example of successful resistance to despotism — in one corner of Europe a flame would have been kept alive, at which the other nations might have rekindled, among themselves, the light of liberty. Hungary was subdued; but does any one who hears me believe that the present state of things in Europe will last? The despots themselves that it will not; and made cruel by their fears, are heaping chain on chain around the limbs of their subjects.

They are hastening the event they dread. Every added shackle galls, into a more fiery impotence, those who wear them. I look with mingling hope and horror to the day — a day bloodier, perhaps, than we have yet seen — when the exasperated nations shall snap their chains and start to their feet. It may well be that Hungary, made less patient of the yoke by the remembrance of her own many and glorious struggles for

我記得俄國軍隊像颶風一樣從北方捲向匈牙利本土之時，德國人民以最關切焦慮的心情注視着事態演變的過程。當時我在巴伐里亞雄偉的首都慕尼黑。那時候，德國人民似乎一反他們原有的性格，爭看油墨未乾的每日新聞，其焦急熱切的程度幾乎使我以爲置身美國。最後終於傳來了噩耗：喬治伊出賣了匈牙利，屈從了俄國的要求。頓時，全城天昏地暗，一片哀傷。我聽到人民悄聲歎息："一切都完了。歐洲得到自由的最後希望已經熄滅。"

俄國判斷對了。如果她讓匈牙利得到獨立或自由，有利於極權主義的反應就會出現缺口；匈牙利會成爲反抗專制主義得到成功的危險先例，歐洲的一隅就留下一把自由火種，其他國家可以用來重新點燃自己解放的明燈。匈牙利被鎮壓下去了。但是在座諸君有誰會相信歐洲的現狀會繼續下去呢？連專制主義者自己也不相信。恐懼的心理使他們更殘忍，他們在自己臣民手脚上套上更多的鎖鏈。

他們正在催促自己害怕的時刻更快到來。每一條新加的鎖鏈都把披枷帶鎖的手脚磨得痛徹心脾，無法忍受。我懷着希望與恐懼注視着那個日子——可能是未曾有過的大流血日子——到了那一天，被激怒的各民族將扭斷身上的鎖鏈，挺立起來。由於匈牙利有無數次爭取獨立的光榮鬥爭記憶，她對身上的桎梏更難於

independence, and better fitted than other nations, by the peculiar structure of her institutions, for founding the liberty of her citizens on a rational basis, will take the lead. In that glorious and hazardous enterprise, in that hour of care, need, and peril, I hope she will be cheered and strengthened with aid from this side of the Atlantic; aid given not with the stinted hand, not with a cowardly and selfish apprehension, last we should not err on the safe side — wisely if you please. I care not with how broad a regard to the future, but in large, generous, effectual measure.

And you, our guest, fearless, eloquent, large of heart and of mind, whose one thought is the salvation of oppressed Hungary, unfortunate but undiscouraged, struck down in the battle of liberty, but great in defeat and gathering strength for future triumphs, receive this action at our hands, that in this great attempt of man to repossess himself of the rights which God gave him, though the strife be waged under a distant belt of longitude, and with the mightiest despotism of the world, the press of America takes part with you and your country. I give you — "Louis Kossuth."

忍受，同時，由於匈牙利國家體制的特殊結構，使她比別的民族更有基礎建立起公民的自由；因此，匈牙利可能首先發難。到了那一天，在那光榮而艱辛的事業中，在他們憂慮危難，需要幫助時，我希望匈牙利會從大西洋此岸得到支持，使她精神奮發，堅強有力；我們的支持不是吝嗇的，沒有怯懦和自私的顧慮。最後，我們不要錯在過份謹慎──如果你們願意，也可以叫作明智。我不考慮將來怎麼做，只是要大規模的、慷慨的、有效的措施。

您，我們的客人，您勇敢無畏，雄才善辯，心胸廣闊。您心中只有一件事，就是解放被壓迫的匈牙利。您際遇坷坎，但絕不氣餒。您在爭取獨立的戰場上被擊倒，但是雖敗猶榮，正積聚力量爭取未來的勝利。你們為重獲上帝賦予的權利而作的鬥爭，實在偉大。雖然這場鬥爭發生在遠隔萬里的地方，雖然敵人是世界上最強大的專制政府，請接受我們美國新聞界對於您和您的國家的支持。現在讓我向你們介紹：路易斯・柯蘇特。

34 An Ex-Slave Discusses Slavery

Frederick Douglass

. . .

Fellow citizens, above your national, tumultuous joy, I hear the mournful wail of millions! Whose chains, heavy and grievous yesterday, are, today, rendered more intolerable by the jubilee shouts that reach them. If I do forget, if I do not faithfully remember those bleeding children of sorrow this day, "may my right hand forget her cunning, and may my tongue cleave to the roof of my mouth"! To forget them, to pass lightly over their wrongs, and to chime in with the popular theme would be treason most scandalous and shocking, and would make me a reproach before God and the world. My subject, then, fellow citizens, is *American slavery*. I shall see this day and its popular characteristics from the slave's point of view. Standing there identified with the American bondman, making his wrongs mine. I do not hesitate to declare with all my soul that the character and conduct of this nation never looked blacker to me than on this Fourth of July! Whether we turn to the declarations of the past or to the professions of the present, the conduct of the nation seems equally hideous and revolting. America

三十四 一個前為奴隸的人論奴隸制

弗列德里克·道格拉斯

……

同胞們，在你們舉國歡騰的作樂聲中，我聽到千萬人的悲慟號哭。昨天，他們在沉重的鎖鏈下輾轉呻吟，今天你們雷動的歡聲使他們身上的枷鎖更覺沉重難耐。如果我今天忘記了親人的悲痛，不把它牢記心上，"情願我的右手忘記技巧，情願我的舌頭貼於上膛！"[1]忘記了他們，對他們的冤屈處之泰然，相反，去參加慶祝歌唱，這將是最醜惡最駭人聽聞的背叛事情，將受到上帝和世人的指責。因此，同胞們，今天我要講的題目是：美國的奴隸制，我要從一個奴隸的觀點來看今天這個日子和它那為眾人所知的獨特面貌。我要以此立場，把美國奴隸的蒙冤受屈當作我自己的冤屈。我要直言不諱地說出我心靈深處的感受：在我看來，這國家的品格與行為再也沒有像今天七月四日這樣黑暗的了！不管過去發過多少宣言，今天又有多少表白，這國家的行為還是顯得同樣醜

道格拉斯（1817～1895），美國著名的廢奴主義者，父親是白人，母親是黑奴。本篇為1852年7月4日他在紐約州羅徹斯特市國慶節大會上的演說。

（1）引自聖經舊約詩篇。

is false to the past, false to the present, and solemnly binds herself to be false to the future. Standing with God and the crushed and bleeding slave on this occasion, I will, in the name of humanity which is outraged, in the name of liberty which is fettered, in the name of the Constitution and the Bible which are disregarded and trampled upon, dare to call in question and to denounce, with all the emphasis I can command, everything that serves to perpetuate slavery — the great sin and shame of America! "I will not equivocate; I will not excuse"; I will use the severest language I can command; and yet not one word shall escape me that any man, whose judgment is not blinded by prejudice; or who is not at heart a slaveholder, shall not confess to be right and just.

. . . There are seventy-two crimes in the state of Virginia which, if committed by a black man (no matter how ignorant he be), subject him to the punishment of death; while only two of the same crimes will subject a white man to the like punishment. What is this but the acknowledgment that the slave is a moral, intellectual, and responsible being? The manhood of the slave is conceded. It is admitted in the fact that Southern statute books are covered with enactments forbidding, under severe fines and penalties, the teaching of the slave to read or to write. When you can point to any such laws in reference to the beasts of the field, then I may consent to argue the manhood of the slave. When the dogs in your streets, when the fowls of the air, when the cattle on your hills, when the fish of the sea and the reptiles that crawl shall be unable to distinguish the slave from a brute, then will I argue with you that the slave is a man!

. . .

惡，同樣令人憎恨。美國失信於過去，失信於
現在，也就必然失信於將來。在這個場合裏，
我和上帝站在一起，與被壓榨流血的奴隸站在
一起，我要以人性遭到踐躪的名義，以自由被
禁錮的名義，以憲法與聖經被無視踐踏的名義，
最強烈地質問和譴責使奴隸制度得以存在的一
切！奴隸制是美國最深重的罪惡和最大的恥
辱！"我決不閃爍其詞，我也絕不寬恕原宥"；
我要用最嚴厲的詞句，然而，只要不被偏見蒙
蔽，只要不是天生的奴隸主，就不會不承認我
說的每一句話，每一個字都是正確的，公道的。

　　……弗吉尼亞州的法例中有七十二種罪，
黑人犯了其中一條，即使他不是明知故犯，也
要判處死刑；但同樣的罪中却只有兩條才會令
白人受相同的懲罰。這意味着什麼？難道這不正
是承認了黑人是有道德、有知識、有責任的人
嗎？奴隸也是人這一點是受承認的。南方各州
的法律典籍中充斥着禁止教育黑人讀書寫字的
條文，違者罰以巨款或處以重刑，他們就是這
樣承認奴隸是人。如果你能指出有哪一條法律
條文規定不許教野獸讀書寫字，我就同意去論
證奴隸是不是人。如果連街邊的狗、天空的鳥、
山上的牛羣、海裏的魚類和爬行的蛇蝎都區別
不出奴隸和野獸，那時我再和你們辯論到底奴
隸是不是人吧！

　　……

What, am I to argue that it is wrong to make men brutes, to rob them of their liberty, to work them without wages, to keep them ignorant of their relations to their fellow men, to beat them with sticks, to flay their flesh with the lash, to load their limbs with irons, to hunt them with dogs, to sell them at auction, to sunder their families, to knock out their teeth, to burn their flesh, to starve them into obedience and submission to their masters? Must I argue that a system thus marked with blood, and stained with pollution, is wrong? No! I will not. I have better employment for my time and strength than such arguments would imply.

. . .

At a time like this, scorching iron, not convincing argument, is needed. O! had I the ability, and could I reach the nation's ear, I would today pour out a fiery stream of biting ridicule, blasting reproach, withering sarcasm, and stern rebuke. For it is not light that is needed, but fire; it is not the gentle shower, but thunder. We need the storm, the whirlwind, and the earthquake. The feeling of the nation must be quickened; the conscience of the nation must be roused; the propriety of the nation must be startled; the hypocrisy of the nation must be exposed; and its crimes against God and men must be proclaimed and denounced.

What, to the American slave, is your Fourth of July? I answer: a day that reveals to him, more than all other days in the year, the gross injustice and cruelty to which he is the constant victim. To him, your celebration is a sham; your boasted liberty, an unholy license; your

你們把人當作野獸，剝奪人的自由，強迫他們去做無酬的勞動，不讓他們知道同胞之間的親密關係，用棍棒敲打他們，用皮鞭把他們抽得皮開肉綻，用鐵鏈鎖住他們的手腳，放狗追趕他們，在集市上拍賣他們，拆散他們的家庭，敲落他們的牙齒，灼烙他們的身體，要他們忍受飢餓，迫使他們屈服聽命於主人。如此種種，難道你們竟還要我去論證這沾滿鮮血，極端腐朽的制度是錯的？不，我不做這種事！我還不如省點時間和精力來做些有用的事呢！

……

現在這種時候，需要的不是有說服力的論理，而是熾熱的烙鐵。啊，要是我有能力使全國的人都聽到我的聲音，我今天就會滔滔不絕地傾吐出尖刻的嘲笑、強烈的譴責、無情的譏刺和嚴厲的申斥。因為現在需要的不是光，而是火；不是和風細雨，而是雷電霹靂；我們需要暴雨，需要颶風，需要地震。我們必須觸動這個國家的感情，喚起她的良知，震撼她的禮義之心，揭露她的偽善，公開譴責她違反上帝和人類的罪行。

你們的七月四日對於美國奴隸來說是個什麼日子？我要回答說：這日子比一年之中其他日子更使他清楚看見他經年累月所受的不公正和殘酷待遇。你們的慶祝對於他們是一場欺騙；你們鼓吹的自由不過是瀆神的放縱；你們所謂

national greatness, swelling vanity; your sounds of rejoicing are empty and heartless; your denunciation of tyrants, brass-fronted impudence; your shouts of liberty and equality, hollow mockery; your prayers and hymns, your sermons and thanks-givings, with all your religious parade and solemnity, are, to Him, mere bombast, fraud, deception, impiety, and hypocrisy — a thin veil to cover up crimes which would disgrace a nation of savages. There is not a nation of savages. There is not a nation on the earth guilty of practices more shocking and bloody than are the people of the United States at this very hour.

Go where you may, search where you will, roam through all the monarchies and despotisms of the Old World, travel through South America, search out every abuse, and when you have found the last, lay your facts by the side of the everyday practices of this nation, and you will say with me that, for revolting barbarity and shameless hypocrisy, America reigns without a rival.

民族的偉大精神不過是自欺欺人的虛榮自負；
你們的歡呼是虛張聲勢；你們對專制的譴責是
厚顏無恥的胡扯；你們高喊的自由平等是空洞
虛假的冒牌貨；你們的禱詞和讚美詩；你們那
喋喋不休的佈道說教和滔滔不絕的感恩祈禱，
加上你們那些宗教遊行和隆重儀式，都只不過
是對上帝的吹牛、撒謊、蒙蔽、不敬和偽善，
只是為了把你們的罪惡遮掩起來的一層薄紗。
哪怕是野蠻人的國家也會因這樣的罪惡蒙受恥
辱。但是，現在沒有野蠻人的國家。此時此刻，
在地球上沒有哪一個民族比美國民族的所作所
為更駭人聽聞，更有血腥味了。

你們可以走遍海角天涯，找遍舊大陸[1] 所
有君主專制的集權國家，訪遍南美洲，到處去
挑出一切陋規惡習，然後把那些東西放在這個
民族每天所幹的事情旁邊比較一下，你們就會
像我這樣說：在極端野蠻和最無恥的偽善方面，
美國確實首屈一指，舉世無匹。

（1）指歐洲。

35 The Idea of a University (I)

John Henry, Cardinal Newman

. . .

I protest to you, gentlemen, that if I had to choose between a so-called university which dispensed with residence and tutorial superintendence, and gave its degrees to any person who passed an examination in a wide range of subjects, and a university which had no professors or examinations at all, but merely brought a number of young men together for three or four years, and then sent them away as the University of Oxford is said to have done some sixty years since, if I were asked which of these two methods was the better discipline of the intellect — I do not say which is *morally* the better, for it is plain that compulsory study must be a good and idleness an intolerable mischief — but if I must determine which of the two courses was the more successful in training, molding, enlarging the mind, which sent out men the more fitted for their secular duties, which produced better public men, men of the world, men whose names would descend to posterity, I have no hesitation in giving the preference to that university which did nothing, over that which exacted of its members an acquaintance with every science under the sun. . . .

. . . When a multitude of young persons, keen, open-hearted, sympathetic, and observant, as young persons

---

約翰・亨利（ 1801～1890 ），就學於牛津大學，
1846年成爲紅衣主教。

1854年都柏林成立天主教大學，約翰・亨利任校

三十五 關於大學的概念(一)

約翰‧亨利(紐曼紅衣主教)

……

各位先生,我向你們聲明,如果有兩種大學,一種是所謂的大學,它不提供住宿,不督察學習,對修滿許多課程考試及格的任何人都授予學位。還有一種大學則既無教授亦無考試,只是把一定人數的年輕人召集在一起過三、四年,之後把他們送出學校,像人們所說牛津大學近六十年來所做的那樣。如果要我在這兩種大學中選擇,問我這兩種方法中哪一種更有利於知識的訓練——我並不從道德的角度說哪一種更好,因為顯而易見地強制性的學習必定好而懶散則極有害——如果我必須斷定這兩條道路中哪一條在訓練、塑造、啟發人的頭腦方面更為成功,哪種方法培養出來的人更適合現實的任務,訓練出更好的公職人員,產生出通曉世情的人和名傳後世的人,我將毫不猶豫地選擇那無教授亦不考試的學校,它優於那種強求學生熟悉天底下每一門科學的學校。……

……當一大羣年輕人,具有青年所有的敏銳、心胸開闊、富於同情心、善於觀察等等特

長。為準備該校成立,約翰‧亨利發表了一系列演說,本文與下篇為其中兩篇。

are, come together and freely mix with each other, they are sure to learn one from another, even if there be no one to teach them; the conversation of all is a series of lectures to each, and they gain for themselves new ideas and views, fresh matter of thought, and distinct principles for judging and acting, day by day. An infant has to learn the meaning of the information which its senses convey to it, and this seems to be its employment. It fancies all that the eye presents to it to be close to it, till it actually learns the contrary, and thus by practice does it ascertain the relations and uses of those first elements of knowledge which are necessary for its animal existence. A parallel teaching is necessary for our social being, and it is secured by a large school or a college, and this effect may be fairly called in its own department an enlargement of mind. ... Here then is a real teaching, whatever be its standards and principles, true or false; and it at least tends towards cultivation of the intellect; it at least recognizes that knowledge is something more than a sort of passive reception of scraps and details; it is a something, and it does a something, which never will issue from the most strenuous efforts of a set of teachers, with no mutual sympathies and no intercommunion, of a set of examiners with no opinions which they dare profess, and with no common principles, who are teaching or questioning a set of youths who do not know them, and do not know each other, on a large number of subjects, different in kind, and connected by no wide philosophy, three times a week, or three times a year, or once in three years, in chill lecture-rooms or on a

點，來到一起，自由密切交往時，即使沒有人教育他們，他們也必定能互相學習；所有人的談話，對每個人來說就是一系列的講課，他們自己逐日學得新的概念和觀點，簇新的思想以及判斷事物與決定行動的各種不同原則。嬰兒需要學會理解由他的感覺傳遞給他的信息，這就是他本分要做的事。他以為眼睛看見的一切事物都近在身旁，後來才了解到情況不盡如此。這樣，他就從實踐中得知他最早學到的那些基本知識的關係和用處，這是他生存必需的知識。我們在社會上的生存也需要有類似的教育，這種教育由一所大的學校或學院提供。它的作用在本身領域中可以公平地稱之為開擴心胸。……姑勿論它的標準與原則為何，是真是偽，這是一種真正的教育。至少它有培養才智的意圖，承認學習知識並不僅僅是被動地接受那些零星、繁瑣的細節。這是有意義的教育，也能做出某種有意義的事來。一批最賣力氣的教師在沒有相互的同情與了解，沒有思想的交流情況下，絕不可能作出這樣的成績。一批沒有意見敢於發表、沒有共同原則，只是教導提問的主考官也同樣達不到上述目的。那些被教被問的青年不認識主考官，他們彼此也不相識，他們的主考官只在冷冰冰的教室裏或在盛大的週年紀念日上向他們教授或詢問一大堆種類不同、相互間並無哲理聯繫的題目，每星期三次或一年三

pompous anniversary.

. . .

. . . How much more profitable for the independent mind, after the mere rudiments of education, to range through a library at random, taking down books as they meet him, and pursuing the trains of thought which his mother wit suggests! How much healthier to wander into the fields, and there with the exiled prince to find "tongues in the trees, books in the running brooks!" . . .

次或三年一次。

……

……受到初步的基礎教育之後，對於願意
獨立思考的人來說，在圖書館裏隨意涉獵，順
手取下一本書來，興之所至，深入鑽研，這該
有多大的好處啊！在田野中徜徉，和被放逐的
王子[1]一同欣賞"樹木的說話和溪中流水的大
好文章！"[2]這該是多麼健康有益啊！……

（1）指莎士比亞《皆大歡喜》中遭篡位放逐的公爵。
（2）引自《皆大歡喜》第二幕第一場第十六及十七行。

36 The Idea of a University (II)

John Henry, Cardinal Newman

. . .

Now from these instances, to which many more might be added, it is plain, first, that the communication of knowledge certainly is either a condition or the means of that sense of enlargement or enlightenment, of which at this day we hear so much in certain quarters: this cannot be denied; but next, it is equally plain, that such communication is not the whole of the process. The enlargement consists, not merely in the passive reception into the mind of a number of ideas hitherto unknown to it, but in the mind's energetic and simultaneous action upon and towards and among those new ideas, which are rushing in upon it. It is the action of a formative power, reducing to order and meaning the matter of our acquirements; it is a making the objects of our knowledge subjectively our own, or, to use a familiar word, it is a digestion of what we receive, into the substance of our previous state of thought; and without this no enlargement is said to follow. There is no enlargement, unless there be a comparison of ideas one with another, as they come before the mind, and a systematizing of them. We feel our minds to be growing and expanding *then*, when we not only learn, but refer what we learn to what we know already. It is not a mere addition to our knowledge which is the illumination; but the locomotion, the movement onwards, of that mental center, to which both what we know and what we are learning, the accumulating mass of our

三十六　關於大學的概念（二）

約翰・亨利（紐曼紅衣主教）

……

　　首先，最明顯不過的是，這些例子，還可以有更多的例子足以說明知識的交流，必然是擴增知識、啟發思想的條件，或從那個意義上說是造成這種條件的手段。關於擴增知識與啟發思想近年來在某些地方談論很多，這是不容否認的事實。但另一方面，同樣明顯的是，知識的交流並不是擴增知識、啟發思想的全部過程。擴增知識所包含的意思，不僅是被動地將一堆原來不知道的觀念接納到腦子裏，而是對湧來的新觀念即時所作積極有力的腦部活動。這是一種具有創造性的行動，將我們取得的知識素材轉化爲有條理和有意義；這是使我們的知識客體成爲我們自己的主體事物，通俗地說，就是將我們接收的事物加以消化，使之與我們原先的思想融爲一體；沒有這些，就不會隨之而生所謂知識擴增。各種觀念來到腦裏時，如果不把一種觀念與另一種觀念比較並爲之建立系統，就沒有知識擴增可言，我們不僅學習，而且將所學的與已知的進行對照，只有這樣，我們才會感到心智在生長、在擴展。所謂啟蒙，不僅是增加一點知識，而是將我們已經學到的和正在學習的大量知識吸收積聚起來，在我們

acquirements, gravitates. And therefore a truly great intellect, and recognized to be such by the common opinion of mankind, such as the intellect of Aristotle, or of St. Thomas, or of Newton, or of Goethe (I purposely take instances within and without the Catholic pale, when I would speak of the intellect as such), is one which takes a connected view of old and new, past and present, far and near, and which has an insight into the influence of all these one on another; without which there is no whole, and no center. It possesses the knowledge, not only of things, but also of their mutual and true relations; knowledge, not merely considered as acquirement, but as philosophy.

Accordingly, when this analytical, distributive, harmonizing process is away, the mind experiences no enlargement, and is not reckoned as enlightened or comprehensive, whatever it may add to its knowledge. For instance, a great memory, as I have already said, does not make a philosopher, any more than a dictionary can be called a grammar. There are men who embrace in their minds a vast multitude of ideas, but with little sensibility about their real relations towards each other. These may be antiquarians, annalists, naturalists; they may be learned in the law; they may be versed in statistics; they are most useful in their

的思考中心不斷運轉前進。因此，真正偉大並為人類普遍承認的才智之士，像亞里斯多德[1]、聖託馬斯[2]、牛頓或歌德（我說到這類才智時，有意同時舉出天主教教會內外的例子），能夠將新與舊、過去與現在、遠與近聯繫起來看，因而能洞察這些事物之間的互相影響。沒有這種觀點，就看不到整體，看不到本質和中心。用這種觀點掌握的知識就不僅看到一件件事，而且可以看到它們之間的本質聯繫。因此這樣的知識便不僅是學得某樣事物而且是一種哲理。

由此類推，如果摒棄了這種分析、分類、彼此協調的過程，即使再加上多少知識，人的心智也談不上擴展，也不能算是得到了啟發或具有了綜合的理解能力。舉例來說，我曾指出記憶力極好的人並不就是一個哲學家，正如一本字典不能稱為語法書一樣。有些人腦裏有包羅萬象的各種思想概念，但對這些思想概念之間的實際關係却一無所知。這些人可能是古玩收藏家，纂寫編年史的人，或是動物標本剝製者；他們可能通曉法律，精通統計學，在各自

（1）亞里斯多德（公元前384～322），古希臘哲學家、
科學家。

（2）即托馬斯·阿奎那 （ Thomas Aquinas, 1227-
1274 ），中世紀神學家及政治思想家。

own place; I should shrink from speaking disrespectfully of them; still, there is nothing in such attainments to guarantee the absence of narrowness of mind. If they are nothing more than well-read men, or men of information, they have not what specially deserves the name of culture of mind, or fulfills the type of liberal education.

In like manner we sometimes fall in with persons who have seen much of the world, and of the men who, in their day, have played a conspicuous part in it, but who generalize nothing, and have no observation, in the true sense of the world. They abound in information in detail, curious and entertaining, about men and things; and, having lived under the influence of no very clear or settled principles, religious or political, they speak of every one and everything, only as so many phenomena, which are complete in themselves, and lead to nothing, not discussing them, or teaching any truth, or instructing the hearer, but simply talking. No one would say that these persons, well informed as they are, had attained to any great culture of intellect or to philosophy.

的職位上都很有用。提到他們時，我不敢表示不敬。可是，即使有這些成就也不能保證思想不流於狹隘。如果他們只是一些博覽羣書的人，或是見聞甚廣的人，那麼他們還配不上" 造詣高深 " 的美稱，也不能算是受到了開明的教育。

同樣，我們有時會碰到一些見過大世面的人或是曾在他們的時代有顯赫成就的人，但是這些人不會概括歸納，也不懂得如何觀察。他們掌握大量有關人和事詳盡的、新奇的、引人入勝的資料。同時，由於受到不十分清楚確定的宗教、政治原則影響，他們說及一切的人和事，完全是一些就事論事的現象，引不出結論。他們對這些事物沒有分析、討論，說不出什麼道理，對聽者並無教益，只是單純地說話而已，儘管這些人見聞很廣，但沒有人會說他們具有淵博的學識或精通哲理。

37 Reply to the U.S. Government

Chief Seattle

Yonder sky that has wept tears of compassion upon my people for centuries untold, and which to us appears changeless and eternal, may change. Today is fair. Tomorrow may be overcast with clouds. My words are like the stars that never change. Whatever Seattle says the great chief at Washington can rely upon with as much certainty as he can upon the return of the sun or the seasons. The White Chief says that Big Chief at Washington sends us greetings of friendship and good-will. That is kind of him for we know he has little need of our friendship in return. His people are many. They are like the grass that covers vast prairies. My people are few. They resemble the scattering trees of a storm-swept plain. The great, and — I presume — good, White Chief sends us word that he wishes to buy our lands but is willing to allow us enough to live comfortably. This indeed appears just, even generous, for the Red Man no longer has rights that he need respect, and the offer may be wise also, as we are no longer in need of an extensive country. . . . I will not dwell on, nor mourn

---

西雅圖（1786～1866）是德沃米希（Dwamish）和蘇國米希（Suquamish）等部落的酋長。美國政府要將當地土人驅逐到"保留地"定居。本文是西雅圖在美國政府壓力下的答覆。

三十七 給美國政府的答覆

西雅圖酋長

數不盡的世代以來，渺渺蒼天曾爲我族灑下多少同情之淚；這在我們看來像是永恒不變的蒼天還是會變的。今天天色晴朗，明天又密佈陰雲。我的說話却像天空的星辰，永遠不變。西雅圖說的話，正如日出東方，季節更迭，華盛頓的大酋長[1]可以確信無疑。白人酋長[2]說，華盛頓的大酋長向我們友好致意。我們感謝他的好意，因爲我們知道他無所求於我們，不用我們以友情回報。他的人民衆多，猶如覆蓋着廣闊原野的靑草。我的人民稀少，像風摧雨襲過後平原上稀疏的樹木。那偉大的——我還假定他是善良的——白人酋長[3]派遣人告訴我們，願意買下我們的土地，但同時也願意留下適量的土地讓我們舒適生活。這看來確實很公道，甚至很慷慨，因爲紅種人已經再也沒有什麼他要尊重的權利了，他出的買價可能也是周到合宜的，因爲我們現在已經不再需要遼闊的地域。……我不再詳述我們民族過早的衰微，也不再

（1）指當時的美國總統皮爾斯（Franklin Pierce，1804～1869）。
（2）指史蒂芬斯州長。
（3）指美國總統。

over, our untimely decay, nor reproach our paleface brothers with hastening it, as we too may have been somewhat to blame.
. . .

Day and night cannot dwell together. The Red man has ever fled the approach of the White Man, as the morning mist flees before the morning sun. However, your proposition seems fair and I think that my people will accept it and will retire to the reservation you offer them. Then we will dwell apart in peace, for the words of the Great White Chief seem to be the words of nature speaking to my people out of dense darkness.

It matters little where we pass the remnant of our days. They will not be many. A few more moons; a few more winters — and not one of the descendants of the mighty hosts that once moved over this broad land or lived in happy homes, protected by the Great Spirit, will remain to mourn over the graves of a people once more powerful and hopeful than yours. But why should I mourn at the untimely fate of my people? Tribe follows tribe, and nation follows nation, like the waves of the sea. It is the order of nature, and regret is useless. Your time of decay may be distant, but it will surely come, for even the White Man whose God walked and talked with him as friend with friend, cannot be exempt from the common destiny. We may be brothers after all. We will see.

We will ponder your proposition, and when we decide we will let you know. But should we accept it,

為此哀歎，不責備白種兄弟加速了我們的衰敗，因為我們或許多少也要責怪一下自己。

……

白晝與黑夜不能同時在一起。紅種人對白種人從來就是敬而遠之的，就像朝霧在旭日升起前就要消散一樣。然而，你們的建議看來是公道的，我想我的人民會接受建議，退居到你給他們的保留地。這樣我們就能分處兩地、和平共存，因為白人大酋長對我人民所說的話，有如大自然從沉沉黑暗中發出來的聲音。

我們在什麼地方度過我們的餘年已經無關重要。我們的來日不多了。再過幾月，再過幾冬，這個民族再也沒有一個後裔留下來在墓前致哀。這原來是一個比你們更強大、更有希望的民族，曾經人數眾多，受大神的庇護，在這廣闊的土地上幸福地安居樂業。但我又何必為我的民族夭折的命運哀嘆呢？一個部落沒落，另一個部落就會振興，一個民族衰亡，另一個民族便會崛起，像海水一樣，後浪逐前浪。這是自然的法則，悲嘆惋惜是無用的。你們衰落的時間可能還很遙遠，卻必定到來，因為即使是能夠同上帝像朋友一樣親密無間的白人，也不能免於同樣的命運。我們終究會成為兄弟的，等着瞧吧。

我們會考慮你們的建議，等到我們作出決定就會通知你們。但是如果我們接受這建議，

I here and now make this condition that we will not be denied the privilege without molestation of visiting at any time the tombs of our ancestors, friends and children. Every part of this soil is sacred in the estimation of my people. Every hillside, every valley, every plain and grove, has been hallowed by some sad or happy event in days long vanished. . . . The very dust upon which you now stand responds more lovingly to their footsteps than to yours, because it is rich with the blood of our ancestors and our bare feet are conscious of the sympathetic touch. . . . Even the little children who lived here and rejoiced here for a brief season will love these somber solitudes and at eventide they greet shadowy returning spirits. And when the last Red Man shall have perished, and the memory of my tribe shall have become a myth among the White Men, these shores will swarm with the invisible dead of my tribe, and when your children's children think themselves alone in the field, the store, the shop, upon the highway, or in the silence of the pathless woods, they will not be alone. . . . At night when the streets of your cities and villages are silent and you think them deserted, they will throng with the returning hosts that once filled and still love this beautiful land. The White Man will never be alone.

Let him be just and deal kindly with my people, for the dead are not powerless. Dead, did I say? There is no death, only a change of worlds.

我現在在這裏就要提出一個保留條件：我們隨時有權不受干擾地掃謁我們祖先、朋友和兒女的墳墓。這裏每一寸土地對於我的人民都是神聖的。每一片山坡、每一個河谷、每一塊平原、每一叢小樹都由於往日的哀愁與歡樂而變得無比聖潔。……地上的塵土在他們脚下比在你們脚下更柔軟舒適，因為那上面浸滿了我們祖先的鮮血，我們赤裸的脚板能夠觸之生情。……甚至只是短期在這裏居住、嬉戲過的幼童也會熱愛這陰沉沉的荒地。在暮色降臨之時，他們會迎接那些幽暗朦朧的陰魂歸來。當最後一個紅種人死去，白人對這個部落的回憶已經成為神話之時，我部落的那些看不見的亡靈仍將密密地聚集在這片土地上。當你們的子孫以為他們獨自在田野、倉庫、商店、公路或寂靜的無路可通的森林中時，他們也不是孑然一身。……夜深人靜，你以為城鎮村落闃無一人時，街上將是滿坑滿谷歸來的故主。他們過去曾住在這裏，他們仍然熱愛這塊美麗的土地。白人永遠不會單獨在這裏。

願他公平、正直、善意地對待我的人民，因為死者並沒有失去力量。不，我說的死者並沒有死，只不過到了另一個世界罷了。

38   On Being Sentenced to Be Hanged

John Brown

I have, may it please the court, a few words to say. In the first place, I deny everything but what I have all along admitted — the design on my part to free the slaves. I intended certainly to have made a clean thing of that matter, as I did last winter when I went into Missouri and there took slaves without the snapping of a gun on either side, moved them through the country, and finally left them in Canada. I designed to have done the same thing again on a larger scale. That was all I intended. I never did intend murder, or treason, or the destruction of property, or to excite or incite slaves to rebellion, or to make insurrection.

I have another objection; and that is, it is unjust that I should suffer such a penalty. Had I interfered in the manner which I admit, and which I admit has been fairly proved (for I admire the truthfulness and candor of the greater portion of the witnesses who have testified in this case) — had I so interfered in behalf of the rich, the powerful, the intelligent, the so-called great, or in behalf of any of their friends — either father, mother, brother, sister, wife, or children, or any of that class — and suffered, and sacrificed what I have in this interference, it would have been all right; and every man in this court would have deemed it an act worthy of reward rather than punishment.

三十八　被判絞刑時發表的說話

約翰・布朗

在這法庭上我只想說幾句話，首先，除去我一直承認確實有計劃要解放黑奴之外，我否認一切其他指控。我確實有意完全消滅奴隸制，去冬我就到過密蘇里接運黑奴，雙方未發一槍就將黑奴運出，送至加拿大。我曾打算擴大這行動的規模。這就是我想做的一切。我從未圖謀殺人、叛國、毀壞私有財產或鼓勵、煽動奴隸謀反作亂。

我還要提出一項異議，那便是：我受到這樣的刑罰是不公平的。我在法庭上所承認的事實已經得到相當充分的證明，我對於證人提供的大部分事實的真確和公允是很欽佩的。但是，假如我的所為，是代表那些有錢有勢、有如識的人或所謂大人物的利益，或是代表他們的朋友、父母、兄弟、姊妹、妻子、兒女或他們所屬的階級其他任何人的利益，並因此而受到我在這件事上所受到的痛苦和犧牲[1]，那就會萬事大吉。這法庭上的每個人都會認為我的行為

布朗（1800～1859），美國廢奴主義的著名領袖。1855年及1859年兩度率領農民及移民革命，1859年11月2日被弗吉尼亞州法院控以叛國，判處絞刑。

（1）布朗在1855年的一次鬥爭中犧牲了三個兒子。

This court acknowledges, as I suppose, the validity of the law of God, I see a book kissed, which I suppose to be the Bible, or at least the New Testament. That teaches me that all things whatsoever I would that men should do to me I should do even so to them. It teaches me, further, to "remember them that are in bonds as bound with them." I endeavored to act up to that instruction. I say I am yet too young to understand that God is any respecter of persons, I believe that to have interfered as I have done — as I have always freely admitted I have done — in behalf of His despised poor was not wrong, but right. Now, if it is deemed necessary that I should forfeit my life for the furtherance of the ends of justice, and mingle my blood further with the blood of my children and with the blood of millions in this slave country whose rights are disregarded by wicked, cruel, and unjust enactments — I submit: so let it be done!

. . .

不但不應受罰，反而值得獎賞了。

我想，這法庭也承認上帝的法律，我看到開庭時你們親吻一本書，那大概是《聖經》吧，至少也是《新約全書》。這本書教導我要以己所欲，施之於人。還教導我"要像自己也被囚禁那樣，不忘身陷囹圄的人們"。我曾努力實踐這訓條。我要說我還太年輕，不懂得上帝竟會不公平待人。我相信，我一直坦率承認曾為上帝窮苦子民所做的事，並沒有做錯，相反，完全正確。如果為了伸張正義，我必須獻出生命，必須在這個被邪惡、殘暴與不義的法制剝奪了一切權利的蓄奴國家裏，把我的鮮血和我的幾個孩子以及千千萬萬人的鮮血流在一起，就請便吧！

……

39 Speech of Farewell

Abraham Lincoln

My friends: No one not in my situation can appreciate my feeling of sadness at this parting. To this place, and the kindness of these people, I owe everything. Here I have lived a quarter of century, and have passed from a young to an old man. Here my children have been born, and one is buried. I now leave, not knowing when or whether ever I may return, with a task before me greater than that which rested upon Washington. Without the assistance of that Divine Being who ever attended him, I cannot succeed. With that assitance, I cannot fail. Trusting in Him who can go with me, and remain with you, and be everywhere for good, let us confidently hope that all will yet be well. To His care commending you, as I hope in your prayers you will commend me, I bid you an affectionate farewell.

三十九　告別演說

阿伯拉罕·林肯

朋友們：不是處在我這地位上的人，很難體味到我此刻的惜別之情。這地方和這裏的人民的友情給了我一切。我在這裏渡過了四分之一世紀；從青春歲月到了暮年。我的孩子在這裏出生，其中一個埋葬在這裏。我現在要離開你們，不知何年何月再回來，甚至不知是否能再回來。我面臨的任務比當年華盛頓肩負的還要重大。上帝曾一直庇護着華盛頓。沒有上帝的扶持，我不會成功。有了他的扶持，我就不會失敗。我們都信賴能與我同行，也與你們同在並無所不在的上帝，讓我們滿懷信心地希望，一切都將好起來。願上帝賜福於你們，願你們祈求上帝賜福於我。我向你們依依道別。

林肯(1809～1865)，美國第十六屆總統，1865年贏得內戰勝利，廢除了黑奴制。內戰結束後被暴徒刺死。1861年2月11日林肯當選總統赴華盛頓就職前，在伊利諾斯州發表本篇演說。

40 His First Inaugural Address

Abraham Lincoln

This country, with its institutions, belongs to the people who inhabit it. Whenever they shall grow weary of the existing government, they can exercise their *constitutional* right of amending it, or their *revolutionary* right to overthrow it. I cannot be ignorant of the fact that many worthy and patriotic citizens are desirous of having the national Constitution amended. While I make no recommendation of amendments, I fully recognize the rightful authority of the people over the whole subject to be exercised in either of the modes prescribed in the instrument itself; and I should under existing circumstances favor rather than oppose a fair opportunity being afforded the people to act upon it. . . .

The chief magistrate derives all his authority from the people, and they have conferred none upon him to fix terms for the separation of the states. The people themselves can do this also if they choose; but the executive, as such, has nothing to do with it. His duty is to administer the present government, as it came to his hands, and to transmit it, unimpaired by him, to his successor.

Why should there not be a patient confidence in the ultimate justice of the people? Is there any better or equal hope in the world? In our present differences, is either party without faith of being in the right? If the Almighty Ruler of nations, with His eternal truth and justice, be on your side of the North, or on yours of

四十　第一次就職演說

阿伯拉罕・林肯

我們的國家，連同她的行政機構，都屬於定居其上的人民。任何時候他們只要對現政府感到厭倦，便可以行使憲法賦與的權利改造政府，或使用革命的權利推翻政府。我知道許多德高望重的愛國公民希望修改國家憲法。我雖然沒有提出修改憲法的具體建議，但是我完全承認，在這整個問題上，人民有權按憲法規定以上述兩種方式去行使他們的權利；在當前的情況下，我並不是反對而是贊成給予人民公平的機會去行使這種權力。……

最高行政長官[1]的一切權力來自人民，人民並未賦予任何權力訂立分裂各州的條件。如果人民願意，他們也可以賦予這樣的權力。但最高行政長官本人無權過問此事。他的職責只是接任管理現政府，在卸任時把政府機構完好地移交繼任人。

人民是最公正的，我們為什麼不對這點抱有最堅定的信心呢？在世界上，我們還能對別的什麼寄予同樣的或更大的希望嗎？在目前南北分歧中，難道哪一方會不堅信公理在自己方面？倘若掌握永恒真理與正義的萬能之主站在你北

（1）指總統。

the South, that truth, and that justice, will surely prevail, by the judgment of this great tribunal, the American people.

By the frame of the government under which we live, this same people have wisely given their public servants but little power for mischief; and have, with equal wisdom, provided for the return of that little to their own hands at very short intervals.

While the people retain their virtue and vigilance, no administration, by any extreme of wickedness or folly, can very seriously injure the government in the short space of four years.

My countrymen, one and all, think calmly and *well* upon this whole subject. Nothing valuable can be lost by taking time. If there be an object to *hurry* any of you, in hot haste, to a step which you would never take *deliberately,* that object will be frustrated by taking time; but no good object can be frustrated by it. Such of you as are now dissatisfied still have the old Constitution unimpaired, and, on the sensitive point, the laws of your own framing under it; while the new administration will have no immediate power, if it would, to change either. If it were admitted that you who are dissatisfied hold the right side in the dispute, there still is no single good reason for precipitate action.

方一面，或站在你南方一面，那麼美國人民這偉大的法官必會作出裁決，將眞理與正義判與該方。

同樣還是這些人民，他們明智地規定了我國的政體，使人民公僕的權力十分有限，不能爲非作歹；他們還同樣明智地規定了每隔一段很短的時間，便可將這極有限的權力收回自己手中[1]。

只要人民保持道德情操和警惕戒備，任何行政管理人員，縱使極端腐敗或愚蠢，亦不能在短期的四年對這政體造成嚴重損害。

全體同胞們，請你們冷靜認眞地把整個問題考慮一下。眞正有價值的東西是不會因花費一點時間而失去的。如果有一個目標，促使你們在頭腦發熱時匆忙地採取了某些行動。這些行動如經深思熟慮是絕不會採取的，那麼時間稍延就不會使這目標得到實現；但是，眞正有價值的目標是不會因時間拖延而得不到實現的。你們當中那些不滿現狀的人絲毫未能改變舊憲法，更主要的是未能改變由你們自己根據舊憲法制定的各項法律。新上任的政府即使願意，也無直接權力去修改憲法或法律。就算我們承認在爭論中，不滿現狀的人是正確的，我們仍然沒有理由急促行事。上帝從未棄我們這

（1）美國憲法規定每四年舉行一次總統選舉。

Intelligence, patriotism, Christianity, and a firm reliance on Him who has never yet forsaken this favored land are still competent to adjust, in the best way, all our present difficulty.

In *your* hands, my dissatisfied fellow countrymen, and not in *mine,* is the momentous issue of civil war. The government will not assail *you.* You can have no conflict, without being yourselves the aggressors. *You* have no oath registered in heaven to destroy the government; while I shall have the most solemn one to "preserve, protect, and defend" it.

I am loath to close. We are not enemies, but friends. We must not be enemies. Though passion may have strained, it must not break our bonds of affection. The mystic chords of memory, stretching from every battlefield, and patriot grave, to every living heart and hearthstone, all over this broad land, will yet swell the chorus of the Union, when again touched, as surely they will be, by the better angels of our nature.

得天獨厚的國家於不顧，聰明的才智、愛國的熱忱、基督徒的虔誠以及對上帝堅定的信賴，所有這一切，仍然是解決我們當前困難的最有效方法。

不滿現狀的同胞們，內戰的命運掌握在你們手中，而不是我的手中。政府不會攻擊你們。如果你們不主動進攻，就不會引起衝突。你們沒有對天盟誓要摧毀這政府，但是我却要最莊嚴地宣誓"維繫、保護和捍衛"政府。

我不願結束我的講話。我們是朋友，不是敵人。我們一定不要彼此為敵。雖然我們會一時衝動，但千萬不要反目成仇。那神秘的懷念心弦將聯結起每一個戰場，每一個愛國志士的墳墓，我們遼闊國土上每一顆跳動的心和每一個溫暖的家庭。我們善良的天性將再次撥動這根心弦，使聯邦團結的大合唱響徹雲霄。

41 Emancipation Proclamation

Abraham Lincoln

Whereas, on the twenty-second day of September, in the year of our Lord one thousand eight hundred and sixty-two, a proclamation was issued by the President of the United States, containing, among other things, the following, to wit:

That on the first day of January, in the year of our Lord one thousand eight hundred and sixty-three, all persons held as slaves within any State, or designated part of a State, the people whereof shall then be in rebellion against the United States, shall be then, thenceforward, and forever free; and the Executive Government of the United States, including the military and naval authority thereof, will recognize and maintain the freedom of such persons, and will do no act or acts to repress such persons, or any of them, in any efforts they may make for their actual freedom.

That the Executive will, on the first day of January aforesaid, by proclamation, designate the States and parts of States, if any, in which the people thereof respectively shall then be in rebellion against the United States; and the fact that any State, or the people thereof, shall on that day be in good faith represented in the Congress of the United States by members chosen thereto at elections wherein a majority of the qualified voters of such State shall have participated, shall in the absence of strong countervailing testimony be deemed conclusive evidence that such State and the people thereof are not then in rebellion against the United States.

Now, therefore, I, Abraham Lincoln, President of

四十一　解放宣言

阿伯拉罕·林肯

有鑒於公元一千八百六十二年九月二十二日，聯邦總統已公佈了一項宣言，包含如下內容，即：

自公元一千八百六十三年元月一日起，任何一州或州內指定地區要是仍蓄有奴隸，當地人民將被視為反叛合眾國政府。一切被蓄為奴的人應獲得自由，並永享自由。合眾國政府，包括陸海軍當局，承認並維護上述人員之自由。對於此種人或其中任何一人為爭取實際自由而作的努力，不採取任何壓制行動。

從上述的元月一日起，總統將認定並宣佈那些為反叛合眾國政府的州或州內地區。其他各州及當地人民如於該日確有由該州多數合格選民選出的代表真誠地參加合眾國國會，倘無其他有力之反證，該州及其人民將被確認為不反叛合眾國政府。

因此，我，合眾國總統阿拉伯罕·林肯，

1861年美國內戰爆發後，林肯於1862年9月22日，在國會發表了"解放宣言"的第二稿。1863年1月1日，正式向全世界公佈。本文是1863年1月1日的定稿。

the United States, by virtue of the power in me vested as Commander-in-Chief of the Army and Navy of the United States, in time of actual armed rebellion against the authority and government of the United States, and as a fit and necessary war measure for suppressing said rebellion, do, on this first day of January, in the year of our Lord one thousand eight hundred and sixty-three, and in accordance with my purpose so to do, publicly proclaimed for the full period of 100 days from the day first above mentioned, order and designate as the States and parts of States wherein the people thereof, respectively, are this day in rebellion against the United States, the following, to wit:

Arkansas, Texas, Louisiana (except the parishes of St. Bernard, Plaquemines, Jefferson, St. John, St. Charles, St. James, Ascension, Assumption, Terre Bonne, Lafourche, St. Mary, St. Martin, and Orleans, including the city of New Orleans), Mississippi, Alabama, Floride, Georgia, South Carolina, North Carolina, and Virginia (except the forty-eight counties designated as West Virginia, and also the counties of Berkeley, Accomac, Northampton, Elizabeth City, York, Princess Anne, and Norfolk, including the cities of Norfolk and Portsmouth), and which excepted parts are for the present left precisely as if this proclamation were not issued.

And by virtue of the power and for the purpose aforesaid, I do order and declare that all persons held as slaves within said designated States and parts of States are, and henceforward shall be, free; and that the Executive Government of the United States, including the military and naval authorities thereof, shall recognize and maintain the freedom of said persons.

際此合衆國政府及其權威受到武裝叛亂反對時期，依據合衆國陸海軍總司令的職權，為剿滅上述叛亂而採取適當與必須的軍事手段，在此公元一千八百六十三年元月一日，於上次為此目的而發表之宣言滿一百日之際[1]，正式宣佈並認定下列各州、州內地區及其人民反叛合衆國政府，即：

阿肯色州、德克薩斯州、路易斯安娜州（以下除外：聖伯納、帕拉奎明斯、傑弗遜、聖約翰、聖查理士、聖詹姆士、阿克森、阿森姆遜、特里本、拉孚切、聖瑪麗、聖馬丁和奧爾艮各教區、新奧爾艮市）、密西西比州、亞拉巴馬州、佛羅里達州、佐治亞州、南卡羅來納州、北卡羅來納州及弗吉尼亞州（除指定為西弗吉尼亞的四十八個縣以及柏克萊、阿康瑪克、諾斯漢姆頓、伊麗莎白市、約克、安公主與諾福克，包括諾福克市及撲茨茅斯市）。明確規定，對上述除外的各地區目前保持本宣言公佈前之原狀。

根據上述目的及我享有之權力，我正式命令並宣佈，在上述指明的各州及州內地區，所有被蓄為奴隸的人，從現在起，獲得自由，並永享自由。合衆國政府，包括其陸海軍當局，承認及維護上述人員之自由。

（1）從1862年9月22日到1863年1月1日是一百天。

And I hereby enjoin upon the people so declared to be free to abstain from all violence, unless in necessary self-defense; and I recommend to them that, in all cases where allowed, they labor faithfully for reasonable wages.

And I further declare and make known that such persons of suitable condition will be received into the armed service of the United States to garrison forts, positions, stations, and other places, and to man vessels of all sorts in said service.

And upon this act, sincerely believed to be an act of justice, warranted by the Constitution upon military necessity, I invoke the considerate judgment of mankind and the gracious favor of Almighty God.

我在此責成上述宣告獲得自由之人員，除必須之自衛，應避免使用任何暴力；同時勸告他們，只要可能，在任何情況下都應忠實工作，取得合理的薪金。

　　我還要宣佈周知，上述人員如條件符合，可爲合衆國徵集入伍以警衛堡壘要塞、據點兵站及其他地方；亦可在各種軍艦上服務。

　　我眞誠地認爲，這是一個正義的行動，此行動由於軍事之必須，爲憲法所認可。我要求人類判斷此行動時予以諒解，請求全能上帝慈悲賜福。

42　The Gettysburg Address

Abraham Lincoln

Fourscore and seven years ago our fathers brought forth upon this continent a new nation, conceived in liberty, and dedicated to the proposition that all men are created equal.

Now we are engaged in a great civil war, testing whether that nation, or any nation so conceived and so dedicated, can long endure. We are met on a great battlefield of that war. We have come to dedicate a portion of that field as a final resting-place for those who here gave their lives that that nation might live. It is altogether fitting and proper that we should do this.

But in a large sense we cannot dedicate, we cannot consecrate, we cannot hallow this ground. The brave men, living and dead, who struggled here, have consecrated it far above our poor power to add or detract. The world will little note nor long remember what we say here; but it can never forget what they did here.

四十二　葛底斯堡演説詞

阿伯拉罕・林肯

八十七年前，我們的先輩在這個大陸上建立起了一個嶄新的國家。這個國家以自由為理想，以致力於實現人人享有天賦的平等權利為目標。

目前我們正在進行一場偉大的國內戰爭。我們的國家或任何一個有着同樣理想與目標的國家能否長久存在，這次戰爭就是一場考驗。現在我們在這場戰爭的一個偉大戰場上聚會在一起。我們來到這裏，將這戰場上的一小塊土地奉獻給那些為國家生存而英勇捐軀的人們，作為他們最後安息之地。我們這樣做是完全適當的，應該的。

然而，在深一層的意義上說來，我們沒有能力奉獻這塊土地，沒有能力使這塊土地變得更為神聖。因為在這裏進行過鬥爭的，活着和已經死去的勇士們，已經使這塊土地變得這樣聖潔，我們的微力已不足以對它有所揚抑了。我們今天在這裏說的話，世人不會注意，也不會

葛底斯堡在美國賓夕法尼亞州。1863年7月1日至3日，北軍在此重創了南軍，扭轉了戰爭局勢。此戰役後這裏修了一個戰爭犧牲者的公墓。本篇是1863年11月19日公墓落成典禮上的演說詞。

It is for us, the living, rather, to be dedicated here to the unfinished work which they who fought here have thus far so nobly advanced. It is rather for us to be here dedicated to the great task remaining before us: that from these honored dead we take increased devotion to that cause for which they gave the last full measure of devotion; that we here highly revolve that these dead shall not have died in vain; that this nation, under God, shall have a new birth of freedom; and that government of the people, by the people, and for the people, shall not perish from the earth.

記住，但是這些英雄們的業績，人們將永誌不忘。我們後來者應該做的是獻身於英雄們曾在這裏爲之奮鬥、努力推進、但尚未竟的工作。我們應該做的是獻身於他們遺留給我們的偉大任務。我們的先烈已將自己的全部精誠付與我們的事業，我們應從他們的榜樣中汲取更多的精神力量，努力使他們的鮮血不致白流。在上帝的護佑下，自由將在我國得到新生。我們這個民有、民治、民享的政府將永存於世上。

43 His Second Inaugural Address

Abraham Lincoln

Fellow Countrymen:

At this second appearing to take the oath of the presidential office, there is less occasion for an extended address than at the first. Then a statement somewhat in detail of the course to be pursued seemed very fitting and proper; now, at the expiration of four years, during which public declarations have constantly been called forth concerning every point and place of the great contest which still absorbs attention and engrosses the energies of the nation, little that is new could be presented. The progress of our arms, upon which all else chiefly depends, is as well known to the public as to myself. It is, I trust, reasonably satisfactory and encouraging to all. With a high hope for the future, no prediction in that regard is ventured. On the occasion corresponding to this four years ago, all thoughts were anxiously directed to an impending civil war. All dreaded it. All sought to avoid it. While the Inaugural Address was being delivered from this place, devoted altogether to saving the Union without war, the insurgent agents were in the city seeking to destroy it without war — seeking to dissolve the Union and divide the effects by negotiating. Both parties deprecated war,

四十三 第二次就職演說

阿伯拉罕 · 林肯

同胞們：在第二次宣誓就職總統的時候，我不必像第一次那樣作長篇大論的演講。第一次就職典禮上，較爲詳盡地叙述我們要採取的方針和道路，看來比較恰當。現在，在我的四年任期結束之時，有關這場至今仍爲舉國矚目的大鬥爭[1]的每個方面，時時有公開的宣告，因此沒有新的內容向各位奉告了。我們的一切都依靠武裝力量，有關這方面的進展大家知道得和我一樣清楚。我相信，大家對此頗感滿意和鼓舞。我們對未來抱着很大希望，在軍事方面就無庸多作預測。四年前我初次就職之際，大家的思慮都集中在即將爆發的內戰之上。大家對內戰都懷有恐懼，均想設法避免這場內戰的發生。當時我在這個講壇上發表的就職演說，全部內容就是爲了不戰而拯救聯邦。與此同時，城裏的叛逆分子却企圖不用戰爭而摧毀聯邦，企圖通過談判來瓦解聯邦，瓜分國家所有。雙方都反對戰爭，但其中一方[2]却寧願戰爭也不

本篇演說發表於1865年 3 月 4 日。

（1）指1861～1865年的內戰。

（2）指北方。南方先發動戰爭，攻佔了政府軍守衛的薩姆特。

but one of them would make war rather than let it perish, and war came. One eighth of the whole population were colored slaves, not distributed generally over the Union, but located in the Southern part. These slaves contributed a peculiar and powerful interest. All knew the interest would somehow cause war. To strengthen, perpetuate, and extend this interest was the object for which the insurgents would rend the Union by war, while the government claimed no right to do more than restrict the territorial enlargement of it. Neither party expected the magnitude or duration which it has already attained; neither anticipated that the cause of the conflict might cease even before the conflict itself could cease. Each looked for an easier triumph and a result less fundamental and astonishing. Both read the same Bible and pray to the same God. Each invokes His aid against the other. It may seem strange that any man should dare to ask a just God's assistance in wringing bread from the sweat of other men's faces; but let us judge not, that we be not judged. The prayer of both should not be answered; that of neither has been answered fully, for the Almighty has His own purposes. "Woe unto the world because of offenses, for it must needs be that offense come; but woe unto that man by whom the offense cometh." If we shall suppose American slavery one of those offenses which, in the providence of God, must needs come, but which, having continued through his appointed time, He now wills

---

（1）最初林肯採取妥協政策，承認南方的奴隸制，只是限制令其不擴展到北方。

（2）戰爭的起因是奴隸制。1863年1月1日，林肯發表了《解放宣言》。本篇演說發表時，內戰還未願聯邦毀滅，於是內戰爆發了。我國黑奴佔人口八分之一，他們不是普遍分佈於全國各地，而是集中在南部。這些黑奴，構成一種特殊而重要的利益。盡人皆知，這種利益遲早會成為戰爭的起因。叛逆分子不惜發動戰爭分裂聯邦，以達到增強、擴展這種利益、使之永存的目的，政府却除去要求將奴隸制限於原來區域，不使擴大之外，不要求其他任何權利[1]，雙方都不曾預料到戰爭會有這樣大的規模；持續這麼久，也不曾預料到引起衝突的原因在衝突停止前會消失[2]。雙方都尋求輕而易舉的勝利，不求徹底或驚人的結果。雙方信奉同一宗教，敬拜同一上帝，都祈求上帝幫助戰勝對方。說來奇怪，竟有人敢於要求公正的上帝幫助自己去榨取別人的血汗；但讓我們不要去品評他人吧，以免受到別人的評論[3]。雙方的祈求都不應得到滿足，也沒有任何一方得到完全的滿足，因為全能的上帝自有主張。＂禍哉斯世，以其陷人故也，夫陷人於罪，事所必有，但陷人者禍矣。＂[4]如果我們把美國的奴隸制當成是上帝要降給我們的災禍，它必定要降臨，但是這災禍已經到了上帝指定期限，祂現在要免去這場災禍了，

結束。

（3）《聖經》新約全書馬太福音第七章第一節。

（4）《聖經》新約全書馬太福音第十八章第七節。

to remove, and that He gives to both North and South this terrible war, as was due to those by whom the offense came, shall we discern that there is any departure from those divine attributes which believers in the living God always ascribe to Him? Fondly do we hope, fervently do we pray, that this mighty scourge of war may speedily pass away; yet if it be God's will that it continue until the wealth piled by bondsmen by two hundred and fifty years' unrequited toil shall be sunk, and until every drop of blood drawn with the lash shall be paid by another drawn with the sword, as was said three thousand years ago, so still it must be said that the judgments of the Lord are true and righteous altogether.

With malice toward none, with charity for all, with firmness in the right, as God gives us to see the right, let us strive on to finish the work we are in, to build up the nation's wounds, to care for him who shall have borne the battle, and for his widow and orphans; to do all which may achieve and cherish a just and a lasting peace among ourselves and with all nations.

於是他把這場可怕的戰爭降給南北雙方，懲罰那些帶來災禍的人。那麼，難道不能將那些篤信耶穌基督並將美德歸於基督的人跟其他人區別分開嗎？我們滿懷希望，熱誠祈禱，願這場懲罰我們的戰爭早日過去；但假若天意要這場戰爭延續下去，直至二百五十年來利用奴隸無償勞動辛苦積聚下來的財富銷毀淨盡，直至奴隸在皮鞭下流淌的鮮血用刀劍下的鮮血來償還，如同三千年前古語所說的那樣，我們仍然要稱頌上帝的判決是公允合理的。

我們對任何人不懷惡意，對所有人都抱有善心，對上帝使我們認識的正義無限堅定，讓我們努力完成我們正在進行的任務，癒合國家的戰爭傷痕，關懷戰死的烈士及其遺屬，盡一切力量為我國及全世界爭取並維護正義持久的和平。

44 At the Dedication of the National Cemetery at Gettysburg

Edward Everett

. . .

And now, friends, fellow citizens of Gettysburg and Pennsylvania, and you from remoter states, let me again, as we part, invoke your benediction on these honored graves. You feel, though the occasion is mournful, that it is good to be here. You feel that it was greatly auspicious for the cause of the country that the men of the East, and the men of the West, the men of nineteen sister states, stood side by side on the perilous ridges of the battle. You now feel it a new bond of union that they shall lie side by side till a clarion, louder than that which marshaled them to the combat, shall awake their slumbers. God bless the Union; it is dearer to us for the blood of brave men which has been shed in its defense. The spots on which they stood and fell; these pleasant heights; the thriving village whose streets so lately rang with the strange din of war; the fields beyond the ridge, where the noble Reynolds held the advancing foe at bay, and, while he gave up his own life, assured by his forethought and self-sacrifice the triumph of the two succeeding days; the little streams which

---

埃弗雷特（1794~1865），曾任美國衆議員、馬薩諸塞州州長、哈佛大學校長、國務卿等職。本篇是他在公墓落成典禮上講話的結束部分。

（1）當時美國只有十九個州。

四十四　在葛底斯堡公墓落成典禮上的講話

愛德華・埃弗雷特

……

朋友們，葛底斯堡和賓夕法尼亞的公民們，還有你們從遠處各州來的同胞們，在我們分手之前，讓我再次懇求你們爲這些神聖的墳墓祝福。雖然這是一個氣氛悲傷的場合，但是，在這裏聚會，你們覺得欣慰。你們感到，東部人、西部人、十九個姊妹州[1]的人，當年在激烈戰鬥中曾在危險的山脊上並肩作戰，實預告了國家的昌盛繁榮。現在，你們感到，他們又將並排安息在這裏，體現一種新的結合，直到比當年列隊出征的軍號聲更爲響亮的號角吹起，把他們從沉睡中喚醒[2]。願上帝保佑我們的聯邦；我們勇敢的同胞爲了捍衛這聯邦而流洒熱血，使我們覺得這聯邦更加珍貴。我們懷念他們奮起戰鬥而又倒下去的地方；這些景色怡人的高地；不久前還迴響着叫人聽不慣的巷戰槍聲，如今已是熙來攘往的村莊；山脊外的原野（在那裏高貴的雷諾茲[3]曾阻止敵人前進；在他捨身成仁時已能預見他的自我犧牲會帶來兩天後

（2）基督教徒相信，上帝的天使吹響號角時，將把每一個死去的人從墓中召回天國。

（3）雷諾茲（1820～1863），北方部隊將領，1863年7月1日在葛底斯堡戰役中陣亡。

wind through the hills, on whose banks in after-times the wandering plowman will turn up, with the rude weapons of savage warfare, the fearful missiles of modern artillery; Seminary Ridge, the Peach Orchard, Cemetery, Culp, and Wolf Hill, Round Top, Little Round Top, humble names, henceforward dear and famous — no lapse of time, no distance of space, shall cause you to be forgotten. "The whole earth," said Pericles, as he stood over the remains of his fellow citizens, who had fallen in the first year of the Peloponnesian War — "the whole earth is the sepulcher of illustrious men." All time, he might have added, is the millennium of their glory. Surely I would do no injustice to the other noble achievements of the war, which have reflected such honor on both arms of the service, and have entitled the armies and the navy of the United States, their officers and men, to the warmest thanks and the richest rewards which a grateful people can pay. But they, I am sure, will join us in saying, as we bid farewell to the dust of these martyr-heroes, that wheresoever throughout the civilized world the accounts of this great warfare are read, and down to the latest period of recorded time, in the glorious annals of our common country there will be no brighter page than that which relates to *the battles of Gettysburg*.

的勝利）；山間蜿蜒的小溪（將來有一天會從兩岸的泥土裏同時發現可怕的現代戰爭炮彈和古代戰爭的粗陋武器）；神學院山脊、桃園、公墓、卡爾普、狼山、園頂坡、小圓頂坡，這些過去是無名的小地方，從今以後將聞名遐邇，人心嚮往，千秋萬代，令人永誌不忘。在伯羅奔尼撒之戰[1]的第一年，培里克利曾經站在陣亡的同胞遺骸前說過：“整個大地是傑出人物的墳墓。”他應該再加上一句：“無盡的時間長流是他們光榮的慶典。”當然，我不會看輕戰爭中其他的光輝成就，這些成就反映了我們海、陸軍的榮譽，理應使兩軍的官兵受到我們整個民族致以最熱烈的感謝和最豐厚的報答。但是，我們向先烈遺骸告別之時，我肯定海陸兩軍官兵會和我們同聲說：整個文明世界任何地方的人，讀到這次偉大戰役實況時，均會感到，翻遍古今光榮的歷史記載，都不能找到比葛底斯堡戰役更為輝煌燦爛的一頁了。

． ． ． ． ． ． ． ．

45 The Return of the Massachusetts Battle Flags

Darius Nash Couch

May it please your Excellency: We have come here today as the representatives of the army of volunteers furnished by Massachusetts for the suppression of the rebellion, bringing these colors in order to return them to the State which intrusted them to our keeping. You must, however, pardon us if we give them up with profound regret — for these tattered shreds forcibly remind us of long and fatiguing marches cold bivouacs, and many hard-fought battles. The rents in their folds, the battle-stains on their escutcheons, the blood of our comrades that has sanctified the soil of a hundred fields, attest the sacrifices that have been made, the courage and constancy shown, that the nation might live. It is, sir, a peculiar satisfaction and pleasure to us that you, who have been an honor to the State and nation, from your marked patriotism and fidelity throughout the war, and have been identified with every organization before you, are now here to receive back, as the State custodian of her precious relics, these emblems of the devotion of her sons. May it pleasure your Excellency, the colors of the Massachusetts volunteers are returned to the State.

四十五　歸還馬薩諸塞州的戰旗

達里厄斯・納緒・柯奇

州長閣下：今天，作爲馬薩諸塞州平叛志願軍[1]的代表，我們來到這裏將本州交托給我們的戰旗奉還給您。請原諒我們在交還這些旗幟時深感遺憾的心情，因爲這些殘破的戰旗不能不使我們記起長途跋涉、餐風宿露、輾轉激戰的情景。旗上楯形紋章[2]的戰跡斑痕，使千百個戰場變得更爲神聖的同志們的血跡，還有旗上的皺摺裂口，這一切，都是曾經作出犧牲、充滿勇氣和堅忍精神的表徵，這一切，曾使我國得以生存。閣下，由您來收回這些象徵着本州兒女忠誠的珍貴文物，使我們特別滿意和高興，因爲您是我州我國的光榮，您在戰爭中表現出高度的愛國誠忱，過去又勞績卓著。州長閣下，現在我謹將馬薩諸塞州志願軍戰旗奉還本州。

本篇演說詞發表於美國南北戰爭結束後，1865年12月22日，波士頓。

（1）指美國南北戰爭中的北軍。

（2）馬薩諸塞州軍旗上的標誌。

46 Acceptance of the Battle Flags

John Albion Andrew

General: This pageant, so full of pathos and of glory, forms the concluding scene in the long series of visible actions and events in which Massachusetts has borne a part for the overthrow of rebellion and the vindication of the Union.

These banners return to the government of the Commonwealth through welcome hands. Borne, one by one, out of this Capital during more than four years of civil war as the symbols of the nation and the Commonwealth, under which the battalions of Massachusetts departed to the field, they come back again, borne hither by surviving representatives of the same heroic regiments and companies to which they were intrusted.

At the hands, General, of yourself, the ranking officer of the volunteers of the Commonwealth (one of the earliest who accepted a regimental command under appointment of the governor of Massachusetts) and of this grand column of scarred and heroic veterans who guard them home, they are returned with honors becoming relics so venerable, soldiers so brave, and citizens so beloved.

Proud memories of many a field: sweet memories alike of valor and friendship; sad memories of fraternal strife; tender memories of our fallen brothers and sons, whose dying eyes looked last upon their flaming folds;

四十六 接受戰旗

約翰・阿卑安・安德魯

將軍：這一面面飽含苦難、滿載光榮的莊嚴戰旗行列，組成了平叛過程中重大活動的最後一幕。馬薩諸塞州在平叛和衛護聯邦方面，曾盡了自己的一分力量。

這些旗由您歸還給州政府，使我們感到高興。在四年多的內戰期間，馬薩諸塞州的一支支部隊曾在這象徵着國家和本州的旗幟下，先後離開本州首府，開赴前綫；現在，戰旗又由這些英雄部隊生還者的代表高舉着回來了。

將軍，您是最早接受馬薩諸塞州州長任命指揮志願部隊的高級將領，您率領的英雄戰士身帶傷痕。這些戰旗在您和上述龐大的戰士縱隊手裏高舉着凱旋歸來了。它們上面閃爍着的光榮，正配得上軍旗這珍貴的文物、英勇的戰士和受到敬重的公民。

在這一面面旗幟上，交織着種種值得驕傲的作戰回憶：豪情與友誼的回憶使我們感到親切甘美；兄弟鬩墻[1]的回憶使我們感到悲傷；對為國捐軀的子弟的懷念使我們心中充滿柔情，還記得他們彌留的目光停在閃爍飄動的戰

安德魯（1818～1867），馬薩諸塞州州長。

（1）指內戰。

grand memories of heroic virtues sublimed by grief; exultant memories of the great and final victory of our country, our Union, and the righteous cause; thankful memories of a deliverance wrought out for human nature itself, unexampled by any former achievement of arms — immortal memories with immortal honors blended, twine around these splintered staves, weave themselves along the warp and woof of these familiar flags, war-worn, begrimed, and baptized with blood. Let "the brave heart, the trusty heart, the deep, unfathomable heart," in words of more than mortal eloquence, uttered though unexpressed, speak the emotions of grateful veneration for which these lips of mine are alike too feeble and unworthy.

General, I accept these relics in behalf of the people and the government. They will be preserved and cherished amid all the vicissitudes of the future as mementoes of brave men and noble actions.

旗上；對於捨身成仁的英雄美德的回憶使我們壯懷激烈；對於我國聯邦和正義行爲取得偉大的最後勝利的回憶使我們喜不自勝；對於人類本性得到解放的回憶使我們感激滿懷，這種解放是過往任何戰爭勝利所未有的。永恒的記憶與永恒的光榮交融在一起，密密地編織在這幾面熟悉的、經歷戰火洗禮、沾滿灰塵和血跡的破舊戰旗上。讓那" 勇敢的心、可靠的心和深邃的心"說出凡人不能表達於萬一的話來吧，我的聲音太微弱，不足以表達我們的感謝崇敬之情。

將軍，我代表人民與州政府接受這些珍貴的文物。在未來的歲月中，儘管滄桑變幻，它們都將作爲記錄勇敢的人們與高尚行爲的紀念品而加以保存，受到珍護。

47 In Support of the "Origin of Species"

Thomas Henry Huxley

. . .

I have said that the man of science is the sworn interpreter of nature in the high court of reason. But of what avail is his honest speech, if ignorance is the assessor of the judge, and prejudice the foreman of the jury? I hardly know of a great physical truth, whose universal reception has not been preceded by an epoch in which most estimable persons have maintained that the phenomena investigated were directly dependent on the Divine Will, and that the attempt to investigate them was not only futile, but blasphemous. And there is a wonderful tenacity of life about this sort of opposition to physical science. Crushed and maimed in every battle, it yet seems never to be slain; and after a hundred defeats it is at this day as rampant, though happily not so mischievous, as in the time of Galileo.

But to those whose life is spent, to use Newton's noble words, in picking up here a pebble and there a pebble on the shores of the great ocean of truth — who watch, day by day, the slow but sure advance of that mighty tide, bearing on its bosom the thousand treasures wherewith man ennobles and beautifies his life —

赫胥黎（1825～1895），英國生物學家、教育家。
其名著有《進化論與倫理學》（舊譯《天演論》）。
本文是他在許多權威學者的一片反對聲中爲達爾文的
進化論辯護。

四十七　支持"物種起源"的學説

托馬斯·亨利·赫胥黎

……

我曾經說過，科學家是在理性的最高法庭上對自然界最忠實的詮釋者。但是，假如無知成爲法官的顧問，偏見成爲陪審團的審判長時，科學家誠實的發言又有什麼用處呢？就我所知，幾乎所有偉大的科學眞理，在得到普遍接受以前，那些最有地位的大人物總堅持認爲各種現象應直接以神意爲依據，誰要是企圖去研究這些現象，不但枉費心機，而且簡直是對神的褻瀆。這種反對自然科學的態度，具有異常頑固的生命力。在每次戰役中，上述的反對態度都被擊潰、受到重創，但却似乎永遠不會被消滅。今天，這種反對態度已經遭到上百次的挫敗，但是仍然像在伽利略時代[1]那樣猖獗橫行，幸而危害性已經不那麼大了。

請讓我借用牛頓的一句名言：有些人一生在偉大眞理海洋的沙灘上拾集晶瑩的卵石。他們日復一日地注視着那雖然緩慢，但却確定無疑地上漲的氣勢磅礴的海潮，這股海潮的胸懷

---

(1)伽利略（1564～1642），意大利天文學家、數學學、物理學家。他的科學發現使他受到殘酷迫害，以致雙目失明。

it would be laughable, if it were not so sad, to see the little Canutes of the hour enthroned in solemn state, bidding that great wave to stay, and threatening to check its beneficent progress. The wave rises and they fly; but, unlike the brave old Dane, they learn no lesson of humility: the throne is pitched at what seems a safe distance, and the folly is repeated.

Surely it is the duty of the public to discourage anything of this kind, to discredit these foolish meddlers who think they do the Almighty a service by preventing a thorough study of His works.

The Origin of Species is not the first, and it will not be the last, of the great questions born of science, which will demand settlement from this generation. The general mind is seething strangely, and to those who watch the signs of the times, it seems plain that this nineteenth century will see revolutions of thought and practice as great as those which the sixteenth witnessed. Through what trials and sore contests the civilised world will have to pass in the course of this new reformation, who can tell?

But I verily believe that come what will, the part

包藏着無數能把人類生活裝點得更高尚美好的珍寶。要是他們看到那些現代的克紐斯⁽¹⁾式小人物，儼然坐在寶座上，命令這股巨大的海潮停止前進，並揚言要阻止那造福人類的進程時，他們會覺得這種做法即使不那麼可悲，也是可笑的。海潮漲上來了，現代的克紐斯們只好逃跑。但是，他們不像古時那位勇敢的丹麥人⁽²⁾，學得謙虛一些。他們只是把寶座挪到似乎是安全的遠處，便又重複地幹着同樣的蠢事。

大衆當然有責任阻止這類事情發生，使這些多管閒事的蠢人聲譽掃地。這些蠢人以爲不許人徹底研究全能上主所創造的世界，就是幫了上主的忙。

物種起源的問題並不是在科學方面要求我們這一代人解決的第一個大問題，也不會是最後一個。當前人類的思潮異常活躍，注視着時代跡象的人看得很清楚，十九世紀將如十六世紀般發生偉大的思想革命與實踐革命⁽³⁾。但是，又有誰能知道在這新的改革過程中，文明世界要經受什麼樣的考驗與痛苦的鬥爭呢？

然而，我眞誠地相信，無論發生什麼情況，

（1）克紐斯，古英王，同時也是丹麥王。他爲了向臣
　　下說明自己並非全能，便命令海潮停止前進。
（2）指克紐斯。
（3）指十四到十六世紀在歐洲發生的文藝復興。

which England may play in the battle is a grand and a noble one. She may prove to the world that, for one people, at any rate, despotism and demagogy are not the necessary alternatives of government; that freedom and order are not incompatible; that reverence is the hand-maid of knowledge; that free discussion is the life of truth, and of true unity in a nation.

Will England play this part? That depends upon how you, the public, deal with science. Cherish her, venerate her, follow her methods faithfully and implicitly in their application to all branches of human thought, and the future of this people will be greater than the past.

Listen to those who would silence and crush her, and I fear our children will see the glory of England vanishing like Arthur in the mist; they will cry too late the woeful cry of Guinever.

在這場鬥爭中，英國會起到偉大而崇高的作用。英國將向全世界證明，至少有一個民族認為，專制政治和煽動宣傳並不是治國的必要選擇，自由與秩序並非必然互相排斥，知識高於威嚴，自由討論是真理的生命，也是國家真正統一的生命。

英國是否會起這樣的作用呢？這就取決於你們大眾對科學的態度了。珍惜科學、尊重科學吧，忠實地、準確地遵循科學的方法，將之運用到一切人類思想領域中去，那麼，我們這個民族的未來就必定比過去更加偉大。

假如聽從那些窒息科學、扼殺科學的人的意見，我恐怕我們的子孫將要看到英國的光輝像亞瑟王[1]在霧中消失那樣黯淡下來。等到他們發出像基妮法[2]那樣的哀哭時，後悔已經來不及了。

（1）傳說中的古代英王，一位半人半神的人物。
（2）亞瑟王的王后，與亞瑟王的部下相戀，被送到修道院關禁終身。

48　The Lamps of Fiction

Goldwin Smith

Ruskin has lighted seven lamps of Architecture
to guide the steps of the architect in the worthy practice
of his art. It seems time that lamps should be lighted
to guide the steps of the writer of fiction. Think what
the influence of novelists now is, and how some of them
use it! Think of the multitudes who read nothing but
novels; and then look into the novels which they read!
I have seen a young man's whole library consisting of
thirty or forty of those paper-bound volumes, which are
the bad tobacco of the mind. In England, I looked over
three railway bookstalls in one day. There was hardly
a novel by an author of any repute on one of them.
There were heaps of nameless garbage, commended by
tasteless, flaunting woodcuts, the promise of which
was no doubt well kept within. Fed upon such food
daily, what will the mind of a nation be? I say that
there is no flame at which we can light the Lamp of
Fiction purer or brighter than the genius of him in
honor to whose memory we are assembled here today.
Scott does not moralize. Heaven be praised that he does
not. He does not set a moral object before him, nor lay

史密斯（1823～1910），英國敎育家、歷史學家。
本文發表於1871年司各脫誕生一百周年紀念會上。
（1）約翰‧羅斯金（John Ruskin, 1819～1900），英
　　國批評家與理論家。他的藝術理論在19世紀中葉
　　對英國有極大影響，他的名著《建築學的七盞明

四十八　小說寫作的指路明燈

戈德文・史密斯

　　羅斯金[1]，點燃了建築學的七盞明燈，引導建築家在高尚的藝術實踐中一步步向前。看來，現在是爲小說家點燃明燈以指引道路的時候了。請想一想，現在的小說家有多大的影響力，而其中有些人是怎樣利用這種影響力的！想想有多少人除了小說以外，什麼都不看；再仔細看看他們所讀的小說內容！我曾看見一個年靑人的全部藏書是三、四十本平裝書，都是些精神毒品。有一天，我在英國瀏覽過三個車站書亭，其中幾乎沒有一個書亭裏的書是知名作者的小說。那是一堆堆無名作家粗製濫造的糟粕，封面是趣味低下、花花綠綠的木刻畫。畫面上的內容無疑在書裏應有盡有。每天用這種精神食糧填塞、餵養出來的民族心靈，會變成什麼樣子？我們今天在此集會紀念的這位天才[2]，我以爲他所發出的火焰比任何人都更純淨、更明亮，更適合用於點燃那照亮小說寫作道路的明燈。司各脫不喜歡道德說敎。讚美上天，他沒有那樣做。他沒有把道德目標擺在自己面前，

　　燈》（The Seven Lamps of Architecture）寫成於1849年。

（2）指華特・司各脫（1771～1832），蘇格蘭小說家和詩人，近代西歐歷史小說的創始人。

down moral rules. But his heart, brave, pure, and true, is a law to itself; and by studying what he does, we may find the law for all who follow his calling. If seven lamps have been lighted for architecture, Scott will light as many for fiction.

I. *The Lamp of Reality.* The novelist must ground his work in faithful study of human nature. . . . For some writers, and writers dear to the circulating libraries too, might, for all that appears in their works, lie in bed all day, and write by night under the excitement of green tea. Creative art, I suppose they call this, and it is creative with a vengeance. Not so, Scott. The human nature which he paints, he has seen in all its phases, gentle and simple, in burgher and shepherd, Highlander, Lowlander, Borderer, and Islesman; he had come into close contact with it; he had opened it to himself by the talisman of his joyous and winning presence; he had studied it thoroughly with a clear eye and an all-embracing heart. When his scenes are laid in the past, he has honestly studied history. . . .

II. *The Lamp of Ideality.* The materials of the novelist must be real; they must be gathered from the field of humanity by his actual observation. But they must pass through the crucible of the imagination; they must be idealized. . . . Of course, this power of idealization is the great gift of genius. It is that which dis-

也沒有規定道德條規。但他那勇敢、純潔，眞誠的心就是心靈自身的準繩。我們研究他做的事，就可以爲所有願意聽從他召喚的人找出一條應該遵循的法則。如果說羅斯金曾經給建築學點起了七盞明燈，那麼，司各脫也會爲小說點起七盞明燈。

第一是現實之燈。小說家必須忠實地研究人類的本性，以此作爲他寫作的基礎。……因爲有些作家，包括有些巡迴圖書館最熟悉的作家，雖然在他們的作品裏寫了那些東西，但他們都很可以白天整天躺在床上，晚上起來用綠茶刺激寫作。他們大概把這稱爲創造藝術吧。是的，創造得過了頭了。司各脫可不是這樣做的。他所勾劃的人類本性，都是他從各個柔和而簡樸的側面親眼看到的。他觀察平民、牧羊人、蘇格蘭高地人和低地人、邊境居民、島上居民，從他們中看到人類的天性。他和人類的天性有密切的接觸。與人相處時，他帶來歡樂，贏得人心，好像身上有靈符法寶，使人類的天性向他開放。他用明亮的眼光和包容一切的心胸對人類的天性進行透徹的探究。如果寫的背景是過去的時代，他就實實在在地鑽研歷史。……

第二是理想之燈。小說家的素材必須眞實，必須通過他對人類親身的體察收集得來。然而這些素材又必須經過想象的冶煉，變得理想化。……自然，這種理想化的能力是一種偉大

tinguishes Homer, Shakespeare, and Walter Scott from ordinary men. . . . Scott's character are never monsters or caricatures. They are full of nature; but it is universal nature. Therefore they have their place in the universal heart, and will keep that place forever. And mark that even in his historical novels he is still ideal. . . .

III. *The Lamp of Impartiality.* The novelist must look on humanity without partiality or prejudice. His sympathy, like that of the historian, must be unbounded, and untainted by sect or party. He must see everywhere the good that is mixed with evil, the evil that is mixed with good. And this he will not do, unless his heart be right. It is in Scott's historical novels that his impartiality is most severely tried and is most apparent, though it is apparent in all his works. . . .

IV. *The Lamp of Impersonality.* Personality is lower than partiality. . . . Novelists, however, often debase fiction by obtruding their personal vanities, favoritisms, fanaticisms, and antipathies. . . . Not only is Scott not personal, but we cannot conceive his being so. We cannot think possible that he should degrade his art by the indulgence of egotism, or crotchets, or party piques. Least of all can we think it possible that his high and gallant nature should use art as a cover for striking a foul blow.

V. *The Lamp of Purity.* . . . Impure novels have brought and bringing much misery on the world. Scott's purity is not that of cloistered innocence and inexperience, it is the manly purity of one who had seen the

的天賦。荷馬、莎士比亞、華特‧司各脫正是由於有了這種天賦才異於常人。……司各脫的小說人物從沒有誇張到怪誕或滑稽程度。他的人物充滿了自然。但這是普遍天性的自然。因此，這些人物在普天下人們的心中佔有自己的地位，並能永遠保持這個地位。請注意，甚至是歷史小說，司各脫依然是用理想化的寫法。……

第三是公正之燈，小說家必須以無偏私無成見的眼光去看待人類。他必須和歷史學家一樣懷有最深厚的同情心，不受宗派情緒的影響。不論任何地方，他必須在邪惡中看到善良，在善良中看到邪惡。如果他沒有一顆公正的心，他就做不到這一點。司各脫公正的心在其歷史小說裏受到最嚴峻的考驗，但也表現得最明顯，儘管這在他的所有作品裏都明顯地表現出來。……

第四是忘我之燈。強調個人比偏私還要低級。……然而小說家却往往把個人的虛榮心、好惡和狂熱放到小說裏去，貶低了小說的價值。……司各脫不僅不强調個人，而且我們也很難想象他會這樣。我們無法想象他會沉湎於自我中心或非非之想或黨派之爭，以致貶低他的藝術。我們更不能想象以他高尚豪爽的品格，會將藝術當作暗箭，傷害別人。

第五是純潔之燈。……不潔的小說已經給世界帶來不幸，還將帶來更多的不幸。司各脫的純潔，不是修道院式與世隔絕的天眞無邪和

231

world, mingled with men of the world, known evil as well as good; but who, being a true gentleman, abhorred filth, and teaches us to abhore it too.

VI. *The Lamp of Humanity.* . . . Scott would have recoiled from the blood as well as from the ordure, he would have allowed neither to have defiled his noble page. . . . He knew that a novelist had no right even to introduce the terrible except for the purpose of exhibiting human heroism, developing character, awakening emotions which, when awakened, dignify and save from harm. It is want of genius and of knowledge of their craft that drives novelists to outrage humanity with horrors. . . .

VII. *The Lamp of Chivalry.* Of this briefly. Let the writer of fiction give us humanity in all its phases, the comic as well as the tragic, the ridiculous as well as the sublime; but let him not lower the standard of character or the aim of life. . . . Scott, like Shakespeare, wherever the thread of his fiction may lead him, always keeps before himself and us the highest ideal which he knew, the ideal of a gentleman. If any one says there are narrow bounds wherein to confine fiction, I answer there has been room enough within them for the highest tragedy, the deepest pathos, the broadest humor, the widest range of character, the most moving incident that the world has ever enjoyed. . . .

未經世事的純潔，而是一個堂堂男子的純潔；他見過世面，與世人相處，認得清善與惡。然而作為一個真正的正派人，他憎惡淫猥，也教導我們憎惡淫猥。

第六是人性之燈。……司各脫絕不會描寫流血和淫穢的東西。他不會讓這些東西玷污他那高潔的篇幅。……司各脫知道，除了為表現人類的英雄主義，或展開一個人物性格，或喚醒某種高尚而無害的感情之外，一個小說家無權將恐怖的場面展示給讀者。窘於沒有天資和寫作技巧知識的小說家，才不得不用恐怖情節來蹂躪人性。……

第七是高尚之燈。關於這點，說得簡要一些。讓小說的作者向我們描寫有關人類的一切吧。給我們寫人類的喜劇，也給我們寫人類的悲劇，給我們寫人類荒唐可笑的一面，也給我們寫人類崇高的一面。但是，請他們一定不要降低人物的情操，也不要降低生命的目標。……司各脫和莎士比亞一樣，不管他的小說的綫索把他引向何處，他永遠在他和我們的面前樹立起他所熟知的典範，那就是一個高尚正派的人的典範。假如有人說這樣對小說的限制太窄，我就要回答說，在這限制的範圍裏，有足夠廣闊之地容納世人所曾欣賞的最崇高的悲劇、最深沉的哀傷、最開懷的幽默、最多樣的各種人物和最動人的情節。……

49 On Woman's Right to Suffrage

Susan Brownell Anthony

Friends and fellow citizens: — I stand before you tonight under indictment for the alleged crime of having voted at the last presidential election, without having a lawful right to vote. It shall be my work this evening to prove to you that in thus voting, I not only committed no crime, but, instead, simply exercised my *citizen's rights,* guaranteed to me and all United States citizens by the National Constitution, beyond the power of any State to deny.

The preamble of the Federal Constitution says:

"We, the people of the United States, in order to form a more perfect union, establish justice, insure *domestic* tranquillity, provide for the common defense, promote the general welfare, and secure the blessings of liberty to ourselves and our posterity, do ordain and establish this Constitution for the United States of America."

It was we, the people; not we, the white male citizens; nor yet we, the male citizens; but we, the whole people, who formed the Union. And we formed it, not to give the blessings of liberty, but to secure them; not to the half of ourselves and the half of our posterity, but to the whole people — women as well as men. And it is a downright mockery to talk to women of their enjoy of the blessings of liberty while they are

四十九 論婦女選舉權

蘇珊・寶萊・安東尼

朋友們、同胞們：我今晚站在你們面前，被控在上次總統選舉中犯有所謂無投票權而參加投票的罪。今天晚上我想向你們證明，我投票選舉，不但無罪，相反，我只是行使了我的公民權。這項權利是國家憲法確保我和一切美國公民所有的，無論哪一州政府都無權剝奪。

聯邦憲法的序言有如下詞句：

"我們，合眾國的人民，為組成一個更完美的聯邦，確立公理，保障國內安寧，提供共同防務，促進普遍福利，永保我們及子孫後代得享自由，特制定此美利堅合眾國憲法。"

組成這個聯邦的，是我們，是人民，不是男性白人公民，也不是男性公民，而是我們全體人民。我們組成這個聯邦，不僅為了使人民得享自由，而且要保障自由；不僅為了給我們中的一半及子孫後代的一半人以自由，而是給全體人民，給男子，同時也給婦女以自由。投票權是這個民主共和政府保障公民自由的唯一

安東尼（1820～1906），美國反對黑奴制與爭取女權的著名人士。當時美國法律規定婦女無選舉權，1872年安東尼在總統選舉中投票被捕，判處罰款。本篇演講在1873年發表。

denied the use of the only means of securing them provided by this democratic-republican government — the ballot.

For any State to make sex a qualification that must ever result in the disfranchisement of one entire half of the people is to pass a bill of attainder, or an *ex post facto* law, and is therefore a violation of the supreme law of the land. By it the blessings of liberty are for ever withheld from women and their female posterity. To them this government has no just powers derived from the consent of the governed. To them this government is not a democracy. It is not a republic. It is an odious aristocracy; a hateful oligarchy of sex; the most hateful aristocracy ever established on the face of the globe; an oligarchy of wealth, where the rich govern the poor, an oligarchy of learning, where the educated govern the ignorant, or even an oligarchy of race, where the Saxon rules the African, might be endured; but this oligarchy of sex, which makes father, brothers, husband, sons, the oligarchs over the mother and sisters, the wife and daughters of every household — which ordains all men sovereigns, all women subjects, carries dissension, discord and rebellion into every home of the nation.

Webster, Worcester and Bouvier all define a citizen to be a person in the United States, entitled to vote and hold office.

The only question left to be settled now is: Are

---

(1)美國著名律師,曾任國務卿,主張南北聯合,解放黑奴。

(2)伍斯特(1758~1837),美國公理會教派牧師,手段，要是婦女不得運用投票權，那麼，向婦女侈談自由的賜福就是莫大的諷刺。

任何州政府，如果以性別爲參加選舉的條件，必然會剝奪整整半數人民的選舉權。這等於通過一項剝奪公民權的法律或一項事後追認的法律，因此這樣做實在是違犯了我國的最高法律，令婦女及其後代的所有女性永遠被剝奪自由。對於女性來說，這個政府並未具有得自人民贊同的正當權力。對於她們來說，這個政府不是民主政體，也不是共和政體。它是可憎的專制，是可恨的性別獨裁，是地球上所有專制中最可恨的專制制度。相形之下，有錢人統治窮人的富人獨裁，受教育者統治未受教育者的勞心者獨裁，甚至撒克遜人統治非洲人的種族獨裁，人們或許還稍能忍受。但是，這種性別獨裁却使每家人的父親、兄弟、丈夫、兒子得以統治母親、姊妹、妻子、女兒，使一切男子成爲統治者，一切婦女成爲奴婢。這種獨裁給全國的每一個家庭帶來不和、紛爭和反叛。

韋伯斯特[1]、伍斯特[2]和保維爾[3]都認爲，公民的定義是有權投票和有權在政府供職的美國人。

那末，現在要解決的唯一問題是：婦女是

以主張和平著稱。

（3）保維爾（1787～1851），美國著名法學家。

women persons? And I hardly believe any of our opponents will have the hardihood to say they are not. Being persons, then, women are citizens; and no State has a right to make any law, or to enforce any old law, that shall abridge their privileges or immunities. Hence, every discrimination against women in the constitutions and law of the several States is today null and void, precisely as in every one against negroes.

不是人？我很難相信，反對我們的人中有誰敢說她們不是。婦女既然是人，也就是公民。無論哪一個州都無權制定新法或重新執行舊法以剝奪婦女的權利或特權。因此，現今，無論哪一州的憲法或法律，一切歧視婦女的法律，正如以往一切歧視黑人的法律，都是無效的、非法的。

50 Introducing Charles Kingsley

Mark Twain

Ladies And Gentlemen: I am here to introduce Mr. Charles Kingsley, the lecturer of the evening, and I take occasion to observe that when I wrote the book called "Innocents Abroad" (applause) I thought it was a volume which would bring me at once into intimate relation with the clergy. But I could bring evidences to show that from that day to this, this is the first time that I have ever been called upon to perform this pleasant office of vouching for a clergyman (laughter) and give him a good unbiased start before an audience. (Laughter.) Now that my opportunity has come at last, I am appointed to introduce a clergyman who needs no introduction in America. (Applause.) And although I haven't been requested by the committee to indorse him, I volunteer that (laughter), because I think it is a graceful thing to do; and it is all the more graceful from being so unnecessary. But the most unnecessary thing I could do in introducing the Rev. Charles Kingsley would be to sound his praises to you, who have read his books and know his high merits as well as I possibly can, so I waive all that and simply say that in welcoming him cordially to this land of ours, I believe that I utter a sentiment which would go nigh to surprising him or possibly to deafen him, if I could concentrate in my voice the utterance of all those in America who feel

---

馬克・吐溫（1835～1910），美國著名作家。代表作有《湯姆・索亞歷險記》及《哈克貝利・芬歷險記》等。本篇發表於1874年 2 月17日，爲歡迎金斯萊而作的演說。金斯萊（1819～1875），英國作家與牧

五十 介紹查理士・金斯萊

馬克・吐溫

各位先生、女士：我現在向你們介紹今天晚上的演講人查理士・金斯萊先生。我還要就便提一下，當我寫那本《老實人出國旅遊記》[1]（鼓掌）時，我想，這本書一定會使我立刻同教會牧師的關係密切起來。但是我可以向你們保證，從那一天到現在，這可是我第一次有幸受命給一位牧師作保人（笑聲），並向聽衆作一個不偏不倚的介紹（笑聲）。現在我終於得到機會，我被指定來介紹一位在美國不需要介紹的牧師（鼓掌）。雖然委員會沒有要求我作他的保人，我却自告奮勇來做了（笑聲），因爲我想那是一件很高雅的事，唯其因爲沒有必要，所以就更高雅了。但是最用不着我做的事却要算向你們讚美查理士・金斯萊牧師了，因爲你們都讀過他的書，比我更了解他的高才盛德，所以我現在要省下這些話，只是簡單地說，我們熱烈歡迎他來到我們的國家。我相信，假如我能夠將我國人民對他的眞摯情誼傾注到我的聲音裏，我的聲音會使他嚇一跳，

_____

師，曾任劍橋大學敎授。

（1）馬克・吐溫1869年出版的遊記體小說，其中的人物有牧師。

that sentiment. (Applause.) And I am glad to say that this kindly feeling toward Mr. Kingsley is not wasted, for his heart is with America, and when he is in his own home, the latchstring hangs on the outside of the door for us. I know this from personal experience; perhaps that is why it has not been considered unfitting that I should perform this office in which I am now engaged. (Laughter.) Now for a year, for more than a year, I have been enjoying the hearty hospitality of English friends in England, and this is a hospitality which is growing wider and freer every day toward our countrymen. I was treated so well there, so undeservedly well, that I should always be glad of an opportunity to extend to Englishmen the good offices of our people; and I do hope that the good feeling, the growing good feeling between the old mother country and her strong, aspiring child will continue to extend until it shall exist over the whole great area of both nations. I have the honor to introduce to you Rev. Charles Kingsley.

甚至可能震聾他的耳朵（鼓掌）。我可以高興地說，我們對金斯萊先生的這種美好情誼不是白費的，因為他的心向着美國。他在家時，我們要是去作客，他的大門總是向我們敞開的。這一點，我曾親身體驗；也許正是因為這樣，今晚由我來接待、介紹他，也還不算不稱職吧（笑聲）。有一年的時間，比一年還要多的時間，我曾經在英國受到英國朋友的熱情款待，這種對我們美國人廣泛而又熱誠的感情正在與日俱增。我在那裏受到這樣盛情的接待，使我當之有愧，所以我常常高興有機會向英國人表達我國人民的熱情歡迎；我衷心期望我們的故國母親和她茁壯成長、胸懷壯志的孩子之間的親密感情繼續發展，直至遍及我們兩國的遼闊國土。我現在榮幸地向你們介紹查理士．金斯萊牧師。

51 Unconscious Plagiarism

Mark Twain

Mr. Chairman, Ladies and Gentlemen: I would have traveled a much greater distance than I have come to witness the paying of honors to Dr. Holmes. For my feeling toward him has always been one of peculiar warmth. When one receives a letter from a great man for the first time in his life, it is a large event to him, as all of you know by your own experience. You never can receive letters enough from famous men afterward to obliterate that one, or dim the memory of the pleasant surprise it was, and the gratification it gave you. Lapse of time cannot make it commonplace or cheap.

Well, the first great man who ever wrote me a letter was our guest — Oliver Wendell Holmes. He was also the first great literary man I ever stole anything from (laughter), and that is how I came to write to him and he to me. When my first book was new a friend of mine said to me, "The dedication is very neat." "Yes," I said, "I thought it was." My friend said: "I always admired it, even before I saw it in the 'Innocents Abroad.'" I naturally said, "What do you mean? Where did you ever see it before?" "Well, I saw it first some

---

這是荷默斯七十壽辰（ 1879年12月 3 日 ）時，馬
克‧吐溫在波士頓為他祝壽的致詞。荷默斯（ Oliver
Wendell Holmes, 1809-1894 ）是美國雜誌《大西洋

五十一 無意的剽竊

主席先生、各位女士、先生：爲了親臨對荷默斯博士的祝壽，再遠的路程我也要前來。因爲我一直對他懷有特別親切的感情。一個人一生中初次接到一位大人物的信時，總是把這當成一件大事。你們所有的人都會有這樣的體驗。不管你後來接到多少名人的來信，都不會使這第一封失色，也不會使你淡忘當時那種又驚喜又感激的心情。流逝的時光也不會湮滅它在你心底的價值。

第一次給我寫信的偉大人物正是我們的貴客——奧列弗・溫德爾・荷默斯。他也是第一位被我從他那裏偷得了一點東西的大文學家。（笑聲）這正是我給他寫信以及他給我回信的原因。我的第一本書[(1)]出版不久，一位朋友對我說："你的卷首獻詞寫得漂亮簡潔。"我說："是的，我認爲是這樣。"我的朋友說："我一直很欣賞這篇獻詞，甚至在你的《老實人出國旅遊記》出版前，我讀到這篇獻詞時就很欣賞了。"我當然感到吃驚，便問："你這話什麼意思？你以前在什麼地方看到這篇獻詞？"

月刊》的創始人。

（1）即《老實人出國旅行記》。

years ago as Dr. Holmes's dedication to his 'Songs in Many Keys.'" Of course, my first impulse was to prepare this man's remains for burial (laughter), but upon reflection I said I would reprieve him for a moment or two, and give him a chance to prove his assertion if he could. We stepped into a bookstore, and he did prove it. I had really stolen that dedication, almost word for word. I could not imagine how this curious thing had happened; for I knew one thing, for a dead certainty, — that a certain amount of pride always goes along with a teaspoonful of brains, and that this pride protects a man from deliberately stealing other people's ideas. That is what a teaspoonful of brains will do for a man, — and admirers had often told me I had nearly a basketful, though they were rather reserved as to the size of the basket. (Laughter.)

However, I thought the thing out and solved the mystery. Two years before I had been laid up a couple of weeks in the Sandwich Islands, and had read and reread Dr. Holmes's poems until my mental reservoir was filled up with them to the brim. The dedication lay on top and handy (laughter), so by and by I unconsciously stole it. Perhaps I unconsciously stole the rest of the volume, too, for many people have told me that my book was pretty poetical, in one way or another. Well, of course, I wrote Dr. Holmes and told him I hadn't meant to steal, and he wrote back and said in the kindest way that it was all right and no harm done;

"唔，幾年前我讀荷默斯博士的《多調之歌》一書獻詞時就看過了。"當然啦，我一聽之下，第一個念頭就是要了這小子的命（笑聲），但是想了一想之後，我說可以先饒他一、兩分鐘，給他個機會，看看他能不能拿出證據證實他的話。我們走進一間書店，他果真證實了他的話。我確確實實偷了那篇獻詞，幾乎一字未改。我當時簡直想象不出怎麼會發生這種怪事；因為我知道一點，絕對無庸置疑的一點，那就是，一個人若有一茶匙頭腦，便會有一分傲氣。這分傲氣保護着他，使他不致有意剽竊別人的思想。那就是一茶匙頭腦對一個人的作用——可有些崇拜我的人常常說我的頭腦幾乎有一隻籃子那麼大，不過他們不肯說這隻籃子的尺寸（笑聲）。

後來我到底把這事想清楚了，揭開了這謎。在那以前的兩年，我有兩、三個星期在三明治島休養。這期間，我反覆閱讀了荷默斯博士的詩集，直到這些詩句填滿我的腦子，快要溢了出來。那獻詞浮在最上面，信手就可拈來（笑聲），於是不知不覺地，我就把它偷來了。說不定我還偷了那集子的其餘內容呢，因為不少人對我說我那本書在有些方面頗有點詩意。當然啦，我給荷默斯博士寫了封信，告訴他我並非有意偷竊。他給我回了信，十分體諒地對我說，那沒有關係，不礙事；他更表示相信我

and added that he believed we all unconsciously worked over ideas gathered in reading and hearing, imagining they were original with ourselves. He stated a truth, and did it in such a pleasant way, and salved over my sore spot so gently and so healingly, that I was rather glad I had committed the crime, for the sake of the letter. I afterward called on him and told him to make perfectly free with any ideas of mine that struck him as being good protoplasm for poetry. (Laughter.) He could see by that that there wasn't anything mean about me; so we got along right from the start.

I have met Dr. Holmes many times since; and lately he said, — however, I am wandering wildly away from the one thing which I got on my feet to do: that is, to make my compliments to you, my fellow teachers of the great public, and likewise to say I am right glad to see that Dr. Holmes is still in his prime and full of generous life; and as age is not determined by years, but by trouble and infirmities of mind and body, I hope it may be a very long time yet before any can truthfully say, "He is growing old." (Applause.)

們所有的人都會不知不覺地運用讀到的或聽來的思想，還以爲這些思想是自己的創見呢。他說出了一個眞理，而且說得那麼令人愉快，幫我順順當當地下了台階，使我甚至慶幸自己虧得犯了這剽竊罪，因而得到了這封信。後來我拜訪他，告訴他以後如果看到我有什麼可供他作詩的思想原料，他儘管隨意取用好了（笑聲）。那樣，他可以看到我是一點也不小氣的；於是我們從一開始就很合得來。

從那以後，我多次見過荷默斯博士；最近，他說——噢，我離題太遠了。我本該向你們，我的同行、廣大公衆的教師們說出我對荷默斯的祝詞。我應該說，我非常高興地看到荷默斯博士的風采依然不減當年。一個人之所以年邁非因年歲而是身心的衰弱。我希望許多許多年之後，人們還不能肯定地說："他已經老了。"（鼓掌）

52 Voltaire

Victor Marie Hugo

A hundred years today a man died. He died immortal. He departed laden with years, laden with works, laden with the most illustrious and the most fearful of responsibilities, the responsibility of the human conscience informed and rectified. He went cursed and blessed, cursed by the past, blessed by the future; and these are the two superb forms of glory. On the death-bed he had, on the one hand, the acclaim of contemporaries and of posterity; on the other, that triumph of hooting and of hate which the implacable past bestows upon those who have combated it. He was more than a man; he was an age. He had exercised a function and fulfilled a mission. He had been evidently chosen for the work which he had done by the Supreme Will, which manifests itself as visibly in the laws of destiny as in the laws of nature.

The eighty-four years which this man lived span the interval between the Monarchy at its apogee and the Revolution at its dawn. When he was born, Louis XIV still reigned; when he died, Louis XVI already wore the crown; so that his cradle saw the last rays of the great throne, and his coffin the first gleams from the great abyss.

. . .

五十二　伏爾泰

維克多・瑪麗・雨果

一百年前的今天，一顆巨星隕落了。但他是永生的。他離開人世時已年登耄耋，他著述極富，肩負着最榮耀也最艱巨的責任，那就是：培育良知，敎化人類。他在咒罵與祝福聲中溘然長逝；被舊時代所詛咒，又受到未來的祝福。這二者都是至高無上的光榮。在他彌留之際，一方面，他受到同時代人和後世子孫的歡呼讚美，另一方面，像其他曾經和舊時代搏鬥過的人一樣，那對他懷有深仇大恨的舊時代也得意洋洋地發出了叫罵聲。他不僅是一個人，他是整整一個時代。他曾盡己任，完成了一項使命。他已完成的工作顯然是天意選派他去完成的，命運的法則和自然的法則都同樣明白地體現出上天的意旨。

這位偉人所生活的八十四個年頭，經歷了達到極點的專制時期和剛剛露出一綫晨曦的革命年代。他誕生時，路易十四尙在王位，他去世時，路易十六已經戴上了王冠。他的襁褓映照着王朝盛世的餘輝，他的靈柩則投射着從大深淵裏透出的最初光芒。

……

雨果（1802～1885），法國文學家。本文爲1878年伏爾泰逝世一百周年的講話。

In the presence of this society, frivolous and dismal, Voltaire alone, having before his eyes those united forces, the court, the nobility, capital; that unconscious power, the blind multitude; that terrible magistracy, so severe to subjects, so docile to the master, crushing and flattering, kneeling upon the people before the king; that clergy, vile *melange* of hypocrisy and fanaticism; Voltaire alone, I repeat, declared war against that coalition of all the social iniquities, against that enormous and terrible world, and he accepted battle with it. And what was his weapon? That which has the lightness of the wind and the power of the thunderbolt — a pen.

With that weapon he fought; with that weapon he conquered.

Let us salute that memory.

Voltaire conquered; Voltaire waged the splendid kind of warfare, the war of one alone against all; that is to say, the grand warfare. The war of thought against matter, the war of reason against prejudice, the war of the just against the unjust, the war for the oppressed against the oppressor, the war of goodness, the war of kindness. He had the tenderness of a woman and the wrath of a hero. He was a great mind and an immense heart.

He conquered the old code and the old dogma. He conquered the feudal lord, the Gothic judge, the Roman priest. He raises the populace to the dignity of people. He taught, pacificated, and civilized. He fought for Sirven and Montbailly, as for Calas and La Barre; he accepted all the menances, all the outrages, all the persecutions, calumny, and exile. He was indefatigable and immovable. He conquered violence by a smile,

在這輕薄無聊、淒慘憂鬱的時世下，伏爾泰獨自一人，面對宮廷、貴族和資本的聯合力量，面對那股毫無意識的強力——羣盲；面對那些無惡不作的官吏，他們專門媚上欺下，俯伏於國王之前，凌駕於人民之上；面對那些教士，他們是僞善與宗教狂的邪惡混合體。讓我再說一遍，伏爾泰獨自一人，向社會上一切邪惡的聯合力量宣戰，向這茫茫的恐怖世界宣戰，並與之搏鬥。他的武器是什麽呢？是那輕若微風而重如霹靂的———一枝筆。

　　他用這武器進行戰鬥，用這武器贏得勝利。

　　讓我們一齊向伏爾泰的英靈致敬吧。

　　伏爾泰勝利了。他發動了一場非同尋常的戰爭，一場以一敵衆的戰爭，一場氣壯山河的戰爭。這是思想向物質作戰，理性向偏見作戰，正義向不義作戰，被壓迫者向壓迫者作戰；這是善之戰，仁愛之戰。伏爾泰具有女性的溫柔和英雄的怒火，他具有偉大的頭腦和浩瀚無際的心胸。

　　他戰勝了陳舊的秩序和陳舊的敎條，他戰勝了封建君主、中古時代的法官和羅馬的敎士。他把黎民百姓提高到尊嚴的地位。他敎化、慰撫、播種文明。他爲西爾旺和蒙貝利而戰，也爲卡萊斯和拉·巴利而戰。他承受了一切威脅、辱罵、迫害、誣謗。他還遭到了流放。但是他不屈不撓，堅定不移。他以微笑戰勝暴力，以

despotism by sarcasm, infallibility by irony, obstinacy by perseverance, ignorance by truth.

I have just pronounced the word *smile*. I pause at it. Smile! It is Voltaire.

. . .

To sum up epochs, by giving them the names of men, to name ages, to make of them in some sort human personages, has only been done by three peoples, Greece, Italy, France. We say, the Age of Pericles, the Age of Augustus, the Age of Leo X, the Age of Louis XIV, the Age of Voltaire. These appellations have a great significance. This privilege of giving names to periods belonging exclusively to Greece, to Italy, and to France, is the highest mark of civilization. Until Voltaire, they were the names of the chiefs of states; Voltaire is more than the chief of a state; he is a chief of ideas; with Voltaire a new cycle begins. We feel that henceforth the supreme governmental power is to be thought. Civilization obeyed force; it will obey the ideal. It was the scepter and the sword broken, to be replaced by the ray of light; that is to say, authority transfigured into liberty. Henceforth, no other sovereignty than the law for the people, and the conscience for the individual. For each of us, the two aspects of progress separate themselves clearly, and they are these: to exercise one's right; that is to say, to be a man; to perform one's duty; that is to say, to be a citizen.

諷刺戰勝專橫，以嘲弄戰勝宗教的自命一貫正
確，以堅韌戰勝頑固偏執，以真理戰勝愚昧無
知。

我剛才說到微笑，我要在這裏停一停。微
笑！這就是伏爾泰。

......

只有希臘、意大利和法蘭西這三個民族曾
經用人的名字來總結和命名時代，使這些時代
具有某種人的品格。我們說，培里克利時代，
奧古斯都[1]時代，列奧十世[2]時代，路易十四
時代，伏爾泰時代。這些稱號有重大的意義。
只有希臘、意大利和法蘭西民族享有以人物來
命名時代的特權，這正是文明的最高標誌。在
伏爾泰之前，只有以某國元首來命名時代的先
例。伏爾泰比國家元首更高，他是各派思想的
元首，一個新的紀元以伏爾泰開始。從此我們
感到，最高的統治力量就是讓一切被理性思考。
文明曾服從於武力，以後，文明將服從於思想。
王杖和寶劍折斷了，光明取而代之。這就是說，
權威已經變換為自由。自此以往，高於一切的
是人民的法律和個人的良心。作為一個人，我
們要行使權利；作為一個公民，我們要克盡職
責。對於我們每一個人來說，這兩方面的進步
是明確分開的。

（1）古羅馬皇帝。

（2）羅馬教皇。

. . .

. . . Let us turn toward that great death, toward that great life, toward that great spirit. Let us bend before the venerated sepulcher. Let us take counsel of him whose life, useful to men, was extinguished a hundred years ago, but whose work is immortal. Let us take counsel of the other powerful thinkers, the auxiliaries of this glorious Voltaire — of Jean Jacques, of Diderot, of Montesquieu. Let us give the word to those great voices. Let us top the shedding of human blood. Enough! enough! despots. Ah! barbarism persists; very well, let civilization be indignant. Let the Eighteenth century come to the help of the Nineteenth. The philosopher our predecessors, are the apostles of true; let us invoke those illustrious shades; let them, before monarchies meditating war, proclaim the right of man to life, the right of conscience to liberty, the sovereighty of reason, the holiness of labor, the blessedness of peace; and since night issues from the thrones, let light come from the tombs.

……

……我們要面向伏爾泰那偉大的死亡，偉大的生命和偉大的精神。讓我們在他神聖的墓前鞠躬致敬。他在一百年前與世長辭，但他曾造福人類因而永垂不朽，讓我們向他請教吧。讓我們也向其他偉大的思想家請教，向讓·雅克[1]、狄德羅和孟德斯鳩請教，他們是光榮的伏爾泰的輔翼者。讓我們與這些偉大的聲音共鳴。讓我們在人類所流的血上再加上我們自己的血吧。夠了！夠了！暴君們。既然野蠻冥頑不化。好吧，讓文明激起義憤吧，讓十八世紀來幫助十九世紀吧。我們的先驅哲人都是真理的倡導者。讓我們喚起那些光輝的亡靈，請他們在策劃戰爭的君主們面前公開宣佈人類生存的權利，艮知爭取自由的權利。請他們宣佈理性支配一切；宣佈勞動神聖；宣佈和平應受到祝福。既然黑暗來自帝王的寶座，讓墳墓中放出光明吧！

（1）即盧梭。

53 On the Cultivation of the Imagination

George Joachim Goschen

I address these words in favor of the cultivation of the imagination to the poorest and most humble in the same way that I address them to the wealthiest and those who have the best prospects in life. I will try not to make the mistake which doctors commit when they recommend patients in receipt of two pounds a week to have recourse to champagne and a short residence at the seaside.

In what sense, then, do I use the word "imagination"? Johnson's dictionary shall answer. I wish you particularly to note the answer Johnson gives as regards the meaning of "imagination." He defines it as "the power of forming ideal pictures"; "the power of representing absent thing to ourselves and to others."

Such is the power which I am going to ask you, confidently, to cultivate in your schools, by your libraries at home, by every influence which I can gain for the cause; and I hope I shall be able to carry you with me and show you why you should cultivate that power. I repeat it is the power of forming ideal pictures and of representing absent things to yourselves and to others. That is the sense in which I shall use the word

五十三　論想象力的培養

喬治・喬埃金・戈申

我的講話是主張培養想象力。我的話既是對那些最富足的、前程遠大的人說的，也是對最貧窮最卑微的人說的。我要努力不犯一些醫生有時會犯的錯誤，那就是他們向每週收入兩鎊的病人建議喝香檳酒和到海濱作短期休養[1]。

那麼，我是從什麼意義上使用"想象力"這個字呢？約翰遜字典上有答案。我希望你們特別注意約翰遜如何解說"想象力"一詞。他對"想象力"下的定義是"構想出理想圖畫的能力"；"向自己或他人描述不在眼前的事物的能力。"

這就是我要求你們在學校中、在家庭藏書室裏以及用一切我能得到的手段影響你們去培養的能力，我確信這是做得到的；我希望我能引導你們，並向你們說清楚爲什麼應該培養這種能力。我重複一遍，這是構想出理想的圖畫以及向你們自己和他人描述不在眼前的事物的能力。我在下面的講話使用"想象力"這個字

戈申（1831～1907），英國政治家，曾任國會議員、駐土耳其大使、愛丁堡大學校長等職。本文爲他1877年在利物浦學院所作的演說詞。

（1）香檳酒和海濱休養都要昂貴的花費。

"imagination" in the course of my address.

Now follow out this thought and I think I can make my meaning clear. Absent things! Take history. History deals with the things of the past. They are absent in a sense, from your minds — that is to say you cannot see them; but the study of history qualifies you and strengthens your capacity for understanding things that are not present to you, and thus I wish to recommend history to you as a most desirable course of study.

Then again take foreign countries — travels. Here again you have matters which are absent, in the physical sense, from you; but the study of travels will enable you to realize things that are absent to your own minds. And as for the power of forming ideal pictures, there I refer you to poets, dramatists, and imaginative writers, to the great literature of all times and of all countries. Such studies as these will enable you to live, and to move, and to think, in a world different from the narrow world by which you are surrounded. These studies will open up to you sources of amusement which, I think I may say, will often rise into happiness.

. . .

時，就具有這樣的含義。

沿着這條思路，我相信可以把我的意思講清楚。不在眼前的事物是什麼呢？例如歷史就是了。歷史講的是過去的事情。從某一意義來說歷史並不存在你腦中——那就是說，你不能親眼看見過去的事情；但是學習歷史使你得到並增強理解不在眼前的事物的能力。因此我願向你們推薦歷史科，那是一門最值得學習的課程。

又例如各種外國遊記。這又是一些不在你身旁的事物，因為你觸摸不到它們。但閱讀各種遊記會使你認識那些不存在於你自己腦中的事物。至於構想出理想圖畫的能力，我建議你們請教詩人、戲劇家和想象力豐富的作家，閱讀一切時代一切國家的偉大文學作品。這種學習能夠令你們在一個新天地中生活、活動與思考，這天地有別於你們現在身處的狹小世界。這種學習會給你開闢各種新的樂趣源泉，這種樂趣，我可以說，往往會上升為幸福。

……

54 The Scholar in a Republic

Wendell Phillips

. . .

We all agree in the duty of scholars to help those less favored in life, and that this duty of scholars to educate the mass is still more imperative in a republic, since a republic trusts the state wholly to the intelligence and moral sense of the people. The experience of the last forty years shows every man that law has no atom of strength, either in Boston or New Orleans, unless, and only so far as, public opinion indorses it, and that your life, goods, and good name rest on the moral sense, self-respect, and law-abiding mood of the men that walk the streets, and hardly a whit on the provisions of the statute book. Come, any one of you, outside of the ranks of popular men, and you will not fail to find it so. Easy men dream that we live under a government of law. Absurd mistake! we live under a government of men and newspapers. Your first attempt to stem dominant and keenly cherished opinions will reveal this to you.

But what is education? Of course it is not book learning. Book learning does not make five per cent of that mass of common sense that "runs" the world, transacts its business, secures its progress, trebles its power over nature, works out in the long run a rough average justice, wears away the world's restraints, and

---

菲立普斯（ 1811～1884 ），生於美國波士頓，著
名的廢奴主義者和演說家。本文爲1881年 6 月30日在

五十四 論共和國的學者

溫德爾‧菲立普斯

……

我們都同意有學識的人有責任幫助那些生活中不甚得志的人。在一個共和國中，有學識的人負責教育羣衆的任務則更爲緊迫，因爲一個共和國的國家命運完全取決於人民掌握知識的程度和道德感。過去四十年的經驗告訴每一個人，不論在波士頓或是新奧爾良，若是沒有公衆輿論的支持，法律是沒有絲毫力量的。你的生活、貨財、令譽，全都得依靠普通老百姓的道德感，依靠他們的自重和守法精神，一點也不能依靠什麼法典條例。你們當中任何一人，只要走出普通人的行列，便不會看不到這種情況。圖安逸的人夢想我們在法律治理下生活，眞是荒謬絕倫！殊不知我們是在人和報紙的治理下生活。只要你試圖去違反一下那佔支配地位的人們一致持有的輿論，你就會明白這一點。

但是什麼是教育呢？那當然不是書本知識。在所謂"管理世界"，處理世界上各種事務，保證世界進步，幾倍地增加世界征服自然的力量，使世界從長遠來看大體能執法公正，逐漸消滅束縛世界的羈絆，卸下世界的重擔──從

──────────

哈佛大學全國優秀生聯誼會成立百周年紀念會上的講話。

lifts off its burdens. The ideal Yankee, who "has more brains in his hand than others have in their skulls," is not a scholar; and two thirds of the inventions that enable France to double the world's sunshine, and make Old and New England the workshops of the world, did not come from colleges or from minds trained in the schools of science, but struggled up, forcing their way against giant obstacles, from the irrepressible instinct of untrained natural power. Her workshops, not her colleges, made England, for a while, the mistress of the world; and the hardest job her workman had was to make Oxford willing he should work his wonders.

So of moral gains. As shrewd an observer as Governor Marcy, of New York, often said he cared nothing for the whole press of the seaboard, representing wealth and education (he meant book learning), if it set itself against the instincts of the people. Lord Brougham, in a remarkable comment on the life of Romilly, enlarges on the fact that the great reformer of the penal law found all the legislative and all the judicial power of England, its colleges and its bar, marshaled against him, and owed his success, *as all such reforms do*, says his lordship, to public meetings and popular instinct. It would be no exaggeration to say that government itself began in usurpation, in the feudalism of the soldier and the bigotry of the priest; that liberty and civilization are only fragments of rights wrung from the

事上述活動所需要的大量普通知識中，書本知識所佔的比例還不到百分之五。理想的美國人，"雙手比別人的大腦更善於思考"，他們並不是學者；使法國能夠把照在世上的陽光增加一倍，使新、舊英格蘭成為世界工廠的這些發明，其中三分之二不是由大學裏的人或是科學院校訓練出來的人發明的，而是由那些未經訓練的自然力量，他們那不可抑制的本能，通過艱苦奮鬥，排除巨大障礙而發明得來的。那是英國的工廠而不是她的大學，使得英國一度成為世界霸主。英國勞動者最艱難的事情是使牛津大學同意創造奇蹟。

道德精神上的成就亦是如此。像紐約州長馬西那樣精明的觀察家便常常說，如果沿海的出版界與人民本能對立的話，他將對代表着財富和教育（他指書本知識）的整個沿海地區出版界不屑一顧。勃拉哈姆爵士[1]在對洛米里一生的重要評論中，詳述了這位偉大的刑法改革者在世時如何遭到了英國所有立法和司法權力機構，和各學會、社團的一致反對。勃拉哈姆爵士說，正如一切改革一樣，洛米里的成功全靠公共會議和羣眾本能的支持。如果說政府始於篡奪、軍人的封建主義和教士的偏執，並不算過甚其詞；如果說自由與文明不過是從有錢

（1）撒母耳·勃拉哈姆（1757～1818），英國的法律
　　改革家。

strong hands of wealth and book learning. Almost all the great truths relating to society were not the result of scholarly meditation, "having up wisdom with each curious year," but have been first heard in the solemn protests of martyred patriotism and the loud cries of crushed and starving labor. When common sense and the common people have stereotyped a principle into a statute, then bookmen come to explain how it was discovered and on what ground it rests. The world makes history, and scholars write it, — one half truly and the other half as their prejudices blur and distort it.

. . .

Hence, I do not think the greatest things have been done for the world by its bookmen. Education is not the chips of arithmetic and grammar, — nouns, verbs, and the multiplication table; neither is it that last year's almannac of dates, or series of lies agreed upon, which we so often mistake for history. Education is not Greek and Latin and the air pump. Still, I rate at its full value the training we get in these walls. Though what we actually carry away is little enough, we do get some training of our powers, as the gymnast or the fencer does of his muscles; we go hence also with such general knowledge of what mankind has agreed to consider proved and settled, that we know where to reach for the weapon when we need it.

. . .

人和讀書人有力的手中強奪過來的權利碎片，
也不算過份。幾乎一切關係到社會的偉大眞
理，都不是那種" 年復一年地求索探尋，積聚
起才識和智慧"[1]的學究式冥思默想結果，而
是最先發自奮鬥犧牲的愛國者的莊嚴抗議聲和
遭受壓迫、忍餓受餓的勞動者的大聲疾呼。
當普通常識和普通人把一項原則制成法律條文
時，文人學者便出來解釋這條文的來歷及依據。
世界創造歷史，學者把歷史寫下來── 一半眞
實，另一半却因學者的偏見而被塗汚或歪曲。

......

因此，我不認爲世界上最偉大的事業是文
人學者做出來的。教育不是算術和語法的零星
知識──名詞、動詞和乘法表；也不是去年的年
鑑，更不是我們常誤認爲是歷史而其實只是人
們一致認同的一系列謊言。教育不是希臘文、
拉丁文和空氣泵。但是，我仍然充分肯定在校園
墻內所受的訓練的價值。儘管我們事實上從學
校得到的很有限，但學校還是訓練了我們的才
能，正如體育家和劍擊家使他們的肌肉得到訓
練一樣。有了這種人類認爲已得到證實和有了
定論的一般知識，我們在鬥爭中需要武器時，
便知道從什麼地方去取得。

......

────────────

（1）這是拜倫《恰爾德·哈羅爾德游記》第三篇中的
第 996 行詩句。

55 Education for the Peasantry in France

Leon Gambetta

The peasantry is intellectually several centuries behind the enlightened and educated classes in the country. The distance between them and us is immense. We have received a classical or scientific education — even the imperfect one of our day. We have learned to read our history, to speak our language, while (a cruel thing to say) so many of our countrymen can only babble! Ah! that peasant, bound as he is to the tillage of the soil, who bravely carries the burden of his day, with no other consolation than that of leaving to his children the paternal fields, perhaps increased an acre in extent; all his passions, joys, and fears concentrated in the fate of his patrimony. Of the external world, of the society in which he lives, he apprehends only legends and rumors. He is the prey of the cunning and fraudulent. He strikes, without knowing it, the bosom of the revolution, his benefactress; he gives loyally his taxes and his blood to a society for which he feels fear as much as respect. But there his role ends, and if you speak to him of principles, he knows nothing of them.

It is to the peasantry, then, that we must address ourselves. We must raise and instruct them. Epithets which partizans have bandied of "rurality" and "rural chamber" must not become the cause of injustice. It

五十五　論法國農民教育

里昂・甘貝塔

我國農民在文化知識方面比其他受過教育有文化的階級落後了幾個世紀。他們和我們之間距離很大。我們曾接受文藝的或科學的教育；雖則我們那時代的教育還不算完善。我們學會讀歷史，學會了使用語言說話。然而，說來痛心，我們的同胞竟有這麼多人連話也說不清楚！啊，農民儘管終年勞碌，從事耕作，却任勞任怨，肩負起每日勞作的重擔，唯一的安慰就是把祖傳那點土地留給子孫，最好能再增添一分半畝。他們的所有熱情、歡樂與畏懼都圍繞着這份祖傳產業的命運。對於外界社會，他聽到的只是些街談巷議，鄉里傳聞。他受害於奸詐狡猾之徒。他不自覺地打擊了使他受惠的革命，却忠心耿耿地向他既敬且畏的社會交上自己的血汗和租稅。但他的作用也就到此為止了，如果你和他談原則，他會茫茫然一無所知。

因此，我們必須着手為農民做一些工作。我們要喚起他們，教育他們。黨內[1]不少人譏誚地談論"鄉土氣"和"鄉村議院"。這類字

甘貝塔（1838～1882），法國政治家，曾任內政部長、衆議院院長、總理、外交部長等職。
（1）指當時的共和派。

is to be wished that there were a "rural chamber" in the profound and true sense of the term; for it is not with hobble-de-hoys that a "rural chamber" can be made, but with enlightened and free peasants who are able to represent themselves. Instead of becoming a cause of raillery, this reproach of a "rural chamber" should be a tribute rendered to the progress of the civilization of the masses. This new social force should be utilized for the general welfare.

Unfortunately we have not yet reached that point. Progress will be denied us as long as the French democracy fail to demonstrate that if we would remake our country, if we would bring back her grandeur, her power, and her genius, it is of vital interest to her superior classes to elevate and emancipate this people of workers, who hold in reserve a force still virgin but able to develop inexhaustible treasures of activity and aptitude. We must learn and then teach the peasant what he owes to Society and what he has the right to ask of her.

On the day when it shall be well understood that we have no grander or more pressing work; that we should put aside and postpone all other reforms; that we have but one task — the instruction of the people, the diffusion of education, the encouragement of science — on that day a great step will have then taken in our regeneration. But our action needs to be a double one, that it may bear upon the body as well as the mind. To be exact, each man should be intelligent, trained not only to think, read, and reason, but made able to act and fight. Everywhere beside the teacher we should

眼不應當成為貶義詞，要是有一個真實而深刻意義的＂鄉村議院＂，那正是我們求之不得的。因為並非幾個少不更事的年輕人就能組成＂鄉村議院＂，而是要由有知識的，能代表他們自己的自由農民才能組成。這種對於所謂＂鄉村議院＂的批評，不但不應引起嘲笑，相反，應該使之轉變為對於大眾文明進步的禮讚。這種新的社會力量應該用來謀求普遍的福利。

不幸的是，我們還沒有做到這一點。假如我們要改造我們的國家，要恢復我國的尊嚴和威力，恢復她的民族精神，最重要的是上層階級喚起並解放勞動者。這些勞動者蘊含着一股潛在力量，一經開發，便會成為活力與才能的無盡寶藏。如果法國民主不能表明這一點，那麼我們就不會得到進步。我們要自己懂得，並教育農民使他們懂得他們對社會負有何等責任，使他們懂得他們有權向社會要求些什麼。

如果有一天大家都能理解到我們沒有其他更崇高更緊迫的工作，我們應該把其他一切改革先放下，我們只有一項任務，就是教育人民、普及知識、倡導科學。這一天到來之時，便是我們在重建法國的任務上邁進一大步之日。然而我們必須同時採取兩方面的行動，既要注意智力訓練又要注意體力訓練。準確地說，就是每個人不僅應該學到知識，學會思考、閱讀和邏輯推理，而且應該能行動與戰鬥。在任何

place the gymnast and the soldier, to the end that our children, our soldiers, our fellow citizens, may be able to hold a sword, to carry a gun on a long march, to sleep under the canopy of the stars, to support valiantly all the hardships demanded of a patriot. We must push to the front education. Otherwise we only make a success of letters, but do not create a bulwark of patriots.

. . .

地方，除教師之外，還應有體育家和軍人，使我們的兒童、兵士與公民都能夠拿起刀劍，扛起槍桿，長途跋涉，餐風宿露，勇敢地應付愛國者可能遇到的一切艱難困苦。我們必須將教育推廣到前線去。否則，我們就只能在文學上有所成就，不能築起一道由愛國者組成的鋼鐵長城。

......

56 Speech at the Graveside of Karl Marx

Friederich Engels

On the 14th of March, at a quarter to three in the afternoon, the greatest living thinker ceased to think. He had been left alone for scarcely two minutes, and when we came back we found him in his armchair, peacefully gone to sleep — but forever.

. . .

Just as Darwin discovered the law of development of organic nature, so Marx discovered the law of development of human history, the simple fact, hitherto concealed by an overgrowth of ideology, that mankind must first of all eat, drink, have shelter and clothing, before it can pursue politics, science, art, religion, etc.; that, therefore the production of the immediate material means of subsistence and consequently the degree of economic development attained by a given people or during a given epoch form the foundation upon which the state institutions, the legal conceptions, art, and even the ideas on religion, of the people concerned have been evolved, and in the light of which they must, therefore, be explained, instead of vice versa, as had hitherto been the case.

But that is not all. Marx also discovered the special law of motion governing the present-day capitalist mode of production and the bourgeois society that this mode of production has created. The discovery of surplus value suddenly threw light on the problem, in

五十六 在馬克思墓前的講話

弗里德里希・恩格斯

3月14日下午兩點三刻，當代最偉大的思想家停止思想了。讓他一個人留在房裏總共不過兩分鐘，我們再進去的時候，發現他在安樂椅上安詳地睡着了——永遠地睡着了。

……

正如達爾文發現有機自然界的發展規律一樣，馬克思發現了人類歷史的發展規律，即歷來爲繁茂蕪雜的意識形態所掩蓋着的一個簡單事實：人們首先必須吃、喝、住、穿，然後才能從事政治、科學、藝術、宗教等等；所以，生產直接與生活有關的物質用品，會爲一個民族或一個時代帶來一定的經濟發展，這兩者又構成了國家制度、法制觀念、藝術以至宗教思想的基礎。因此，我們必須從這個方向來解釋上述種種觀念和思想，而不是依隨那一直以來的相反方向。

不僅如此，馬克思還發現了現代資本主義生產方式和由此產生的資產階級社會的特殊運動規律。剩餘價值的發現，使前此一切資產階

馬克思（1818～1883）和恩格斯（1820～1895），馬克思主義的創始人。這是恩格斯1883年3月17日在倫敦海格特公墓安葬馬克思時的講話。

trying to solve which all previous investigations, of both bourgeois economists and socialist critics, had been groping in the dark.

Two such discoveries would be enough for one lifetime. Happy the man to whom it is granted to make even one such discovery. But in every single field which Marx investigated — and he investigated very many field, none of them superficially — in every field, even in that of mathematics, he made independent discoveries.

. . .

For Marx was before all else a revolutionist. His real mission in life was to contribute, in one way or another, to the overthrow of capitalist society and of the state institutions which it had brought into being, to contribute to the liberation of the modern proletariat, which *he* was the first to make conscious of its own position and its needs, conscious of the conditions of its emancipation. Fighting was his element. And he fought with a passion, a tenacity and a success such as few could rival. His work on the first *Rheinische Zeitung* (1842), the *Paris Vorwarts* (1844), the *Deutsche Brusseler Zeitung* (1847), the *Neue Rheinische Zeitung* (1848–49), the *New York Tribune* (1852–61), and in addition to these a host of militant pamphlets, work in organizations in Paris, Brussels and London, and finally, crowning all, the formation of the great International Working Men's Association — this was indeed an achievement of which its founder might well have been proud even if he had done nothing else.

級經濟學家和社會主義批評家在黑暗中摸索、探求的問題豁然開朗，得到解決。

一生中能有這樣的兩項發現，該是很夠了。甚至只要能有一項這樣的發現，也已經是幸福的了。但是馬克思在他所研究的每一個領域，甚至是數學方面，都有獨到的發現。他研究的領域很廣，其中沒有一個領域他是膚淺地研究的。

……

馬克思始終以革命事業為首。他畢生的真正使命是以各種方式參加推翻資本主義社會及其國家制度，協助現代無產階級得到解放。這些現代無產階級有賴馬克思才第一次意識到自身的地位和需求，意識到自身的解放條件。鬥爭是他的基本精神。他鬥爭時所具的熱忱、頑強精神和成就，無人能及。他最早參與《萊茵報》（1842年）[1]、巴黎《前進報》（1844年）、《德意志-布魯塞爾報》（1847年）、《新萊茵報》（1848～1849年）、《紐約每日論壇報》（1852～1861年）等報紙，以及許多富有戰鬥性的小冊子的工作，其後參與巴黎、布魯塞爾和倫敦各組織的工作，最後創立了偉大的國際工人協會[2]。作為這協會的始創人，即使別的

（1）德國科倫出版的報紙，1943年被政府查封。

（2）即第一國際，1864年秋由馬克思創立，鞏固各國工人的團結。

And, consequently, Marx was the best hated and most calumniated man of his time. Governments, both absolutist and republican, deported him from their territories. Bourgeois, whether conservative or ultra-democratic, vied with one another in heaping slanders upon him. All this he brushed aside as though it were cobweb, ignoring it, answering only when extreme necessity compelled him. And he died beloved, revered and mourned by millions of revolutionary fellow workers — from the mines of Siberia to California, in all parts of Europe and America — and I make bold to say that though he may have had many opponents he had hardly one personal enemy.

His name will endure through the ages, and so also will his work!

什麼也沒有做，也足夠以此成果引爲自豪了。

正因爲這樣，馬克思成爲當代最遭嫉恨和最受誣蔑的人。各國政府，無論是專制政府或共和政府都驅逐他；無論保守派或極端民主派的資產者，都紛紛爭先恐後地誹謗他，詛咒他。他對這一切毫不在意，把它們當做蛛絲一樣輕輕抹去，只是在萬分必要時才作答覆。現在他逝世了，在整個歐洲和美洲，從西伯利亞礦井到加利福尼亞，千百萬革命工人戰友無不對他表示尊敬、愛戴和悼念。我敢大膽地說：他可能有許多敵人，但却難得一個私敵。

他的英名和事業將永垂不朽！

57 Gladstone, England's Greatest Leader

Whitelaw Reid

Gentlemen: — I am pleased to see that since this toast was sent me by your committee, it has been proof read. As it came to me, it describes Mr. Gladstone as England's greatest Liberal leader. I thought you might well say that and more. It delights me to find that you have said more — that you have justly described him as England's greatest leader. ("Hear! Hear!") I do not forget that other, always remembered when Gladstone is mentioned, who educated his party till it captured its opponents' place by first disguising and then adopting their measures. That was in its way as brilliant party leadership as the century has seen, and it placed an alien adventurer in the British peerage and enshrined his name in the grateful memory of a great party that vainly looks for Disraeli's successor. (Applause.) . . .

But this man whom you toast honors, after a career that might have filled any man's ambition, became the head of the Empire whose morning drumbeat heralds the rising sun on its journey round the world. That

---

里德（1837～1912），美國記者、外交家。本文爲1886年在紐約市愛爾蘭裔美國人舉行的晚餐會上的講話。

威廉‧愛華德‧格拉斯頓（William Ewart Gladstone, 1809～1898），英國政治家。1868～1894

五十七　英國最偉大的領導人格拉斯頓

懷德羅・里德

各位先生：我很高興，祝詞是由你們委員會送給我的，說明委員會已經批准這篇祝詞了。祝詞把格拉斯頓先生稱爲英國最偉大的自由黨領袖。我認爲你們那樣說，不但不過份，而且還不夠。使我高興的是，你們確實不但稱他爲最偉大的自由黨領袖，而且還很公正地稱他爲英國最偉大的領袖。（對啊！對啊！）我沒有忘記另外的那一位，提到格拉斯頓時，我總會記起他[1]。他教會了他的黨先把他們的各項議案僞裝起來，然後通過，以此攫取對手的地位。這是本世紀領導黨派的一種絕妙手法，這種辦法把一個外國冒險家[2]提升到了英國貴族的地位，使他的名字感恩戴德地放在那個大黨的記憶神龕中。這個黨在代斯雷里之後，後繼無人了。（鼓掌）……

但是你們在這篇祝詞中頌揚的這個人，在經歷了一段可以滿足任何人野心的政治生涯以後，成了英帝國的首腦。這個日不落帝國每天以晨鐘迎來東升的旭日。他冒了風險，丟了職

年爲英國自由黨領袖，推行不少開明的改革。

（1）指代斯雷里（Benjamin Disraeli），曾任英國首相，保守黨領袖，格拉斯頓的政敵。

（2）代斯雷里的父祖是猶太人，故稱他爲外國冒險家。

place he risked and lost, and risked again to give to an illtreated powerless section of the Empire, not even friendly to his sway, *Church Reform, Educational Reform, Land Reform, Liberty!* (Cheers.) It was no sudden impulse and it is no short or recent record. It is more than seventeen years since Mr. Gladstone secured for Ireland the boon of disestablishment. It is nearly as long since he carried the first bill recognizing and seriously endeavoring to remedy the evils of Irish land tenure.

He has rarely been able to advance as rapidly or as far as he wished; and more than once he has gone by a way that few of us liked. But if he was not always right, he has been courageous enough to set himself right. If he made a mistake in our affairs when he said Jefferson Davis had founded a nation, he offered reparation when he secured the Geneva Arbitration, and loyally paid its award. If he made a mistake in Irish affairs in early attempts at an unwise coercion he more than made amends when he led that recent magnificent struggle in Parliament and before the English people, which ended in a defeat, it is true, but a defeat more

---

（ 1 ）指愛爾蘭。

（ 2 ）英國法律規定愛爾蘭天主教教會必須向英格蘭教
會納稅。格拉斯頓力爭下，此法於1869年廢除。

（ 3 ）指格拉斯頓在第一、二任首相期間通過的愛爾蘭位，又再次冒着風險為英帝國中這個無權而又受到不公正待遇的地區[1]——雖則這地區並不支持他當政——爭取宗教改革、教育改革和土地改革，爭取自由！（歡呼）他這樣做並非出於一時衝動，也不是近期才開始的了。格拉斯頓為愛爾蘭爭取得廢除向英格蘭教會納稅[2]已經不止十七年了。他努力使第一個租佃法案[3]得到通過，承認而且認真彌補了英格蘭地主佔有愛爾蘭土地的罪過。他在這方面的努力，也有同樣長的時間了。

他的工作很少按照他希望的速度進行，也很少能達到預期的結果；他的作法有時不為我們所取。但是如果說他不是一貫正確，他却總有足夠的勇氣糾正自己的錯誤。如果說他在我們美國的問題上犯過錯誤，說杰弗遜戴維斯建立了一個國家，但是後來他却恪守了日內瓦裁決[4]，彌補了他的過失。如果說他早期在愛爾蘭問題上曾經犯過錯誤，企圖實行不明智的高壓政策，那麼他最近在英國國會上以及在英國人民面前進行的卓越鬥爭，已經彌補他的錯誤有餘了。不錯，這次鬥爭以失敗告終，但是這

————————————

土地改革法案。

（4）美國內戰期間，英國破壞了美國若干商船。1871～1872年為此在日內瓦舉行談判，英國同意賠償美國的損失。

brilliant than many victories and more hopeful for Ireland. (Applause.)

. . .

More than any other statesman of his epoch, he has combined practical skill in the conduct of politics with a steadfast appeal to the highest moral considerations. To a leader of that sort defeats are only stepping-stones, and the end is not in doubt. A phrase once famous among us has sometimes seemed to me fit for English use about Ireland. A great man, a very great man, whose name sheds lasting honor upon our city, said in an impulsive moment — that he "never wanted to live in a country where the one half was pinned to the other by bayonets." If Mr. Gladstone ever believed in thus fastening Ireland to England, he has learned a more excellent way. Like Greeley he would no doubt at the last fight, if need be, for the territorial integrity of his country. But he has learned the lesson Charles James Fox taught nearly a hundred years before: "The more Ireland is under Irish government, the more she will be bound to English interests." That precept he has been trying to reduce to practice. God grant the old statesman life and light to see the sure end of the work he has begun! (Loud applause.)

（ 1 ）指下文的格里萊。

（ 2 ）賀拉斯・格里萊（ Horace　Greeley,　1811 ～

1872)，美國《紐約論壇報》的創始人，激進的

種失敗比許多勝利更爲光榮，它給愛爾蘭帶來
更多的希望（鼓掌）。

......

　　比起同時代其他任何政治家，他更能把政
治行爲的實踐技巧和高度道德標準的堅定要求
結合起來。對於那樣的領袖人物，失敗只不過
是前進的階梯，最後勝利是無庸置疑的。在我
們當中一度傳誦過一句名言，有時候我覺得英
國人用來談論愛爾蘭也很適合。一位偉大的、
十分偉大的人，他[1]的英名永遠光耀我們的城
市，曾在一個激動人心的時刻說過，他“決不
住在用刺刀把各人釘在一起的國家裏。”即使
格拉斯頓先生曾經認爲愛爾蘭應該這樣附着英
格蘭，他也懂得用更好的方式。像格里萊[2]一
樣，如有需要，他肯定會爲國家的領土統一而
戰鬥到底。但是，格拉斯頓記住了查爾斯·詹
姆士·伐斯[3]將近一百年前的教導：“愛爾蘭
愈是由自己的政府管理就愈於英國有利。”格
拉斯頓一直致力於這句格言的實現。願上帝賜
給這位老政治家生命與光明，使他能看到他所
開創的業績得到完成！（熱烈鼓掌）

廢奴主義者。

（3）伐斯（1749～1806），英國的開明政治家，英王
　　喬治三世時任外交大臣。

58　War and Armaments in Europe

Otto von Bismarck

. . .

Since the great war of 1870 was concluded has there been any year, I ask you, without its alarm of war? Just as we were returning, at the beginning of the seventies, they said: When will we have the next war? When will the "revanche" be fought? In five years at latest. They said to us then: "The question of whether we will have war, and of the success with which we shall have it (it was a representative of the center who upbraided me with it in the Reichstag), depends today only on Russia. Russia alone has the decision in her hands."

In these days we must be as strong as we can; and if we will, we can be stronger than any other country of equal resources in the world. And it would be a crime not to use our resources. If we do not need an army prepared for war, we do not need to call for it. It depends merely on the not very important question of the cost — and it is not very important, though I mention it incidentally. When I say that we must strive continually to be ready for all emergencies, I advance the proposition that, on account of our geographical posi-

---

俾斯麥（1815~1898），全名爲鄂圖・愛德華・萊奧波德・馮・俾斯麥（Otto Eduard Leopold von Bismarck），出身貴族，德國國王威廉一世的首相。他擁護君主主義，力主以武力鎮壓革命，有"鐵血宰

五十八 歐洲的戰爭與戰備

鄂圖·馮·俾斯麥

......

　　試問，自從1870年的大戰結束以來，哪一年不曾有過戰爭的警報？就在七十年代初我們結束戰爭[1]回來的時候，他們就已經說了：我們什麼時候再開戰？什麼時候我們與"復仇之師"？最遲不過五年。當時他們對我們說："我們是否會發生戰爭以及能否取得勝利（這正是中間派一位代表在國會上用來責備我的話），現今完全取決於俄國了。唯有俄國手裏掌握着決定權。"

　　在現在這種時刻，我們必須盡力壯大自己。只要我們願意，我們就能比世界上有着同樣資源的任何國家更加強大。因此，不利用我們的資源就是一種罪過。如果我們不需要一支隨時可作戰的軍隊，我們就無需建立一支軍隊。這事只取決於並不十分重要的費用問題。費用問題的確無關重要，我只是順帶提提而已。我說我們必須繼續努力，以便應付一切緊急情況。鑑於我國的特殊地理位置，爲了達到上述目的，

相"之稱。本文是他1888年在德國國會上發表的演說。

（1）指1870年至1871年的普法戰爭，法國在這次戰爭敗於德國。

287

tion, we must make greater efforts than other powers would be obliged to make in view of the same ends. We lie in the middle of Europe. We have at least three fronts on which we can be attacked. France has only an eastern boundary; Russia only its western, exposed to assault. We are, moreover, more exposed than any other people to the danger of hostile coalition because of our geographical position, and because, perhaps, of the feeble power of cohesion which, until now, the German people has exhibited when compared with others. At any rate, God has placed us in a position where our neighbors will prevent us from falling into a condition of sloth — of wallowing in the mire of mere existence.

The bill will bring us an increase of troops capable of bearing arms a possible increase, which, if we do not need it, we need not call out, but can leave the men at home. But we will have it ready for service if we have arms for it. And that is a matter of primary importance. I remember the carbine which was furnished by England to our landwehr in 1813, and with which I had some practise as a hunter — that was no weapon for a soldier. We can get arms suddenly for an emergency, but if we have them ready for it, then this bill will count for a strengthening of our peace forces and a reenforcement of the peace league as great as if a fourth great power had joined the alliance with an army of seven hundred thousand men — the greatest yet put in the field.

. . .

I am never for an offensive war, and if war can come only through our initiative, it will not begin. Fire must be kindled by some one before it can burn, and we will not kindle it. Neither the consciousness of our strength,

我建議我們必須作出比其他大國家更大的努力才行。我國位於歐洲中部。我們至少在三條邊界綫上可能受到襲擊。法國和俄國分別只有東部和西部是無掩護的國界。由於我們的地理位置，或許加上直到現在德國人民所顯示的團結力量比其他民族薄弱，使我們比任何其他國家的人民更直接地受到敵對聯盟國家的威脅。不管怎麼說，上帝已經把我們放在這樣一個地位，我們的鄰里不允許我們稍有懈怠，不允許我們在只求苟存的泥潭中打滾。

這項法案將增加我國能隨時武裝起來的士兵數目。在我們不用增加士兵人數時，增加的士兵無需徵集入伍，可以在家安居樂業。一旦我們有了足夠武器，他們就隨時可以裝備起來。武器是頭等重要的事，我還記得1813年英國供給我國後備軍的卡賓槍，我用那些槍打過獵，那不是軍人用的武器。當然，遇有緊急情況，我們可以很快地得到武器，但如果我們現在能準備好，這項法案就能加強我們的和平力量，也能給予和平聯盟以强大的支援。那就簡直有如一個擁有七十萬軍隊的第四强國加入聯盟。這是迄今在戰場上最大的隊伍。

......

我從不主張侵略戰爭。我們決不發動戰爭。火必須有人去燃點才會燃燒，我們決不去點火。無論我們怎樣意識清楚上述自己的力量，也無

as I have just represented it, nor the trust in our alliances, will prevent us from continuing with our accustomed zeal and our accustomed efforts to keep the peace. We will not allow ourselves to be led by bad temper; we will not yield to prejudice. . . .

We Germans fear God, and nothing else in the world.

It is the fear of God which makes us love peace and keep it. He who breaks it against us ruthlessly will learn the meaning of the warlike love of the Fatherland which in 1813 rallied to the standard the entire population of the then small and weak kingdom of Prussia; he will learn, too, that this patriotism is now the common property of the entire German nation, so that whoever attacks Germany will find it unified in arms, every warrior having in his heart the steadfast faith that God will be with us.

論我們相信盟國多麼可靠，都不會因此而妨礙我們以固有的熱忱與努力去繼續保衛和平。我們不會意氣用事，也不會衝動偏激。……

我們德國人除了上帝之外，不畏懼世界上任何人！

正是由於我們敬畏上帝，所以我們熱愛和平，保衛和平。誰要是殘忍地破壞我們的和平，他就會受到教訓，知道我們德國人的尚武愛國感情意味着什麼！1813年，當普魯士還是一個弱小的王國時，這種精神就曾使我們全體人民一致團結在我們的國旗下。他還會知道，這種愛國主義精神現已成為全德意志民族的共同財富。因此，誰要想進攻德國，都會看到我們團結一致，武裝起來，每一個戰士都抱定上帝與我們同在的必勝信心。

59 The Race Problem in the South

Henry Woodfin Grady

. . .

Far to the south, Mr. President, separated from this section by a line, once defined in irrepressible difference, once traced in fratricidal blood, and now, thank God, but a vanishing shadow, lies the fairest and richest domain of this earth. It is the home of a brave and hospitable people. There, is centered all that can please or prosper humankind. A perfect climate above a fertile soil yields to the husbandman every product of the temperate zone. There, by night the cotten whitens beneath the stars, and by day the wheat locks the sunshine in its bearded sheaf. In the same field the clover steals the fragrance of the wind, and the tobacco catches the quick aroma of the rains. There, are mountains stored with exhaustless treasures; forests vast and primeval; and rivers that, tumbling or loitering, run wanton to the sea. Of the three essential items of all industries — cotton, iron, and wood — that region has easy control. In cotton, a fixed monopoly; in iron, proven supremacy; in timber, the reserve supply of the Republic. From this assured and permanent advantage, against which artificial conditions cannot much longer prevail, has grown an amazing system of industries.

五十九 南方的種族問題

……

主席先生，在南方的遠處，有一塊地球上最秀麗最富饒的土地，被一條界線同這個地區分開。這條界線一度標明了無法和解的矛盾，一度灑滿了兄弟相殘的鮮血，現在，感謝上帝，這界線已經漸漸消失，只留下一絲陰影了。那裏是一個勇敢而友善的民族的家園。那裏集中了人類帶來歡樂與繁榮的一切條件。那裏氣候和煦，土壤肥沃，出產溫帶的一切農產品。在那裏，雪白的棉花在星光下泛出銀光，金色的陽光在小麥的麥芒中閃耀。風吹苜蓿偷香，雨灑烟葉送馥。那裏的崇山峻嶺儲埋着無盡寶藏；原始森林廣闊無垠；江河汩汩，迤邐入海。那區域穩握整個工業必需的三要素：棉花、鐵與木材。棉花佔固定的壟斷地位，鐵礦經探明首屈一指；木材足以供應全國。由於有了這種永久固定的有利因素，雖然存在暫時的人爲不利條件，那裏已經發展起一個驚人龐大的工業體

格里底（1851～1889），美國新聞記者、編輯。本文是1889年12月13日在波士頓商會的年會宴會上的講話，說明南北戰爭結束了二十多年，美國的種族問題仍然很嚴重。

Not maintained by human contrivance of tariff or capital, afar off from the fullest and cheapest source of supply, but resting in Divine assurance, within touch of field and mine and forest; not set amid costly farms from which competition has driven the farmer in despair, but amid cheap and sunny lands, rich with agriculture, to which neither season nor soil has set a limit, — this system of industries is mounting to a splendor that shall dazzle and illumine the world.

. . .

If this does not invite your patient hearing tonight, hear one thing more. My people, your brothers in the South — brothers in blood, in destiny, in all that is best in our past and future — are so beset with this problem that their very existence depends upon its right solution. Nor are they wholly to blame for its presence. The slave ships of the Republic sailed from your ports, the slaves worked in our fields. You will not defend the traffic, nor I the institution. But I do hereby declare that in its wise and humane administration, in lifting the slave to heights of which he had not dreamed in his savage home, and giving him a happiness he has not yet found in freedom, our fathers left their sons a saving and excellent heritage. In the storm of war this institution was lost. I thank God as heartily as you do that human slavery is gone forever from the American soil.

But the freedman remains. With him a problem

系。這個工業體系不靠人為的關稅和資本來維持，更不靠充足而低廉的資源供應，而是靠神賜的保證，靠周圍的原野、礦山和森林。這個工業體系不是建立在花銷很大的農場之中（這些農場之間的競爭使農人絕望破產），而是建立在陽光充足的廉價土地之上。這些土地農產豐富，廣闊無垠，四季如春。這個工業體系日益發展，將光照人寰，舉世矚目。

……

如果我剛才的這番話提不起你們的興趣，那麼請聽我再說一點。我的人民，你們南方的兄弟——與我們共命運、共有過去與將來最美好一切的骨肉兄弟——現在正為這問題苦惱。這問題能否得到正當的解決，關係到他們的生死存在。這問題的出現並不完全是他們的過失。共和國販運奴隸的船隻從你們的港口啓航，運來的奴隸在我們的土地工作勞動。你們不會為奴隸販運申辯，我也不衛護奴隸制度。但是我要在這裏聲明，我們的祖先已把奴隸提攜到他們在野蠻故鄉時從未夢想到的高度地位，給他們享受到成為奴隸前也沒有過的幸福。我們先輩這種既明智又有人道的做法，給兒孫留下一份極寶貴的儲備遺產。奴隸制度在一場戰爭的風暴中消失了。我像你們一樣衷心地感謝上帝，人類的奴隸制已從美國國土上絕跡。

但是解放了的奴隸還在。伴隨着他們的是

without precedent or parallel. Note its appalling conditions. Two utterly dissimilar races on the same soil, with equal political and civil rights, almost equal in numbers, but terribly unequal in intelligence and responsibility, each pledged against fusion, one for a century in servitude to the other, and freed at last by a desolating war, the experiment sought by neither, but approached by both with doubt, — these are the conditions.

. . .

The resolute, clear-headed, broad-minded men of the South, the men whose genius made glorious every page of the first seventy years of American history, whose courage and fortitude you tested in five years of the fiercest war, whose energy has made bricks without straw and spread splendor amid the ashes of their war-wasted homes, — these men wear this problem in their hearts and their brains, by day and by night. They realize, as you cannot, what this problem means — what they owe to this kindly and dependent race — the measure of their debt to the world in whose despite they defended and maintained slavery. And though their feet are hindered in its undergrowth and their march encumbered with its burdens, they have lost neither the patience from which comes clearness nor the faith from which comes courage. Nor, Sir, when in passionate moments is disclosed to them that vague and

一個空前的難題。請注意這問題的驚人情況：兩個完全不同的種族生活在同一塊土地上，享有同樣的政治權利與公民權利。雙方人數大約相等，但掌握的知識與負有的責任却極不平等。雙方都竭力反對互相溶化，其中一個種族在一百年中充當另一個種族的奴隸，最後在一場毀滅性的戰爭中得到了解放。這場戰爭是雙方都不打算進行，但又帶着懷疑地採用的一個試驗。……

　　果斷的、頭腦清醒、心胸開闊的南方人，他們的天才曾經使美國開國七十年的每一頁歷史都熠熠發光，他們的勇氣與剛毅精神你們已在那最殘酷的五年戰爭[1]中考驗過，他們過人的精力曾經白手起家，在炮火餘燼、斷壁頹垣上建造起錦綉繁華的家園。這些人日日夜夜把上述的種族問題放在心中，記在腦裏。他們意識到這問題很嚴重，那是你們認識不到的。他們知道欠下這友好仁慈的從屬種族的債，他們知道全世界都仇恨奴隸制，而他們由於過去維護與保持了奴隸制，欠下世界的債有多麼深重。雖然他們的脚步在荆棘中蹒跚，他們的行進受重擔的拖累，然而他們並未因此而失去忍耐與信心。忍耐使他們頭腦清醒，信心使他們勇氣百倍。先生，即使在感情衝動的時刻，在他們

─────────────

（1）指美國的南北戰爭。

awful shadow, with its lurid abysses and its crimson stains, into which I pray God they may never go, are they struck with more of apprehension than is needed to complete their consecration!

Such is the temper of my people. But what of the Problem itself? Mr. President, we need not go one step farther unless you concede right here the people I speak for are as honest, as sensible, and as just as your people, seeking as earnestly as you would in their place, rightly to solve the problem that touches them at every vital point. If you insist that they are ruffians, blindly striving with bludgeon and shotgun to plunder and oppress a race, then I shall sacrifice my self-respect and tax your patience in vain. But admit that they are men of common sense and common honesty, wisely modifying an environment they cannot wholly disregard, guiding and controlling as best they can the vicious and irresponsible of either race, compensating error with frankness and retrieving in patience what they lose in passion, and conscious all the time that wrong means ruin, — admit this, and we may reach an understanding to-night.

. . .

心中出現地獄和殷紅血跡的模糊可怕陰影時——
我禱告上帝使他們永遠不要進去——他們也沒
有被恐怖懾服而不去為事業獻身！

　　這就是我的人民的性格。但是問題本身的
情況如何？我為他們說話的南方人民和你們的
人民一樣誠實、公正、通情達理，他們和你們
一樣具有尋求正確解決問題的熱情，而這問題
與他們息息相關。主席先生，除非你就在此承
認南方人民的上述各點，否則我們無需再說下
去了。如果你堅持要說他們是暴徒，指責他們
盲目地用棍棒與槍枝去掠奪、壓迫另一個種族，
那麼我就是白白地犧牲了我的自尊並浪費了你
們的耐性。但是如果你們承認他們是有常識和
具有一般誠實品質的人，他們正在運用智慧改
造一個他們不能完全置之不顧的環境，盡一切
努力去引導和控制兩個種族中兇惡的、不負責
任的人，坦率地承認錯誤，用耐心重新挽回感
情衝動時所失去的東西，時時刻刻意識到一着
失誤將毀去全局——如果承認這些，我們今晚
就可能達到互相諒解。

　　……

60 Work Done for Humanity

Frences E.C. Willard

I wish we were all more thorough students of the mighty past, for we should thus be rendered braver prophets of the future, and more cheerful workers in the present. History shows us with what tenacity the human race survives. Earthquake, famine, and pestilence have done their worst, but over them rolls a healing tide of years and they are lost to view; or sweeps the great procession, and hardly shows a scar. Rulers around whom clustered new forms of civilization pass away, but greater men succeed them. Nations are rooted up; great hopes seem blighted; revolutions rise and rivers run with the blood of patriots; the globe itself seems headed toward the abyss; new patriots are born; higher hopes bloom out like stars; humanity emerges from the dark ages vastly ahead of what it was on entering that cave of gloom, and ever the right comes uppermost; and now is Christ's kingdom nearer than when we first believed.

Only those who have not studied history lose heart in great reforms; only those unread in the biography of genius imagine themselves to be original. Except in the

六十　爲人類而做的工作

　　我希望我們對氣勢磅礴的過去歷史研究得
更徹底，這樣，我們對未來就敢於作更大膽的
預言，對當前的工作就更樂觀、歡快。歷史告
訴我們，人類有着何等堅韌的生存力量。地震、
饑饉、瘟疫可以肆虐一時，但隨後流過的歲月
又治癒一切創傷，使它們消失不見；又或偉大
的歷史進程橫掃大地，把一切傷痕都抹去。新
形式的文明圍繞着顯赫的帝王建立起來，這些
帝王逝世後，又有更偉大的人物繼起。有些民
族被消滅殆盡，殷切的希望化爲泡影；革命一
次又一次發生，愛國志士血流成河；地球本身
似乎就要沉入毀滅的深淵；然而新的愛國者又
湧現出來，更高的希望像繁星般閃現；人類大
步走出了黑暗時代，比當初進入那陰森洞穴中
時大大地進步了。從此，公理被承認爲至高無
上。現在，基督王國比我們最初預想到的更爲
臨近了。

　　只有那些不懂歷史的人才在偉大的改革中
灰心喪氣，只有那些不讀天才人物傳記的人才

　　薇爾拉德（1839～1898），全名爲Frances E-
lizabeth Caroline Willard，美國的慈善家和社會活
動家。本文是她1890年發表的演說。

realm of material invention, there is nothing new under the sun. There is no reform which some great soul has not dreamed of centuries ago; there is not a doctrine that some father of the church did not set forth. The Greek philosophers and early Christian Fathers boxed the compass once for all; we may take our choice of what they have left on record. Let us then learn a wise humility, but at the same time a humble wisdom, as we remember that there are but two classes of men — one which declares that our times are the worst the world has seen, and another which claims our times as best — and he who claims this, all revelation, all science, all history, witnesses is right and will be right forevermore.

The most normal and the most perfect human being is the one who most thoroughly addresses himself to the activity of his best powers, gives himself most thoroughly to the world around him, flings himself out into the midst of humanity, and is so preoccupied by his own beneficent reaction on the world that he is practically unconscious of a separate existence. . . .

. . .

會自以為是首創者。除了物質領域裏的發明之外，天下沒有什麼新東西。沒有哪一種改革不是早在幾個世紀以前就有偉大的心靈憧憬過，沒有哪一種教義不是某位神父早就訂立過的。希臘哲學家和早期的神父早已一勞永逸地為後人指明了方向，我們盡可以在他們留下的記載中去任意挑選。因此，讓我們學會明智的謙虛，也同時學會謙虛的智慧。讓我們記住，世上只有兩類人：一類人宣稱我們的時代是這世界歷來最壞的時代，另一類人却認為這是最好的時代。一切新發明、一切科學和全部歷史都證明了持後一種意見的人是正確的，而且永遠、永遠正確。

最正常、最完美的人就是那徹底獻身於自己最擅長的活動的人，是那徹底投身周圍世界和眾人當中去的人。他完全專心致志於他對世界的有利作用，以致幾乎意識不到自己與世界還有什麼距離。……

……

61 Eulogy of Ulysses S. Grant

Horace Porter

. . .

General Grant possessed in a striking degree all the characteristics of the successful soldier. His methods were all stamped with tenacity of purpose, with originality and ingenuity. He depended for his success more upon the powers of invention than of adaptation, and the fact that he has been compared at different times to nearly every great commander in history is perhaps the best proof that he was like none of them. He was possessed of a moral and physical courage which was equal to every emergency in which he was placed; calm amidst excitment, patient under trials, never unduly elated by victory or depressed by defeat. While he possessed a sensitive nature and a singularly tender heart, yet he never allowed his sentiments to interfere with the stern duties of the soldier. He knew better than to attempt to hew rocks with a razor. He realized that paper bullets cannot be fired in warfare. He felt that the hardest blows bring the quickest results; that more men die from disease in sickly camps than from shot and shell in battle.

His magnanimity to foes, his generosity to friends, will be talked of as long as manly qualities are honored. You know after Vicksburg had succumbed to him he said in his order: "The garrison will march out tomorrow. Instruct your commands to be quiet and

---

波特（1837～1921），美國南北戰爭中的北軍將領，曾任格蘭特的助手。

尤里塞斯·格蘭特（1822～1885），美國南北戰爭中北軍的主帥，1869至1877年任第十八屆總統。1891

六十一 獻給尤里塞斯‧格蘭特的
頌詞

賀拉斯‧波特

......

　　格蘭特將軍具有一位成功軍人所應有的一切品格，而且表現得異常出色。他一生的業績表明他堅韌不拔，富有創建，足智多謀。他的成功主要是靠獨創能力而不是靠適應能力。差不多歷史上的每一位偉大統帥，人們都曾拿來跟他作過比較，這也許恰好證明他有別於任何一人。無論處身何種緊急情況，他都具有精神上和肉體上的勇氣以應付該情況：在激動中鎮靜，在艱苦中忍耐，勝不驕矜，敗不氣餒。他感情豐富，心地柔和，却從不讓自己的感情影響軍人應有的嚴明職責。他知道刀片不能劈石頭，紙彈不能打仗。他明白最猛力的打擊會帶來最速效的結果，死於疾病蔓延的營房中的兵士多於死在戰場的槍炮之下。

　　他對敵人寬大，對朋友慷慨。只要豪俠的品質受到尊崇，他便會一直為人傳頌。你們知道，攻陷威克斯堡[1]後，他下令說："衞戍部隊明日撤離本城，應指示所屬部隊在俘虜經過

年10月 8 日，田納西州陸軍為格蘭特騎馬塑像落成舉行宴會，這是波特在會上的講話。

（1）威克斯堡戰役是美國南北戰爭中的一次重大戰役，雙方為爭奪密西西比河而戰。

305

orderly as the prisoners pass by, and make no offensive remarks." After Lee's surrender at Appomattox, when our batteries began to fire triumphal salutes, he at once suppressed them, saying in his order: "The war is over; the rebels are again our countrymen; the best way to celebrate the victory will be to abstain from all demonstrations in the field." . . . So that he penned no idle platitude, he fashioned no stilted epigram, he spoke the earnest convictions of an honest heart when he said, "Let us have peace." He never tired of giving unstinted praise to worthy sub-ordinates for the work they did. Like the chief artists who weave the Gobelin tapestries, he was content to stand behind the cloth and let those in front appear to be the chief contributors to the beauty of the fabric.

If there be one single word in all the wealth of the English language which best describes the predominating trait of General Grant's character, that word is "loyalty." Loyal to every great cause and work he was engaged in; loyal to his friends, loyal to his family, loyal to his country, loyal to his God. This produced a reciprocal effect in all who came in contact with him. It was one of the chief reasons why men became so loyally attached to him. It is true that this trait so dominated his whole character that it led him to make mistakes, it induced him to continue to stand by men who were no longer worthy of his confidence; but after all, it was a trait so grand, so noble, we do not stop to count the errors which resulted. It showed him to be

之時保持安靜，嚴守紀律，切勿惡言相加。"李將軍在愛坡默托斯投降後，我軍鳴炮慶祝，格蘭特將軍立即下令制止說："戰事已經結束；叛亂分子又已成為我們的同胞；慶祝勝利的最好方式是避免在戰場上的一切行動。"……同樣，他從不寫出陳詞濫調，也不追求誇張的警句。當他說"讓我們共同享有和平吧"[1]他表達的是一顆誠實的心最真摯的信念。他從不厭煩或吝嗇讚揚有功下屬所作的貢獻。一如編織哥白林雙面掛毯[2]的首要藝匠，格蘭特將軍情願把自己隱在掛毯的後面，讓掛毯前面的其他工匠充當這幅精美作品的主要創造者。

　　如果英語的語言寶庫裏有一個單字可以描畫出格蘭特將軍的性格特點，那麼這個字就是"忠"。他忠於自己參予的一切偉大事業和工作，忠於他的朋友，忠於他的家庭，忠於他的國家，忠於他的上帝。他的忠誠令所有和他有接觸的人不期然作出回報。這就是他的兵士對他如此忠誠的主要原因之一。不錯，他是這樣地忠誠，以至於因此而犯錯誤，使他繼續和那些已經不值得他信任的人站在一起。但這種性格是如此高尚而光明磊落，我們也就不去計較它帶來的不良後果了。這一點表明他是一個有

（1）這是格蘭特接受南方投降時的說話。
（2）法國巴黎出產的一種編織物。

a man who had the courage to be just, to stand between worthy men and their unworthy slanderers, and to let kindly sentiments have a voice in an age in which the heart played so small a part in public life. Many a public man has had hosts of followers because they fattened on the patronage dispensed at his hands; many a one has had troops of adherents because they were blind zealots in a cause he represented; but perhaps no man but General Grant had so many friends who loved him for his own sake, whose attachment strengthened only with time, whose affection knew neither variableness nor shadow of turning, who stuck to him as closely as the toga of Nessus, whether he was captain, general, President, or simply private citizen.

. . .

勇氣主持正義的人，有勇氣站在值得尊敬的人一邊，去反對誣謗他們的卑劣小人。在人心對公衆生活起的作用如此微小的年代，他使仁愛的感情還能有些影響。許多公職人員有大批追隨者，因爲這些追隨者能憑借公職人員手中的權力得到厚利；不少公職人員有一伙伙黨羽，因爲這些人盲從他們所代表的主義；然而除了格蘭特將軍之外，也許沒有人有如此衆多的忠實朋友了。他們只是愛他的爲人，他們對他的深情與時俱增，他們對他的熱愛不會轉變。他們像耐薩斯的袍服[1]，永遠貼附於他，不論他是軍官，是將軍，是總統或只是一個普通公民。

……

（1）耐薩斯是希臘神話中半人半馬的怪物，騙大力神海克拉斯（Hercules）穿上他的血衣，結果血衣粘在海克拉斯身上起火，把海克拉斯燒死。

62 Eulogy of Robert E. Lee

. . .

He was born in the same county, and descended
from the same strains of English blood from which
Washington sprang, and was united in marriage with
Mary Custis, the daughter of his adopted son. He had
been reared in the school of simple manners and lofty
thoughts which belonged to the elder generation; and
with Washington as his examplar of manhood and his
ideal of wisdom, he reverenced his character and fame
and work with a feeling as near akin to worship as any
that man can have for aught that is human.

. . .

Years of his professional life he had spent in
Northern communities, and, always a close observer of
men and things, he well understood the vast resources
of that section, and the hardy, industrious, and resolute
character of its people; and he justly weighed their
strength as a military power. When men spoke of how
easily the South would repel invasion he said: "You
forget that we are all Americans." And when they
prophesied a battle and a peace, he predicted that it
would take at least four years to fight out the impending conflict. None was more conscious than he that
each side undervalued and misunderstood the other.
He was, moreover, deeply imbued with the philosophy
of history and the course of its evolutions, and well
knew that in an upheaval of government deplorable

丹尼.爾（1842－？），南北戰爭中南方的將領，
後曾當選議員。羅伯特‧李（1807～1870），南北戰
爭時的南軍總司令。本文是1883年6月在弗吉尼亞州

310

六十二　獻給羅伯特·李的頌詞

約翰·華威克·丹尼爾

……

他和華盛頓出生於同一個縣，同屬英國血統，又同華盛頓養子的女兒瑪麗·科絲蒂斯聯姻。他在一所禮儀簡省、思想高尚的舊式學校受教育。他以華盛頓的為人作他的典範，以華盛頓的才智為他的楷模。他以一種對凡人所能有的，接近於崇拜的感情敬仰華盛頓的品格、名聲和事業。

……

他多年在北方任職，又秉性好仔細觀察人和事，故能清楚了解北方的巨大資源以及當地人民刻苦耐勞、堅決果斷的性格；他能夠正確地估計到北方作為一支軍事力量有多大。當人們說到南方可以輕易地擊退北軍的入侵時，他說："你忘記了我們都是美國人。"當人們預言打一仗便會得到和平時，他却預測至少要有四年，那場將臨的戰事才能打出結果。沒有一個人比他更清楚地意識到雙方都低估了對方、誤解了對方的情況。此外，他完全掌握歷史哲學，了解歷史的進程，深知隨着政府大亂而來的必定是令人痛悔的種種後果。這些後果開始

華盛頓與李大學（Washington and Lee University）
李將軍卧像揭幕典禮上的講話。

results would follow which were not thought of in the beginning, or, if thought of, would be disavowed, belittled and deprecated. And eminently conservative in his cast of mind and character, every bias of his judgment, as every tendency of his history, filled him with yearning and aspiration for the peace of his country and the perpetuity of the Union. Is it a wonder then, as the storm of revolution lowered, Colonel Lee, then with his regiment, the Second Cavalry, in Texas, wrote thus to his son in January, 1861:

"The South, in my opinion, has been aggrieved by the acts of the North as you say. I feel the aggression, and am willing to take any proper steps for redress. It is the principle I contend for, not individual or private benefit. As an American citizen, I take great pride in my country, her prosperity and institutions, and would defend any state if her rights were invaded. But I can anticipate no greater calamity for the country than a dissolution of the Union. It would be an accumulation of all evils we complain of, and I am willing to sacrifice everything but honor for its preservation. I hope, therefore, that all constitutional means will be exhausted before there is a resort to force. Secession is nothing but revolution. . . . Still, a Union that can only be maintained swords and bayonets, and in which strife and civil war are to take the place of love and kindness, has no charm for me. I shall mourn for my country and for the welfare and progress of mankind. If the Union is dissolved, and the government is disrupted, I shall return to my native state and share the miseries of my people, and, save in defense, will draw my sword on none."

時未有人想到，即使想到，也會或是不肯承認，或是將後果說得較輕，或是反對有這樣的後果。他的頭腦和性格屬於突出的穩健型。他的觀點和行為表現出的一切傾向，都使他充滿對國家太平和聯邦久存的熱望。因此，1861年1月，革命的風暴平息下去後，當時正在德克薩斯州第二騎兵隊服務的李上校，給兒子的信中寫了如下的話，又有什麼奇怪呢？

"我認為，正如你所說，北方的行動使南方受到了侵害。我感到北方的侵入行動，我願意採取任何適當的步驟為南方伸雪冤屈。我奮鬥爭取的是原則而不是個人的私利。作為一個美國公民，我以國家及其繁榮和制度而自豪，任何一州的權利遭到侵害，我都要起而捍衛。但是我可以預見到，對於我們的國家，沒有什麼災難比聯邦分裂更大了。聯邦分裂將是我們現在所抱怨的一切惡果的總和。為了維護聯邦，除了榮譽之外，我願犧牲一切。因此，我希望，在一切憲法手段都用盡之前，絕不使用武力。脫離聯邦只能帶來革命……。然而，一個只能靠劍和刺刀來維繫的聯邦，在其中只有爭吵和內戰而沒有愛和善，這對我沒有吸引力。我只好為國家和人類的福利進步受到破壞而哀悼。如果聯邦分裂，政府瓦解，我將回到我出生的弗吉尼亞州分擔我的人民的不幸，同時，除了自衛，絕不用刀劍對付任何人。"

. . .

On the twentieth of April, as soon as the news of Virginia's secession reached him, he resigned his commission in the army of the United States, and thus wrote to his sister who remained with her husband on the Union side: "With all my devotion to the Union, and the feeling of loyalty and duty of an American citizen, I have not been able to make up my mind to raise my hand against my relatives, my children, my home. I have therefore resigned my commission in the army, and save in the defense of my native state (with the sincere hope that my poor services may never be needed) I hope I may never be called upon to draw my sword."

Bidding an affectionate adieu to his old friend and commander, General Scott, who mourned his loss, but nobly expressed his confidence in his motives, he repaired to Richmond. Governor John Letcher immediately appointed him to the commander in chief of the Virginia forces, and the Convention unanimously confirmed the nomination. . . .

. . .

Thus came Robert E. Lee to the state of his birth and to the people of his blood in their hour of need! Thus, with as chaste a heart as ever plighted its faith until death, for better or for worse, he came to do, to suffer, and to die for us who today are gathered in awful reverence and in sorrow unspeakable to weep our blessings upon his tomb.

. . .

......

4月20日⁽¹⁾，弗吉尼亞脫離聯邦的消息傳
來，他立刻辭去美國的軍職。他的妹妹和妹夫
留在聯邦那邊，他給妹妹的信中寫道："儘管
懷着對聯邦的一片赤誠和美國公民的忠心與責
任感，我至今還是不能下決心舉手反對我們的
親屬、孩子和我的故鄉。因此我已辭去我在軍
隊中的職務。除非爲了保衞我出生的弗吉尼亞
州（我眞誠地希望永不需要我來擔任此項任
務），我希望永不需要拔出佩劍。"

他向他的老朋友和司令官司各脫將軍依依
道別。司各脫將軍雖然痛惜失去良將，但表示
信任他的眞誠動機，於是他回到里士蒙。約翰·
列奇州長立即任命他爲弗吉尼亞州部隊總司
令。州議會一致贊同這項任命。……

......

羅伯特·李就這樣在他血肉相連的人民需
要的時刻，來到他出生的弗吉尼亞州！這樣，他
懷着一顆同過去一樣純潔的心，懷着矢誓生死
不渝、禍福與共的忠誠，來到我們當中，爲我
們工作、受苦以至赴難。我們今天懷着無比敬
畏的心情聚集在他的墓前，流淚含哀，對他致
敬祝福。

......

（1）1861年4月20日。

63 Presentation of the Cheney-Ives Gateway to Yale University

Henry Johnson Fisher

President Hadley and Yale men: I am here as a representative of the class of ninety-six, to present to you this gate. In its stone and iron it typifies the rugged manliness of those to whose lasting memory it has been erected. That is our wish. To you who are now gathered beneath these elms, and those Yale men who shall follow after us, we wish this memorial to stand first of all for the manhood and courage of Yale. In the evening shadows the softer lights may steal forth and infold it, but through the daylight hours of toil and accomplishment let the sun shine down upon it, and bring out each line of strength, that every Yale man may be imbued with that dauntless spirit which inspired these two sons of Yale in their lives and in their deaths.

We do not wish you merely to stand before this memorial and gaze upon it as a monument. We want everyone of you, whether graduate at Commencement time or undergraduate in term time, to come to it and to sit upon its benches, just as we of ninety-six shall come to it during the advancing years, and, in the coming, keep always alive in our hearts the spirit of these two who did their work and held their peace,

六十三　將邁尼與埃弗斯門樓獻給耶魯大學

亨利・約翰遜・費舍

赫德萊校長和耶魯人：我在這裏代表九六級學生向你們獻上這座門樓。門樓的石塊和鐵架象徵着剛毅精神和丈夫氣概，這座門樓就是為了永遠紀念具有這種精神的兩位同學而建造的。這是我們的願望。對於你們，現在聚集在榆蔭下的人們以及後來的耶魯人，我們希望這座紀念碑首先代表豪邁英勇的耶魯精神。黃昏來臨時，夕陽的殘照或會偷偷地把它遮掩起來；但是當辛勤勞動的白日來到，照在它上面的燦爛陽光，將使它發出一股股力量，使每個耶魯人的心中充滿了大無畏的精神。這兩位耶魯男兒的一生以及他們死亡的時刻，都曾得到這種大無畏的精神激勵。

我們不願你們站在這座門樓之前，只把它當做一座紀念碑來欣賞。我們要求你們每一個人，無論是畢業典禮上的畢業生還是在學期中的大學生，都像我們九六級的同學在未來的歲月那樣，來到這座門樓前，坐在凳子上，心中常保有這兩個人的精神。他們完成任務後，心

本文為耶魯大學1896級畢業生代表費舍在耶魯大學校慶二百周年紀念會上的演說。邁尼和埃弗斯是已去世的1896級學生。

and had no fear to die. That is the lesson these two careers are singularly fitted to teach us. To the one came the keenest disappointment which can come to a soldier, the disappointment of staying behind, and after that the toil, the drudgery, and the sickness, — all bravely borne. To the other it was given to meet death with that steadfast courage which alone avails to men who die in the long quiet after the battle. It is no new service these two have given to Yale. Looking back to-day through the heritage of two centuries, these names are but added to the roll of those who have served Yale because they have served their country.

The stone and iron of this gate will keep alive the names of these two men. It is our hope that the men of Yale will, in their own lives, perpetuate their manhood and courage.

情平靜，從容就死。這就是他們的業績對我們最好的教育。他們中的一位是軍人，但滯留後方，未能參戰，這對一個軍人來說是最大的失望。但這種失望以及後來勞頓艱苦的生活和疾病的磨難，他都勇敢地承受了。另一位則以最鎮定果敢的態度迎接了死亡，這種態度是只有在激戰後，在長久寧靜中死去的人才有的。他們兩人對耶魯所做的不算是新的貢獻了。回顧兩個世紀來耶魯的傳統，他們只是為耶魯效勞的光榮行列中增添的兩個名字而已。他們為國效勞，也就是為耶魯效勞了。

他們的名字將和這座門樓的石塊與鐵架共存，永垂不朽。我們願一切耶魯人一生都能永遠保持他們這種豪邁精神與勇氣。

64 Acceptance of the Cheney-Ives Gateway

Arthur Twining Hadley

Of all the memorials which are offered to a university by the gratitude of her sons, there are none which serve so closely and fully the purposes of her life as those monuments which commemorate her dead heroes. The most important part of the teaching of a place like Yale is found in the lessons of public spirit and devotion to high ideals which it gives. These things can in some measure be learned in books of poetry and of history. They can in some measure be learned from the daily life of the college and the sentiments which it inculcates. But they are most solemnly and vividly brought home by visible signs, such as this gateway furnishes, that the spirit of ancient heroism is not dead, and that its highest lessons are not lost.

It seems as if the bravest and best in your class, as well as in others, had been sacrificed to the cruel exigencies of war. But they are not sacrificed. It is through their death that their spirit remains immortal. It is through men like those whom we have loved, and whom we here commemorate, that the life of the republic is kept alive. As we have learned lessons of heroism from the men who went forth to die in the Civil War, so will our children and our children's children learn the same lesson from the heroes who have a little while lived with us and then entered into an immortality of glory.

六十四　接受遷尼與埃弗斯門樓

阿瑟·吐溫寧·赫德萊

　　一切爲了表示感激而贈送給母校的紀念品當中，沒有哪一樣比紀念死去的英雄紀念碑更緊密完美地代表學校生活宗旨的了。在耶魯這樣的學府裏，最重要的課程部分是爲公衆服務和獻身於崇高理想的精神。在一定程度上，這種精神可以從詩歌與歷史的書籍學得，也可以從大學的日常生活及大學教誨的情操中學到。然而像這座門樓這樣可見的形象，最莊嚴最生動地反映了這種精神，說明古代的英雄主義精神不死，說明這種精神的最深教育意義不會消失。

　　表面看來，似乎你們班級中，還有其他一些班級，最勇敢最優秀的人已經在殘酷危險的戰爭中犧牲了。但是他們並未白白犧牲。死亡使他們的精神永生。正是這些我們所熱愛、我們在這裏紀念的人們，使我們的共和國得以生存。我們過去曾經從內戰中壯烈犧牲的人們學到了英雄主義，我們的子孫後代也將從這些人學到同樣的精神。這些人曾經短暫地和我們生活在一起，現在則進入了不朽的光榮。

65 Salt

Henry van Dyke

"Ye are the salt of the earth." Matthew 5:13.

This figure of speech is plain and pungent. Salt is savory, purifying, preservative. It is one of those super-fluities which the great French wit defined as "things that are very necessary." From the very beginning of human history men have set a high value upon salt and sought for it in caves and by the seashore. The nation that had a good supply was counted rich. A bag of salt, among the barbarous tribes, was worth more than a man. The Jews prized it especially, because they lived in a warm climate where food was difficult to keep, and because their religion laid particular emphasis on cleanliness, and because salt was largely used in their sacrifices.

Christ chose an image which was familiar, when He said to His disciples, "Ye are the salt of the earth." This was His conception of their mission, their influence. They were to cleanse and sweeten the world in which they lived, to keep it from decay, to give a new and more wholesome flavor to human existence. Their function was not to be passive, but active. The sphere of its action was to be this present life. There is no use in saving salt for heaven. It will not be needed there. Its mission is to permeate, season, and purify things on earth.

六十五 鹽

亨利·范·戴克

"你們是世上的鹽。"《馬太福音》,第五章第十三節。

這個比喻平凡而發人深省。鹽食之有味,又可潔物、防腐。鹽並非必需品,但那位偉大的法國才智之士却稱之為"頭等必需品"。人類有史之初,就對鹽有很高的評價,並在山洞和海灘採集鹽。盛產鹽的國家曾被目為富國。在原始部落裏,一袋鹽比一個人還要貴重。猶太人尤其珍視鹽,因為他們居住的地方氣候炎熱,食物難於保藏。此外,他們的宗教特別強調潔淨,向神獻祭時又需大量用鹽。

基督對他的門徒說"你們是世上的鹽"時,選用了一個大家都熟悉的物喻。他以此說明他認為眾門徒該肩負的使命和應發生的影響。他們到世上來就是要淨化、美化他們所在的世界,使它免於腐敗,給人新的、更健康的生存意味。他們的作用不是消極的,而是積極的。他們任務的活動範圍是今世,不必把鹽省下來帶到天國去。天國不需要鹽。鹽的使命是滲入、調和與淨化世界的事物。

范·戴克(1852~1933),美國作家、教育家和傳道士,酷愛描寫自然、友誼與信仰。本文於1898年6月在哈佛大學發表。

. . .

Men of privilege without power are waste material. Men of enlightenment without influence are the poorest kind of rubbish. Men of intellectual and moral and religious culture, who are not active forces for good in society, are not worth what it costs to produce and keep them. If they pass for Christians they are guilty of obtaining respect under false pretenses. They were meant to be the salt of the earth. And the first duty of salt is to be salty.

This is the subject on which I want to speak to you today. The saltiness of salt is the symbol of a noble, powerful, truly religious life.

You college students are men of privilege. It costs ten times as much, in labor and care and money, to bring you out where you are today, as it costs to educate the average man, and a hundred times as much as it costs to raise a boy without any education. This fact brings you face to face with a question: Are you going to be worth your salt?

You have had mental training, and plenty of instruction in various branches of learning. You ought to be full of intelligence. You have had moral discipline, and the influences of good example have been steadily brought to bear upon you. You ought to be full of principle. You have had religious advantages and abundant inducements to choose the better part. You ought to be full of faith. What are you going to do with your intelligence, your principle, your faith? It is your duty to make active use of them for the seasoning, the cleansing, the saving of the world. Don't be sponges. Be the salt of the earth.

Think, first, of the influence for good which men of intelligence may exercise in the world, if they will only

……

享有特權而無力量的人是廢物。受過教育而無影響的人是一堆一文不值的垃圾。有些人在知識、道德、宗教信仰方面受過教養，但沒有成為社會上行善的積極力量，這些人就對不起為培育和供養他們而花費的代價。如果他們也算是基督徒，他們就犯了因偽裝而受尊敬的罪。他們本應成為世上的鹽，而鹽的首要責任應當有鹽味。

這就是今天我要對你們講的題目。鹽的鹽味象徵高尚的、有力的、真正虔誠的生活。

你們大學生是享有特權的人。把你們培養成今天這樣，所花費的勞力、心血與金錢，十倍於教育一般人，百倍於撫養大一個未受教育的兒童。這事實使你們面對這樣的一個問題：你們是否打算做有用的鹽。

你們受過智力訓練，受過各科學問的教育，應該很有知識。你們受過德育訓練，不斷受到良好典範的影響，應該極有原則。你們在宗教上得天獨厚，不斷得到引導向善，應該極有信仰。你們準備用你們的知識、原則和信仰去做些什麼呢？你們有責任積極地調劑、淨化世界，使世人得救。不要做只取不予的海綿，要做世上的鹽。

首先想想，有知識的人只要願意將自己的文化用於正途，就可能產生善的影響。人類的

put their culture to the right use. Half the troubles of mankind come from ignorance, — ignorance which is systematically organized with societies for its support and newspapers for its dissemination, — ignorance which consists less in not knowing things, than in willfully ignoring the things that are already known. There are certain physical diseases which would go out of existence in ten years if people would only remember what has been learned. There are certain political and social plagues which are propagated only in the atmosphere of shallow self-confidence and vulgar thoughtlessness. There is a yellow fever of literature specially adapted and prepared for the spread of shameless curiosity, incorrect information, and complacent idiocy among all classes of the population. Persons who fall under the influence of this pest become so triumphantly ignorant that they cannot distinguish between news and knowledge. They develop a morbid thirst for printed matter, and the more they read the less they learn. They are fit soil for the bacteria of folly and fanaticism.

Now the men of thought, of cultivation, of reason, in the community ought to be an antidote to these dangerous influences. Having been instructed in the lessons of history and science and philosophy they are bound to contribute their knowledge to the service of society. As a rule they are willing enough to do this for pay, in the professions of law and medicine and teaching and divinity. What I plead for today is the wider, nobler, unpaid service which an educated man renders to society simply by being thoughtful and by helping other men to think.

. . .

Think, in the second place, of the duty which men of moral principle owe to society in regard to the evils which corrupt and degrade it. Of the existence of these

煩惱，一半來自無知。這種無知為了使自己延續下去，便與社會有系統地結成一體，而為了四處擴散又利用報刊的力量；這種無知不僅不去認識事物，而且故意抹殺已經認識的事物。如果人們能夠記住已經學到的東西，某些危害身體的疾病在十年內就會絕迹。某些政治和社會瘟疫，只在淺薄的自信和庸俗輕率的氣氛裏才會傳播開來。還有一類壞書特別適於各個階層中散佈無恥的邪念、訛誤的消息和自負的愚蠢。受到這種惡劣影響的人變得愚昧無知、洋洋得意，以致分不清什麼是道聽途說，什麼是真正的知識。他們對所有印刷品有一種病態的饑渴，但他們讀得愈多，知道得愈少。他們正是培育愚昧與狂熱盲從細菌的肥沃土壤。

社會上有思想、有教養、有理性的人們，應該成為這類危險影響的解透劑。他們學習過歷史、科學與哲學，有責任用他們的知識來服務社會。一般說來，他們做律師、醫生、教員或神父，為換取職業的報酬而樂於服務社會。但我今天要求你們去做的，却是更廣泛、更高尚而且無報酬的服務，那很簡單，就是一個受過教育的人多思考，並且幫助別人學會思考。

……

其次，由於邪惡腐蝕社會，有道德原則的人要想到自己對社會的責任。正因為我們是比較乾淨、高尚和正直的人，我們要一再地提醒

evils we need to be reminded again and again, just because we are comparatively clean and decent and upright people. Men who live an orderly life are in great danger of doing nothing else. We wrap our virtue up in little bags of respectability and keep it in the storehouse of a safe reputation. But if it is genuine virtue it is worthy of a better purpose than that. It is fit, nay, it is designed and demanded, to be used as salt, for the purifying of human life.
. . .

自己注意這些邪惡事物的存在。生活正派的人最怕是潔身自好。我們爲了明哲保身，往往把美德裝在一包包用尊敬包起來的小包裹裏，束之高閣。但是，眞正的美德應該用於更好的目的。它不僅適宜於，而且本來就計劃好必須像鹽那樣，用來淨化人類的生活。

……

66 The Apostle of Peace Among the Nations

Andrew Dickson White

Your Excellencies, Mr. Burgomaster, Gentlemen of the University Faculties, My Honored Colleagues of the Peace Conference, Ladies and Gentlemen: The Commission of the United States comes here this day to discharge a special duty. We are instructed to acknowledge, on behalf of our country, one of its many great debts to the Netherlands.

This debt is that which, in common with the whole world, we owe to one of whom all civilized lands are justly proud, — the poet, the scholar, the historian, the statesman, the diplomatist, the jurist, the author of the treatise "De Jure Belli ac Pacis."

Of all works not claiming divine inspiration, that book, written by a man proscribed and hated both for his politics and his religion, has proved the greatest blessing to humanity. More than any other it has prevented unmerited suffering, misery, and sorrow; more than any other it has ennobled the military profession; more than any other it has promoted the blessings of peace and diminished the horrors of war.

六十六　一位倡導國際和平的偉人

安德魯・狄克遜・懷特

諸位閣下、勃戈馬斯脫先生、來自各大學的諸位先生、尊敬的和平會議同事們，諸位女士、先生：

美國代表團今天來到這裏執行一項特殊的任務。我們受惠於荷蘭甚多，現在我們按照指示，代表我國對我們欠下荷蘭的一份情意表示感謝。

這份謝意是對一位所有文明國家都理應引為驕傲的人而言，全世界和我們一同感謝他。他是一位詩人、學者、歷史學家、政治家、外交家、法學家，也是《論戰爭與和平的法律》的作者。

在一切並不自詡為由神啟而寫成的著作中，這部由一位在政治與宗教上都受到擯斥和憎恨的人寫成的書，已被證明是人類最大的福音。它比別的任何著作更能使人類少受無謂的苦難、悲痛與憂愁；它比別的任何著作更能使軍人的職業變得高尚；它比別的任何著作更能促進和平的賜福，減少戰爭的恐怖。

懷特（1832~1918），美國教育家與外交家，1899年海牙和平會議的主席。本文發表於會議期間，讚揚荷蘭法學家修果・格羅提烏斯（1583~1645）。

On this tomb, then, before which we now stand, the delegates of the United States are instructed to lay a simple tribute to him whose mortal remains rest beneath it — Hugo de Groot, revered and regarded with gratitude by thinking men throughout the world as "Grotius."

. . .

In the vast debt which all nations owe to Grotius, the United States acknowledges its part gladly. Perhaps in no other country has his thought penetrated more deeply and influenced more strongly the great mass of the people. It was the remark of Alexis de Tocqueville, the most philosophic among all students of American institutions, that one of the most striking and salutary things in American life is the widespread study of law. De Tocqueville was undoubtedly right. In all parts of our country the law of nations is especially studied by large bodies of young men in colleges and universities; studied, not professionally merely, but from the point of view of men eager to understand the fundamental principles of international rights and duties.

The works of our compatriots, Wheaton, Kent, Field, Woolsey, Dana, Lawrence, and others, in developing more and more the ideas to which Grotius first gave life and strength, show that our country has not cultivated in vain this great field which Grotius opened.

因此，在這座墓前，美國代表團受命向長眠在墓中，被全世界有思想的人們尊崇感謝、並稱他爲格羅提烏斯的修果‧德‧格魯特[1]獻上我們簡樸的禮讚。

……

一切國家都深受惠於格羅提烏斯，美國樂於承認其中有她的一份。他的思想在我國廣大人民中影響巨大，深入人心，大概沒有別的國家可以相比擬。阿歷克賽‧德‧托克維爾[2]是研究美國制度最有哲理思想的學者，他說過：美國人生活中最顯著而又令人讚賞的事情莫過於對法律的廣泛研究了。德‧托克維爾無疑是正確的。在我國各地的大學和學院中，有大批青年正在從事各國法律的專門研究；他們不僅從職業觀點進行研究，並且是從人類熱切希望了解國際權利與義務的基本原則這角度去研究。

我的同胞韋頓、肯特、費文特、伍爾西、達納、勞倫斯[3]和其他人的許多著作都不斷地發展最先由格羅提烏斯給予生命與力量的思想。在格羅提烏斯開闢的這片偉大園地裏，我們的國家並沒有白白地耕耘。

（1）格羅提烏斯荷蘭文的名字。

（2）法國法官，曾訪問美國，著有《美國的民主》

　　（De la Démocratie en Amérique）一書。

（3）都是美國著名的國際法學者。

As to the bloom and fruitage evolved by these writers out of the germ ideas of Grotius I might give many examples, but I will mention merely three:

The first example shall be the act of Abraham Lincoln. Amid all the fury of civil war he recognized the necessity of a more humane code for the conduct of our armies in the field; and he intrusted its preparation to Francis Lieber, honorably known to jurists throughout the world, and at that time Grotius's leading American disciple.

My second example shall be the act of General Ulysses Grant. When called to receive the surrender of his great opponent, General Lee, after a long and bitter contest, he declined to take from the vanquished general the sword which he had so long and so bravely worn; imposed no terms upon the conquered armies save that they should return to their homes; allowed no reprisals; but simply said, "Let us have peace."

My third example shall be the act of the whole people of the United States. At the close of that most bitter contest, which desolated thousands of homes, and which cost nearly a million of lives, no revenge was taken by the triumphant Union on any of the separatist statesmen who had brought on the great struggle, or on any of the soldiers who had conducted it; and, from that day to this, North and South, once every year,

這些作家從格羅提烏斯思想的幼芽中開出的花朵和結成的果實，我可以舉出許多例證，但現在我只舉其三：

第一個例子是阿伯拉罕・林肯的行為。在內戰激烈進行期間，他就認識到需要制訂一部更富有人性的法典，以指導我們南北兩方的軍隊在戰場上的行為。他把這部法典的起草工作委託給弗朗西斯・里伯爾。里伯爾受全世界法學家敬重，是當時格羅提烏斯在美國最重要的門徒。

第二個例子是尤里西斯・格蘭特將軍的行為。經過長期劇烈戰爭，他受命接受大敵李將軍投降時，拒絕接受這位敗將長期來勇敢地佩帶着的佩劍[1]。格蘭特將軍除去要求敗軍解甲回家外，沒有提出任何其他條件。他不允許報復行動，只是簡單地說："讓我們得享和平。"

第三個例子是整個美國民族的行為。當那場使千百個家園荒蕪、使近百萬人犧牲生命的殘酷戰爭[2]結束時，得勝的聯邦沒有對發動戰爭、主張分裂的任何一個政治家或任何一個作戰的兵士進行報復。從那一天起，直到現在，

（1）按習慣，敗軍的主將要將自己的佩劍交給勝利的一方以示投降。

（2）指美國的南北戰爭。

on Decoration Day, the graves of those who fell wearing the blue of the North and the gray of the South are alike strewn with flowers. Surely I may claim for my countrymen that, whatever other shortcomings and faults may be imputed to them, they have shown themselves influenced by those feelings of mercy and humanity which Grotius, more than any other, brought into the modern world.

. . .

每年內戰停戰紀念日[1]到來之時，從南方到北方，不論穿藍色制服的北軍軍士的墓地或是穿灰色制服的南軍軍士的墳頭，都綴飾着簇簇鮮花。我可以肯定地說，儘管我的同胞可能有這樣的缺點和那樣的錯誤，但他們却顯示出深受仁慈與人道精神的影響。這種精神正是由格羅提烏斯帶到現代世界來，沒有人可以在這方面和他相比。

······

67 Farewell to England

Edward John Phelps

My Lord Mayor, My Lords, and Gentlemen: I am sure you will not be surprised to be told that the poor words at my command do not enable me to respond adequately to your most kind greeting, nor the too flattering words which have fallen from my friend, the Lord Mayor, and from my distinguished colleague, the Lord Chancellor. But you will do me the justice to believe that my feelings are not the less sincere and hearty if I cannot put them into language. I am under a very great obligation to your Lordship not merely for the honor of meeting this evening an assembly more distinguished I apprehend than it appears to me has often assembled under one roof, but especially for the opportunity of meeting under such pleasant circumstances so many of those to whom I have become so warmly attached, and from whom I am so sorry to part.

. . .

And so I have gone in and out among you these four years and have come to know you well. I have taken part in many gratifying public functions; I have been the guest at many homes; and my heart has gone out with yours in memorable jubilee of that sovereign lady whom all Englishmen love and all Americans honor. I

六十七 告別英倫

愛德華・約翰・費爾普斯

市長先生、各位爵士、各位先生：諸位對我的親切致意，還有我的朋友市長先生和我的尊敬同行大法官閣下剛才對我的過譽之詞，對於這一切，要是我說自己拙於詞令，無法用語言表達我的感謝，想必你們不會覺得奇怪。但是儘管我無法用言語表達，你們一定會相信，我的感情完全是眞摯的、由衷的。我感謝你們，各位先生，不僅因爲今天晚上你們在此爲我舉行的宴會極其特別，遠非我所想的那些千篇一律的宴會，尤其因爲你們使我有機會在這友好的氣氛中會晤衆多的良友。對於他們，我懷着深深的惜別之情。

……

在這四年內，我出入你們之間，對你們有了很好的了解。我曾參加許多令人滿意的公開活動，到過許多家庭作客。英女王陛下受全國人民愛戴和美國人民尊敬，在她那次令人難忘的大典[1]裏，我的心和你們一同歡忻慶祝。我

費爾普斯（1822～1900），美國律師，1885～1890年間出任美國駐英大使。本文爲他卸任離開英國前在餞別宴會上的講話。

（1）1887年維多利亞女王舉行即位五十周年大慶典禮。

have stood with you by some unforgotten grave; I have shared in many joys; and I have tried as well as I could through it all, in my small way, to promote constantly a better understanding, a fuller and more accurate knowledge, a more genuine sympathy between the people of the two countries.

And this leads me to say a word on the nature of these relations. The moral intercourse between the governments is most important to be maintained, and its value is not to be overlooked or disregarded. But the real significance of the attitude of nations depends in these days upon the feeling which the general intelligence of their inhabitants entertain toward each other. The time has long passed when kings or rulers can involve their nations in hostilities to gratify their own ambition or caprice. There can be no war nowadays between civilized nations, nor any peace that is not hollow and delusive unless sustained and backed up by the sentiment of the people who are parties to it. Before nations can quarrel their inhabitants must seek war. The men of our race are not likely to become hostile until they begin to misunderstand each other. There are no dragon's teeth so prolific as mutual misunderstandings. It is in the great and constantly increasing intercourse between England and America, in its reciprocities, and its amenities, that the security against misunderstanding must be found. While that continues, they cannot be otherwise than friendly. Unlucky incidents may sometimes happen; interests may conflict; mistakes may be made on one side or on the other,

曾和你們一同站在你們的不朽名人墓前默哀；我分享你們的快樂。我一直盡我的微薄力量以增強我們兩國人民之間的了解，促進彼此更全面、更準確的認識，加深他們之間眞誠的感情。

這使我要就我們之間這種關係說幾句話。維繫政府之間精神上的交流是最重要的，其價值不容忽視。但是，在現代，有關各國的立場態度，主要繫於各國民衆之間全面了解的感情。歷代帝王或統治者爲滿足個人的野心和狂想而把國家捲入敵對行爲之中的時代早已過去。現在在文明國家之間，如果得不到本國人民眞情的支持，就發動不起戰爭，彼此的和平也只是空洞而渺茫的。只是雙方人民要戰爭，兩國才能動武。除非產生誤解，我們這個民族的人民是不會輕易彼此懷有敵意的。沒有任何龍牙比互相誤解更能種出仇恨了[1]。要保障避免發生誤解，就必須加強英美兩國之間大量的、不斷增長的友好往來聯繫。只要這種交往繼續下去，我們兩國的關係就必然是友好的。有時我們可能遇到不幸的意外事件，我們的利益可能互相衝突，一方或他方可能犯錯誤，輕率或

（1）希臘神話裏，卡德莫斯（Cadmus）殺死一條龍，把龍牙種在地裏，這些龍牙變成武士從地裏冒出來殺他。因此，" 種龍牙 "在西方即播下仇恨與敵意的意思。

and sharp words may occasionally be spoken by un-guarded or ignorant tongues. The man who makes no mistakes does not usually make anything. The nation that comes to be without fault will have reached the millennium, and will have little further concern with the storm-swept geography of this imperfect world. But these things are all ephemeral; they do not touch the great heart of either people; they float for a moment on the surface and in the wind, and then they disappear and are gone — "in the deep bosom of the ocean buried."

. . .

無知的人有時會口出刺耳之言。但是，不犯錯誤的人往往只是什麼事也不做。同樣，一個不犯錯誤的國家只能在極樂世界中才找得到，在這個有瑕疵的、風吹雨打、坎坷不平的塵世上是沒有的。不如人意的種種終究是轉瞬即逝的東西，它們不會觸及我們兩個民族的偉大心懷。它們只是一時隨風飄動，然後便永遠消失——"埋葬在滔滔大海的深處。"

......

68 Abraham Lincoln

Booker Taliaferro Washington

. . .

Says the Great Book somewhere, "Though a man die, yet shall he live." If this is true of the ordinary man, how much more true is it of the hero of the hour and the hero of the century — Abraham Lincoln! One hundred years of the life and influence of Lincoln is the story of the struggles, the trials, ambitions, and triumphs of the people of our complex American civilization. Interwoven into the warp and woof of this human complexity is the moving story of men and women of nearly every race and color in their progress from slavery to freedom, from poverty to wealth, from weakness to power, from ignorance to intelligence. Knit into the life of Abraham Lincoln is the story and success of the nation in the blending of all tongues, religions, colors, races, into one composite nation, leaving each group and race free to live its own separate social life, and yet all a part of the great whole.

If a man die, shall he live? Answering this question as applied to our martyred president, perhaps you expect me to confine my words of appreciation to the great boon which, through him, was conferred upon

---

勃克・華盛頓（ 1858～1915 ），生於弗吉尼亞州，
其母爲黑奴，1881年受聘爲阿拉巴馬州一所師範學校

六十八 阿伯拉罕·林肯

勃克·泰利亞費勞·華盛頓

……

《聖經》某處寫道："人死後仍能得生。"假如這句說話適用於一個普通人，那麼，對於這位此刻受人紀念、本世紀的英雄阿伯拉罕·林肯來說，這句話就更加確切了！林肯出生已經有一百年了，他在世時以及死後的影響包含了我們美國人民的歷史，其中充滿鬥爭、考驗、雄心和勝利，形成了我們的複雜文明。編織在這個人類複雜體系經緯線的是一部動人的歷史，其中幾乎包括了每個種族、每種膚色的男人女人，呈現了他們從奴役到自由、從貧窮到富裕、從弱小到強大、從下愚到上智的進展過程。織入阿伯拉罕·林肯一生的是我國的一段成功歷史，那就是把一切不同的語言、宗教、膚色和種族連結起來成爲一個混和的國家，其中各個團體和種族的人可以分別過着自己的社會生活，但同時又是組成這偉大整體的一部分。

　　一個人死後還能活着嗎？就我們這位已殉職的總統來回答這問題，也許你們以爲我會將頌詞限於他對我們種族的巨大恩惠上。然而我

的校長。本文是他在1909年紀念林肯誕生100周年時的講話。

my race. My undying gratitude and that of ten millions of my race for this and yet more! To have been the instrument used by Providence through which four millions of slaves, now grown into ten millions of free citizens, were made free, would bring eternal fame within itself, but this is not the only claim that Lincoln has upon our sense of gratitude and appreciation.

. . .

But, again, for a higher reason he lives tonight in every corner of the Republic. To set the physical man free is much. To set the spiritual man free is more. So often the keeper is on the inside of the prison bars and the prisoner on the outside.

As an individual, grateful as I am to Lincoln for freedom of body, my gratitude is still greater for freedom of soul — the liberty which permits one to live up in that atmosphere where he refuses to permit sectional or racial hatred to drag down, to warp and narrow his soul.

The signing of the Emancipation Proclamation was a great event, and yet it was but the symbol of another, still greater, and more momentous. We who celebrate this anniversary should not forget that that same pen which gave freedom to four millions of African slaves, at the same time struck the shackles from the souls of twenty-seven millions of Americans of another color.

. . .

In abolishing slavery, Lincoln proclaimed the principle that, even in the case of the humblest and weakest of mankind, the welfare of each is still the good of all. In reestablishing in this country the principle that, at bottom, the interests of humanity and of the individual

和我族一千萬人對他永遠感激之情，遠不止此！他受上天差遣，通過他，四百萬奴隸得到解放，增長為現今一千萬個自由公民。這件功業本身已足以彪炳千秋，然而這還不是我們對林肯感激讚美的一切。

......

但是，他現在仍然活在共和國的每一個角落，還有一個更重要的原因。從肉體上解放一個人已經夠偉大的了，使一個人精神得到解放則更偉大。獄卒的肉身在坐牢，囚犯的精神却在牢檻之外，這是常有的事。

以個人來說，我為得到人身自由而感謝林肯，但對於靈魂得到解放，我更要感激他。靈魂的解放使人在自由自在的環境中生活，不允許宗派或種族的仇恨使靈魂變得墮落、扭曲、狹隘。

解放宣言的簽署是一件大事，然而它更標誌着另一件更偉大更重要的事情。我們在此慶祝這周年紀念的人不應忘記，正是那枝使四百萬非洲黑奴獲得自由的筆，同時擊碎了二千七百萬另一膚色的美國人靈魂上的枷鎖。

......

林肯廢除奴隸制時，宣佈了一項原則，那就是，即使在人類處於最卑下最弱小的情況，一個人的幸福仍然是所有人的幸福。他為這個國家重新樹立起原則，令全人類的利益實際上

are one, he freed men's souls from spiritual bondage; he freed them to mutual helpfulness. Henceforth no man of any race, either in the North or in the South, need feel constrained to fear or hate his brother.

By the same token that Lincoln made America free, he pushed back the boundaries of freedom, and fair play will never cease to spread and grow in power till throughout the world all men shall know the truth, and the truth shall make them free.

. . .

To my race, the life of Abraham Lincoln has its special lesson at this point in our career. In so far as his life emphasizes dogged determination and courage; courage to avoid the superficial, courage to persistently seek the substance instead of the shadow, it points the road for my people to travel.

As a race we are learning, I believe, in an increasing degree, that the best way for us to honor the memory of our emancipation is by seeking to imitate him. Like Lincoln, the negro race should seek to be simple without bigotry, and without ostentation. There is great power in simplicity. We, as a race, should, like Lincoln, have moral courage to be what we are, and not pretend to be what we are not. We should keep in mind that no one can degrade us except ourselves; that if we are worthy, no influence can defeat us. Like other races, the negro will often meet obstacles, often be sorely tried and tempted; but we must keep in mind that freedom, in the broadest and highest sense, has never been a bequest; it has been a conquest.

In the final test, the success of our race will be in

同個人利益完全一致，把人的靈魂從精神桎梏中解放出來，使各人能夠互相幫助。從此，不論在南方或是北方，不論是哪個種族，沒有人會感到被迫去害怕或是仇恨自己的兄弟。

林肯使美國得到了自由，也藉此把自由的界限擴大了。正直公平的原則將不斷加強和推廣，直至全世界一切人都掌握了這真理，而這真理使他們得到自由。

……

林肯的一生對我們種族現階段的發展，有着特殊的教益。他一生表示出執着的決心與勇氣，克服淺薄，堅定地求實避虛。這樣，他為我國人民指出了前進的道路。

我相信我們全族正愈來愈懂得，紀念我們解放的最好方法是努力效法林肯。像他一樣，黑種人應該追求樸素純真而不尚偏激浮誇。簡樸自身就具有巨大的力量。我們全族應該像林肯那樣，具有道德上的勇氣以我們的本來面目出現而不偽裝成原非我們的面目。我們應該記住，除了我們自己以外，沒有人能貶低我們。我們要記住，如果我們自己堅強，就沒有什麼不良影響能夠打敗我們。正如別的種族一樣，黑人會經常遇到障礙、受到嚴重的考驗與誘惑，但是我們必須記住，從最廣最深的意義上說，自由永遠不是一種恩賜，却必須以鬥爭求得。

歸根結底，考核我們種族所得成就的大小

proportion to the service that it renders to the world. In the long run, the badge of service is the badge of sovereignty.

With all his other elements of strength, Abraham Lincoln possessed in the highest degree patience and, as I have said, courage. The highest form of courage is not always that exhibited on the battlefield in the midst of the blare of trumpets and the waving of banners. The highest courage is of the Lincoln kind. It is the same kind of courage, made possible by the new life and the new possibilities furnished by Lincoln's Proclamation, displayed by thousands of men and women of my race every year who are going out from Tuskegee and other negro institutions in the South to lift up their fellows. When they go, often into lonely and secluded districts, with little thought of salary, with little thought of personal welfare, no drums beat, no banners fly, no friends stand by to cheer them on; but these brave young souls who are prolonging school terms, teaching the people to buy homes, build houses, and live decent lives, are fighting the battles of this country just as truly and bravely as any persons who go forth to fight battles against a foreign foe.

In paying my tribute of respect to the Great Emancipator of my race, I desire to say a word here and now in behalf of an element of brave and true white men of the South, who, though they saw in Lincoln's policy the ruin of all they believe in and hope for, have loyally accepted the results of the Civil War, and are today working with a courage few people in the North can understand, to uplift the negro in the South and complete the emancipation that Lincoln began.

And, finally, gathering inspiration and encouragement from this hour and Lincoln's life, I pledge to you and to the nation that my race, in so far as I can speak

將看它對世界的貢獻。長遠來說,我們服務世界的獎賞將是我們的主權。

除去其他力量的素質,阿伯拉罕·林肯還具有高度的耐心和上面說到的勇氣。勇氣的最高表現不常在號聲響亮、旗幟飛揚的戰場上表現出來。最大的勇氣是林肯式的勇氣。林肯宣言為我們帶來新生和希望,使我族得到最大的勇氣。我族每年有幾千名男女畢業於塔斯基給和其他南方黑人學校,他們為提高本族人的教育學識表現出最大的勇氣。他們往往去到偏僻的地區,不計工資的多少,不計個人的福利,沒有敲鑼打鼓、旗幟招展,也沒有朋友列隊歡呼鼓勵他們,但這些勇敢的年輕人主動延長教學年限,教導人們建立家園、蓋造房屋,過高尚的生活。他們真誠勇敢地為我國努力奮鬥,一如任何人抵禦外敵時的表現。

當我向我族的偉大解放者致敬時,我願意在此時此地為勇敢真誠的南方白人的品質說一句話。這些人雖然在林肯的政策中看到了自己所信仰所希望的全部歸於毀滅,但仍然忠誠地接受了內戰的結果,現今更勇敢地為提高南方黑人的地位、為完成林肯始創的解放事業而工作。他們的這份勇氣,很少北方人能夠明白理解。

受到這節日和林肯一生事迹的激勵,我想最後在此就我所能為我的種族向你們和國家作

for it, which in the past, whether in ignorance or intelligence, whether in slavery or in freedom, has always been true to the Stars and Stripes and to the highest and best interests of this country, will strive to so deport itself that it shall reflect nothing but the highest credit upon the whole people in the North and in the South.

一點保證。我的種族在過去，無論是處於無知或有識之時，無論是在奴役下還是得到了自由，都一直忠於星條旗[1]和我國的最高最大利益，今後我族仍將致力於此，使我的行為完全無愧於北方南方的全體人民。

_____

（1）美國國旗。

69 Makers of the Flag

Franklin Knight Lane

This morning, as I passed into the Land Office, The Flag dropped me a most cordial salutation, and from its rippling folds I heard it say: "Good morning, Mr. Flag Maker."

"I beg your pardon, Old Glory," I said, "aren't you mistaken? I am not the president of the United States, nor a member of Congress, nor even a general in the army. I am only a government clerk."

"I greet you again, Mr. Flag Maker," replied the gay voice, "I know you well. You are the man who worked in the swelter of yesterday straightening out the tangle of the farmer's homestead in Idaho, or perhaps you found the mistake in that Indian contract in Oklahoma, or helped to clear that patent for the hopeful inventor in New York, or pushed the opening of that new ditch in Colorado, or made that mine in Illinois more safe, or brought relief to the old soldier in Wyoming. No matter; whichever one of these beneficent individuals you may happen to be, I give you greeting, Mr. Flag Maker."

I was about to pass on, when The Flag stopped me with these words:

"Yesterday the president spoke a word that made happier the future of ten million peons in Mexico;

萊恩（1864～1921），曾任美國內政部長。本文為他1914年6月14日美國國旗制定日對國務院內政部工作人員的講話。

六十九　製造國旗的人們

佛蘭克林・耐特・萊恩

今天早晨，我走進土地管理局的時候，國旗飄揚着，似乎向我熱情敬禮。從那旗面的皺摺中，我彷彿聽到它說：" 早上好，製旗者先生。"

" 請原諒，光榮的老友， " 我說，"你搞錯了吧？我不是合衆國總統，也不是國會議員，連部隊裏的將軍也不是。我不過是個政府職員罷了。"

" 我再次向你致敬，製旗者先生， " 它高高興興地回答，" 我對你熟悉得很。你就是昨天在埃達荷爲移民家宅地基問題費盡心血解紛排難的那個人，或者你就是那個發現和俄克拉荷馬印第安人簽訂的契約中有弊病的人，要不然你就是幫助了那位有前途的紐約發明家解決專利權的人，或許是開辦了科羅拉多一項新的挖渠工程的人，或許是使伊利諾斯礦山更安全的人，或許是使懷俄明老兵得到救濟的人。沒有關係，不管你是上述那一位做好事的人，我要向你這位製旗者先生問好。"

我正要走過去，國旗把我叫住，對我說：

" 昨天總統說了一句話，使千百萬在墨西哥欠債的傭工得到未來幸福[1]。但是總統呈現

(1)指總統伍德羅・威爾遜通過外交途徑，爲美國在墨西哥的傭工爭得了一些權利。

but that act looms no larger on the flag than the struggle which the boy in Georgia is making to win the Corn Club prize this summer.

"Yesterday the Congress spoke a word which will open the door of Alaska; but a mother in Michigan worked from sunrise until far into the night, to give her boy an education. She, too, is making the flag.

"Yesterday we made a new law to prevent financial panics, and yesterday, maybe, a school-teacher in Ohio taught his first letters to a boy who will one day write a song that will give cheer to the millions of our race. We are all making the flag."

"But," I said impatiently, "these people were only working!"

Then came a great shout from The Flag:

"The work that we do is the making of the flag.

"I am not the flag: not at all. I am but its shadow.

"I am whatever you make me, nothing more.

"I am your belief in yourself, your dream of what a people may become.

"I live in a changing life, a life of moods and passions, of heartbreaks and tired muscles.

在國旗上的這個行動，並不一定大於今年夏天一個男孩在喬治亞洲贏得玉米俱樂部獎所作的努力。

"昨天國會說了一句話，這句話將把阿拉斯加的大門打開[1]；但是密歇根的一位母親爲了使兒子受到教育，從早到晚辛勞工作，這位母親也同樣是在製造國旗。

"昨天，我們通過了一項新的法律，防止發生經濟恐慌；也可能是昨天，俄亥俄州一位小學教師教他的學生學寫最初幾個字母，這學生也許有一天會譜出一首使我們民族千萬人振奮的歌曲。我們都在製造國旗。"

我不耐煩地說："可是這些人不過是在做工作呀！"

國旗大聲喊起來：

"我們做的工作就是製造國旗。

"我不是國旗，根本就不是，我只不過是它的影子。

"你們把我做成什麼樣子，我就是什麼樣子。

"我是你們對自己的信心，我是你們對民族發展方向的理想。

"我生活在變化之中，心緒起伏，感情多變，有時傷心，有時疲勞。

（1）指美國國會通過決定把阿拉斯加的鐵路收歸政府所有。

"Sometimes I am strong with pride, when men do an honest work, fitting the rails together truly.

"Sometimes I droop, for then purpose has gone from me, and cynically I play the coward.

"Sometimes I am loud, garish, and full of that ego that blasts judgment.

"But always I am all that you hope to be, and have the courage to try for.

"I am song and fear, struggle and panic, and ennobling hope.

"I am the day's work of the weakest man, and the largest dream of the most daring.

"I am the constitution and the courts, statutes and the statute makers, soldier and dreadnaught, drayman and street sweep, cook, counselor, and clerk.

"I am the battle of yesterday, and the mistake of tomorrow.

"I am the mystery of the men who do without knowing why.

"I am the clutch of an idea, and the reasoned purpose of resolution.

"I am no more than what you believe me to be and I am all that you believe I can be.

"I am what you make me, nothing more.

"I swing before your eyes as a bright gleam of color, a symbol of yourself, the pictured suggestion of that big thing which makes this nation. My stars and my

"有時我會滿懷豪情，感到堅強，這是人們誠實工作、井然有序的時候。

　　"有時我嗒然懊喪，因爲我那時失去了目標，可悲地成爲懦夫。

　　"有時我趾高氣揚，華而不實，自我中心，完全失去了判斷力。

　　"但是，你們希望我成爲什麼樣子，並且有勇氣努力去做，我就永遠是你們希望的樣子。

　　"我是歡歌，我是恐懼，我是鬥爭，我是驚惶，我是使人高尚的希望。

　　"我是最弱小者的日常工作，又是最強大者的最高夢想。

　　"我是憲法和法庭，我是法規和立法者，我是士兵和大無畏的人，我是運貨的馬車夫，我是掃街的工人，我是厨子、律師和職員。

　　"我是昨天的戰爭和明天的失誤。

　　"我是一個謎，衆人不知其所以然而爲之的一個謎。

　　"我執着與把握一種理想，我是下定決心的人們冷靜考慮去爭取的目標。

　　"你們相信我成爲什麼，我就只能成爲什麼；你們相信我能成爲什麼，我就能成爲什麼。

　　"你們把我造成什麼樣子，我就是什麼樣子。

　　"我在你們的眼前飄揚，像一束五彩的光，象徵着你們自己，上面畫出創造我們國家的偉

stripes are your dream and your labors. They are bright with cheer, brilliant with courage, firm with faith, because you have made them so out of your hearts. For you are the makers of the flag and it is well that you glory in the making."

大精神。我的星條[1]是你們的夢想和勞動。它們振奮明亮，果敢光輝，信仰堅定，因為那是你們用心做成的。你們是國旗的製造者，所以你們應當為製造國旗而感到無上光榮。"

---

[1] 美國國旗是星條旗，其上的五十顆星代表五十個州。

70 Address to the German People

Kaiser Wilhelm II

Since the founding of the Empire, during a period of forty-three years, it has been my zealous endeavor and the endeavor of my ancestors to preserve peace to the world and in peace to promote our vigorous development. But our enemies envy us the success of our toil. All professed and secret hostility from East and West and from beyond the sea, we have till now borne in the consciousness of our responsibility and power. Now, however, our opponents desire to humble us. They demand that we look on with folded arms while our enemies gird themselves for treacherous attack. They will not tolerate that we support our ally with unshaken loyalty, who fights for its prestige as a great power, and with whose abasement our power and honor are likewise lost. Therefore the sword must decide. In the midst of peace the world attacks us. Therefore up! To arms! All hesitation, all delay were treachery to the Fatherland. It is a question of the existence or non-existence of the Empire which our fathers bounded anew. It is the question of the existence or the non-existence of German might and German culture. We shall defend ourselves to the last breath of man and beast. And we shall survive this fight, even though it were against a world of enemies. Never yet was Germany conquered when she was united. Then forward march with God! He will be with us as He was with our fathers.

威廉二世（1859～1941），德國皇帝，竭力鼓吹武裝德國，結果導致第一次世界大戰。本文發表於 1914年 8 月 6 日。

七十 致德國人民

德皇威廉二世

自帝國建立以來這四十三年中，諸位先王和我本人始終竭力維護世界和平，在和平中欣欣向榮地發展我國。但是，我們的敵人嫉妒我們辛勤努力換來的成就。由於我們意識到自己的責任和力量，對來自東方、西方以及大洋彼岸的一切公開和暗藏的敵意，我們至今一直忍耐着。但是，現在我們的敵人却企圖羞辱我們。當敵人全副武裝準備背信棄義進攻時，他們却要求我們袖手旁觀。他們不讓我們堅定忠誠地支援我們的盟友[1]，而我們的盟友正在為維護她的大國地位而鬥爭。一旦我們盟友的地位降低，我們的力量和榮譽亦將喪失。因此只能用刀劍來裁決了。全世界在和平的烟幕下向我們進擊。因此，起來吧！武裝起來！一切猶疑，一切遷延都是對祖國的背叛。這是關乎我們父兄重新界定的帝國能否存在下去的問題。這是關乎德國武力和德國文化能否存在下去的問題。只要一息尚存，我們就要為保衛自己而戰。儘管我們的敵人是全世界，我們必定能戰鬥到底。德國只要團結一致，就從未被征服過。前進吧，上帝和我們同在。他曾降福我們的祖先，也將降福我們。

（1）指奧匈帝國。當時德國與奧匈帝國一同支持土耳其。

71 "A Scrap of Paper"

David Lloyd George

There is no man in this room who has always regarded the prospect of our being engaged in a great war with greater reluctance, with greater repugnance than I have done throughout the whole of my political life. There is no man more convinced that we could not have avoided this war without national dishonour. I am fully alive to the fact that every nation which has ever engaged in any war has always invoked the sacred name of honour. Many a crime has been committed in its name. There are some crimes being committed now. All the same, national honour is a reality, and any nation that disregards it is doomed. Why is our honour as a country involved in this war? It is because we are bound by honourable obligations to defend the independence, the liberty, the integrity of a small neighbor. She could not have compelled us. She was weak. But the man who declines to discharge his duty because his creditor is too poor to enforce it is a blackguard.

We entered into a solemn treaty to defend Belgium, but our signatures did not stand alone there. Why are not Austria and Germany performing the obligations of their bond? It is suggested that when we quote this treaty it is purely an excuse on our part; it is our low

---

喬治（1863～1945），英國政治家。1914年9月
2日英德兩方談判時，德國首相提出："你們是否要

七十一　"一張廢紙"

大衛・勞伊德・喬治

在座諸位沒有人會比我更不情願、更反感地看到我們被捲入一場大戰的前景了。在我的一生政治生涯中，我一直抱着上述的態度。沒有人會比我更堅信，我們不可能既不使我國榮譽受到損害，又避免這場戰爭的發生。我完全看得清楚，一個國家只要捲入戰爭，就必然要乞靈於榮譽這個堂而皇之的名義。不少罪行都是在榮譽的名義下犯的。現在就有些犯罪活動正在進行。然而，國家的榮譽畢竟是一個客觀存在的現實，任何國家無視這個現實，都是註定要滅亡的。為什麼這場戰爭牽涉到我國的榮譽問題？這是因為我們承擔着光榮的責任，要保衛一個弱小鄰國的獨立、自由與領土完整。這國家很弱小，不可能強迫我們這樣做。但是如果有人因債權人太窮，無力強迫他還債，便拒絕清償債務，此人便是一個卑鄙的惡棍。

我們簽訂過一項保衛比利時的光榮條約，但是在條約上簽字的不僅是我們。為什麼奧地利和德國不履行他們應守的條約義務？有人提出說我國引用這項條約純粹是藉口，指我們施

為一張廢紙（指保證比利時中立的條約）和我們開戰？"本文是喬治的回答講話。

craft and cunning to cloak our jealousy of a superior civilization which we are attempting to destroy. Our answer is our action in 1870. We called then upon France and Prussia to respect the treaty.

At that time the greatest danger to Belgium came from France and not from Germany, and we invited both belligerent Powers to state that they had no intention of violating Belgian territory. What was the answer given by Bismarck? He said it was superfluous to ask Prussia such a question in face of the treaties in force. France gave a similar answer. We received the thanks of the Belgian people for our intervention in a remarkable document addressed by the municipality of Brussels to Queen Victoria. In 1870 the French army was wedged up against the Belgian front, with every means of escape shut off by a ring of flame from Prussian cannon. The one way out was by violating the neutrality of Belgium, and the French preferred ruin and humiliation to the breaking of their bond. The French emperor, the French marshals, a hundred thousand gallant Frenchmen preferred captivity rather than dishonour the name of their country. When it was to the interest of France to break the treaty she did not do it. It was the interest of Germany today to break it, and Germany had done it.

She avows it with cynical contempt. She says that treaties only bind you when it is to your interest to keep them. What is a treaty, says the German Chancellor, but a scrap of paper? Have you any £5 notes about you? Have you any of those neat little Treasury one-

詭計、耍手腕，有意掩飾我們對更爲文明發達的國家的妒忌心，而我們企圖摧毀這個國家。我們對此的回答是我們在1870年的行動。當時我們也曾呼籲法國和普魯士遵守這項條約。

那時比利時的最大威脅來自法國而不是德國。我們要求德、法兩個交戰大國同時聲明他們無意侵佔比利時領土。俾斯麥怎樣回答呢？他說，旣然有生效的條約，向普魯士提出這樣一個問題，便是多此一舉。法國也作出了類似的回答。在布魯塞爾[1]市政府給維多利亞女王的一份著名文件中，比利時人民對我們干預此事表達了感謝。1870年，法國軍隊在比利時國境受到普魯士炮火的嚴密封鎖，斷絕了一切突圍的出路。唯一的辦法是破壞比利時的中立，進入比利時國境。但當時法國人情願滅亡與屈辱，也不願破壞條約。當時法國皇帝和將軍們以及成千上萬英勇的法國人寧願被俘，也不願國家聲譽受損。在撕毀條約有利於法國的時候，法國沒有這樣做。但今天，撕毀條約有利於德國，德國却這樣做了。

她以一種侮慢的態度公開承認這一點，她說條約只是在有利於你時才對你有約束力。德國首相說，條約不就是一張廢紙？你們身上帶有五鎊的紙幣嗎？帶有印刷精美的小張一鎊紙

（1）比利時首都。

pound notes? If you have, burn them. They are only scraps of paper. What are they made of? Rags! What are they worth? The whole credit of the British Empire! Scraps of paper! I have been dealing with scraps of paper in the last few weeks. We suddenly found the commerce of the world coming to a standstill. The machine had stopped. Why? The machinery of commerce was moved by bills of exchange. I have seen some of them; wretched, crinkled, scrawled over, blotted, frowzy; and yet those scraps of paper moved great ships, laden with thousands of tons of precious goods from one end of the world to the other. The motive power behind them was the honour of commercial men.

Treaties are the currency of international statesmanship. German traders have the reputation of being as upright and straight-forward as any traders in the world, but if the currency of German commence is to be debased to the level of that of her statesmanship, no trader from Shanghai to Valparaiso will ever look at a German signature again. That is the doctrine of the scrap of paper; that is the doctrine which is proclaimed by Bernhardi — that treaties only bind a nation as long as it is to its interest. It goes to the root of all public law. It is the straight road to barbarism. Just as if you removed the magnetic pole whenever it was in the way of a German cruiser, the whole navigation of the

幣嗎？要是有的話，燒了它吧。還不是幾張廢
紙！它們是用什麼造成的？殘片碎布罷了！可
是它們價值幾何？等於不列顛帝國的全部信譽
啊！幾張廢紙！這幾個星期我一直在和幾張廢
紙打交道。我們發現全世界的商業突然停頓下
來，機器停止了運轉。爲什麼？因爲商業機構
是由股票來推動運轉的。我也見過一些股票，
破破爛爛、皺皺巴巴、上面亂塗亂畫、斑斑點
點、骯髒不堪。但是這些廢紙却開動了載滿千
萬噸珍貴貨物的巨大海輪，往返航行於世界各
地。這些廢紙後面的動力是商人的信譽。

條約是代表國際政治家信譽的錢幣。德國
商人和世界上任何其他國家的商人一樣有着同
樣誠實正直的名譽。但是如果德國錢幣貶值到
和她的政治家的信譽一樣的水平，那末從上海
到瓦爾帕萊索 [1]，再也沒有一個商人會對德國
商人的簽字看上一眼了。這就是所謂一張廢紙
的理論。這就是伯恩哈廸 [2] 公開宣揚的理論：
條約只在於有利一國時才有其約束力。這關係
到一切公共法律的根本問題。這樣走下去，就
直通野蠻時代了。正如你嫌地球的磁極妨礙了
一艘德國巡洋艦，便把它拿開一樣，各個海洋

（1）智利港口。
（2）弗里德利克・馮・伯恩哈廸（Friedrich　von
　　　Berndardi, 1849～1930），德國將軍。

seas would become dangerous, difficult, impossible; the whole machinery of civilization will break down if this doctrine wins in this war. We are fighting against barbarism. There is only one way of putting it right. If there are nations that say they will only respect treaties when it is to their interest to do so, we must make it to their interest to do so.

. . .

的航行就會變得危險、困難，甚至不可能。如果在這次戰爭中，這種主張佔上風，整個文明世界的運作便要土崩瓦解。我們正在跟野蠻作戰。只有一個辦法能扭轉這種情況：如果有哪些國家說他們只在條約對他們有利時才守約，我們就不得不使局勢變得只有守約才對他們有利。

......

72 Ask Congress to Declare War Against Germany

Woodrow Wilson

. . .

It is a war against all nations. American ships have been sunk, American lives taken, in ways which it has stirred us very deeply to learn of, but the ships and people of other neutral and friendly nations have been sunk and overwhelmed in the waters in the same way. There has been no discrimination. The challenge is to all mankind. Each nation must decide for itself how it will meet it. The choice we make for ourselves must be made with a moderation of counsel and a temperateness of judgment befitting our character and our motives as a nation. We must put excited feeling away. Our motive will not be revenge or the victorious assertion of the physical might of the nation, but only the vindication of right, of human right, of which we are only a single champion.

When I addressed the Congress on the twenty-sixth of February last I thought that it would suffice to assert our neutral rights with arms, our right to use the seas against unlawful interference, our right to keep our people safe against unlawful violence. But armed neutrality, it now appears, is impracticable. Because sub-

七十二 要求國會對德宣戰

伍德羅・威爾遜

......

這是一場對抗全世界各國的戰爭。美國的船隻被擊沉，美國人的生命被殺戮，所採用的方式駭人聽聞，但其他中立友好國家的船隻和人民在各個公海上也被同樣的方式擊沉、殺戮。不分皂白，一律對待。這是對全人類的挑戰。每個國家必須自行決定如何應付此種情況。我們的決策必須經過深思熟慮，我們的判斷必須穩重適宜，符合我國民族的品格與宗旨。我們必須心平氣和。我們不應以復仇或勝利地顯示我國的實力為目的，我們的目的只能是維護權利，維護人的權利，我們不過是為此而奮鬥的一名真純戰士。

今年2月26日我在國會演說時，本以為我們只要以武力保證我們的中立，保證我們在公海航行不受非法干擾，保證我們有權衛護我國人民，使之不受非法的暴力攻擊就夠了。然而在目前看來，武力保衛中立是行不通的。雖然國

威爾遜（1856～1924），美國第二十八任總統。第一次世界大戰初期，美國宣佈中立，但美國船隻不斷被德國潛艇擊沉，美國國會於是對德宣戰。這是1917年4月2日威爾遜對國會的演說。

marines are in effect outlaws when used as the German submarines have been used against merchant shipping, it is impossible to defend ships against their attacks as the law of nations has assumed that merchantmen would defend themselves against privateers or cruisers, visible craft giving chase upon the open sea. It is common prudence in such circumstances, grim necessity indeed, to endeavor to destroy them before they have shown their own intention. They must be dealt with upon sight, if dealt with at all. The German government denies the right of neutrals to use arms at all within the areas of the sea which it has proscribed, even in the defense of rights which no modern publicist has ever before questioned their right to defend. The intimation is conveyed that the armed guards which we have placed on our merchant ships will be treated as beyond the pale of law and subject to be dealt with as pirates would be. Armed neutrality is ineffectual enough at best; in such circumstances and in the face of such pretensions it is worse than ineffectual; it is likely only to produce what it was meant to prevent; it is practically certain to draw us into the war without either the rights or the effectiveness of belligerents. There is one choice we cannot make, we are incapable of making: we will not choose the path of submission and suffer the most sacred rights of our nation and our people to be ignored or violated. The wrongs against which we now array ourselves are no common wrongs; they cut to very roots of human life.

With a profound sense of the solemn and even tragical character of the step I am taking and of the grave responsibilities which it involves, but in unhesitating obedience to what I deem my constitutional duty, I advise that the Congress declare the recent course of the imperial German government to be in fact nothing less than war against the government and people of

際法規定商船出於自衛可還擊在公海上追擊自
己的武裝民船、巡洋艦及其他可見船隻，但是
現在德國使用潛艇襲擊商船，因此這些潛艇事
實上已經是海盜船。在這樣的情況下，不等到
這些潛艇顯示出攻擊意向，就努力擊沉他們，
不僅是慎重的，事實上已成為必需的了。你如
果打算同它們交手，就必須在它們一出現之時
就立刻予以攻擊。德國根本否定中立國有權在
德國所劃定的海域內使用武器，即使是為了捍
衛現代國際法專家們一直認為毫無疑義地應該
捍衛的權利也不允許。他們宣稱將把我們在商
船上設置的武裝衛隊視為非法，並按海盜對待。
武裝中立本來就缺乏效力。在德國上述主張面
前，武裝中立比缺乏效力更糟。它很可能只
能產生原來想避免的結果；實際上肯定會把我
們捲入戰爭，卻又得不到交戰國的權力與實效。
有一條道路是我們不應選擇也不能選擇的：我
們不能走屈服的道路，不能走上把國家和人民
最神聖的權利置之不顧、受到破壞的道路。我
們一致起來反抗的邪惡並非一般的邪惡，而是
損害到人類生活根基的邪惡。

　　我深深感到我現在要採取的步驟十分嚴
重，甚至會帶來悲痛後果。採取這一步驟責任
十分重大，但是我認為這是憲法賦予我的責任，
我應該毫不猶豫地執行。我建議國會宣佈德帝
國政府近來對美國政府和人民的行為事實上就

the United States; that it formally accept the status of belligerent which has thus been thrust upon it; and that it take immediate steps not only to put the country in a more thorough state of defense, but also to exert all its power and employ all its resources to bring the government of the German Empire to terms and end the war.

. . .

It is a distressing and oppressive duty, gentlemen of the Congress, which I have performed in thus addressing you. There are, it may be, many months of fiery trial and sacrifice ahead of us. It is a fearful thing to lead this great peaceful people into war, into the most terrible and disastrous of all wars, civilization itself seeming to be in the balance. But the right is more precious than peace, and we shall fight for the things which we have always carried nearest our hearts — for democracy, for the right of those who submit to authority to have a voice in their own governments, for the dominion of right by such a concert of free peoples as shall itself at last free. To such a task we can dedicate our lives and our fortunes, everything that we are and everything we have, with the pride of those who know that the day has come when American is privileged to spend her blood and her might for the principles that gave her birth and happiness and the peace which she has treasured. God helping her, she can do no other.

是發動了戰爭；建議國會宣佈正式接受強加於我國的交戰國地位，建議國會立即採取步驟，以使國家更全面地處於防禦狀態，並且動員我國一切財力物力，迫使德帝國政府屈服並結束戰爭。

……

各位議員先生，向你們提出這樣的建議，對我來說，是一個痛苦而沉重的任務。我們面前可能是嚴重考驗和犧牲的艱苦歲月。把這個偉大的和平民族引入一場空前可怕的戰爭中去，是一件思之令人恐懼的事情。全人類文明處於岌岌可危的關頭。但是正義比和平更珍貴，我們將為心中最珍貴的事物奮勇作戰——為民主，為那些爭取在自己政府中有發言地位的人的權利，為各自由民族一致贊同的自由正義統治而戰。為了實現這一任務，我們可以驕傲地獻出我們的生命財產，獻出我們一切所有，連同我們自己在內，因為我們認識到美國人有權用自己的熱血和力量去捍衛自己原則的時刻已經來臨，正是這些原則賦予我國生命、幸福與她所珍惜的和平。願上帝降福美國。這是美國的唯一出路。

73 The League of Nations

Woodrow Wilson

Mr. chairman:— I consider it a distinguished privilege to be permitted to open the discussion in this Conference on the League of Nations. We have assembled for two purposes: to make the present settlements which have been rendered necessary by this war, and also to secure the peace of the world, not only by the present settlements, but by the arrangements we shall make at this Conference for its maintenance. The League of Nations seems to me to be necessary for both of these purposes. There are many complicated questions connected with the present settlements which perhaps cannot be successfully worked out to an ultimate issue by the decisions we shall arrive at here. I can easily conceive that many of these settlements will need subsequent consideration, that many of the decisions we make shall need subsequent alteration in some degree; for, if I may judge by my own study of some of these questions, they are not susceptible of confident judgments at present.

It is, therefore, necessary that we should set up some machinery by which the work of this Conference should be rendered complete. We have assembled here for the purpose of doing very much more than making the present settlements that are necessary. We are assembled under very peculiar conditions of world opinion. I may say, without straining the point, that we are not representatives of governments, but representatives of peoples. It will not suffice to satisfy

七十三　關於國際聯盟

伍德羅・威爾遜

主席先生：我能夠在本屆會議上就成立國際聯盟最先發言，感到莫大的光榮。我們在此集會有兩個目的：一是就解決此次戰爭引起的問題，提出若干當前必要的措施；另一是通過當前的這些措施，並在本屆會議上作出各種安排，以保證持久和平。我認為，成立國際聯盟對於上述兩個目的都是必需的。當前的具體措施牽涉到許多複雜問題，或許不能根據我們本屆會議上的決定得到最終解決。這些措施當中，不難看出，有許多還需要繼續審議；某些決定也還要事後作某些程度的修改。因為，我經過研究，認為對於某些問題的判斷，目前還沒有可靠的依據。

所以，我們必須設立一定的機構，使本屆會議進行的工作得以進一步完善。我們在此集會的目的，除去提出一些必需的措施而外，還有更多的事情要做。我們是在國際輿論十分獨特的情況下召集這次會議的。我可以毫不牽強地說，我們不僅是各國政府的代表，我們還是各國人民的代表。無論在什麼地方，僅使政府

本文為威爾遜於第一次世界大戰後，1919 年 1 月 25 日在巴黎和會上的講話。

governmental circles anywhere. It is necessary that we should satisfy the opinion of mankind. The burdens of this war have fallen in an unusual degree upon the whole population of the countries involved. I do not need to draw for you the picture of how the burden has been thrown back from the front upon the older men, upon the women, upon the children, upon the homes of the civilized world, and how the real strain of the war has come where the eye of government could not reach, but where the heart of humanity beat. We are bidden by these people to make a peace which will make them secure. We are bidden by these people to see to it that this strain does not come upon them, and I venture to say that it has been possible for them to bear this strain because they hoped that those who represented them could get together after this war and make such another sacrifice unnecessary.

. . .

Therefore, it seems to me that we must concert our best judgment in order to make this league of Nations a vital thing — not merely a formal thing, not an occasional thing, not a thing sometimes called into life to meet an exigency, but always functioning in watchful attendance upon the interests of the nations, and that its continuity should be a vital continuity; that it should have functions that are continuing functions, and that do not permit an intermission 'of its watchfulness and of its labor; that it should be the eye of the nations to keep watch upon the common interest, an eye that did not slumber, an eye that was everywhere watchful and attentive.

. . .

You can imgine, gentlemen, I dare say, the sentiments and the purpose with which representatives of the United States support this great project for a League

階層滿意是不夠的，必須使全人類滿意。這次戰爭的負擔，極大程度落在各有關國家的人民身上。我無需向你們描述這副重擔如何由前方轉到了後方的老弱婦孺身上，轉到了文明世界的千家萬戶頭上，也不需解釋這次戰爭的眞正耗竭程度，非政府目力所及，只有人心能感到。我們正是受這些人民的囑托，來此謀求一個使他們安心的和平。我們正是受到這些人民的囑托，來設法保證這種緊張耗竭不再落在他們身上。我可以大膽地說，他們在戰爭期間所以能夠忍受這種緊張耗竭，只因爲寄望他們的代表在戰後能夠聚在一起共商大計，使他們不必重受這樣的痛苦犧牲。

……

因此，我以爲我們必須協力作出最佳的判斷，使得國際聯盟成爲一個活生生的東西。國際聯盟不應徒具形式，不應是一個暫時的權宜機構，不是爲了應急，而是爲了各國利益而常備不懈的機構。國際聯盟的繼續不斷運作應是充滿活力的；它的作用是持久不息的作用，不能間歇，不能稍存懈怠。國際聯盟應成爲保護各國共同利益的眼睛，在一切地方都永遠清醒、警覺、從不睏倦。

……

各位先生，我想你們一定能想象出美國代表在支持建立國際聯盟這一偉大計劃中的感情

of Nations. We regard it as the keystone of the whole program which expressed our purposes and ideals in this war and the associated nations accepted as the basis of the settlement. If we return to the United States without having made every effort in our power to realize this program, we should return to meet the merited scorn of our fellow-citizens. For they are a body that constitutes a great democracy. They expect their leaders to speak their thoughts and no private purpose of their own. They expect their representatives to be their servants. We have no choice but to obey their mandate. But it is with the greatest enthusiasm and pleasure that we accept that mandate; and because this is the keystone of the whole fabric, we have pledged our every purpose to it, as we have to every item of the fabric. We would not dare abate a single item of the program which constitutes our instruction. We would not dare compromise upon any matter as the champion of this thing — this peace of the world, this attitude of justice, this principle that we are the masters of no people, but are here to see that every people in the world shall choose its own masters and govern its own destinies, not as we wish but as it wishes. We are here to see, in short, that the very foundations of this war are swept away.

和目的。對於這次戰爭的目的和理想，我們有整套規劃。我們把國際聯盟看成是這套規劃的基石，希望有關各國接受國際聯盟作為解決措施的基礎。如果我們沒有盡一切努力實現這個規劃，回國之時就會受到我國公民理應對我們的蔑視。因為他們是構成一個偉大民主國家的主體。他們指望領袖說出他們的想法而不存私人目的，期望他們的代表成為公僕。我們只能聽命於他們，但是我們是懷着最大的熱忱，最愉快的心情接受他們的命令的。由於這是整個結構的奠基石，我們保證決心實現它，也保證決心完成整個結構中的一切項目。我們不敢不完成規劃中規定我們完成的任何一個項目。作為這件事的倡議者，我們不敢妥協。這是一件關係到世界和平、關係到正義的態度、關係到一個原則的問題。這原則就是：我們不是人民的主人，我們到這裏來，只不過為了努力保證世界上一切民族有權按照自己的意願而非我們的意願選擇自己的主人，掌握自己的命運。簡而言之，我們到這裏來是為了保證消除發生這次戰爭的一切根源。

74 Peace

James Ramsay MacDonald

Today, as I read about the Peace, as I hoped and prayed about the Peace, I thought of the almost countless graves scattered in the centre of Europe. Many of our children are lying there. It must be in the hearts of all of us to build a fair monument to those men who will never come back to bless us with their smiles. Do they not want a grand and magnificent monument built for them so that the next generations, even if they forget their names, shall never forget their sacrifice? That is what I want. I almost felt I heard the grass growing over them in a magnificent, soothing hormony, and that simple soothing peace of the growing grass seemed to grow louder and more magnificent until the riot and distractive sound of the guns were stifled and stilled by it. Can we not have that sentiment today, that feeling in our hearts? Can we not go in imagination to where our children lie, and feel that, in Europe, in our own hearts, that same peace shall rule, and through sorrow and through sacrifice we shall obtain that wisdom and light which will enable Europe to possess peace for ever?

七十四　論和平

詹姆斯・拉姆齊・麥克唐納

今天，當我閱悉和平已經到來，當我盼望和平、爲和平祈禱，我想到遍佈歐洲中心各地幾乎數不清的墳墓。我們許多兒女長眠在這些墳墓之中。我們所有人都會在自己的心頭許願，要爲這些再也不能含笑歸來和我們重逢的人樹立起一座紀念碑。難道不應該建立一座雄偉壯麗的紀念碑，使後世子孫即使忘記了他們的姓名，也能永遠記住他們的犧牲嗎？我認爲應該這樣做。我彷彿聽到他們墓上的青草在簌簌生長，發出莊嚴而又使人慰藉的和聲，這種簡單而使人安慰的和平之音彷彿逐漸響亮起來，更加莊嚴肅穆，把一切紛亂的槍炮聲淹沒下去。在今天這個日子，我們難道心內沒有這種感情嗎？我們難道能不在神游我們孩子們長眠之所時，感到和平將植根於我們心中，也將主宰歐洲？難道通過這些哀痛與犧牲，我們不會變得聰明、得到啓示，使歐洲永保和平嗎？

麥克唐納（1866～1937），英國工黨右翼領袖，曾任內閣首相。第一次世界大戰中，反對英國參戰。本文是1919年大戰結束後他在英國工黨會議上的演說。

75 Theses and Report on Bourgeois Democracy and the Dictatorship of the Proletariat

Nikolai Lenin

. . .

. . . The main thing that socialists fail to understand and that consitutes their short-sightedness in matters of theory, their subservience to bourgeois prejudices and their political betrayal of the proletariat is that in capitalist society, whenever there is any serious aggravation of the class struggle intrinsic to that society, there can be no alternative but the dictatorship of the bourgeoisie or the dictatorship of the porletariat. Dreams of some third way are reactionary, petty-bourgeois lamentations. That is borne out by more than a century of development of bourgeois democracy and the working-class movement in all the advanced countries, and notably by the experience of the past five years. This is also borne out by the whole science of political economy, by the entire content of Marxism, which reveals the economic inevitability, wherever commodity economy prevails, of the dictatorship of the bourgeoisie that can only be replaced by the class which the very growth of capitalism develops, multiplies, wields together and strengthens, that is, the proletarian class.

Another theoretical and political error of the socialists is their failure to understand that ever since the rudiments of democracy first appeared in antiquity, its forms inevitably changed over the centuries as one ruling class replaced another. Democracy assumed different forms and was applied in different degrees in

七十五　關於無產階級民主和無產階級專政

尼古拉伊・列寧

……

……社會黨人所以在理論上短視、被資產階級偏見俘虜並在政治上背叛無產階級，主要是因爲他們不了解在資本主義社會中，當作爲這個社會基礎的階級鬥爭發展至相當尖銳時，除了資產階級專政或無產階級專政外，不可能有其他可行之道。幻想走第三條道路是反動的小資產者的悲嘆。一切先進國家百多年來資產階級民主和工人運動發展的經驗，尤其近五年來的經驗均證明了上述的一點。全部政治經濟學、馬克思主義的所有內容也證明了這一點。馬克思主義闡明了在商品經濟統治下資產階級專政的經濟必然性，能夠代替資產階級專政的，沒有別的階級，只有由資本主義本身所發展、擴大、團結、鞏固起來的階級，即無產階級。

社會黨人在理論上和政治上的另一錯誤，在於不懂得從古代民主萌芽時期起，在幾千年過程中，民主形式必然隨着統治階級的更換而

列寧（1870～1924），1917年9月領導俄國革命，當選爲第一屆蘇維埃主席。本文爲1919年列寧在共產國際第一次代表大會上的報告。

the ancient republics of Greece, the medieval cities and the advanced capitalist countries. It would be sheer nonsense to think that the most profound revolution in human history, the first case in the world of power being transferred from the exploiting minority to the exploited majority, could take place within the time-worn framework of the old, bourgeois, parliamentary democracy, without drastic changes, without the creation of new forms of democracy, new institutions that embody the new conditions for applying democracy, etc.

Proletarian dictatorship is similar to the dictatorship of other classes in that it arises out of the need, as every other dictatorship does, to forcibly suppress the resistance of the class that is losing its political sway. The fundamental distinction between the dictatorship of the proletariat and the dictatorship of other classes — landlord dictatorship in the Middle Ages and bourgeois dictatorship in all the civilised capitalist countries — consists in the fact that the dictatorship of the landowners and bourgeoisie was the forcible suppression of the resistance offered by the vast majority of the population, namely, the working people. In contrast, proletarian dictatorship is the forcible suppression of the resistance of the exploiters, i.e., an insignificant minority of the population, the landowners and capitalists.

It follows that proletarian dictatorship must inevitably entail not only a change in democratic forms and institutions, generally speaking, but precisely such a change as provides an unparalleled extension of the actual enjoyment of democracy by those oppressed by capitalism — the toiling classes.

. . .

有所改變。民主以不同的形式、不同的程度出現於古代希臘各共和國、中世紀各城市，以及先進的資本主義國家。世界上政權首次由少數剝削者手裏轉到多數被剝削者手裏，將是人類歷史上最深刻的革命。如果認爲這革命能夠在舊式的、資產階級的議會制民主範圍內發生，不需要急劇的轉變，不需要建立新的民主形式，不需要新機關體現運用民主的新條件，那就荒謬絕倫了。

無產階級專政同其他階級專政相似的地方，在於它同任何專政一樣，必須用暴力鎮壓那失去政治統治權的階級的反抗。無產階級專政同其他階級專政（中世紀的地主專政，一切文明的資本主義國家中的資產階級專政）根本不同的地方，在於地主和資產階級專政是用暴力鎮壓絕大多數勞動人民的反抗。相反地，無產階級專政是用暴力鎮壓極少數人的反抗，即地主和資本家等剝削者。

由此可以得出結論說，無產階級專政必然使民主的形式和機關發生變化，而且，一般說來，正是這種變化使得受資本主義壓迫的勞動階級能在世界上空前廣泛地實際享有民主。

……

76 Napoleon

Ferdinand Foch

If one considers that Napoleon revealed his powers in 1796 at the age of twenty-seven, it is plain that nature endowed him extraordinarily. These talents he applied unceasingly through the whole length of his prodigious career.

Through them he marks out his way along a re-splendent path in the military annals of humanity. He carries his victorious eagles from the Alps to the Pyramids, and from the banks of the Tagus to those of the Moskova, surpassing in their flight the conquests of Alexander, of Hannibal and of Caesar. Thus he remains the great leader, superior to all others in his prodigious genius, his need of activity, his nature, ardent to excess, which is always favorable to the profits of war but dangerous to the equilibrium of peace.

Thus he lifts the art of war far above all known heights, but this carries him to regions of dizziness. Identifying the greatness of the country with his own, he would rule the destinies of nations with arms, as if one could bring about the prosperity of the people from a succession of victories at grievous sacrifices. As if this people could live by glory instead of by labor.

福克（1851～1929），法國元帥。本文為1921年5月5日拿破崙逝世一百周年時，福克在拿破崙墓前發表的演說。

（1）法國的軍旗，以鷹為標誌。

（2）在西班牙與葡萄牙交界處。

（3）今蘇聯首都莫斯科附近的河流。

七十六 拿破崙

費汀納德·福克

只要想一想，1796年，拿破崙年僅二十七歲已經嶄露頭角，就不難知道他天賦非凡的資質。他把自己的天才不斷地用於一生的豐功偉業之中。

由於秉賦這種天才，他在人類軍事史上走出了一條光輝的道路。他高舉戰無不戰的鷲旗[1]從阿爾卑斯山進軍到埃及的金字塔，從塔古斯河[2]之濱到莫斯科河[3]兩岸。在飛舞的軍旗下，他建立的赫赫武功超越亞歷山大大帝[4]、漢尼拔大將和凱撒大帝[5]。這樣，他以驚人的天才，不甘守成和好大喜功的本性成為勝過一切其他人的最偉大領袖人物。這種本性，有利於戰爭，但對維持和平的均勢却很危險。

他把戰爭藝術提高到從未有過的高度，而這就把他推到了岌岌可危的巔峯。他把國家的榮耀和他個人的榮耀視為一體，他要以武力控制各國的命運。他以為一個個人能夠以慘痛的犧牲為代價得到一系列的勝利，換來本民族的繁榮；以為這個民族可以靠光榮而不是靠勞動

（4）亞歷山大（公元前356～323），馬其頓王腓力二世之子，建立了東起印度河，西至尼羅河與巴爾干半島的亞歷山大帝國。

（5）凱撒(公元前100～44)，古羅馬統帥，稱凱撒大帝。

As if the conquered nations, deprived of their independence, would not rise some day to reconquer it, putting an end to a regime of force and presenting armies strong in numbers and invincible in the ardor of outraged justice. As if in a civilized world, moral right should not be greater than a power created entirely by force, however talented that force might be. In attempting this Napoleon himself goes down, not for lack of genius, but because he attempted the impossible, because he undertook with a France exhausted in every way, to bend to his laws a Europe already instructed by its misfortunes, and soon entirely in arms.

Decidedly, duty is common to all. Higher than commanding armies victoriously, there is our country to be served for her good as she understands it; there is justice to be respected everywhere. Above war there is peace.

Assuredly, the most gifted man errs who, in dealing with humanity, depends upon his own insight and intelligence and discards the moral law of society, created by respect for the individual, and those principles of liberty, equality and fraternity, the basis of our civilization, and the essence of Christianity.

Sire, sleep in peace; from the tomb itself you labor continually for France. At every danger to the country, our flags quiver at the passage of the Eagle. If our legions have returned victorious through the triumphal arch which you built, it is because the sword of Austerlitz marked out their direction, showing how to unite

獲得生存；以為那些被征服而失去獨立的國家不會一朝奮起，列出陣容強大、士氣高昂、戰無不勝的義師，推翻武力統治，重新贏得獨立；以為在文明世界裏，道德公理不應比完全靠武力形成的力量為強大，不管這支武力有多大。由於這樣的企圖，拿破崙走了下坡路。他不是缺乏天才，而是由於他想做那不可能的事。他想以當時財枯力竭的法國使整個歐洲屈膝，豈知當時歐洲已經總結了失敗的教訓，很快就全面武裝起來。

當然，每個人都有自己的責任。但是，比指揮軍隊克敵制勝更重要的是，按照祖國的需要為祖國服務，使正義在一切地方受到尊重。和平高於戰爭。

的確，在處理人的問題時，如果只依賴個人的見識與才智，歪曲為尊重個人而制定的社會道德法律，歪曲作為我們文明基礎和基督教本質的自由、平等、博愛的原則，那麼，即使是最有天才的人，也肯定會犯錯誤。

陛下，請安息吧。你英靈未泯，你的精神仍然在為法蘭西服務。每次國家危難的時刻，我們的鷲旗依然迎風招展。如果我們的軍隊能在你建造的凱旋門下勝利歸來，那是因為奧斯特列茨[1]的寶劍為他們指引了方向，教導他們

（1）捷克地名，1805年12月4日拿破崙在此打敗了俄國和奧地利的聯軍。

and lead the army that won the victory. Your masterly lessons, your determined labors, remain indefeasible examples. In studying them and meditating on them the art of war grows daily greater. It is only in the reverently and thoughtfully gathered rays of your immortal glory that generations of the distant future shall succeed in grasping the science of combat and the management of armies for the sacred cause of the defense of the country.

如何團結起來帶領軍隊取得勝利。你高深的敎誨，你堅毅的努力，永遠是我們不可磨滅的榜樣。我們研究思索你的言行，戰爭的技藝便日益發展。只有恭謹地、認眞地學習你不朽的光輝思想，我們的後代子孫才能成功地掌握作戰的知識和統軍的策略，以完成保衞我們祖國的神聖事業。

77 Appeal to America

Mohandas Karamchand Gandhi

In my opinion, the Indian struggle for freedom bears in its consequences not only upon India and England but upon the whole world. It contains one-fifth of the human race. It represents one of the most ancient civilizations. It has traditions handed down from tens of thousands of years, some of which, to the astonishment of the world, remain intact. No doubt the ravages of time have affected the purity of that civilization as they have that of many other cultures and many institutions.

If India is to revive the glory of her ancient past, she can only do so when she attains her freedom. The reason for the struggle having drawn the attention of the world I know does not lie in the fact that we Indians are fighting for our liberty, but in the fact the means adopted by us for attaining that liberty are unique and, as far as history shows us, have not been adopted by any other people of whom we have any record.

The means adopted are not violence, not bloodshed, not diplomacy as one understands it nowadays, but they are purely and simply truth and non-violence. No wonder that the attention of the world is directed toward this attempt to lead a successful bloodless revolution. Hitherto, nations have fought in the manner of the brute. They have wreaked vengeance upon those

七十七 向美國呼籲

莫罕達斯・卡拉姆紀德・甘地

我以為印度爭取自由的鬥爭，其後果不僅影響印度與英國，而且影響全世界。印度有全人類五分之一的人口，是最古老的文明國家之一。印度有數萬年流傳下來的傳統，其中一部分至今保存完整，使世界詫異。正如其他的文化和傳統因年深日久受到損壞一樣，印度文明的純淨無疑也因年代久遠而受到了侵蝕。

印度若要恢復古時的光榮，就只有獲得自由以後才可以。就我所知，我們的鬥爭之所以引起全世界的注意，並不是因為印度正在為自己的解放而戰，而是因為我們為爭取解放而採取的手段是獨一無二的，不曾為歷史上我們有過記錄的任何民族所採用。

我們採用的手段不是暴力，不必流血，也無需採取時下人們所理解的那種外交手段，我們運用的是純粹的真理和非暴力。我們企圖成功地進行不流血革命，無怪乎全世界的注意力都轉向我們。迄今為止，所有國家的鬥爭方式

甘地（1869～1948），印度民族運動領袖。早年留學倫敦，第一次世界大戰後返回印度，提倡"不合作運動"（即非暴力抵抗運動）。1948年為印度教極右派分子刺死。

whom they have considered to be their enemies.

We find in searching national anthems adopted by great nations that they contain imprecations upon the so-called enemy. They have vowed destruction and have not hesitated to take the name of God and seek divine assistance for the destruction of the enemy. We in India have endeavored to reverse the process. We feel that the law that governs brute creation is not the law that should guide the human race. That law is inconsistent with human dignity.

I, personally, would wait, if need be, for ages rather than seek to attain the freedom of my country through bloody means. I feel in the innermost of my heart, after a political extending over an unbroken period of close upon thirty-five years, that the world is sick unto death of bloodspilling. The world is seeking a way out, and I flatter myself with the belief that perhaps it will be the privilege of the ancient land of India to show the way out to the hungering world.

都是野蠻的。他們向自己心目中的敵人報復。

　　查閱各大國的國歌，我們發現歌詞中含有對敵人的詛咒。歌詞中發誓要毀滅敵人，而且毫不猶豫地引用上帝的名義並祈求神助以毀滅敵人。我們印度人正努力扭轉這種進程。我們感到統治野蠻世界的法則不應是指導人類的法則。統治野蠻世界的法則有悖人類尊嚴。

　　就我個人來說，如果需要的話，我寧願長時期地等待，也不願用流血手段使我的國家得到自由。在連續不斷地從政近三十五年之後，我由衷地感到，全世界對於流血已經深惡痛絕。世界正在尋找出路，我敢說，或許印度古國會有幸為這飢渴的世界找到出路。

78 The Strength of Satyagraha

Mohandas Karamchand Gandhi

You will forgive me for saying the few words that I want to say just now, sitting in the chair. I am under strict medical orders not to exert myself, having a weak heart. I am, therefore, compelled to have some assistance and to have my remarks read to you. But before I call upon Mr. Deasi to read my remarks, I wish to say one word to you. Take thought before you sign the Pledge. But if you sign it, see to it that you never violate the Pledge you have signed. May God help you and me in carrying out the Pledge.

(The Pledge)

Being conscientiously of the opinion that the Bills known as the Indian Criminal Law (Amendment) Bill No. I, of 1919, and the Criminal Law (Emergency Powers) Bill No. II, of 1919, are unjust, subversive of the principle of liberty and justice, and destructive of the elementary rights of individuals on which the safety of the community as a whole and the State itself is based, we solemnly affirm that in the event of these Bills becoming laws until they are withdrawn, we shall refuse civilly to obey these laws and such other laws as a committee to be hereafter appointed may think fit and further affirm that in this struggle we will faithfully follow truth and refrain from violence to life, person or property.

(Mr. Deasi, after a few words of introduction, read the following message:—)

七十八　非暴力抵抗主義的力量

莫罕達斯・卡拉姆紀德・甘地

　　請你們原諒我坐在椅子上說幾句話。我心臟衰弱，醫生嚴格囑咐不能過度疲勞，因此，不得不請人代爲宣讀我的講話。但未請達西先生宣讀我的講話之前，我想說一句話：簽署誓詞之前請你們務必愼重考慮。但是簽字以後，就決不要違反誓詞了。願上帝幫助你我使誓詞實現。

誓　詞

　　我們眞心誠意地認爲稱作印度刑法（修正案）1919年第一號以及刑法（緊急件）1919年第二號的這兩個文件是不正義的，破壞了自由與正義的原則及個人的基本權利。這些個人基本權利是全體居民與國家自身安全的基礎。因此，我們嚴正申明，若此二項法案生效，則在其生效直至撤銷期間，我們將以和平方式拒絕遵守此二項法案以及爾後指定成立的委員會認爲不應遵守的其他法律。我們還要申明，在鬥爭中我們將忠實地遵從眞理，作出克制，不採取危及個人生命、人身與財產安全的暴力行動。

　　（達西先生作了簡短的說明之後，朗讀下列講話稿）：

　　本文發表於1919年。

I regret that because of a heart weakness I am unable to speak to you personally. You have no doubt attended many meetings, but those of you who have been attending recently are different from others, in that at these meetings some immediate, tangible action, some definite sacrifice has been demanded of you for the purpose of averting the serious calamity that has overtaken us in the shape of what are known as the Rowlatt Bills. One of them — Bill No. I — has undergone material alterations and its further consideration has been postponed. In spite, however, of the alterations, it is mischievous enough to demand opposition. At this very moment, in all probability, the Second Bill has finally been passed by the Council — if, in reality, you can say that the Bill has been passed by that august body when all its non-official members have unanimously and vociferously opposed it!

The Bills must be resisted, not only because they are in themselves bad, but also because the Government, which is responsible for their introduction, has seen fit to ignore public opinion — and some of its members have boasted of so ignoring that opinion. Resistance to these bills is a common cause between the different schools of thought of the country. For my part, after much prayerful consideration, and after very careful examination of the Government's position, I have pledged myself to offer Satyagraha against the Bills, and have invited all men and women who think and feel as I to do likewise.

. . .

Let us see, therefore, wherein lies the strength of Satyagraha. As the name implies, it is an insistence upon truth which, dynamically expressed, means love; and by the law of love we are required not to return hatred for hatred, violence for violence, but to return

我很遺憾，由於心臟衰弱，不能親自向你們講話。無疑你們參加過許多會議，但最近參加過會議的人和其他人有所不同，因為這些會議要求你們立即採取某些實際行動，作出一定犧牲，使以勞列特法案形式出現而降臨到我們頭上的這場大難得以避免。其中的第一號法案，現已作出實質的修改並延期審議。但是，僅僅修改還不夠，這項法案為害太大，需要根本否定。同時，此刻議會完全可能已通過了第二號法案——如果莊嚴的議會在所有非官守議員一致激烈反對的情況下通過也可以算是通過的話！

　　這兩項法案必須受到抵制，原因不僅是法案本身不好，更且因為提出法案的政府認為可以無視公眾輿論——某些官員甚至以此誇耀於人。抵制此二項法案是全國各種不同思想派別的共同事業。我的態度是，經過有如對上帝祈禱般的深思熟慮，又仔細考察了政府的立場後，我立誓以非暴力抵抗主義反對這兩項法案，並顧請一切和我有共同思想感情的男女同胞和我一同行動起來。

　　……

　　因此，讓我們看非暴力抵抗主義的力量所在。顧名思義，它的力量在於對真理堅韌不拔的追求。這種真理，用強有力的字眼來表達就是愛。愛的法則要求我們不要以怨報怨，以暴

403

good for evil. As Shrimati Sarojuni Devi told you yesterday. The strength lies in a definite recognition of the true religious spirit and of the action corresponding to that spirit. And when once you introduce the religious elements into politics, you revolutionize the whole of your political outlook. You then achieve reform, not by imposing suffering on those who resist reform, but by taking the suffering upon yourselves. And so in this movement we hope, by the intensity of our sufferings, to affect and laten the Government's resolution not to withdraw these objectionable Bills.

. . .

But I have no desire to argue. As the English proverb says, the proof of the pudding is in the eating. The movement, for better or for worse, has been launched. We shall be judged, not by our words, but solely by our deeds. It is, therefore, not enough that we sign the Pledge. Our signing is but an earnest of our determination to live up to it, and if all who sign the Pledge live up to it, I make bold to promise that we shall bring about the withdrawal of the two Bills and that neither the Government nor our critics will have a word to say against us. The cause is great, the remedy is equally great; let us prove worthy of them both.

力對暴力，而要像司里買提‧沙路祝尼‧戴維昨天告訴你們的那樣，以德報怨。非暴力抵抗主義的力量在於確認眞正的宗敎精神以及與這種精神相協調的行動。一旦你將宗敎信仰的因素引進政治，你就使你的全部政治觀點完全改變了。於是你就能夠進行改革，不是通過把苦難强加給抵抗改革的人，而是通過自己承受苦難而達到改革的目的。因此，我們希望，在這個行動中，通過我們所受的深重苦難，可以影響政府，使政府推遲不撤銷這兩項受到反對的法案的決定。

……

但是，我不願再爭辯下去了。正如一句英國諺語所說：布丁好不好，嚐嚐才知道。無論好壞，非暴力抵抗運動已經發動起來。人們應該只是根據我們的行爲而不是根據我們的語言來評判我們。因此，僅在誓詞上簽字是不夠的。我們的簽字只是表示我們決心忠於誓言，如果所有簽名者都確能忠於這誓言，我可以大膽保證我們將使上述兩個法案撤銷，而不論政府或批評我們的人都不敢置一詞以反對我們。我們的事業是偉大的，我們的改革方法也同樣是偉大的，讓我們無愧於我們偉大的事業和改革方法吧。

79 On His Seventieth Birthday

George Bernard Shaw

Of late years the public have been trying to tackle me in every way they possibly can, and failing to make anything of it they have turned to treating me as a great man. This is a dreadful fate to overtake anybody. There has been a distinct attempt to do it again now, and for that reason I absolutely decline to say anything about the celebration of my seventieth birthday. But when the Labor Party, my old friends the Labor Party, invited me here I knew that I should be all right. We have discovered the secret that there are no great man, and we have discovered the secret that there are no great nations or great states.

. . .

According to the capitalist, there will be a guarantee to the world that every man in the country would get a job. They didn't contend it would be a well-paid job, because if it was well paid a man would save up enough one week to stop working the next week, and they were determined to keep a man working the whole time on a bare subsistence wage — and, on the other hand, divide an accumulation of capital.

They said capitalism not only secured this for the working man, but, by insuring fabulous wealth in the hands of a small class of people, they would save money

七十九　在七十壽辰宴會上的講話

喬治・蕭伯納

　　近年來公衆輿論一直千方百計想要把我整垮。此計不成，又反過來把我捧成一個偉人。誰碰上了這種事都是極爲倒霉的。現在出於另一企圖，有人又在幹同樣的事了。爲了這個緣故，對於慶祝我七十歲生日的活動，我完全拒絕發表任何意見。但是，當我的老朋友工黨請我到這裏來時，我知道一切都沒有問題。我們發現了一個秘密，那就是世界上沒有什麼偉人。我們還發現另一秘密，那就是，世界上沒有什麼偉大的民族，也沒有什麼偉大的國家。

　　……

　　資本主義者說，將向全世界保證，在這國家裏，每人都能得到一份職業。他們並不主張那是一份收入很好的職業，因爲假如收入很好，這個人只要做一星期的工，就能節餘足夠的錢，下星期就不工作了。他們要使每個人全時工作來掙得僅能維持生計的工薪，另外，他們還要分得一份積累的資本。

　　他們說，資本主義不僅爲工人提供了上述的保證，而且由於確保巨大的財富集中在一小

　　蕭伯納（1856～1950），英國戲劇家，生於愛爾蘭。這篇演說詞發表於1926年。

whether they liked it or not, and would have to invest it. That is capitalism, and this Government is always interfering with capitalism. Instead of giving a man a job or letting him starve they are giving him doles — after making sure he has paid for them first. They are giving capitalists subsidies and making all sorts of regulations that are breaking up their own system. All the time they are doing it, and we are telling them it is breaking up, they don't understand.

We say in criticism of capitalism: Your system has never kept its promises for one single day since it was promulgated. Our production is ridiculous. We are producing eighty horse-power motor cars when many more houses should be built. We are producing most extravagant luxuries while children starve. You have stood production on its head. Instead of beginning with the things the nation needs most, you are beginning at just the opposite end. . . .

We are opposed to that theory. Socialism, which is perfectly clear and unmistakable, says the thing you have got to take care of is your distribution. We have to begin with that, and private property, if it stands in the way of good distribution, has got to go.

A man who holds public property must hold it on the public condition on which, for instance, I carry my walking stick, I am not allowed to do what I like with it. I must not knock you on the head with it. We say that if distribution goes wrong, everything else goes wrong — religion, morals, government. And we say, therefore (this is the whole meaning of our socialism), we must begin with distribution and take all

階層人手裏，那麼，不論這些人自己願意與否，都必須將錢儲蓄起來，用於投資。這就是資本主義，而我們政府的政策却常常和資本主義相抵觸。政府旣不爲人提供工作，又不讓他們餓死，而是給他們一點救濟——當然，首先得肯定受施者已經爲這點救濟付足了錢。政府給資本主義者津貼，却又訂出各種各樣規定，破壞他們的制度。政府一直在做這樣的事。我們告訴他們這是破壞，他們却不懂。

我們批評資本主義時說道：你們的制度自公佈以來，就從未有哪一天實踐過你們的諾言。我們的生產是荒唐的，我們本需要蓋更多的房屋，却去生產八十匹馬力的汽車。孩子們在挨餓，我們却生產各種最豪華的奢侈品。你們把生產本末倒置了，不首先生產國民最需要的東西，却恰恰相反。……

我們反對這種資本主義理論。明白無誤的社會主義理論指出需要注意的是分配制度。我們必須從這個問題入手。如果私有財產妨礙分配制度的實行，那麼就必須廢除私有財產。

掌握公共財產的人必須遵守公共條件，就像我拿手杖一樣，我不能願意用它幹什麼就幹什麼，我不能用它來敲你的腦袋。我們說，如果分配制度出了差錯，那麼，宗敎、道德、政府等，一切都會跟着出問題。因此，我們說，必須從分配着手，並採取一切必要的步驟，這

the necessary steps.

I think we are keeping it in our minds because our business is to take care of the distribution of wealth in the world: and I tell you, as I have told you before, that I don't think there are two men, or perhaps one man, in our 47,000,000 who approves of the existing distribution of wealth. I will go even further and say that you will not find a single person in the whole of the civilized world who agrees with the existing system of the distribution of wealth. It has been reduced to a blank absurdity. . . .

. . .

I think the day will come when we will be able to make the distinction between us and the capitalists. We must get certain leading ideas before the people. We should announce that we are not going in for what was the old-fashioned idea of redistribution, but the redistribution of income. Let it always be a question of income.

I have been very happy here tonight. I entirely understand the distinction made by our chairman tonight when he said you hold me in social esteem and a certain amount of personal affection. I am not a sentimental man, but I am not insensible to all that, I know the value of all that, and it gives me, now that I have come to the age of seventy (it will not occur again and I am saying it for the last time), great feeling of pleasure that I can say what a good many people can't say.

I know now that when I was a young man and took the turning that led me into the Labor Party, I took the right turning in every sense.

就是我們的社會主義理論的全部意義。

我以為，我們應當記住上述的一點，因為我們的任務是要處理好世界財富的分配問題。我告訴過你們，現在還要告訴你們，我認為在我們四千七百萬人口中，沒有兩個人，也許連一個人也沒有，會贊同現存的財富分配制度。我甚至要說，你們在整個文明世界中也找不出一個贊同現存財富分配制度的人來。這分配制度已成為毫無意義、荒謬絕倫的東西了。⋯⋯

⋯⋯

我認為我們能夠將自己和資本主義者區別開的一天終會到來。我們必須將我們的指導思想公之於眾。我們必須宣稱我們要實現的不是舊概念中的再分配，而是收入的再分配。我們始終指的是收入的問題。

今天晚上我很高興，我們的主席說，你們對我的社會地位有很高的評價，也對我有很深的個人感情，我感到非常光榮。我不是一個感情用事的人，但也不能對此無動於衷。我知道這一切的價值。我已經七十歲了，一個人一生只能有一次七十歲，我說這話也就是這一次了。我十分高興能夠在這裏說出了一些許多人不能說的話。

現在我確信，在我年輕時，思想轉變，加入工黨，這轉變從一切方面都可以說，我的道路走對了。

80 The Reichstag Fire Trial — His Final Speech

Dimitrov

· · ·

My Lords, Judges, Gentlemen for the Prosecution and the Defence! At the very beginning of this trial three months ago as an accused man I addressed a letter to the President of the Court. I wrote that I regretted that my attitude in Court should lead to collisions with the judges, but I categorically refuted the suggestion which was made against me that I had misused my right to put questions and my right to make statements in order to serve propagandist ends. Because I was wrongly accused before this Court I naturally used all the means at my disposal to defend myself against false charges.

· · ·

The direction of this trial has been determined by the theory that the burning of the Reichstag was an act of the German Communist Party, of the Communist International. This anti-Communist deed, the Reichstag fire, was actually blamed upon the Communists and declared to be the signal for an armed Communist insurrection, a beacon fire for the overthrow of the present German constitution. An anti-Communist character has been given to the whole proceedings by the use of this theory.

· · ·

Everyone knows that the German Communist Party was in favour of the dictatorship of the pro-

---

季米特洛夫（1882～1949），保加利亞人，國際工人運動活動家。1933年 2 月 27 日，德國法西斯收買偽證人，誣陷季米特洛夫"縱火"，將他逮捕。這是

八十　國會縱火案審訊的最後辯詞

季米特洛夫

……

各位法官、檢察官和辯護人！三個月前，在這審訊剛開始的時候，我，作爲被告人，給法庭庭長寫了一封信。上面寫道：我在法庭上的意見引起了各位法官的一些衝突，我很抱歉。但是因而指責我濫用提出質問的權利和作出聲明的權利以達到宣傳的目的，那是我絕對要加以駁斥的。由於我在本庭受到誣告，我當然要用我所能用的一切方法來爲自己辯護，以免遭到誣陷。

……

這次審訊由一個理論決定，這就是：火燒國會是德國共產黨幹的，是共產國際幹的。火燒國會這一反共行爲事實上被用來誣陷共產黨人，他們宣稱這是共產黨武裝起義的信號，是推翻德國現政府的烽火。由於用了這理論，全部訴訟程序就貫串着反共的性質。

……

任何人都知道德國共產黨贊成無產階級專政，但這絕不是本案訴訟程序中決定性的一點。

季米特洛夫在法庭上的發言。德國法西斯後來不得不宣佈被告無罪。

letariat, but that is by no means a point decisive for these proceedings. The point is simply this: was an armed insurrection aimed at the seizure of power actually planned to take place on February 27, 1933, in connection with the Reichstag fire?

What, my Lords, have been the results of the legal investigations? The legend that the Reichstag fire was a Communist act has been completely shattered. Unlike some counsel here, I shall not quote much of the evidence.

To any person of normal intelligence at least this point is now made completely clear, that the Reichstag fire had nothing whatever to do with any activity of the German Communist Party, not only nothing to do with an insurrection, but nothing to do with a strike, a demonstration or anything of that nature. The legal investigations have proved this up to the hilt. The Reichstag fire was not regarded by anyone – I exclude criminals and the mentally deranged – as the signal for insurrection. No one observed any deed, act or attempt at insurrection in connection with the Reichstag fire. The very stories of such things expressly appertain to a much later date. At that moment the working class was in a state of alarm against the attacks of Fascism. The German Communist Party was seeking to organise the opposition of the masses in their own defence. But it was shown that the Reichstag fire furnished the occasion and the signal for unleashing the most terrific campaign of suppression against the German working class and its vanguard the Communist Party.

. . .

Heller, the police official, read in Court a Communist poem out of a book published in 1925 to prove that the Communists set the Reichstag on fire in 1933. Permit me also the pleasure of quoting a poem, a poem by the greatest German poet, Goethe:

414

決定性的一點只是：共產黨實際上是否計劃在1933年2月27日發動與國會縱火有關的武裝起義，以奪取政權？

先生們，依法調查的結果如何？國會縱火是共產黨所爲這一神話已經完全被粉碎了。我不想象其他辯護人一樣援引許多例證。

對於任何具有正常智力的人來說，至少這一點現在是完全清楚了：國會縱火與德國共產黨的活動完全無關，不但與起義無關，而且與罷工、示威或任何其他類似的活動都完全沒有關係。按照法律進行的調查已經徹底證明了這一點。任何人（我不把罪犯和精神病患者算在內）都不認爲國會縱火是起義的信號。沒有人發現與國會縱火有關的任何起義的事實、行爲或企圖，種種捏造都是事後很久才編製出來的。那時工人階級正處於防衞法西斯進攻的狀態。德國共產黨正力圖組織羣衆進行反抗與自衞。但事實證明：國會縱火只是藉口和信號，用以發動預先佈置好的大規模運動，來鎮壓德國工人階級及其先鋒隊共產黨。

……

警官海勒在法庭上讀了一首共產黨員寫的詩，以此證明共產黨員在1933年放火燒國會。該首詩選自一本1925年出版的書。請允許我也引用一首詩，一首由最偉大的德國詩人歌德寫的詩：

"Lerne zeitig kluger sein.
Suf des Gluckes grosser Wage
Steht die Zunge selten ein;
Du musst steigen oder sinken,
Du musst herrschen und Gewinnen
Oder dienen und verkieren,
Leiden oder triumphieren,
Amboss oder Hammer sein."
Victory or defeat! Be hammer or anvil!
. . .

A time will come when these accounts will have to be settled, with interest! The elucidation of the Reichstag fire and the identification of the real incendiaries is a task which will fall to the people's Court of the future proletarian dictatorship.

When Galileo was condemned he declared:
"E pur si muove!"

No less determined than Galileo we Communists declare today: "E pur si muove!" The wheel of history moves on towards the ultimate, inevitable, irrepressible goal of Communism. . . .

(The Court forbade Dimitrov to speak further.)

要及早學得聰明些。

在命運的偉大天秤上，

天秤針很少不動；

你不得不上升或下降；

必須統治和勝利，

否則奴役和失敗，

或者受罪，或者凱旋，

不做鐵鑽，就做鐵錘。

不是勝利，便是失敗，不做鐵鑽，就做鐵錘！

……

清算賬目的時刻終會到來，而且要加上利息！國會縱火案的真相以及真正罪犯的判定，將由未來無產階級專政的人民法庭完成。

伽利略被判刑時，他宣告：

"地球仍然在轉動！"[1]

我們共產黨人今天也懷着同伽利略一樣的決心宣告："地球仍然在轉動！"歷史的車輪滾滾向前，向着最後的、不可避免地、不可遏制地必然要達到的目標——共產主義……。

（法庭禁止季米特洛夫繼續發言。）

（1）伽利略因提出地球繞太陽轉動的學說，受到教會迫害。

81 Blood, Toil, Sweat and Tears

Winston Leonard Spencer Churchill

On Friday evening last I received from His Majesty the mission to form a new administration.

It was the evident will of Parliament and the nation that this should be received on the broadest possible basis and that it should include all parties.

I have already completed the most important part of this task. A war cabinet has been formed of five members, representing, with the Labor, Opposition and Liberals, the unity of the nation.

. . .

I now invite the House by a resolution to record its approval of the steps taken and declare its confidence in the new government. The resolution:

"That this House welcomes the formation of a government representing the united and inflexible resolve of the nation to prosecute the war with Germany to a victorious conclusion."

To form an administration of this scale and complexity is a serious undertaking in itself. But we are in the preliminary phase of one of the greatest battles in history. We are in action at many other points — in Narway and in Holland — and we have to be prepared in the Mediterranean. The air battle is continuing, and

八十一　熱血、辛勞、汗水、眼淚

温斯頓·李安納德·史賓塞·邱吉爾

星期五晚我奉國王陛下之命組織新內閣。

國會與國民顯然希望這內閣在最廣泛的基礎上組成，包括所有黨派在內。

迄今我已完成此項任務中的最重要部分。一個五人戰時內閣經已組成，其中包括工黨、反對黨和自由黨，代表了國家的統一。

……

現在我提請議院作出決議，認可已採取的各項步驟，記錄在案，並宣佈對新政府的信任。決議全文如下：

"本議院歡迎新政府成立。新政府代表了全國團結一致、堅定不移的信心：對德作戰，直至最後勝利。"

組織如此複雜並具有如此規模的內閣，本身就是一項嚴肅的任務。但我們目前正處於有史以來規模最大戰役的最初階段，我們正在其他許多地方，例如挪威與荷蘭，採取行動，我們在地中海也要有所準備。空戰正在繼續進行，

邱吉爾（1874～1965），兩次（1940～1945及1951～1955）為英國首相。他在文學上造詣很深，1953年獲諾貝爾文學獎。本文為邱吉爾1940年5月13日被任命為首相後在國會上的演說詞。

many preparations have to be made here at home.

In this crisis I think I may be pardoned if I do not address the House at any length today, and I hope that any of my friends and colleagues or former colleagues who are affected by the political reconstruction will make all allowances for any lack of ceremony with which it has been necessary to act.

I say to the House as I said to Ministers who have joined this government, I have nothing to offer but blood, toil, tears and sweat. We have before us an ordeal of the most grievous kind. We have before us many, many months of struggle and suffering.

You ask, what is our policy? I say it is to wage war by land, sea and air. War with all our might and with all the strength God has given us, and to wage war against a monstrous tyranny never surpassed in the dark and lamentable catalogue of human crime. That is our policy.

You ask, what is our aim? I can answer in one word. It is victory. Victory at all costs — victory in spite of all terrors — victory, however long and hard the road may be, for without victory there is no survival.

Let that be realized. No survival for the British Empire, no survival for all that the British Empire has stood for, no survival for the urge, the impulse of the ages, that mankind shall move forward toward his goal.

I take up my task in buoyancy and hope. I feel sure that our cause will not be suffered to fail among men.

I feel entitled at this juncture, at this time, to claim the aid of all and to say, "Come then, let us go forward together with our united strength."

我們在國內需要做許多準備工作。

在此非常時期，我相信議院將原諒我今天發言簡短，我還希望我的朋友、同事或受到這次政治改組影響的前任同事們，能體諒省去一般情況下必需的儀節。

我已告訴過組成新政府的各位大臣，在此再告訴諸位議員：我所能奉獻的，只有熱血、辛勞、汗水與眼淚。我們還要經受極其嚴峻的考驗，我們面臨着漫長而艱苦卓絕的鬥爭。

要問我們的政策是什麼？我的回答是：在海、陸、空作戰，盡我們所能、以上帝賜予我們的一切力量作戰。我們的敵人是人類犯罪史上空前暴虐兇殘的暴君，我們要和敵人決一死戰，這就是我們的政策。

要問我們的目的是什麼？我可以用兩個字回答，那就是：勝利。不惜一切代價奪取勝利，不顧一切流血恐怖奪取勝利。不論道路多麼漫長，多麼崎嶇，一定要奪取勝利！因為沒有勝利就不能生存。

希望大家認識到這一點：沒有勝利，英帝國將不能生存，英帝國所代表的一切將不再存在，推動人類歷史不斷前進的動力將不再存在。

我滿懷希望地接受我的任務，我確信人們不會聽任我們的事業遭到失敗。

此時此際，我認為我有權要求所有人的支持，我要說："讓我們團結一致，共赴國難吧。"

82　Report the Miracle of Dunkirk

Winston Leonard Spencer Churchill

. . .

The German eruption swept like a sharp scythe around the right and rear of the armies of the north. Eight or nine armored divisions, each of about four hundred armored vehicles of different kinds, but carefully assorted to be complementary and divisible into small self-contained units, cut off all communications between us and the main French armies. It severed our own communications for food and ammunition, which ran first to Amiens and afterward through Abbeville, and it shored its way up the coast to Boulogne and Calais, and almost to Dunkirk. Behind this armored and mechanized onslaught came a number of German divisions in lorries, and behind them again there plodded comparatively slowly the dull brute mass of the ordinary German Army and German people, always so ready to be led to the trampling down in other lands of liberties and comforts which they have never known in their own. . . .

Meanwhile, the Royal Air Force, which had already been intervening in the battle, so far as its range would allow, from home bases, now used part of its main metropolitan fighter strength, and struck at the German

---

這是 1940 年 6 月 4 日，邱吉爾就 5 月 27 日到 6 月 4 日 " 敦刻爾克大撤退 " 的經過向國會的報告。

（ 1 ）法國西北部城市。

八十二 向議會報告敦刻爾克大撤退的奇跡

溫斯頓‧李安納德‧史賓塞‧邱吉爾

......

德軍突然發動大舉進攻，好像一把鋒利的鐮刀，緊緊圍逼住此部聯軍的右翼和後方。德軍的八、九個裝甲師，每師約有各種裝甲車四百輛，這些車輛分組成一個個精心搭配、相互呼應的獨立作戰單位，插入了我軍，切斷了我軍和法軍主力的一切聯繫。德軍斷絕了我軍的糧食彈藥供應。我們的糧食彈藥補給線直達亞眠[1]，然後又通過阿布維爾[2]。德軍沿岸直抵布洛涅和加萊[3]，逼近敦刻爾克。在這支裝甲機械部隊突擊之後，是用軍車運載的許多個德軍師團，再後面緊跟着的就是大批行動較緩慢、陰沉殘酷的德國常規軍和德國平民了。這些人素來是甘心情願被人牽着鼻子闖進別人的國土，去摧殘別人的自由與安適生活的。這種自由與安適生活，他們在自己的國土上從未享到過......。

與此同時，皇家空軍早已參戰，在航程所及範圍內從國內基地出動打擊敵人；現時並用部分城市空防戰鬥機的主力，襲擊德國轟炸機羣

（2）法國北部一個城市。

（3）布洛涅和加萊都是法國北部港口。

bombers and at the fighters which in large numbers protected them. This struggle was protracted and fierce. Suddenly the scene has cleared, the crash and thunder has for the moment — but only for the moment — died away. A miracle of deliverance, by faultless service, by resource, by skill, by unconquerable fidelity, is manifest to us all. The enemy was hurled back by the retreating British and French troops. He was so roughly handled that he did not hurry their departure seriously. The Royal Air Force engaged the main strength of the German Air Force, and inflicted upon them losses of at least four to one; and the navy, using nearly one thousand ships of all kinds, carried over 335,000 men, French and British, out of the jaws of death and shame, to their native land and to the tasks which lie immediately ahead. We must be very careful not to assign to this deliverance the attributes of a victory. Wars are not won by evacuations. But there was a victory inside this deliverance, which should be noted. . . .

. . .

Nevertheless, our thankfulness at the escape of our army and so many men, whose loved ones have passed through an agonizing week, must not blind us to the fact that what has happened in France and Belgium is a colossal military disaster. The French Army has been weakened, the Belgian Army has been lost, a large part of those fortified lines upon which so much faith had been reposed is gone, many valuable mining districts and factories have passed into the enemy's possession, the whole of the Channel ports are in his hands, with all the tragic consequences that follow from that, and we must expect another blow to be struck almost immediately at us or at France. We are told that Herr Hitler has a plan for invading the British Isles. This

及掩護它們的大批戰鬥機。戰鬥的時間持續很長，也十分激烈。後來，戰場的形勢突然明朗化起來。目前，只是在目前，隆隆的槍炮聲暫時漸漸止息。展現在我們眼前的是，靠着完善的工作、機智、技能和耿耿忠心爭取得來的奇迹般解救。在撤退中的英法聯軍阻擊了敵人，使其受到嚴重挫敗後不能從容撤退。皇家空軍向德國空軍的主力進擊，使之受到至少四倍於我們的損失。我們的海軍動員了各種艦艇近千艘，援救了三十三萬五千餘英法軍兵士，使之脫離虎口，免遭折辱，安返本國，立即投入新的鬥爭。但是我們應該十分謹慎，切不可將此次解救成功說成是一場勝利。在戰爭中，勝利是不能靠撤退贏得的。但是我們應該注意到，在此次援救中我們確是打了一場勝仗。……

……

然而，我們慶幸如此眾多的士兵得免於難之際（在整整一週裏，他們的親屬處在極度緊張痛苦的等待中），切勿因此而看不到法國和比利時領土上軍事慘敗的事實。法國軍隊被削弱，比利時軍隊全軍覆沒，曾經賴以確保安全的防線大部分被破壞，許多寶貴的礦區和工廠已歸敵人所有，海峽港口全部落入敵手，後果嚴重，我們還必須準備承受對我們或對法國接踵而來的第二次打擊。我們已得知希特勒先生計劃入侵英倫三島。這一點我們早就預料到了。

has often been thought of before. When Napoleon lay at Boulogne for a year with his flat-bottomed boats and his Grand Army, he was told by someone, "There are bitter weeds in England." There are certainly a great many more of them since the British Expeditionary Force returned.

. . .

I have, myself, full confidence that if all do their duty, if nothing is neglected, and if the best arrangements are made, as they are being made, we shall prove ourselves once again able to defend our island home, to ride out the storm of war, and to outlive the menace of tyranny, if necessary for years, if necessary alone. At any rate, that is what we are going to try to do. That is the resolve of His Majesty's Government — every man of them. That is the will of Parliament and the nation. The British Empire and the French Republic, linked together in their cause and in their need, will defend to the death their native soil, aiding each other like good comrades to the utmost of their strength. Even though large tracts of Europe and many old and famous states have fallen or may fall into the grip of the Gestapo and all the odious apparatus of Nazi rule, we shall not flag or fail. We shall go on to the end, we shall fight in France, we shall fight on the seas and oceans, we shall fight with growing confidence and growing strength in the air, we shall defend our island, whether the cost may be, we shall fight on the beaches, we shall fight on the landing grounds, we shall fight in the fields and in the streets, we shall fight in the hills; we shall never surrender, and even if, which I do not for

當拿破崙的平底軍艦和大軍在布洛涅駐扎了一年之久時，有人告訴他：" 英國到處有荊棘葵藜。" 是的，英國遠征部隊得救回來後，英國的荊棘葵藜就更多了。

……

如果所有人都忠於職守，如果我們的工作不出紕漏，事事都像現在那樣安排周密,那麼，我是充滿信心的。我們將又一次證明我們能夠抵禦戰爭的風暴，抗擊強暴的威脅，保衛自己的島國。如果必要，我們就進行持久戰，如果必要，就孤軍作戰。無論如何，這就是我們準備做的。這就是英王政府以及政府中每一個人的決心。這就是國會和全國國民的意願。由共同的目標和共同的需要聯繫起來的英帝國和法蘭西共和國，將誓死保衛自己的國土，將親如同志，盡一切力量彼此支援。雖然歐洲的大片土地和許多有名的古國已經或即將淪於蓋世太保[1]及一切可憎的納粹機構之手，我們也不會氣餒，不會屈服。我們要堅持到底，我們要在法國國土上作戰，要在各個海洋上作戰，我們的空軍將愈戰愈強，愈戰愈有信心，我們將不惜一切犧牲保衛我國本土，我們要在灘頭作戰，在登陸地作戰，在田野、在山上、在街巷作戰；我們永不投降，即使整個英倫島或大部

（1）納粹秘密警察。

a moment believe, this island or a large part of it were subjugated and starving, then our Empire beyond the seas, armed and guarded by the British fleet, would carry on the struggle, until, in God's good time, the New World, with all its power and might, steps forth to the rescue and the liberation of the old.

分土地被佔，我們饑寒交迫——這一點我認為是絕不可能的——那時，在英國艦隊守衛下武裝起來的英帝國海外領地將繼續鬥爭下去，直至上帝認為適當的時候已屆，新大陸將挺身而出，以其全部力量支援舊世界，使舊世界得到解放。

83　Anticipates the Battle of Britain

Winston Leonard Spencer Churchill

During the first four years of the last war the Allies experienced nothing but disaster and disappointment. . . . We repeatedly asked ourselves the question, "How are we going to win?" and no one was ever able to answer it with much precision, until at the end, quite suddenly, quite unexpectedly, our terrible foe collapsed before us, and we were so glutted with victory that in our folly we threw it away.

However matters may go in France or with the French government or other French Governments, we in this island and in the British Empire will never lose our sense of comradeship with the French people. . . . If final victory rewards our toils they shall share the gains — aye, and freedom shall be restored to all. We abate nothing of our just demands; not one jot or tittle do we recede. . . . Czechs, Poles, Norwegians, Dutch, Belgians, have joined their causes to our own. All these shall be restored.

What General Weygand called the Battle of France is over. I expect that the Battle of Britain is about to begin. Upon this battle depends the survival of Christian civilization. Upon it depends our own British life, and the long continuity of our institutions and our Empire.

1940年 6 月，巴黎失陷後，邱吉爾於 6 月18日在英國議會發表本篇演說。

(1)馬西姆 · 魏剛(Mascime Weygand, 1867~1965)，

八十三　對不列顛之戰的展望

溫斯頓·李安納德·史賓塞·邱吉爾

在上次大戰的最初四年中，各協約國節節敗退，士氣低落。……當時我們一再自問："我們如何才能贏得勝利?"但無人能確定地回答這問題。直到最後，出乎意料之外，我們的強敵突然在我們眼前瓦解了。這突如其來的勝利衝昏了我們的頭腦，竟使我們做了坐失良機的蠢事。

無論法國出現何種情況，當前的法國政府或其他法國政府會碰到什麼問題，我們英國本土以及整個英帝國的一切人都絕不會失去對法國人民的同志情誼。……待到我們的辛勞換來最後勝利，他們將和我們同享勝利之果——啊，我們都將重新得到自由。我們決不放棄我們的正當要求；對於這，我們一絲一毫也不退讓。……捷克人、波蘭人、挪威人、丹麥人、比利時人已經把他們的事業和我們的事業聯繫在一起。這些國家都將光復起來。

魏剛將軍[(1)]所說的法蘭西戰役已經結束，但我預計不列顛的戰役即將開始。世界文明的存亡繫此一戰。英國人民的生死繫此一戰，我國制度以及英帝國的國祚能否延續亦繫此一

法國將軍，投降希特勒德國，成為法國"維琪政府"的國防部長。

The whole fury and might of the enemy must very soon be turned on us. Hilter knows that he will have to break us in this island or lose the war. If we can stand up to him, all Europe may be free and the life of the world may move forward into broad, sunlit uplands. But if we fail, then the whole world, including the United States, including all that we have known and cared for, will sink into the abyss of a new Dark Age, made more sinister, and perhaps more protracted, by the lights of perversed science. Let us therefore brace ourselves to our duties, and so bear ourselves that, if the British Empire and its Commonwealth last for a thousand years, men will say, "This was their finest hour."

戰。不久敵人將傾全力向我們猛撲過來。希特勒深知如不能在英倫島上擊潰我們，他便將徹底失敗。如果我們能抵禦住他，整個歐洲便可得到自由，全世界便可走上陽光燦爛的廣闊大道。但是，如果我們失敗了，全世界包括美國在內，包括我們所熟悉所熱愛的一切，將陷入一個新黑暗時代[1]的深淵。發達的科學的使這個黑暗時代更險惡，更漫長。因此，讓我們振作精神，克盡職責。倘若英帝國及聯邦得以永世長存，人們將說道：「這是他們最光榮美好的時刻。」

（1）歐洲中世紀，尤指五至十世紀這個時期。

84 Address to the Young Democratic Club

Franklin Delano Roosevelt

I, for one, do not believe that the era of the pioneer is at an end; I only believe that the area for pioneering has changed. The period of geographical pioneering is largely finished. But, my friends, the period of social pioneering is only at its beginning. And make no mistake about it — the same qualities of heroism and faith and vision that were required to bring the forces of Nature into subjection will be required — in even greater measure — to bring under proper control the forces of modern society.

You ought to thank God tonight if, regardless of your years, you are young enough in spirit to dream dreams and see visions — dreams and visions about a greater and finer America that is to be; if you are young enough in spirit to believe that poverty can be greatly lessened; that the disgrace of involuntary unemployment can be wiped out; that class hatreds can be done away with; that peace at home and peace abroad can be maintained; and that one day a generation may possess this land, blessed beyond anything we now know, blessed with these things — material and spiritual — that make man's life abundant. If that is the fashion of your dreaming then I say: "Hold fast to your dream. America needs it."

八十四　對民主黨青年俱樂部的講話

佛蘭克林・狄朗勞・羅斯福

有人不認為拓荒時代已經結束，我就是持這種看法中的一個；我只認為開拓的領域改變了。地理上的拓荒階段大體上已經完成。但是，朋友們，社會的拓荒時期却剛剛開始。我們必須清楚明白，在治理現代社會的鬥爭中，我們需要具有與征服大自然相同的、甚至更高的英雄氣概、忠誠信念和洞察能力。

不論你們年歲幾何，倘若你們能在精神上青春常在，善於夢想，能夠想象出一個未來更偉大優越的美國；相信貧窮現象將大幅度地改善；相信可恥惱人的失業現象將徹底消滅；相信階級仇恨將完全清除；相信國內的安定與國際的和平能永遠保持；相信後代子孫有一天能夠使我們的國家掌握現在想象不到的物質和精神財富，令人類的生活豐富無比；如果你們懷有這樣的青春夢想，今夜你們應該感謝上帝。如果這就是你們的夢想，那麼我要說：“深深地沉入你們的夢想，牢牢地把握住並實現它吧。美利堅需要它。”

羅斯福（1882～1945），1933至1945年間出任美國總統。

本文為羅斯福在1936年4月13日在巴庭莫的講話。

85 Address at University of Pennsylvania

Franklin Delano Roosevelt

. . .

Benjamin Franklin, to whom this University owes so much, realized too that while basic principles of natural science, of morality and of the science of society were eternal and immutable, the application of these principles necessarily changes with the patterns of living conditions from generation to generation. I am certain that he would insist, were he with us today, that it is the whole duty of the philosopher and the educator to apply the eternal ideals of truth and goodness and justice in terms of the present and not terms of the past. Growth and change are the law of all life. Yesterday's answers are inadequate for today's problems — just as the solutions of today will not fill the needs of tomorrow.

Eternal truths will be neither true nor eternal unless they have fresh meaning for every new social situation.

It is the function of education, the function of all of the great institutions of learning in the United States, to provide continuity for our national life — to transmit to youth the best of our culture that has been tested in the fire of history. It is equally the obligation of education to train the minds and the talents of our youth; to improve, through creative citizenship, our American institutions in accord with the requirements of the future.

本文是羅斯福1940年 9 月20日在賓夕法尼亞大學建校 200 周年紀念會上的講話。

(1)本杰明・佛蘭克林 (1708～1790),美國傑出政

八十五　在賓夕法尼亞大學的演説

佛蘭克林・狄朗勞・羅斯福

……

本杰明・佛蘭克林[1]對我們這所大學貢獻
甚大，他也認爲雖然自然科學、道德和社會科
學的基本原則是永恒的、不變的，但是這些原
則的應用則應隨着一代代人生活條件模式的變
化而作必要的變化。倘若他今天仍然健在，我
可以肯定他必然會堅持這樣的觀點：哲學家與
教育家的全部職責在於根據現時的條件而不是
過去的條件將眞理、善良與正義的永恒理想付
諸實用。生長與變化是一切生命的法則。昨日
的答案不適用於今日的問題——正如今天的方
法不能解決明天的需求一樣。

永恒的眞理如果不在新的社會形勢下賦與
新的意義，就旣不是眞理，也不是永恒的了。

教育的作用，美國一切大學術機構的作用，
是使我們國家的生命得以延續，是將我們經得
起歷史烈火考驗的最優秀文化傳給靑年一代。
同樣，教育有責任訓練我們靑年的心智和才能；
通過具有創造精神的公民義務教育，來改進我
們美國的學術機構，適應未來的要求。

治家、科學家和作家。他在美國獨立前，建立了
賓夕法尼亞大學的前身"美國靑年敎育學院"。

We cannot always build the future for our youth, but we can build our youth for the future.

It is in great universities like this that the ideas which can assure our national safety and make tomorrow's history, are being forged and shaped. Civilization owes most to the men and women, known and unknown, whose free, inquiring minds and restless intellects could not be subdued by the power of tyranny.

This is no time for any man to withdraw into some ivory tower and proclaim the right to hold himself aloof from the problems and the agonies of his society. The times call for bold belief that the world can be changed by man's endeavor, and that this endeavor can lead to something new and better. No man can sever the bonds that unite him to his society simply by averting his eyes. He must ever be receptive and sensitive to the new; and have sufficient courage and skill to face novel facts and to deal with them.

If democracy is to survive, it is the task of men of thought, as well as men of action, to put aside pride and prejudice; and with courage and single-minded devotion — and above all with humility — to find the truth and teach the truth that shall keep men free.

We may find in that sense of purpose, the personal peace, not of repose, but of effort, the keen satisfaction of doing, the deep feeling of achievement for something far beyond ourselves, the knowledge that we build more gloriously than we know.

我們不能總是為我們的青年造就美好未來，但我們能夠為未來造就我們的青年一代。

正是一些像這所學校般偉大的學府，冶煉和形成各保證國家安全、創造明天歷史的意識形態。文明的形成有賴於許多知名與不知名的男女公民，他們心胸開闊，孜孜不倦，勇於探索，決不屈服於專制力量。

現在不是鑽進象牙塔裏，空喊自己有權高高在上，置身社會問題與苦難之外的時候了。時代要求我們大膽地相信人經過努力可以改變世界，達到新的、更美好的境界。沒有人能夠僅憑閉目不看社會的現實，就割斷自己同社會的聯繫。他必須永遠保持對新鮮事物的敏感，隨時準備接受新鮮事物；他必須有勇氣與能力去面對新的事實，解決新的問題。

要使民主得以生存，思索着的人與行動着的人都必須放下傲慢與偏見；他們要有勇氣、有全心全意的獻身精神，以及最重要的謙虛精神，去尋求與傳播那使人民永保自由的真理。

朝着上述目標，我們會尋找得個人的平靜，那不是歇息而是經過努力奮鬥後的平靜；我們會對自己的行為感到由衷的滿意；為取得不為一己私利的成就而感到深深喜悅；建立遠非我們所能想到的輝煌知識。

86 Asks for a Declaration of War Against Japan

Franklin Delano Roosevelt

Mr. Vice-President, Mr. Speaker, members of the Senate and the House of Representatives:

Yesterday, December 7, 1941 — a date which will live in infamy — the United States of America was suddenly and deliberately attacked by naval and air forces of the empire of Japan.

The United States was at peace with that nation, and, at the solicitation of Japan, was still in conversation with its government and its Emperor looking toward the maintenance of peace in the Pacific.

Indeed, one hour after Japanese air squadrons had commenced bombing in the American island of Oahu the Japanese Ambassador to the United States and his colleague delivered to our Secretary of State a formal reply to a recent American message. And, while this reply stated that it seemed useless to continue the existing diplomatic negotiations, it contained no threat or hint of war or of armed attack.

It will be recorded that the distance of Hawaii from Japan makes it obvious that the attack was deliberately planned many days or even weeks ago. During the intervening time the Japanese government has deliberately sought to deceive the United States by false statements and expressions of hope for continued peace.

八十六　要求國會對日本宣戰

佛蘭克林・狄朗勞・羅斯福

副總統先生、議長先生、各位參議員和衆議員：

昨天，1941年12月7日，將成爲我國的國恥日。美利堅合衆國遭到了日本帝國海、空軍有預謀的突然襲擊。

在此之前，美國同日本處於和平狀態，並應日本之請同該國政府及天皇談判，指望維持太平洋區域的和平。

日本空軍部隊在美國的阿奧胡島[1]開始轟炸一小時後，日本駐美大使及其同僚居然還向美國國務卿遞交正式覆函，回答美國最近致日本的一封函件。這份文件雖然聲言目前的外交談判已無繼續之必要，但却未有威脅的言詞，也沒有暗示將發動戰爭或採取軍事行動。

夏威夷島距離日本頗遠，說明此次襲擊顯然是許多天前甚至幾星期前所策劃的，此事將記錄在案。在此期間，日本政府有意用虛僞的聲明和表示繼續保持和平的願望欺騙美國。

第二次世界大戰，美國珍珠港受到日本偷襲，羅斯福於1941年12月8日在國會發表本篇演說。美國國會當天通過決定，向日本宣戰。

（1）美國在夏威夷羣島中的一個島。

The attack yesterday on the Hawaiian Islands has caused severe damage to American naval and military forces. I regret to tell you that very many American lives have been lost. In addition, American ships have been reported torpedoed on the high seas between San Francisco and Honolulu.

Yesterday the Japanese government also launched an attack against Malaya.

Last night Japanese forces attacked Hong Kong.

Last night Japanese forces attacked Guam.

Last night Japanese forces attacked the Philippine Islands.

Last night the Japanese attacked Wake Island.

And this morning the Japanese attacked Midway Island.

Japan has therefore undertaken a surprise offensive extending throughout the Pacific area. The facts of yesterday and today speak for themselves. The people of the United States have already formed their opinions and well understand the implications to the very life and safety of our nation.

As Commander-in-Chief of the Army and Navy, I have directed that all measures be taken for our defense.

Always will we remember the character of the onslaught against us.

No matter how long it may take us to overcome this premeditated invasion, the American people, in their righteous might, will win through to absolute victory.

I believe that I interpret the will of the Congress and of the people when I assert that we will not only defend ourselves to the uttermost, but will make it very certain that this form of treachery shall never again endanger us.

日本昨天對夏威夷羣島的襲擊，給美國海陸軍造成了嚴重的破壞。我遺憾地告訴你們：許許多多美國人被炸死。同時，據報告，若干艘美國船隻在三藩市與火奴魯魯[1]之間的公海上被水雷擊中。

昨天，日本政府還發動了對馬來亞的襲擊。

昨夜日本部隊襲擊了香港。

昨夜日本部隊襲擊了關島。

昨夜日本部隊襲擊了菲律賓羣島。

昨夜日本部隊襲擊了威克島。

今晨日本人襲擊了中途島[2]。

這樣，日本就在整個太平洋區域發動了全面的突然襲擊。昨天和今天的情況已說明了事實的眞相。美國人民已經清楚地了解到這是關係我國存亡安危的問題。

作爲海、陸軍總司令，我已指令採取一切手段進行防禦。

我們將永遠記住對我們這次襲擊的性質。

無論需要多長時間去擊敗這次預謀的侵略，美國人民正義在手，有力量奪取徹底的勝利。

我保證我們將完全確保我們的安全，確保我們永不再受到這種背信棄義行爲的危害，我相信這話說出了國會和人民的意志。

（1）夏威夷羣島中的大城市。

（2）威克島和中途島都是美國在太平洋中的島嶼。

Hostilities exist. There is no blinking at the fact that our people, our territory, and our interests are in grave danger.

With confidence in our armed forces, with the unbounding determination of our people, we will gain the inevitable triumph. So help us God.

I ask that the Congress declare that since the unprovoked and dastardly attack by Japan on Sunday, December 7, 1941, a state of war has existed between the United States and the Japanese Empire.

大敵當前。我國人民、領土和利益正處於極度危險的狀態，我們決不可閉目不視。

　　我們相信我們的軍隊，我們的人民有無比堅定的決心，因此，勝利必定屬於我們。願上帝保祐我們。

　　我要求國會宣佈：由於日本在1941年12月7日星期日對我國無故進行卑鄙的襲擊，美國同日本已經處於戰爭狀態。

87　The Four Freedoms

Franklin Delano Roosevelt

. . .

In the future days, which we seek to make secure, we look forward to a world founded upon four essential human freedoms.

The first is freedom of speech and expression — everywhere in the world.

The second is freedom of every person to worship God in his own way — everywhere in the world.

The third is freedom from want — which, translated into world terms, means economic understandings which will secure to every nation a healthy peace time life for its inhabitants — everywhere in the world.

The fourth is freedom from fear — which, translated into world terms, means a world-wide reduction of armaments to such a point and in such a thorough fashion that no nation will be in a position to commit an act of physical aggression against any neighbor — anywhere in the world.

That is no vision of a distant millennium. It is a definite basis for a kind of world attainable in our own time and generation. That kind of world is the very antithesis of the so-called new order of tyranny which

八十七 論四大自由

佛蘭克林・狄朗勞・羅斯福

......

我們努力保證未來的歲月能夠安定，我們期待將來有一個建立在四項人類基本自由基礎之上的世界。

第一是在世界的一切地方，一切人都有言論與表達意見的自由。

第二是在世界的一切地方，一切人都有自由以自己的方式崇拜上帝。

第三是免於匱乏的自由。從世界範圍的意義上說就是在經濟上達到諒解，保證世界一切地方，每一個國家的居民都能過一種健康的和平生活。

第四是免於恐懼的自由。從世界範圍的意義上說就是進行世界性的徹底裁軍，使世界上一切地方，沒有一個國家有能力向任何鄰國發起侵略行動。

這不是對遙遠未來的黃金時代的幻想。這是我們所追求的世界必須具有的基礎，這世界可以在這個時代，由我們這一代人贏得。我們追求的世界，跟獨裁者企圖用炸彈炸出來的所

本文為羅斯福於1941年1月6日致美國國會的諮文中的一段講話。

447

the dictators seek to create with the crash of a bomb.

To that new order we oppose the greater conception — the moral order. A good society is able to face schemes of world domination and foreign revolutions alike without fear.

Since the beginning of our American history we have been engaged in change — in a perpetual peaceful revolution — a revolution which goes on steadily, quietly adjusting itself to changing conditions — without the concentration camp or the quick-lime in the ditch. The world order which we seek is the cooperation of free countries, working together in a friendly, civilized society.

This nation has placed its destiny in the hands and heads and hearts of its millions of free men and women; and its faith in freedom under the guidance of God. Freedom means the supremacy of human rights everywhere. Our support goes to those who struggle to gain those rights or keep them. Our strength is in our unity of purpose.

To that high concept there can be no end save victory.

謂"新秩序"的暴政正好相對立。

我們以道德秩序這偉大的觀念來反對那種新秩序。一個好的社會，能夠毫無恐懼地面對企圖主宰世界以及在別國發動革命的各種計劃。

自有美國歷史以來，我們就從事於改革——從事不間斷的和平革命。我們持久地進行革命，沉靜地使革命不斷適應外間變化的情況。我們的革命沒有集中營，也沒有萬人塚[1]。我們要建立的世界秩序是自由國家之間的合作，是在一個友好文明的社會中共同工作。

我們的國家已經將她的命運交托給千百萬自己的男女公民，由他們的雙手、頭腦和心靈來決定；我們的國家已經將她對自由的信念置於上帝的指引之下。自由就是人權在所有地方高於一切。我們支持一切為了得到並保持這些權利而奮鬥的人們。我們目標一致，使我們得到力量。

這種崇高的觀念捨勝利而外無其他結局。

（1）第二次世界大戰，法西斯國家軍隊屠殺後將屍體拋入溝內，灑上生石灰水。

88 Jefferson Day Address

Franklin Delano Roosevelt

Americans are gathered together this evening in communities all over the country to pay tribute to the living memory of Thomas Jefferson — one of the greatest of all democrats; and I want to make it clear that I am spelling that word "democrats" with a small "d". I wish I had the power, just for this evening, to be present at all of these gatherings.

In this historic year, more than ever before, we do well to consider the character of Thomas Jefferson as an American citizen of the world.

As Minister to France, then as our first Secretary of State and as our third President, Jefferson was instrumental in the establishment of the United States as a vital factor in international affairs.

It was he who first sent our Navy into far distant waters to defend rights. And the promulgation of the Monroe Doctrine was the logical development of Jefferson's far-seeing foreign policy.

Today this nation which Jefferson helped so greatly to build is playing a tremendous part in the battle for the rights of man all over the world.

八十八　在傑弗遜紀念日上的演說

佛蘭克林・狄朗勞・羅斯福

今天晚上，全國各地的美國人都集會紀念永遠活在我們記憶中的湯姆士・傑弗遜——最偉大的民主主義者中的一位；我要說清楚，我說的是"民主主義者"，而不是民主黨人。我多麼希望今天晚上我能夠分身有術，出席所有的集會啊！

今年是具有歷史意義的一年，我們會比以往任何時候都更多地想到湯姆士・傑弗遜，想到他那具有世界性的美國公民品格。

傑弗遜先出使法國、後任我國第一任國務卿及第三屆總統。美國能夠成為國際事務中的決定力量，傑弗遜起了重大作用。

他是第一個把海軍派到遠洋保衛我國權利的人。傑弗遜在外交政策方面卓有遠見，門羅主義的頒佈正是合乎邏輯的發展結果。

傑弗遜為締造我國曾經出過如此大力，今天這個國家在為爭取全世界人權的鬥爭中正起着極其重要的作用。

羅斯福於1945年4月12日正在工作時突然去世。他逝世前正在撰寫本篇演說稿，準備在次日傑弗遜紀念日上發表，故又稱未完成的演說詞。傑弗遜（1743～1826），美國第三任總統。

Today we are part of the vast Allied force — a force composed of flesh and blood and steel and spirit — which is today destroying the makers of war, the breeders of hatred, in Europe and in Asia.

In Jefferson's time our Navy consisted of only a handful of frigates headed by the gallant U.S.S. Constitution — "Old Ironsides" — but that tiny Navy taught nations across the Atlantic that piracy in the Mediterranean — acts of aggression against peaceful commerce and the enslavement of their crews was one of those things which, among neighbors, simply was not done.

We, as Americans, do not choose to deny our responsibility.

Nor do we intend to abandon our determination that, within the lives of our children and our children's children, there will not be a Third World War.

We seek peace — enduring peace. More than an end to war, we want an end to the beginnings of all wars — yes, an end to this brutal, inhuman and thoroughly impractical method of settling the differences between governments.

The once powerful, malignant Nazi state is crumbling. The Japanese war lords are receiving, in their own homeland, the retribution for which they asked when they attacked Pearl Harbor.

But the mere conquest of our enemies is not enough.

We must go on to do all in our power to conquer the doubts and the fears, the ignorance and the greed, which made this horror possible.

今天，我們是廣大同盟國軍事力量的一部分，這力量由血與肉、鋼鐵與意志組成，它正在消滅歐洲和亞洲的戰爭製造者，消滅那些滋生與培育仇恨的人們。

傑弗遜在世的時候，我們的海軍只有以雄姿勃勃的"老鐵邊"⁽¹⁾憲法號為首的幾艘驅逐艦，但是那支小小的艦隊却使大西洋彼岸各國懂得了，地中海上的海盜行為，危害和平貿易和奴役船員的行為是絕不允許在鄰國之間發生的。

作為美國人，我們不願放棄我們的職責。

我們決心制止第三次世界大戰在下一代甚至再下一代發生，這是我們不會改變的決心。

我們致力和平——持久的和平。我們不僅要結束這次戰爭，而且要根絕一切戰爭。是的，我們要永遠結束為解決政府間分歧而採用的這種殘忍的、不人道的、完全行不通的方法。

那個曾經不可一世、兇狠殘暴的納粹國家正在土崩瓦解。日本軍閥曾偷襲珍珠港，現正在他們的本土受到應得的回報。

但是僅僅戰勝敵人是不夠的。

我們必須繼續盡一切努力戰勝懷疑與恐懼，戰勝無知與貪婪，那是這場可怕戰爭的根源。

（1）美國最早的軍艦以鐵皮包邊，故名。

Thomas Jefferson, himself a distinguished scientist, once spoke of "the brotherly spirit of Science, which unites into one family all its votaries of whatever grade, and however widely dispersed throughout the different quarters of the globe."

Today, science has brought all the different quarters of the globe so close together that it is impossible to isolate them one from another.

Today we are faced with the pre-eminent fact that, if civilization is to survive, we must cultivate the science of human relationships — the ability of all peoples, of all kinds, to live together and work together, in the same world, at peace.

Let me assure you that my hand is the steadier for the work that to be done, that I move more firmly into the task, knowing that you — millions and millions of you — are joined with me in the resolve to make this work endure.

The work, my friends, is peace. More than an end of this war — an end to the beginnings of all wars. Yes, an end, forever, to this impractical, unrealistic settlement of the differences between governments by the mass killing of peoples.

Today, as we move against the terrible scourge of war — as we go forward toward the greatest contribution that any generation of human beings can make in this world — the contribution of lasting peace, I ask you to keep up your faith. I measure the sound solid achievement that can be made at this time by the straightedge of your own confidence and your resolve. And to you, and to all Americans who dedicate themselves with us to the making of an abiding peace, I say:

The only limit to our realization of tomorrow will be our doubts of today. Let us move forward with strong and active faith. . . .

托馬斯・傑弗遜本人還是一位卓越的科學家，他曾經說過：" 科學的博愛精神把分散在世界各地各種水平的熱心科學的人聯結成一個大家庭。"

今天，科學已經使地球上的各個部分緊接起來，不可能再把它們孤立、割裂開。

今天，我們面前最重要的事情是：如果要保全文明，就必須傳播、教化人際關係的知識，亦即一切民族、一切種族能夠在同一個地球上一起和平地生活、工作。

讓我向你們保證，我決心完成這項工作，我的步伐愈來愈堅定，因為我知道，你們，千千萬萬的人們，決心和我一起令這項工作變得持久。

朋友們，這項工作就是和平。不僅結束這次戰爭，而且使一切戰爭根本不能發生。是的，永遠結束這種為解決政府間分歧而使各民族受到大屠殺的行不通的、不現實的辦法。

今天，當我們採取行動反對這種可怖的戰爭苦難，當我們向爭取持久和平這個人類各時代最偉大的目標邁進時，我要求你們保持堅定的信念。我要用你們的信念和決心來衡量我們當前可能取得成就的堅實可靠程度。我要對你們，對一切和我們一起獻身於持久和平事業的美國人說：

實現明天理想的唯一障礙是今天的疑慮。讓我們信心百倍，奮勇向前吧。……

89 On the Death of Lenin

Joseph Stalin

Comrades, we Communists are people of a special mould. We are made of a special stuff. We are those who form the army of the great proletarian strategist, the army of Comrade Lenin. There is nothing higher than the honour of belonging to this army. There is nothing higher than the title of member of the Party whose founder and leader was Comrade Lenin. It is not given to everyone to withstand the stresses and storms that accompany membership in such a party. It is the sons of the working class, the sons of want and struggle, the sons of incredible privation and heroic effort who before all should be members of such a party. That is why the Party of the Leninists, the Party of the Communists, is also called the Party of the working class.

. . .

For twenty-five years Comrade Lenin tended our Party and made it into the strongest and most highly steeled workers' party in the world. The blows of tsarism and its henchmen, the fury of the bourgeoisie and the landlords, the armed attacks of Kolchak and Denikin, the armed intervention of Britain and France, the lies and slanders of the hundred-mouthed bourgeois press — all these scorpions constantly chastised our Party for a quarter of a century. But our Party stood

---

史達林（1879～1953），繼列寧後成爲蘇聯的主要領導人。本篇是史達林1924年 1 月26日在列寧追悼會的演說。

（1）亞歷山大・華西里耶夫維奇・高爾察克（1873～

八十九　悼列寧

約瑟夫・史達林

同志們！我們共產黨人具有特種的氣質，由特殊材料製成。偉大的無產階級戰略家的軍隊，列寧同志的軍隊，就是由我們這些人組成的。在這軍隊當戰士，是再光榮不過的了。列寧同志是這個黨的創始人和領導人，能夠成為這個黨的黨員，是再榮幸不過的了。這個黨的黨員必須經歷種種苦難和風暴，不是任何人都能成為黨員。工人階級的兒女，在貧困和鬥爭中成長起來的兒女，在千辛萬苦和英勇奮鬥中成長起來的兒女，應當首先成為這個黨的黨員。因此，列寧主義者的黨，共產主義者的黨，同時也叫做工人階級的黨。

……

二十五年來列寧同志培養了我們的黨，使我們的黨成為世界上最強大和飽經鍛煉的工人黨。沙皇政府及其走狗的打擊，資產階級和地主的瘋狂暴行，高爾察克[1]和鄧尼金[2]的武裝襲擊，英國和法國的武裝干涉，一切資產階級報刊異口同聲的造謠和誣譏，二十五年來所有

1920），沙俄的海軍上將。

（2）安東・伊凡諾維奇・鄧尼金（1872～1947），沙俄將軍。

firm as a rock, repelling the countless blows of its enemies and leading the working class forward, to victory. In fierce battles our Party forged the unity and solidarity of its ranks. And by unity and solidarity it achieved victory over the enemies of the working class.

. . .

Lenin never regarded the Republic of Soviets as an end in itself. He always looked on it as an essential link for strengthening the revolutionary movement in the countries of the West and the East, an essential link for facilitating the victory of the working people of the whole world over capitalism. Lenin knew that this was the only right conception, both from the international standpoint and from the standpoint of preserving the Republic of Soviets itself. Lenin knew that this alone could fire the hearts of the working people of the whole world with determination to fight the decisive battles for their emancipation. That is why, on the very morrow of the establishment of the dictatorship of the proletariat, he, the greatest of the geniuses who have led the proletariat, laid the foundation of the workers' International. That is why he never tired of extending and strengthening the union of the working people of the whole world — the Communist International.

. . .

這一切惡毒的攻擊都落在我們黨的頭上。可是，我們的黨像巖石般屹立，打退了敵人無數次的攻擊，引導工人階級向勝利前進。我們的黨在殘酷戰鬥中鍛煉出自己隊伍的統一和團結，藉此戰勝了工人階級的敵人。

……

列寧從來沒有把成立蘇維埃共和國看作最終目的。他始終把蘇維埃共和國看作加強東西方各國革命運動的重要環節，看作促進全世界勞動者戰勝資本主義的重要環節。列寧知道，不論從國際觀點或是保全蘇維埃共和國本身來看，也只有上述的見解才是正確的。列寧知道，只有這樣，才能鼓舞全世界勞動者堅決進行爭取解放的戰鬥。正因為如此，列寧這位無產階級中最英明的領袖，在無產階級專政成立的第二天，就奠定了工人國際的基礎。因為如此，列寧始終不倦地擴大並鞏固全世界勞動者聯盟——共產國際。

……

90 The Radio Address

Joseph Stalin

Comrades! Citizens! Brothers and sisters! Men of our Army and Navy! I am addressing you, my friends!

A perfidious military attack on our fatherland begun on June 22 by Hilter's Germany is continuing in spite of the heroic resistance of the Red Army, and, although the enemy's finest divisions and finest air force units have already been smashed and have met their doom on the field of battle, the enemy continues to push forward, hurling fresh forces into the attack. . . . Grave danger hangs over our country.

How could it have happened that our glorious Red Army surrendered a number of our cities and districts to the Fascist armies? Is it really true that German Fascist troops are invincible, as is ceaselessly trumpeted by boastful Fascist progagandists?

Of course not! History shows that there are no invincible armies and never have been. Napoleon's army was considered invincible, but it was beaten successively by Russian, English and German armies. Kaiser Wilhelm's German army in the period of the first imperialist war was also considered invincible, but it was beaten several times by Russian and Anglo-French forces and was finally smashed by Anglo-French forces. The same must be said of Hitler's German Fascist army today. This army had not yet met with serious resistance on the continent of Europe. Only in our territory

九十　廣播演說

約瑟夫・史達林

同志們！公民們！兄弟姊妹們！我們的陸海軍戰士們！我的朋友們，我現在向你們講話！

希特勒德國從 6 月22日起向我們祖國發動背信棄義的軍事進攻，現仍持續着。雖然紅軍英勇抵抗，雖然敵人的精銳師團和精銳空軍部隊被擊潰，被埋葬在戰場上，但是敵人又向前線投入了新的兵力，繼續向前進犯。……我們的祖國面臨着嚴重的危險。

我們光榮的紅軍怎麼會讓法西斯軍隊佔領了我們的一些城市和地區呢？難道德國法西斯軍隊眞的像法西斯吹牛宣傳家所不斷吹噓的那樣，是無敵的軍隊嗎？

當然不是！歷史表明無敵的軍隊現在沒有，過去也沒有過。拿破崙的軍隊曾被認爲是無敵的，可是這支軍隊却先後被俄國、英國和德國的軍隊擊潰了。在第一次帝國主義戰爭時期，威廉的德國軍隊也曾被認爲是無敵的軍隊，可是這支軍隊曾經數次敗在俄國軍隊和英法軍隊手中，終於被英法軍隊擊潰了。現在希特勒的德國法西斯軍隊也是這樣。這支軍隊在歐洲大

德國於1941年 6 月22日向蘇聯突然襲擊，本篇爲史達林於1941年 7 月 3 日發表的廣播演說。

has it met serious resistance. And if as the result of this resistance the finest divisions of Hitler's German Fascist army have been defeated by our Red Army, it means that this army, too, can be smashed and will be smashed as were the armies of Napoleon and Wilhelm.

. . .

What is required to put an end to the danger hovering over our country and what measures must be taken to smash the enemy?

Above all, it is essential that our people, the Soviet people, should understand the full immensity of the danger that threatens our country and abandon all complacency, all heedlessness, all those moods of peaceful constructive work which were so natural before the war, but which are fatal today when war has fundamentally changed everything. The enemy is cruel and implacable. He is out to seize our lands, watered with our sweat, to seize our grain and oil, secured by our labor. He is out to restore the rule of landlords, to restore tsarism, to destroy national culture and the national state existence of Russians, Ukrainians, White Russians, Lithuanians, Letts, Estonians, Uzbeks, Tartars, Moldavians, Georgians, Armenians, Azerbaidjanians and the other free peoples of the Soviet Union, to Germanize them, to convert them into the slaves of German princes and barons. Thus the issue is one of life or death for the Soviet state, for the people of the Union of Soviet Socialist Republics; the issue is whether the peoples of the Soviet Union shall remain free or fall into slavery. The Soviet people must realize this and abandon all heedlessness;

陸還沒有遇到重大的抵抗。只是在我國領土上，德國才遇到了重大的抵抗。由於我們的抵抗，德國法西斯軍隊的精銳師團已被我們紅軍擊潰。這就是說，正像拿破崙和威廉的軍隊一樣，希特勒法西斯軍隊也是能夠被擊潰的，而且一定會被擊潰。

……

為了消除我們祖國面臨的危險，需要做些什麼呢？為了粉碎敵人，應該採取哪些措施呢？

首先我們蘇聯人必須了解到威脅我國的嚴重危險程度，堅決克服泰然自若、漠不關心的心理，克服和平建設的情緒；這種情緒在戰前是完全可以理解的，但是現在，戰爭使形勢根本改變了，這種情緒就變得十分有害。敵人是殘酷無情的。他們的目的是要侵佔我們用汗水澆灌出來的土地，掠奪我們憑勞動獲得的糧食和石油。他們的目的是要恢復地主政權，恢復沙皇制度，摧殘俄羅斯人、烏克蘭人、白俄羅斯人、立陶宛人、拉脫維亞人、愛沙尼亞人、烏茲別克人、韃靼人、摩爾達維亞人、格魯吉亞人、亞美尼亞人、阿塞拜疆人以及蘇聯其他各自由民族的民族文化和國家制度，把我們德意志化，使我們變成德國王公貴族的奴隸。因此，這是蘇維埃國家生死存亡的問題，是蘇聯各族人民生死存亡的問題，是蘇聯各族人民繼續享受自由還是淪為奴隸的問題。蘇聯人必須

they must mobilize themselves and reorganize all their work on new, war-time lines, when there can be no mercy to the enemy.

. . .

This war with Fascist Germany cannot be considered an ordinary war. It is not only a war between two armies, it is also a great war of the entire Soviet people against the German Fascist forces. The aim of this national war in defense of our country against the Fascist oppressors is not only the elimination of the danger which hangs over our country but also to aid all European peoples who are groaning under the yoke of German Fascism. In this war of liberation we shall not be alone. . . .

Comrades, our forces are numberless. The overweening enemy will soon learn this to his cost. Side by side with the Red Army and Navy thousands of workers, collective farmers and intellectuals are rising to fight the enemy aggressor. The masses of our people will rise up in their millions. The working people of Moscow and Leningrad have already commenced to form vast popular levies in support of the Red Army. Such popular levies must be raised in every city which is in danger of enemy invasion, all working people must be roused to defend our freedom, our honor, our country — in our patriotic war against German Fascism.

. . .

了解這一點，不要再漠不關心。他們必須動員起來，把自己的全部工作轉到新的戰時軌道上來，拿出對敵人毫不留情的氣概。

……

同法西斯德國的戰爭，絕不能看成普通的戰爭。這場戰爭不僅是兩國軍隊之間的戰爭，也同時是全體蘇聯人民反對德國法西斯軍隊的偉大戰爭。這場反法西斯壓迫者的全民衛國戰爭的目的，不僅是要消除我國面臨的危險，還要幫助那些在德國法西斯主義枷鎖下的歐洲各國人民。在這場解放戰爭中，我們不是孤立的。

……

同志們！我們的力量是無窮無盡的。趾高氣揚的敵人很快就會付出代價學得這一點。同紅軍一道對進犯我國的敵人奮起作戰的，有成千成萬的工人、集體農莊的農民和知識分子。我國千百萬人民羣眾都將奮起作戰。莫斯科和列寧格勒的勞動者已經開始成立有成千上萬人的民兵隊伍來支援紅軍。在我們反對德國法西斯主義的衛國戰爭中，在每一個遭到敵人侵犯危險的城市裏，我們都應當成立這樣的民兵隊伍，發動全體勞動者起來鬥爭，挺身捍衛我們的自由、我們的榮譽、我們的祖國。

……

91 V-E Order of the Day May 9, 1945

Joseph Stalin

On May 8, 1945, in Berlin, the representatives of the German High Command signed the act of unconditional surrender of the forces of the German army.

The Great Patriotic War waged by the Soviet people against the German-fascist invaders has been victoriously concluded; Germany is utterly routed.

Comrades Red Army men, Red Navy men, sergeants, petty officers, officers of the Army and Navy, generals, admirals and marshals! I congratulate you upon the victorious termination of the Great Patriotic War.

To mark the complete victory over Germany, today, on May 9, the Day of Victory, at 10 P.M., the capital of our Motherland — Moscow — on behalf of the Motherland, will salute the gallant troops of the Red Army and the ships and units of the Navy which have won this brilliant victory, by firing thirty artillery salvos from 1,000 guns.

Eternal glory to the heroes who fell in the fighting for the freedom and independence of our Motherland!

Long live the victorious Red Army and Navy!

九十一 1945 年 5 月 9 日給紅軍和 海軍部隊的命令

約瑟夫·史達林

1945年5月8日，德國最高統帥部代表在柏林簽署了德國武裝力量無條件投降書。

蘇聯人民對德國法西斯侵略者進行的偉大衛國戰爭勝利地結束了；德國已經完全被擊敗了。

紅軍和海軍戰士、軍士、下級軍官、軍官、將軍和元帥同志們！我向你們祝賀偉大衛國戰爭的勝利結束。

為了慶祝對德國的完全勝利，我們祖國首都莫斯科於今天，5月9日勝利日晚上十時，以祖國的名義，用一千門大炮齊鳴禮炮三十響，向獲得這次輝煌勝利的英勇紅軍部隊和海軍艦隊和部隊致敬。

為保衛我們祖國自由與獨立而戰鬥犧牲的英雄永垂不朽！

戰無不勝的紅軍和海軍萬歲！

92 Has the Last Word Been Said?

Charles De Gaulle

The chiefs who have been at the head of the Army for many years have formed a Government.

This government, alleging the defeat of our armies, has made contact with the enemy to put an end to the fight.

There is no question that we have been, that we are swamped by the mechanical strength of the enemy on the ground and in the air. Far more than by their numbers, we are thrown back by the tanks, the airplanes, and the strategy of the Germans. It is the tanks, the airplanes, the strategy of the Germans which surprised our Chiefs and brought them to the point where they are today.

But has the last word been said? Is all hope to be lost? Is the defeat final? No!

Believe me, for I speak to you with full knowledge of what I say. I tell you that nothing is lost for France. The very same means that conquered us can be used to give us one day the victory.

For France is not alone. She is not alone! She is not alone! She has a vast empire behind her. She can form a coalition with the British Empire, which holds the seas and is continuing the struggle. She can, like

戴高樂（1890～1970），全名為夏爾·安德烈·瑪麗·約瑟夫·戴高樂（Charles Andŕe Marie Joseph de Gaulle），1945～46年任法國臨時總統，1959～1969年任法蘭西第五共和國的第一任總統。

468

九十二 誰説敗局已定

夏爾·戴高樂

擔任了多年軍隊領導職務的將領們已經組成了一個政府[1]。

這個政府藉口軍隊打了敗仗，便同敵人接觸，謀取停戰。

我們確實打了敗仗，我們已經被敵人陸、空軍的機械化部隊所困。我們之所以落敗，不僅因德軍的人數衆多，更其重要的是他們的飛機、坦克和作戰戰略。正是敵人的飛機、坦克和戰略使我們的將領們驚惶失措，以至出此下策。

但是難道敗局已定，勝利已經無望？不，不能這樣說！

請相信我的話，因爲我對自己所說的話完全有把握。我要告訴你們，法蘭西並未落敗。總有一天我們會用目前戰勝我們的同樣手段使自己轉敗爲勝。

因爲法國並非孤軍作戰。她並不孤立！絕不孤立！她有一個幅員遼闊的帝國作後盾，她可以同控制着海域並在繼續作戰的不列顛帝國

1940年6月18日，他在倫敦英國廣播公司發表本篇廣播演說。

（1）指原法國總理貝當元帥對德投降後組織的"維希政府"。

England, have limitless access to the immense industrial power of the United States.

This war is not limited to the territory of our unhappy land. This war is not decided by the Battle of France. This war is a world war. All mistakes, all delays, all suffering do not alter the fact that there exist in the world all the means needed to crush our enemies some day. Crushed as we are today by mechanized force, we can in the future conquer by superior mechanized force. Therein lies the destiny of the world.

I, General De Gaulle, speaking from London, invite the French officers and soldiers who may be in British territory now or at a later date, with their arms or without their arms — I invite the engineers and the workers skilled in the manufacture of armaments who may be, now or in the future, on British soil — to get in touch with me.

Whatever may come, the flame of French resistance must never be extinguished; and it will not be extinguished.

Tomorrow, as I have today, I shall speak over the London Broadcast.

結成聯盟。她和英國一樣，可以得到美國雄厚工業力量源源不斷的支援。

這次戰禍所及，並不限於我們不幸的祖國，戰爭的勝敗亦不取決於法國戰場的局勢。這是一次世界大戰。我們的一切過失、延誤以及所受的苦難都沒關係，世界上仍有一切手段，能夠最終粉碎敵人。我們今天雖然敗於機械化部隊，將來，却會依靠更高級的機械化部隊奪取勝利。世界命運正繫於此。

我，戴高樂將軍，現在在倫敦發出廣播講話。我籲請目前或將來來到英國國土的法國官兵，不論是否還持有武器，都和我聯繫；我籲請具有製造武器技術的技師與技術工人，不論是目前或將來來到英國國土，都和我聯繫。

無論出現什麼情況，我們都不容許法蘭西抗戰的烽火被撲滅，法蘭西抗戰烽火也永不會被撲滅。

明天我還要和今天一樣在倫敦發表廣播講話。

93 V-E Day Broadcast to the French People

Charles De Gaulle

The war has been won. This is victory. It is the victory of the United Nations and that of France. The German enemy has surrendered to the Allied Armies in the West and East. The French High Command was present and a party to the act of capitulation.

In the state of disorganization of the German public authorities and command it is possible that certain enemy groups may intend here and there to prolong on their own account a senseless resistence. But Germany is beaten and has signed her disaster.

While the rays of glory once again lend brilliance to our flags, the country turns its thoughts and affection first of all toward those who died for her and then toward those who in her service struggled and suffered so much. Not one single act of courage or self-sacrifice of her sons and daughters, not one single hardship of her captive men and women, not one single bereavement and sacrifice, not one single tear will have been wasted in vain.

In the national rejoicing and pride, the French people send brotherly greetings to their gallant Allies, who, like themselves and for the same cause, have sustained so many hardships over such a long period, to their heroic armies and to those commanding them, and to all those men and women who, throughout the world, fought, suffered and worked so that the cause of liberty and justice might ultimately prevail.

九十三 在勝利日對法國人民的廣播 講話

夏爾・戴高樂

戰爭結束了，勝利已經到來。這是同盟國的勝利，也是法國的勝利。德國已經在東西兩線向同盟國軍隊投降。法國最高統帥部以其中一方代表身份出席了受降儀式。

在德國當局和統帥部處於瓦解的情況下，可能還有敵軍的某些零星部隊在各地區擅自進行毫無意義的頑抗。但是德國已經被擊敗而且簽字認輸。

在這國旗高揚、日月重光的時刻，國家首先深切悼念為國捐軀的烈士，並向那些曾為祖國作艱苦鬥爭的人深深致敬。沒有哪一次祖國兒女們所作的自我犧牲勇敢行動，沒有哪一個被俘男女同胞所受的苦楚，沒有哪一次喪亡，沒有哪一滴眼淚會是白費的。

在這舉國歡騰、揚眉吐氣的時刻，法國人民向英勇的同盟國致以兄弟般的敬禮。他們和我們一樣，為了相同的事業，在過去漫長的歲月中，歷盡艱難困苦。法國人民還向盟軍的英勇戰士和指揮官們致敬，向全世界一切為爭取自由和正義最後勝利而戰鬥、受難和工作的兄弟姊妹們致敬。

本文為戴高樂在1945年5月8日的講話。

Honor, eternal honor, to our armies and their leaders. Honor to our nation, which never faltered, even under terrible trials nor gave in to them. Honor to the United Nations, which mingled their blood, their sorrow and their hopes with ours and who today are triumphant with us.

Long live France!

永恒的榮耀歸於我們的軍隊和我們的將領。榮耀歸於我們的國家，即使在最嚴酷的考驗下，她也從未動搖，從未屈服。榮耀歸於各同盟國。他們曾和我們同灑熱血，分甘共苦，今天又和我們共享勝利的歡樂。

法蘭西萬歲！

94 Broadcast on Japanese Surrender

Harry S. Truman

My fellow Americans:

The thoughts and hopes of all America — indeed of all the civilized world — are centered tonight on the battleship *Missouri*. There on that small piece of American soil anchored in Tokyo Harbor the Japanese have just officially laid down their arms. They have signed terms of unconditional surrender.

Four years ago the thoughts and fears of the whole civilized world were centered on another piece of American soil — Pearl Harbor. The mighty threat to civilization which began there is now laid at rest. It was a long road to Tokyo — and a bloody one.

We shall not forget Pearl Harbor.

The Japanese militarists will not forget the U.S.S. *Missouri*.

The evil done by the Japanese warlords can never be repaired or forgotten. But their power to destroy and kill has been taken from them. Their armies and what is left of their Navy are now impotent.

. . .

Our first thoughts, of course — thoughts of gratefulness and deep obligation — go out to those of our loved ones who have been killed or maimed in this terrible

---

杜魯門（1884～1972），1945至1953年任美國總統。1945年羅斯福總統在任內突然病逝，杜魯門以副總統身份繼任。本文是杜魯門1945年日本投降時發表

九十四　在日本投降時發表的廣播演說

哈利·杜魯門

全國同胞們：

全美國的心思和希望——事實上整個文明世界的心思和希望——今天晚上都集中在密蘇里號軍艦上。在這停泊於東京港口的一小塊美國領土[1]上，日本人剛剛正式放下武器，簽署無條件投降。

四年前，整個文明世界的心思與恐懼集中在美國另一塊土地上——珍珠港。那裏曾發生對文明巨大的威脅，現在已經清除了。從那裏通到東京的是一條漫長的、灑滿鮮血的道路。

我們不會忘記珍珠港。

日本軍國主義者也不會忘記美國軍艦密蘇里號。

日本軍閥犯下的罪行是無法彌補，也無法忘却的。但是他們的破壞和屠殺力量已經被剝奪了。現在他們的陸軍以及剩下的海軍已經毫不足懼了。

……

當然，我們首先懷着深深感激之情想到的，是在這場可怕的戰爭中犧牲或受到傷殘的親人

的廣播演說。

（1）根據國際法，停泊在外國或公海上的船隻爲本國領土。

war. On land and sea and in the air, American men and women have given their lives so that this day of ultimate victory might come and assure the survival of a civilized world. No victory can make good their loss.

We think of those whom death in this war has hurt, taking from them husbands, sons, brothers, and sisters whom they loved. No victory can bring back the faces they longed to see.

Only the knowledge that the victory, which these sacrifices have made possible, will be wisely used, can give them any comfort. It is our responsibility — ours, the living — to see to it that this victory shall be a monument worthy of the dead who died to win it.

. . .

This is a victory of more than arms alone. This is a victory of liberty over tyranny.

From our war plants rolled the tanks and planes which blasted their way to the heart of our enemies; from our shipyards sprang the ships which bridged all the oceans of the world for our weapons and supplies; from our farms came the food and fibre for our armies and navies and for our Allies in all the corners of the earth; from our mines and factories came the raw materials and the finished products which gave us the equipment to overcome our enemies.

But back of it all were the will and spirit and determination of a free people — who know what freedom is, and who know that it is worth whatever price they had to pay to preserve it.

It was the spirit of liberty which gave us our armed

們。在陸地、海洋和天空，無數美國男女公民奉獻出他們的生命，換來今日的最後勝利，使世界文明得以保存。但是，無論多麼巨大的勝利都無法彌補他們的損失。

我們想到那些在戰爭中忍受親人死亡的悲痛人們，死亡奪去了他們摯愛的丈夫、兒子、兄弟和姐妹。無論多麼巨大的勝利也不能使他們和親人重逢了。

只有當他們知道親人流血犧牲換來的勝利會被明智地運用時，他們才會稍感安慰。我們活着的人們，有責任保證使這次勝利成為一座紀念碑，以紀念那些為此犧牲的烈士。

……

這次勝利不僅是軍事上的勝利。這是自由對暴政的勝利。

我們的兵工廠源源生產坦克、飛機，直搗敵人的心臟；我們的船塢源源製造出戰艦，溝通世界各大洋，供應武器與裝備；我們的農場生產出食物、纖維，供應我們海陸軍以及世界各地的盟國；我們的礦山與工廠生產出各種原料與成品，裝備我們，戰勝敵人。

然而，作為這一切的後盾是一個自由民族的意志、精神與決心。這個民族知道自由意味着什麼，他們知道為了保持自由，值得付出任何代價。

正是這種自由精神給予我們武裝力量，使

strength and which made our men invincible in battle. We now know that spirit of liberty, the freedom of the individual, and the personal dignity of man, are the strongest and toughest and most enduring forces in all the world.

. . .

Victory always has its burdens and its responsibilities as well as its rejoicing.

But we face the future and all its dangers with great confidence and great hope. America can build for itself a future of employment and security. Together with the United Nations, it can build a world of peace founded on justice and fair dealing and tolerance.

As President of the United States, I proclaim Sunday, September second, 1945 to be V-J Day — the day of formal surrender by Japan. It is not yet the day for the formal proclamation of the end of the war or of the cessation of hostilities. But it is a day which we Americans shall always remember as a day of retribution — as we remember that other, the day of infamy.

From this day we move forward. We move toward a new era of security at home. With the other United Nations we move toward a new and better world of peace and international goodwill and cooperation.

God's help has brought us to this day of victory. With His help we will attain that peace and prosperity for ourselves and all the world in the years ahead.

士兵在戰場上戰無不勝。現在，我們知道，這種自由的精神、個人的自由以及人類的個人尊嚴是世界上最強大、最堅韌、最持久的力量。

……

勝利是值得歡慶的，但同時有其負擔和責任。

但是，我們以極大的信心與希望面對未來及其一切艱險。美國能夠為自己造就一個充分就業而安全的未來。連同聯合國一起，美國能夠建立一個以正義、公平交往與忍讓為基礎的和平世界。

我以美國總統的身份宣佈1945年9月2日星期日——日本正式投降的日子——為太平洋戰場勝利紀念日。這一天還不是正式停戰和停止敵對行為的日子，但是我們美國人將永遠記住這是報仇雪恥的一天，正如我們將永遠記住另一天[1]是國恥日一樣。

從這一天開始，我們將走向一個國內安全的新時期，我們將和其他國家一同走向一個國與國之間和平、友善和合作的更美好新世界。

上帝幫助我們取得了今天的勝利。我們仍將在上帝的幫助下得到我們以及全世界的和平與繁榮。

（1）指1941年12月7日。當天日本偷襲珍珠港。

95 The Atlantic Charter

Clement Richard Attlee

We do not envisage an end to this war save victory. We are determined not only to win the war but to win the peace. Plans must be prepared in advance. Action must be taken now if the end of the war is not to find us unprepared. But the problems of the peace cannot be solved by one nation in isolation. Britain must be fitted in the plans of a post-war world, for this fight is not just a fight between nations. It is a fight for the future of civilization. Its result will affect the lives of all men and women — not only those now engaged in the struggle.

It is certain that until the crushing burden of armaments throughout the world is lifted from the backs of the people, they cannot enjoy the maximum social well-being which is possible. We cannot build the city of our desire under the constant menace of aggression. Freedom from fear and freedom from want must be sought together.

The joint expression of aims common to the United States and the British Commonwealth of Nations known as the Atlantic Charter includes not only purposes covering war but outlines of more distant objectives.

九十五　大西洋憲章

克利門蒂‧理察德‧艾德禮

除得勝之外，我們看不到這次戰爭[1]有其他結局。我們不但決心贏得戰爭，並且決心贏得和平。我們必須預先做好計劃。如果戰爭結束時，我們不至處於毫無準備的狀態，目前就須採取行動。但是有關和平的問題不能由一個國家單獨解決。英國必須配合戰後世界的計劃，因為這次戰爭不僅是國與國之間作戰，而且是為未來的文明而戰。這次戰爭的結果不僅僅影響到參加這場鬥爭的人，而是影響全世界人類的生活。

當然，只有從人民的肩上卸下全世界的軍備重擔，人民才可能享受到最大限度的社會福利。在持續存在的侵略威脅下，我們不可能建設心中理想的城市。我們必須同時爭取免於恐懼和免於貧困的自由。

大西洋憲章表達了美國和英聯邦國家的共同目的，其中不僅包括了有關戰爭的目標，更勾劃出長遠的目標。

艾德禮（1883～1967），1945至1951年任英國首相。艾德禮於1941年10月29日代表英政府出席國際勞工組織會議發表本篇演說。

（1）指第二次世界大戰。

It binds us to endeavor with due respect to our existing obligations to further the enjoyment by all States, great and small, victors and vanquished, of access on equal terms to trade and raw materials which are needed for their economic prosperity. In addition it records our desire to bring about the fullest collaboration between all nations in the economic field with the object of securing for all labor standards, economic advancement and social security. But it is not enough to applaud these objectives. They must be attained. And if mistakes are to be avoided, there must be the closest international collaboration in which we in the United Kingdom will gladly play our part.

We are determined that economic questions and questions of the universal improvement of standards of living and nutrition shall not be neglected as they were after the last war owing to the preoccupation with political problems. The fact is that wars do not enrich but impoverish the world and bold statesmanship will be needed if we are to repair the ravages of war and to insure to all the highest possible measure of labor standards, economic advancement and social security to which the Atlantic Charter looks forward.

大西洋憲章約束我們，使我們努力根據現有的義務協助一切大小國家，不論其為戰勝或戰敗國，均能更好地享受平等權利進行貿易或取得原料，令該國達至經濟繁榮。此外，大西洋憲章還載明了我們願意令一切國家在經濟上得到最充分的合作，我們的目的是要使一切國家的勞動水準、經濟進步和社會安全得到保證。但是，僅僅表示贊成這些目標是不夠的，還要努力爭取達到這些目標。為了避免犯錯誤，我們需要有最密切的國際合作，聯合王國樂於盡力達成國際合作。

　　我們決心使經濟問題、生活水平與營養水平得到普遍改善的問題不被忽略，這些問題在上次世界大戰後因注意力集中在政治問題上而被忽視了。事實上戰爭只會使世界貧窮而不會使之富裕，如果我們要彌補戰爭的破壞，要保證達到大西洋憲章所要求的最高勞動水準，經濟進步和社會安全，我們就需要果斷政治家的膽略。

96 Nobel Prize Acceptance Speech

William Faulkner

I feel that this award was not made to me as a man but to my work — a life's work in the agony and sweat of the human spirit, not for glory and least of all for profit, but to create out of the materials of the human spirit something which did not exist before. So this award is only mine in trust. It will not be difficult to find a dedication for the money part of it commensurate with the purpose and significance of its origin. But I would like to do the same with the acclaim too, by using this moment as a pinnacle from which I might be listened to by the young men and women already dedicated to the same anguish and travail, among whom is already that one who will some day stand here where I am standing.

Our tragedy today is a general and universal physical fear so long sustained by now that we can even bear it. There are no longer problems of the spirit. There is only the question: When will I be blown up? Because of this, the young man or woman writing today has forgotten the problems of the human heart in conflict with itself which alone can make good writing because only that

九十六　接受諾貝爾獎時的演説

威廉‧福克諾

　　我感到這份獎金不是授與我個人而是授與我的工作的，——授與我一生從事關於人類精神的嘔心瀝血工作。我從事這項工作，不是爲名，更不是爲利，而是爲了從人的精神原料中創造出一些從前不曾有過的東西。因此，這份獎金只不過是托我保管而已。爲這份獎金的錢找到與獎金原來的目的和意義相稱的用途並不難，但我還想爲獎金的榮譽找到承受者。我願意利用這個時刻，利用這個舉世矚目的講壇，向那些聽到我說話並已獻身同一艱苦勞動的男女青年致敬。他們中肯定有人有一天也會站到我現在站着的地方。

　　我們今天的悲劇是人們普遍存在一種生理上的恐懼，這種恐懼存在已久，以致我們能夠忍受下去了。現在再沒有精神上的問題了。唯一的問題是：我什麼時候會被炸得粉身碎骨？正因如此，今天從事寫作的男女青年已經忘記了人類內心的衝突。然而，只有接觸到這種內心衝突才能產生出好作品，因爲這是唯一值得

　　福克諾（1897～1962），美國小說家，1949年獲諾貝爾文學獎。他的小說常描寫美國社會生活的黑暗面。

is worth writing about, worth the agony and the sweat.

He must learn them again. He must teach himself that the basest of all things is to be afraid; and, teaching himself that, forget it forever, leaving no room in his workshop for anything but the old verities and truths of the heart, the old universal truths lacking which any story is ephemeral and doomed — love and honor and pity and pride and compassion and sacrifice. Until he does so he labors under a curse. He writes not of love but of lust, of defeats in which nobody loses anything of value, of victories without hope and worst of all without pity or compassion. His griefs grieve on no universal bones, leaving no scars. He writes not of the heart but of the glands.

Until he relearns these things he will write as though he stood among and watched the end of man. I decline to accept the end of man. It is easy enough to say that man is immortal simply because he will endure; that when the last ding-dong of doom has clanged and faded from the last worthless rock hanging tideless in the last red and dying evening, that even then there will still be one more sound: that of his puny inexhaustible voice, still talking. I refuse to accept this. I believe that man will not merely endure: he will prevail. He is immortal, not because he alone among creatures has an inexhaustible voice, but because he has a soul, a spirit capable of compassion and sacrifice and endurance. The poet's, the writer's duty is to write about

寫、值得嘔心瀝血地去寫的。

　　他一定要重新認識這些問題。他必須使自己明白世間最可鄙的事情莫過於恐懼。他必須使自己永遠忘却恐懼，在他的工作室裏除了心底古老的眞理之外，不允許任何別的東西有容身之地。缺了這古老的普遍眞理，任何小說都只能曇花一現，注定要失敗；這些眞理就是愛情、榮譽、憐憫、自尊、同情、犧牲等感情。若是他做不到這樣，他的氣力終歸白費。他不是寫愛情而是寫情慾，他寫的失敗是沒有人感到失去可貴東西的失敗，他寫的勝利是沒有希望、甚至沒有憐憫或同情的勝利。他不是爲有普遍意義的死亡而悲傷，所以留不下深刻的痕跡。他不是在寫心靈而是在寫器官。

　　在他重新懂得這些之前，他寫作時，就猶如站在人類末日中去觀察末日的來臨。我不接受人類末日的說法。因爲人能傳種接代而說人是不朽的，這很容易。因爲即使最後一次鐘聲已經消失，消失在再也沒有潮水冲刷、映在落日的餘暉裏。海上最後一塊無用的礁石之旁時，還會有一個聲音，那就是人類微弱的、不斷的說話聲，這樣說也很容易。但是我不能接受這種說法。我相信人類不僅能傳種接代，而且能戰勝一切。人之不朽不是因爲在動物中唯獨他能永遠發出聲音，而是因爲他有靈魂，有同情心、有犧牲和忍耐精神。詩人和作家的責任就

these things. It is his privilege to help man endure by lifting his heart, by reminding him of the courage and honor and hope and pride and compassion and pity and sacrifice which have been the glory of his past. The poet's voice need not merely be the record of man, it can be one of the props, the pillars to help him endure and prevail.

是把這些寫出來。詩人和作家的特殊光榮就是去鼓舞人的鬥志，使人記住過去曾經有過的光榮——他曾有過的勇氣、榮譽、希望、自尊、同情、憐憫與犧牲精神——以達到不朽。詩人的聲音不應只是人類的記錄，而應是幫助人類永存並得到勝利的支柱和棟樑。

97 Peace in the Atomic Age

Albert Einstein

I am grateful to you for the opportunity to express my conviction in this most important political question.

The idea of achieving security through national armament is, at the present state of military technique, a disastrous illusion. On the part of the United States this illusion has been particularly fostered by the fact that this country succeeded first in producing an atomic bomb. The belief seemed to prevail that in the end it were possible to achieve decisive military superiority.

In this way, any potential opponent would be intimidated, and security, so ardently desired by all of us, brought to us and all of humanity. The maxim which we have been following during these last five years has been, in short: security through superior military power, whatever the cost.

The armament race between the U.S.A. and U.S.S.R., originally supposed to be a preventive measure, assumes hysterical character. On both sides, the means to mass destruction are perfected with feverish haste — behind the respective walls of secrecy. The H-bomb appears on the public horizon as a probably attainable goal.

If successful, radioactive poisoning of the atmosphere and hence annihilation of any life on earth has been brought within the range of technical possibilities.

492

九十七 原子能時代的和平

阿爾伯特・愛因斯坦

感謝你們使我有機會就這個最重要的政治問題發表意見。

在軍事技術已發展到目前狀況的今天，加強國家軍備以保證安全的想法，只是一個會帶來災難後果的幻想。美國首先製成了原子彈，所以特別容易抱有這種幻想。看來多數人相信，美國最終可能在軍事上取得決定性的優勢。

這樣，任何潛在的敵人就會被震懾，而我們和全人類就可以得到大家所熱望的安全了。我們近五年來一直信守的格言，簡而言之，就是：不惜一切代價，通過軍事力量的優勢以保證安全。

美國與蘇聯之間的軍備競賽，最初只是作為一種防止戰爭的手段，現在已經帶有歇斯底里的性質。在保證安全的漂亮帷幕後面，雙方都以狂熱速度改善大規模的破壞手段，在人們的眼光裏；氫彈似乎已是可能達到的目標。

一旦達到這個目標，大氣層的放射性污染以及由此引致地球上一切生命的滅絕，在技術

愛因斯坦（1879～1955），美國籍猶太人，當代偉大科學家。二次世界大戰後，愛因斯坦奔走呼號，要求限制使用核武器。本文是1950年2月12日在美國電視的講話。

The ghostlike character of this development lies in its apparently compulsory trend. Every step appears as the unavoidable consequence of the preceding one. In the end, there beckons more and more clearly general annihilation.

Is there any way out of this impasse created by man himself? All of us, and particularly those who are responsible for the attitude of the U.S. and the U.S.S.R., should realize that we may have vanquished an external enemy, but have been incapable of getting rid of the mentality created by the war.

It is impossible to achieve peace as long as every single action is taken with a possible future conflict in view. The leading point of view of all political action should therefore be: What can we do to bring about a peaceful co-existence and even loyal cooperation of the nations?

The first problem is to do away with mutual fear and distrust. Solemn renunciation of violence (not only with respect to means of mass destruction) is undoubtedly necessary.

Such renunciation, however, can only be effective if at the same time a supra-national judicial and executive body is set up empowered to decide questions of immediate concern to the security of the nations. Even a declaration of the nations to collaborate loyally in the realization of such a "restricted world government" would considerably reduce the imminent danger of war.

In the last analysis, every kind of peaceful cooperation among men is primarily based on mutual trust and only secondly on institutions such as courts of justice and police. This holds for nations as well as for individuals. And the basis of trust is loyal give and take.

方面而言將成為可能。這種發展的可怕之處在於它已明顯地成為不可遏止的趨勢。第一步必然引出第二步。最後,越來越清楚地,必然招致全人類的普遍滅絕。

人類自己走進的這條死胡同還有出路嗎?我們所有人,特別是那些對美國和蘇聯立場負責的人,應該認識到:我們可能戰勝外部的敵人,但却不可能消除由戰爭產生的那種精神狀態。

如果每採取一項行動都考慮將來可能要發生衝突,那要取得和平是不可能的。因此,一切政治行動的指導思想應該是:為了實現國與國之間的和平共存甚至真誠合作,我們能做些什麼?

首先要做到的是去除雙方的恐懼和猜疑。鄭重宣佈廢棄使用武力(不僅是廢棄大規模的破壞手段),無疑是必要的。

然而,只有同時成立一個超國家的司法和執行機構,使它有權決定直接關係到各國安全的問題,才能有效地廢絕使用武力。即使是各國發表共同宣言,保證忠誠地通力合作,使成立這樣一個"權力有限的世界政府"得以實現,也會大為緩和戰爭發生的危險。

總括地說,一切人類和平合作的基礎首先是相互信任,其次才是法庭和警察一類的機構。對於個人是這樣,對於國家也是這樣。信任的基礎是取和予都要正直忠實。

98 Inaugural Address

John Fitzgerald Kennedy

We observe today not a victory of Party but a celebration of freedom, symbolizing an end as well as a beginning, signifying renewal as well as change. For I have sworn before you and Almighty God the same solemn oath our forebears prescribed nearly a century and three-quarters ago.

. . .

Let every nation know, whether it wishes us well or ill, that we shall pay any price, bear any burden, meet any hardship, support any friend, oppose any foe to assure the survival and the success of liberty.

This much we pledge — and more.

To those old allies whose cultural and spiritual origins we share, we pledge the loyalty of faithful friends. United, there is little we cannot do in a host of co-operative ventures. Divided, there is little we can do, for we dare not meet a powerful challenge at odds and split asunder.

To those new states whom we welcome to the ranks of the free, we pledge our word that one form of colonial control shall not have passed away merely to be replaced by a far more iron tyranny. We shall not always expect to find them supporting our view. But

---

約翰·甘迺迪（1917~1963），美國第三十五屆總統。1960年當選，1963年遇刺而死。

（1）1787年美國通過憲法，規定總統就職前應宣誓。

九十八　就職演說

約翰·費滋傑羅·甘迺迪

我們不把今天看作是一黨勝利的日子，而看作慶祝自由的佳節，它既象徵結束，也象徵開始；它意味着繼業，又意味着更新。我在你們和全能上帝面前宣讀的，是將近一百七十五年[1]前我們祖先所宣讀的同一莊嚴誓詞。

……

讓每一個關心我們或對我們懷有敵意的國家知道，我們願付出任何代價，承受任何負擔，迎接任何困難，支持任何朋友，反抗任何敵人，以爭取和維護自由。

我們保證做到這些，我們還要保證做得更多。

對於和我們有共同精神文化的舊盟國，我們保證忠實不渝。團結一致時，我們合作的多項事業將無往不利。一旦分手，我們將一事無成，因爲在不和與分裂中，我們不敢應付任何強有力的挑戰。

我們歡迎加入自由行列的新國家，對於他們，我們保證決不容許以另一種更暴虐的專政去替代殖民統治。我們不能總指望這些國家支

甘迺迪於1961年1月20日發表本篇演說，距離1787年將近一百七十五年。

we shall always hope to find them strongly supporting their own freedom, and to remember that, in the past, those who foolishly sought power by riding the back of the tiger ended up inside.

To those peoples in the huts and villages of half the globe struggling to break the bonds of mass misery, we pledge our best efforts to help them help themselves, for whatever period is required, not because the Communists may be doing it, not because we seek their votes, but because it is right. If a free society cannot help the many who are poor, it cannot save the few who are rich.

To our sister republics south of our border, we offer a special pledge: to convert our good words into good deeds, in a new alliance for progress, to assist free men and free governments in casting off the chains of poverty. But this peaceful revolution of hope cannot become the prey of hostile powers. Let all our neighbors know that we shall join with them to oppose aggression or subversion anywhere in the Americas. And let every other power know that this hemisphere intends to remain the master of its own house.

To that world assembly of sovereign states, the United Nations, our last best hope in an age where the instruments of war have far outpaced the instruments of peace, we renew our pledge of support: to prevent it from becoming merely a forum for invective, to strengthen its shield of the new and the weak, and

持我們的觀點，但是我們却總希望他們有力地支持他們自己的自由，總希望我們能記住，過去想騎在老虎背上攫取權力的蠢人最終必葬身虎腹。

對於半個地球上仍然住在鄉村的草舍茅屋，正在奮鬥以掙脫悲慘處境的各民族，我們保證在任何需要的時刻盡最大努力協助他們幫助自己。我們這樣做，不是為了怕共產主義同我們爭奪陣地，也不是為了爭取他們在聯合國的選票，只是因為這樣做是對的。一個自由的社會如果不能幫助衆多的窮人，也就不能拯救少數的富人。

對於我們邊界以南的各姊妹共和國，我們作出特殊的保證：我們要把說好話變為做好事，為爭取進步結成新的聯盟，幫助自由的人民和自由的政府掙脫貧窮的枷鎖。但是這種和平革命不應成為敵對大國的可乘之機。我們要讓鄰國知道，我們將和這些姊妹國聯合起來，反對在南北美洲任何地方進行侵略與顛覆。我們要讓每一個大國知道，這半球上的人民要繼續做自己的主人。

在戰爭手段的發展遠遠超過和平手段發展的當代，我們對聯合國這個主權國家的世界組織寄予最終和最大的希望，我們重申對聯合國的支持：我們要努力使聯合國不成為單單互相攻訐的講壇，而成為新生和弱小國家的庇護，

to enlarge the area in which its writ may run.

Finally, to those nations who would make themselves our adversary, we offer not a pledge but a request: that both sides begin anew the quest for peace, before the dark powers of destruction unleashed by science engulf all humanity in planned or accidental self-destruction.

. . .

In your hands, my fellow citizens, more than mine, will rest the final success or failure of our course. Since this country was founded, each generation of Americans has been summoned to give testimony to its national loyalty. The graves of young Americans who answered the call to service surround the globe.

Now the trumpet summons us again — not as a call to bear arms, though arms we need; not as a call to battle, though embattled we are; but a call to bear the burden of a long twilight struggle, year in and year out, "rejoicing in hope, patient in tribulation," a struggle against the common enemies of man: tyranny, poverty, disease and war itself.

Can we forge against these enemies a grand and global alliance, North and South, East and West that can assure a more fruitful life for all mankind? Will you join in that historic effort?

In the long history of the world, only a few generations have been granted the role of defending freedom in its hour of maximum danger. I do not shrink from this responsibility; I welcome it. I do not believe that

使聯合國的議決案在更大的範圍內得以實行。

最後，對於同我們敵對的國家，我們不提出保證而提出一項要求：讓我們雙方都開始重新尋求和平吧，不要等到由於科學昌明而發展的毀滅性邪惡力量，有計劃地或偶然地被觸發而吞噬整個人類。

……

同胞們，我們事業的最終成敗，主要不在我手中，而在你們手中。從我國建國伊始，每一代美國人都曾經被召喚為祖國忠誠服務。許許多多美國青年回答了祖國的召喚，他們的忠骨埋遍世界各地。

現在召喚我們的號角又吹響了——不是號召我們拿起武器，雖然我們需要武器；不是號召我們奔赴戰場，雖然我們已在備戰；這號角聲召喚我們去作黎明前漫長的鬥爭，年復一年地“在希望中歡欣，在苦難中忍耐”；這是一場反對專制、貧窮、疾病與戰爭等人類共同敵人的鬥爭。

我們能否在全球東、西、南、北形成一個巨大的聯盟對抗這些敵人，以保證整個人類更美滿的生活呢？你們願意參加這具有歷史意義的事業嗎？

在世界漫長的歷史上，只有少數幾代人有幸在自由處於最危急的關頭被委以捍衛自由的重任。我對這任務當仁不讓，勇於承擔。我不

any of us would exchange places with any other people or any other generation. The energy, the faith, the devotion which we bring to this endeavor will light our country and all who serve it, and the glow from that fire can truly light the world.

And so, my fellow Americans, ask not what your country can do for you, ask what you can do for your country.

My fellow citizens of the world, ask not what America will do for you, but what together we can do for the freedom of man.

Finally, whether you are citizens of America or citizens of the world, ask of us here the same high standards of strength and sacrifice which we ask of you. With a good conscience our only sure reward, with history the final judge of our deeds, let us go forth to lead the land we love, asking His blessing and His help, but knowing that here on earth God's work must truly be our own.

相信我們有人會願意同其他民族或其他時代的人換易我們現在所處的地位。我們付與這事業的精力、信仰與忠誠將照耀我們的祖國和為國效勞的人，我們祖國發出的光芒將真正普照全世界。

因此，我的美國同胞們，請你們對國家只談貢獻，莫計報酬。

世界公民們，請你們勿問何所得於美國，但問共同為人類自由貢獻多少。

最後，美國公民和世界公民，請按照我們向你們所要求的力量與犧牲的崇高標準來要求我們。良心的平靜是我們唯一可靠的報酬，歷史將為我們的作為做最後的裁判，讓我們引導摯愛的祖國勇往直前。我們祈求上帝的祝福與幫助，雖然我們知道上帝在世上的工作就是我們自己的事業。

99　I Have a Dream

Martin Luther King

I am happy to join with you today in what will go down in history as the greatest demonstration for freedom in the history of our nation.

Five score years ago, a great American, in whose symbolic shadow we stand, signed the Emancipation Proclamation. This momentous decree came as a great beacon light of hope to millions of Negro slaves who had been seared in the flames of withering injustice. It came as a joyous daybreak to end the long night of captivity.

But one hundred years later, we must face the tragic fact that the Negro is still not free. One hundred years later, the life of the Negro is still sadly crippled by the manacles of segregation and the chains of discrimination. One hundred years later, the Negro lives on a lonely island of poverty in the midst of a vast ocean of material prosperity. One hundred years later the Negro is still languishing in the corners of American society and finds himself an exile in his own land. So we have come here today to dramatize an appalling condition.

In a sense we have come to our nation's Capital to cash a check. When the architects of our republic wrote the magnificent words of the Constitution and the Declaration of Independence, they were signing a promissory note to which every American was to fall heir. This note was a promise that all men would be guaranteed the unalienable rights of life, liberty, and the pursuit of happiness.

馬丁・路德・金（1929~1968），美國黑人解放
運動的著名領袖，1968年被種族主義者刺殺。1963年
8月28日，美國首都華盛頓舉行大規模的黑人集會，馬

九十九　我有一個夢想

馬丁・路德・金

今天，我很高興能夠參加這次我國歷史上爲爭取自由而舉行的最偉大示威集會。

一百年前，一位美國偉人[1]簽署了《解放宣言》。現在我們站在他紀念像投下的影子裏。這重要的文獻爲千千萬萬在非正義烈焰中煎熬的黑奴點燃起一座偉大的希望燈塔。這文獻有如結束囚室中漫漫長夜的一束歡樂的曙光。

然而一百年後的今天，我們却不得不面對黑人依然沒有自由這一可悲的事實。一百年後的今天，黑人的生活依然悲慘地套着種族隔離和歧視的枷鎖。一百年後的今天，在物質富裕的汪洋大海中，黑人依然生活在貧乏的孤島之上。一百年後的今天，黑人依然在美國社會的陰暗角落裏艱難掙扎，在自己的國土上受到放逐。所以我們今天到這裏來揭露這駭人聽聞的事實。

從某種意義來說，我們是到我國的首都兌現一張支票來了。我們共和國的奠基人寫下憲法和獨立宣言的莊嚴詞句時，就是簽署了一張期票，許諾每一個美國人都得成爲國家的繼承人。這張期票保證一切人具有不可剝奪的生存權、自由權以及追求幸福的權利。

丁・路德・金在會上發表本篇演說。

（1）指阿伯拉罕・林肯。

It is obvious today that America has defaulted on this promissory note insofar as her citizens of color are concerned. Instead of honoring this sacred obligation, America has given the Negro people a bad check; a check which has come back marked "insufficient funds." But we refuse to believe that the bank of justice is bankrupt. We refuse to believe that there are insufficient funds in the great vaults of opportunity of this nation. So we have come to cash this check — a check that will give us upon demand the riches of freedom and the security of justice. We have also come to this hallowed spot to remind America of the fierce urgency of *now*. This is not time to engage in the luxury of cooling off or to take the tranquilizing drug of gradualism. *Now* is the time to make real the promises of Democracy. *Now* is the time to rise from the dark and desolate valley of segregation to the sunlit path of racial justice. *Now* is the time to lift our nation from the quicksands of racial injustice to the solid rock of brotherhood.

. . .

But there is something that I must say to my people who stand on the warm threshold which leads into the palace of justice. In the process of gaining our rightful place we must not be guilty of wrongful deeds. Let us not seek to satisfy our thirst for freedom by drinking from the cup of bitterness and hatred. We must forever conduct our struggle on the high plane of dignity and discipline. We must not allow our creative protest to degenerate into physical violence. Again and again we must rise to the majestic heights of meeting physical force with soul force. The marvelous new militancy which has engulfed the Negro community must not lead us to a distrust of all white people, for many of our

顯然，就有色公民而言，美國並沒有兌付這張期票。美國不但沒有承擔這項神聖義務，反而付給黑人一張失效票，一張打着"現金不足"記號的退票。但我們不相信正義的銀行已經破產。我們不相信在這個倉廩充盈、機會良多的國家裏會發生現金不足的情況。因此我們來要求兌現這張支票——這張能夠給我們所要求的自由財寶與正義保障的支票。我們到這神聖的地方來，還爲了要提醒美國：目前是萬分緊急的時期。現在不是侈談冷靜或以漸進改革爲麻醉劑的時候。現在是實現民主諾言的時候；現在是從種族隔離的黑暗荒谷中走上種族平等的陽光普照大道的時候；現在是使我們國家從種族不平等的泥潭拔足到博愛的堅固岩石上來的時候。

……

　　但是我還有一句話要對站在溫暖門檻上，準備進入正義之宮的同胞們說清楚：在爭取合法地位的進程中，我們不要用錯誤的行動使自己犯罪。我們不要用仇恨的苦酒來緩解熱望自由的乾渴。我們必須永遠站在高處，使我們的鬥爭方式保持尊嚴，堅守紀律。我們一定不能使富有創造性的抗爭淪爲使用暴力的低下行動。我們必須努力不懈站在以靈魂力量來對付肉體力量的神聖高度。已經席捲黑人社會的戰鬥氣氛決不要導致我們對一切白種人的不信

white brothers, as evidenced by their presence here today, have come to realize that their destiny is tied up with our destiny and their freedom is inextricably bound to our freedom. We cannot walk alone.

. . .

I say to you today, my friends, that in spite of the difficulties and frustrations of the moment I still have a dream. It is a dream deeply rooted in the American dream.

I have a dream that one day this nation will rise up and live out the true meaning of its creed: "We hold these truths to be self-evident; that all men are created equal."

. . .

This is our hope. This is the faith with which I return to the South. With this faith we will be able to hew out of the mountain of despair a stone of hope. With this faith we will be able to transform the jangling discords of our nation into a beautiful symphony of brotherhood. With this faith we will be able to work together, to pray together, to struggle together, to go to jail together, to stand up for freedom together, knowing that we will be free one day.

. . .

When we let freedom ring, when we let it ring from every village and every hamlet, from every state and every city, we will be able to speed up that day when all of God's children, black men and white men, Jews and Gentiles, Protestants and Catholics, will be able to join hands and sing in the words of the old Negro spiritual, "Free at last! free at last! thank God almighty, we are free at last!"

任。我們許多白人兄弟今天到這裏來集會，就已經證明了他們認識到他們的命運和我們的命運緊緊聯結在一起，他們的自由和我們的自由完全分不開。我們不能單獨行動。

……

朋友們，今天我要告訴你們：儘管當前還有許多困難挫折，我仍然懷有一個夢想。這是深深扎根於美國人夢想中的夢想。

我夢想有一天這個國家能夠站立起來，實現她信條的眞締："我們把這些看作是不證自明的眞理：一切人生來就是平等的。"

……

這就是我們的希望。這就是我帶回南方的信念。懷着這個信念，我們能夠把絕望的大山鑿成希望的盤石。懷着這個信念，我們能夠將我國種族不和的喧囂變爲一曲友愛的樂章。懷着這個信念，我們能夠一同工作，一同祈禱，一同奮鬥，一同入獄，一同爲爭取自由而鬥爭，因爲我們知道我們終將得到自由。

……

我們使自由之音響徹千村萬戶，響徹每個州郡，每座城池，就會促使那日子盡快到來。到了那一天，上帝的一切兒女，無論黑人、白人、猶太人、非猶太人、基督教徒和天主教徒都將携手同唱那首古老的黑人聖歌："我們終於得到了自由！終於得到了自由！感謝全能的上帝，我們終於得到了自由！"

100 Inaugural Address

Richard Milhous Nixon

Senator Dirksen, Mr. Chief Justice, Mr. Vice President, President Johnson, Vice President Humphrey, my fellow Americans and my fellow citizens of the world community:

I ask you to share with me today the majesty of this moment. In the orderly transfer of power, we celebrate the unity that keeps us free.

Each moment in history is a fleeting time, precious and unique. But some stand out as moments of beginning, in which courses are set that shape decades or centuries.

For the first time, because the people of the world want peace and the leaders of the world are afraid of war, the times are on the side of peace.

The greatest honor history can bestow is the title of peace-maker. This honor now beckons America — the chance to help lead the world at last out of the valley of turmoil and on to that high ground of peace that man has dreamed of since the dawn of civilization.

If we succeed, generations to come will say of us

一〇〇 就職演説

理查德·米豪斯·尼克森

德克遜參議員、最高法院首席法官先生、副總統先生、約翰遜總統、漢弗萊副總統[1]、美國同胞們、全世界的公民們：

今天，在這個時刻裏，我要求你們和我分享這種崇高肅穆的感情。在有秩序的權力交接中，我們歡慶我們的團結一致，它使我們保有自由。

歷史巨輪飛轉，分分秒秒的時間都十分寶貴，也獨特非凡。但是有些瞬間却成為新的起點，定下其後數十年乃至幾個世紀的行程。

現在，由於世界人民要求和平，各國領導人懼怕戰爭，所以在歷史上第一次，時代站到了和平方面。

歷史能授與的最光榮稱號莫過於"和平創造者"。這最高榮譽現正召喚美國。美國有機會引導世界最終從動亂的深淵中拔足，走向人類自有文明以來即夢寐以求的和平寬闊高地。

如果我們能夠成功，後輩子孫提到我們現

尼克森（1913～　），1968 年當選美國第 37 屆總統，1974年因水門事件被彈劾罷免。本文發表於1969年 1 月20日。

（1）約翰遜與漢弗萊分別為第36屆總統及副總統。

now living that we mastered our moment, that we helped make the world safe for mankind.

Standing in this same place a third of a century ago, Franklin Delano Roosevelt addressed the nation ravaged by depression, gripped in fear. He could say in surveying the nation's troubles: "They concern, thank God, only material things."

Our crisis today is in reverse.

We find ourselves rich in goods, but ragged in spirit; reaching with magnificent precision for the moon, but falling into raucous discord on earth.

We are caught in war, wanting peace. We're torn by division, wanting unity. We see around us empty lives, wanting fulfillment. We see tasks that need doing, wanting for hands to do them.

To a crisis of the spirit, we need an answer of the spirit.

And to find that answer, we need only look within ourselves.

As we measure what can be done, we shall promise only what we know we can produce; but as we chart our goals we shall be lifted by our dreams.

No man can be fully free while his neighbor is not. To go forward at all is to go forward together.

This means black and white together, as one nation, not two. The laws have caught up with our conscience. What remains is to give life to what is in the law: to

在活着的人時，將會說我們駕馭了我們的時代，爲人類求得了世界安全。

三分之一世紀以前，佛蘭克林・德蘭諾・羅斯福曾經站在這裏向全國演說，當時國家正受經濟不景氣困擾，陷於惶恐中。他看到國家當時的種種困難，却仍然能夠說：" 感謝上帝，我國的困難畢竟只在物質方面。"

今天我們的危機正相反。

我們物質豐富，却精神貧乏；我們以超卓的準確程度登上了月球，但却陷入了一片混亂地球。

我們捲入了戰爭，沒有和平。我們四分五裂，沒有團結。我們看到周圍的人生活空虛，沒有充實的內容；我們看到許多工作需要完成，但却沒有人手去做。

對於精神的危機，我們需要精神的解決辦法。

爲了找到這解決辦法，我們只需省視自身。

當我們估量要做什麼時，我們只能許諾能做到的事。但在制訂目標時，却要有高遠的理想。

如果你的鄰舍沒有自由，你就不會得到完全的自由。只有共同前進才能前進。

這意味着黑人和白人同爲一個民族，不是分爲兩個。法律是按照我們的良心制訂的。剩下的問題就是賦予法律條文以生命：保證旣然

insure at last that as all are born equal in dignity before God, all are born equal in dignity before man.

As we learn to go forward together at home, let us also seek to go forward together with mankind.

. . .

Only a few short weeks ago, we shared the glory of man's first sight of the world as God sees it, as a single sphere reflecting light in the darkness.

As Apollo astronauts flew over the moon's gray surface on Christmas Eve, they spoke to us of the beauty of earth and in that voice so clear across the lunar distance we heard them invoke God's blessing on its goodness.

In that moment of surpassing technological triumph, men turned their thoughts toward home and humanity — seeing in that far perspective that man's destiny on earth is not divisible; telling us that however far we reach into the cosmos our destiny lies not in the stars but on earth itself, in our own hands, in our own hearts.

Our destiny offers not the cup of despair, but the chalice of opportunity. So let us seize it, not in fear, but in gladness — and "riders on the earth together," let us go forward, firm in our faith, steadfast in our purpose, cautious of the dangers; but sustained by our confidence in the will of God and the promise of man.

一切人在上帝面前生來就有同等的尊嚴，在人的面前也應有同等的尊嚴。

我們在國內要學會和所有人共同前進，讓我們也努力求得全人類的共同前進吧。

……

短短幾個星期以前，我們剛分享了人類第一次像上帝那樣看到地球的光榮，我們看到了地球像一顆星一樣，在黑暗中反射出光芒。

聖誕節前夕阿波羅太空飛行員飛越月球灰色的表面時，他們告訴我們地球是多麼美麗；由太空遠處月球附近傳來的聲音是那麼清晰，我們聽到他們祈求上帝賜福給地球上一切善良的人。

在尖端技術歡奏凱歌的時刻，人們想到自己的家園和人類。從太空的遠處看來，地球上人類的命運是分不開的；這告訴我們，不論我們能到達宇宙的任何遠處，我們的命運並不在那些星星上，而在地球上，掌握在我們自己手裏，決定於我們的內心。

命運給與我們的不是失望之酒，而是機會之杯。因此，讓我們毫無畏懼、充滿歡愉地把握住命運。「乘坐地球的人們」，讓我們堅定信念，認準目標，提防危險，憑着對上帝意旨和人類諾言的信心，一起前進吧。

Bibliography 參考書目

Stewart H. Benedict (ed.), *Famous American Speeches,* New York, Dell, 1967

David Josiah Brewer (ed.), *World Best Orations,* 10 vols., Chicago, F. P. Kaiser Publishing Company, 1923

William Jennings Bryan (ed.), *World's Famous Orations,* 10 vols., New York, Funk and Wagnalls, 1906

Sherwin Cody (ed.), *Selections from the World's Great Orations,* Chicage, A. C. McClurg, 1931

Lewis Copeland (ed.), *The World's Great Speeches,* 2nd rev. ed., New York, Dover Publications, 1958

Arthur Charles Fox-Davies (ed.), *The Book of Public Speaking,* London, Caxton Publishing Co. Ltd., S.D.

Charles Hurd (ed.), *Treasury of Great American Speeches,* New York, Hawthorn Books, 1959

Hebert Paul (ed.), *Famous Speeches,* London, Issac Pitman and Sons, 1912

Houston Peterson (ed.), *A Treasury of the World's Great Speeches,* New York, Simon and Schuster, 1954

Mabel Platz (ed.), *Anthology of Public Speeches,* New York, The H. W. Wilson Company, 1940

世界名人演講集　王義田編譯　台北　名家　1980

一百叢書 2

100 FAMOUS SPEECHES
名人演說一百篇

譯者◆石幼珊

發行人◆施嘉明

總編輯◆方鵬程

叢書編輯◆羅斯

責任編輯◆曾振邦

校對◆張隆溪

出版發行：臺灣商務印書館股份有限公司

台北市重慶南路一段三十七號

電話：(02)2371-3712

讀者服務專線：0800056196

郵撥：0000165-1

網路書店：www.cptw.com.tw

E-mail：ecptw@cptw.com.tw

部落格：http://blog.yam.com/ecptw

臉書：http://facebook.com/ecptw

局版北市業字第 993 號

香港初版：1986 年 3 月

臺灣初版一刷：1988 年 10 月

臺灣初版十二刷：2012 年 2 月

定價：新台幣 280 元

本書經商務印書館(香港)有限公司授權出版

名人演說一百篇＝100 famous speeches／石幼
珊譯. －－臺灣初版. －－臺北市：臺灣商務，
1988 [民 77]
　　面；　公分，－－(一百叢書：2)
參考書目：面
ISBN 957-05-0058-1（平裝）

813.5　　　　　　　　　　　　　　82008193

一百叢書　　100 SERIES

英漢　·　漢英對照

讀者回函卡

姓名：＿＿＿＿＿＿＿＿＿＿＿＿＿＿＿ 性別：□男 □女

出生日期：＿＿＿年＿＿＿月＿＿＿日

職業：□學生 □公務（含軍警） □家管 □服務 □金融 □製造
　　　□資訊 □大眾傳播 □自由業 □農漁牧 □退休 □其他

學歷：□高中以下（含高中） □大專 □研究所（含以上）

地址：＿＿＿＿＿＿＿＿＿＿＿＿＿＿＿＿＿＿＿＿＿＿＿＿
　　　＿＿＿＿＿＿＿＿＿＿＿＿＿＿＿＿＿＿＿＿＿＿＿＿

電話：（H）＿＿＿＿＿＿＿＿＿＿（O）＿＿＿＿＿＿＿＿＿

購買書名：＿＿＿＿＿＿＿＿＿＿＿＿＿＿＿＿＿＿＿＿

您從何處得知本書？
　　　□書店 □報紙廣告 □報紙專欄 □雜誌廣告 □DM廣告
　　　□傳單 □親友介紹 □電視廣播 □其他

您對本書的意見？（A/滿意 B/尚可 C/需改進）
　　　內容＿＿＿＿ 編輯＿＿＿＿ 校對＿＿＿＿ 翻譯＿＿＿＿
　　　封面設計＿＿＿＿ 價格＿＿＿＿ 其他＿＿＿＿＿＿＿＿

您的建議：＿＿＿＿＿＿＿＿＿＿＿＿＿＿＿＿＿＿＿＿
　　　　　＿＿＿＿＿＿＿＿＿＿＿＿＿＿＿＿＿＿＿＿＿＿
　　　　　＿＿＿＿＿＿＿＿＿＿＿＿＿＿＿＿＿＿＿＿＿＿

臺灣商務印書館

台北市重慶南路一段三十七號 電話：（02）23713712轉分機50～57
讀者服務專線：0800056196 傳真：（02）23710274・23701091
郵撥：0000165-1號 E-mail：cptw@cptw.com.tw
網址：www.cptw.com.tw

100臺北市重慶南路一段37號

臺灣商務印書館 收

對摺寄回，謝謝！

傳統現代  並翼而翔

Flying with the wings of tradition and modernity.